# THE EN

The earth shudd—— ——— ——— and all around them, groaning as if stricken a mortal wound. Almost everyone held their breath, waiting.

Then, as if on cue, the entire complex shook violently as the shock wave passed through the earth's crust. Forrest pressed hard against the wall, bracing his feet against the floor as the room jiggled back, forth, and up and down on its shock absorbers. The women and the children screamed in terror, all of them covering their heads, but nothing fell and no cracks appeared in the walls, the entire installation having been purposefully built to absorb this very kind of shock wave. Within a few seconds the earth stopped shaking, and everything grew silent.

"Is it over?" Joann asked, lifting her head.

"Switch on the cameras," Forrest said. "See if we're blind."

Ulrich turned on the monitor, switching to the outside feeds. The grasslands all around the house were burning.

"Is it raining fire?" West asked.

"Sure as hell is," Forrest said. "The asteroid blasted millions of tons of rock into the outer atmosphere."

West looked at Forrest. "And so it begins."

# CANNIBAL REIGN

## THOMAS KOLONIAR

# HARPER

*An Imprint of* HarperCollins*Publishers*

This book is a work of fiction. The characters, incidents, and dialogue are drawn from the author's imagination and are not to be construed as real. Any resemblance to actual events or persons, living or dead, is entirely coincidental.

**HARPER**

*An Imprint of* HarperCollins*Publishers*
10 East 53rd Street
New York, New York 10022-5299

Copyright © 2012 by Thomas Koloniar
ISBN 978-0-06-202582-1

First Harper mass market printing: July 2012

HarperCollins® and Harper® are registered trademarks of Harper-Collins Publishers.

Printed in the United States of America

Visit Harper paperbacks on the World Wide Web
at www.harpercollins.com

10 9 8 7 6 5 4 3 2 1

*For Claudia*
*El amor de mi vida*

"The near-Earth asteroid '2011 $AG_5$' currently has an impact probability of 1 in 625 for Feb. 5, 2040."

— Donald Yeomans, Chief of the Near-Earth Object Observations Program at NASA's Jet Propulsion Laboratory in Pasadena

As of the printing of this book, asteroid 2011 $AG_5$ has been observed for only a little more than half an orbit, and the likelihood of impact is expected to adjust as observations continue; but it remains one of only two near-earth objects (NEOs) to be listed above "0" on the Torino Scale. Discussions are already taking place as to how it might be deflected.

Though the exact composition of 2011 $AG_5$ remains unknown at this time, it is 140 meters wide, and the impact of an object of this size could easily yield as much energy as any of the largest nuclear tests ever carried out by humankind.

# ACKNOWLEDGMENTS

**THANK YOU, TO THE FOLLOWING . . .**

My parents for putting me through college where I came to love this craft, which so many of us slave over, willingly, like oarsmen rowing for our very lives.

Alice Austin of Manchester High School, the first to indulge the earliest scribblings of a fledgling writer.

Professor Robert Pope of the University of Akron for all of his guidance these many years. No writer could ask for a better mentor. No student could expect a finer teacher. And no man could hope for a truer friend.

Elicia Skelton for restoring to me that which I had lost. Mere words cannot adequately express the depth of my appreciation for your appearance on the scene. My finest wishes are with you always.

Lisa Cron and Doug Michael for their many hours of diligent work and, most of all, for believing in me.

My agent, Ian Kleinert, for believing in this story.

And finally, Dr. James Helmuth and Mr. David Lynn Jones . . . for saving my life.

Just as I have attempted to demonstrate within the pages of this novel, no one is an island, and no one does it alone.

# BOOK ONE

# PROLOGUE

"Ed, wake up!" the woman whispered. "There's someone in the house!"

Colonel Ed Lucket sat up in the dark listening. "I don't
hear anything," he said quietly.

"I heard a clunk in your study!"

Lucket listened a moment longer and reached for his cell
phone, only to find that it was gone from the nightstand
where he put it every night before bed. "Shit. Stay here."

"But what are you—"

"Stay here!" he hissed, pulling his arm free of her grasp
before hurriedly stepping into a pair of pants.

"Be careful!"

He waved at her to shut up and poked his head into the
hall, where he saw a light on in the study at the far end, a
thin layer of smoke hanging stagnant in the dim glow. What
the hell was going on? He made his way cautiously along the
wall, a cold sweat breaking out across his chest. His heart
skipped a beat when he heard someone shift in his chair, the
leather creaking. The only firearm in the house was in the
wall safe behind his desk.

He drew a deep breath and stepped boldly into the room,
instantly recognizing the man sitting at the desk. "Reeves!"
he bellowed. "What the hell are you doing? You scared the
billy piss out of me!"

Jerry Reeves sat back in the chair, serenely smoking one of Lucket's fine Cuban cigars taken from the humidor in the corner. He gestured with it to an open folder on the desk. "This file makes for a rather jarring read, Colonel."

The colonel saw his pistol and cell phone resting on the desk near the folder, the door to his wall safe ajar. "That's classified, you son of a bitch! And how did you get past the security system? It's the fucking best!"

"Indeed it is," Reeves chuckled, shaping the smoldering end of the cigar against the crystal ashtray. "Though an alarm system's only as dependable as the man using it."

Lucket felt his face flush. Reeves was a civilian with Army intelligence, attached to the Pentagon, a crafty bastard he'd been trying to subvert for years. "I asked how you got in."

"I strolled into the garage right behind you and the— uh . . . *lady*. That is General Loughton's wife, isn't it? Of course it is, otherwise you'd have gone right for the land-line."

"Get out of my house!" Lucket ordered, pointing at the door, the gray hair on his chest glistening.

Reeves held up the file. "Colonel, who else is privy to this nightmare? Why are they so intent on keeping it a secret?"

Lucket's eyes narrowed. "Isn't that rather obvious? The world would tear itself apart. Now get out!"

"In due time," Reeves said affably. "First, I want the video. The one your CIA pals made of me down in Havana last week."

Lucket was hard-pressed to cover his shock. "I . . . I'd say your illicit real estate deal is irrelevant now . . . given what you've just read."

"Quite the contrary. It's even more relevant now than it was an hour ago when I stood watching you and the general's wife have at it."

Lucket felt a worrisome tightness in his chest, bit back an obscenity. "Why is it more relevant?"

Reeves tapped the file. "It's obvious I'll need someplace warm to weather this storm."

"There's no place to run," Lucket sneered. "No place to hide."

Reeves puffed the cigar as he considered his next move, realizing that Lucket would likely attempt to have him terminated now that he'd read the file. "About the video, Colonel?"

"It's not here," Lucket said thinly.

Reeves took the pistol and shot him in the leg, shattering his left knee. The colonel went down swearing: "You filthy bastard!"

"I may be that," Reeves said, rising, the cigar in his free hand, "but I'm not here to discuss my finer qualities with you. Now where's the video? I'd like to hold onto my position long enough to honor some old debts."

The colonel lay over on his side, his chest constricting, gripping his knee and barely suppressing the urge to vomit. "Middle drawer, you son of a bitch! Take it and get out!"

Reeves took a small unmarked video card from his pocket. He'd already found it in the drawer but wanted to be sure of what it was. "May I assume this is the only copy?" he asked, the cigar caught in the corner of his mouth.

Lucket realized he was a dead man. "You're a filthy coward!" he roared. "Do you hear me? *A filthy coward!*"

Reeves squatted beside him, a frown creasing his face as he put the weapon to the colonel's head. "I didn't come here to kill you," he said solicitously, "but we both know you would have sent someone to kill me for reading that file."

"Burn in hell!" Lucket made a desperate grab for the weapon and was very nearly fast enough, though not quite.

Reeves squeezed off the round in the nick of time, glad to have given the colonel a chance to go out fighting. He then wiped down the pistol along with anything else he had touched, locking it back in the safe and taking the file down the hall to the bedroom. He flicked on the light and knelt down to find Mrs. Loughton hiding under the bed.

"Don't be silly," he said, offering his hand to the terrified woman. "I've never made war on women or children. Come on out of there."

Mrs. Loughton sat sniveling in a chair a short time later, Lucket's robe gathered around her as she sopped at her eyes with a tissue. A blonde with nice skin, she was sexy for being almost fifty, around Reeve's own age. "Is he dead?" she whimpered.

"Very," Reeves said, setting the cigar down in the ashtray on the nightstand and fluffing one of the pillows. "Were you in love with him?"

She shook her head despondently. "Though I liked him a lot— You're going to kill me!" she blurted.

Reeves went around to remake her side of the bed. "I've already told you I'm not going to hurt you. What I'm going to do is take you home. And then you and I are going to keep one another's secrets . . . which I'd say is more than fair."

She watched him tidy up. "Why would you trust me?"

He finished and picked up the cigar, eyeing the file beneath the lamp. "Let's just say I've learned something tonight that makes much me less worried about the immediate future than I might otherwise have been. Now go get dressed while I make a quick call."

General Loughton's wife gathered her clothes and stepped into the master bathroom, closing the door.

Reeves took her chair and pulled a satellite phone from inside his coat pocket, dialing a number from memory. The phone rang a number of times before it was finally answered.

"I hope this is important," said a tired voice.

"Jack? It's Reeves. Listen, I've got a file here you need to see, and soon."

"Classified?"

"Oh, yeah, and then some. Looks like there's a real nightmare headed our way . . . and this one's right up your alley."

# ONE

**JACK FORREST RAISED HIS HEAD IN LAUNCH CONTROL,**
cocking an eyebrow and listening as the heavy steel door
above was pulled to and secured. A slight grin crossed his
face as he returned his attention to a textbook on heavenly
bodies.

Wayne Ulrich trotted down three stories of a steel staircase and crossed through the common areas into Launch
Control, where he stopped in the doorway and stood watching unhappily as Forrest sat reading.

Forrest glanced up from the book just long enough to see
the crease in his friend's face. "What's got your feathers in
a ruffle?"

Ulrich crossed the room and tossed a clipboard onto the
console near Forrest's feet. "Three more names have magi-
cally appeared on the roster," he said, hands on his hips.
"Any idea how that happened?"

"I wrote them in with my magic pen," Forrest said, dropping his feet to the deck and posturing up in the squeaky
old government chair to stretch his back. A lean, muscular
man of medium height, Jack Forrest was thirty-five, with
a relentlessly sarcastic disposition. He had flinty blue eyes
and chiseled features, thick brown hair cut high-and-tight in
military fashion, and a two-inch scar on his chin where he'd

been struck by a rifle butt years earlier during the Second Gulf War. "Got a problem with that, Stumpy?"

Ulrich was the exact opposite. A die-hard pragmatist, he and Forrest had made unlikely friends during their Special Forces training in Fort Bragg, North Carolina. He walked with an almost imperceptible limp, having lost his left foot in Afghanistan to an IED during the summer of 2006. Tall and slender with wispy blond hair, pale blue eyes, and a thin mustache, he was dressed in digital-camouflage trousers and a black underarmor T-shirt.

"You're damn right I do." He pointed at the roster. "Do you realize how much extra food I have to come up with every time you add even a single name to that list? Two meals, every day, for eighteen months. Times *three* people, that's 2,190 goddamn meals, Jack! Do you know how much food that is? I can't just run down to the supermarket, fill up the family station wagon and call it a day."

"So rent another truck," Forrest said, tossing the heavy book on top of the roster, then lighting a Camel cigarette with a brass Zippo lighter. "Come to think of it, rent two and take Kane with you." He tossed the lighter onto the book and rocked back in the chair.

"You're missing the point," Ulrich said. "People are going to notice. So when word finally gets out—and it's gonna get out—somebody could remember us hoarding all that food. And they just might come looking for it."

"Then drive to Colorado for the food," Forrest said, taking a drag from the cigarette. "Hell, drive all the way to Vegas for all I care. Only do me a favor while you're there and visit a hooker, will ya? You get cranky when you haven't had your ashes hauled."

"My ashes haven't got anything to do with it," Ulrich insisted, though both men knew that he would never cheat on his wife Erin, who was waiting back in North Carolina. "There are forty-eight names on that list. And that's not counting the five of us and our families. How many more people do you plan on having down here? Eighty? A hundred? This old septic system's only going to assimilate so much shit, you know."

"What? You haven't crunched the numbers on that yet?"

Ulrich bridled. "I haven't got the slightest idea how much a single person shits in a year."

"Then I suggest you call one of those septic pumper companies and find out."

Ulrich hung his head with a weary sigh. "How many more names, Jack?"

Forrest shrugged. "I keep finding people I want to save."

"You mean women. And how many of them are good-looking?"

"A few."

"Jesus, you're something else."

Forrest stood up from the squeaky chair, exhaling a cloud of bluish smoke as he crushed out the cigarette in a brass ashtray cut from a 76mm cannon shell casing. "Who do *you* suggest we save, Wayne . . . if not women and children? Sweaty biker types who'd kill us all the first chance they got? Old men and women who're gonna be dead in a few years? How about some asshole businessmen? I put single mothers on that list for good reason. We get too much testosterone down here and we're asking for trouble."

"Suppose none of these women are interested in repopulating?"

"Oh, that's got nothing to do with it," Forrest said with a wave. "Whether they are or not, their virtue will be a hell of a lot safer down here than it will up there once this shit kicks off."

Ulrich rubbed the back of his neck, remembering the war-torn Middle East. Both men had seen the type of iniquities a woman could look forward to in the absence of law and order. "It just isn't fair, that's all. A pretty woman's got no more right to—"

"Look, if I could save everybody, I would. So would you. We all would. But we can't. People are going to die up there. They're going to die by the bushel—men, women, children, ugly or not. And for the record, Stumpy, not every woman on that roster is a beauty queen. What do you think I am?"

Before Ulrich could reply, Marcus Kane came around the corner, having heard their voices echoing along the steel blast vestibule leading from one of the Titan missile silos. A six-foot African American, Kane was recruiting-poster handsome, with a shaved head, smooth skin, and gentle almond-shaped eyes.

"Y'all argue enough, you'd think you were married," he said, taking a pretzel rod from a bag on the console.

"Anybody on that list happen to be black?" Ulrich asked, wanting to stir the pot.

"Don't start," Forrest said.

"You didn't pick any sisters?" Marcus said. "Man, come on now."

"As a matter of fact," Forrest replied, "I've picked seven, all with kids."

"Suppose these folks want to bring their extended families or friends along?" Ulrich asked.

"Tough shit," Forrest said, shaking another cigarette from its pack. "Needless to say, anyone chosen will have some tough choices to make, and I expect most of them will choose to stay up there and face what's coming."

Ulrich nodded, looked at Kane. "How are the countermeasures coming?"

Kane considered. "Well, I figure we'd better count on them getting past the first blast door," he said at length. "Somebody good could conceivably cut their way in with an acetylene torch. But if we bore some holes in the overhead concrete of the security vestibule, run a line for the accelerant, we can fit a flame nozzle into each hole. That way we can fill the entire vestibule with liquid fire, burn 'em to the bone like a goddamn dragon."

"I don't really see anybody getting past the first blast door," Ulrich said. "The damn thing is ten inches thick with steel pins all around the jambs. Cutting off the hinges wouldn't even get it open."

"Marcus is right, though," Forrest said. "Somebody good with a torch could cut their way through. It would take a hell of a long time, but remember, they'll be desperate."

Ulrich reached for the pretzel bag. "What I'm worried about is them poisoning the ventilator shafts."

Forrest nodded. "It's a definite chink in the armor. How about the topside silo doors?"

"Those are damn near impregnable," Kane said.

"What about a torch?"

"Through three feet of solid steel?"

Ulrich took a bite from his pretzel. "Suppose somebody shows up with a 'dozer? Digs down deep to the ceiling. Employs a jackhammer."

"That's six feet of reinforced concrete to go through," Kane said.

"Well, like Jack said, they'll be desperate."

Forrest said, "We all know there's no such thing as an impregnable castle. We can only prepare for what we can prepare for. But just in case, we'd better have some kind of Broken Arrow in mind."

All three men pondered the unthinkable. A measure of last resort was not something to be overlooked.

"We could plant topside charges," Ulrich suggested.

"Maybe," Forrest said. "Where's the Dynamic Duo?"

"Still working on the wiring," Kane said. "The generators are in place but they're not hooked into Launch Control yet. The ventilation system probably needs a lot of work too. Those motors haven't been run up in years."

"Well, that goddamn realtor assured me they still run," Forrest said. "Once we're powered up, give them a try."

"You're the man."

"And what *about* that realtor?" Ulrich said. "Say she survives? She knows you went asshole-deep in debt to get this place. She might start asking questions. Might think we knew this was gonna happen all along."

"I hadn't thought of that," Forrest said, taking a moment to consider the point. "Well, we can't take any chances.

Marcus, you'd better kill the real-estate lady. Make it look like an accident. Toss a toaster into the tub with her."

Ulrich couldn't help cracking a smile.

Kane stood chewing. "Know what else we ain't figured out? Vasquez. How much insulin can we store and how long will it keep if we lose power?"

Forrest looked at Ulrich. "I guess we'll have to kill Vasquez too. There's no sense in having him down here eating our food if he's only going to die."

Ulrich snorted. "You're a fucking jerk."

"This is true," Forrest said, dropping back into the chair with a sharp squeak. "We need some new chairs too." He held up the textbook he'd been reading, a work on heavenly bodies by an astronomer named Ester Thorn. "Look guys, prehistoric man already pulled off this exact same mission with nothing more than a double digit IQ and some animal hide. Don't tell me that five battle-tested Green Berets won't be able to think their way through this challenge. That's all this is, another mission, so we knuckle down and we drive on."

# TWO

**MARTY CHITTENDEN STOOD IN THE HALL OUTSIDE A** classroom at the California Institute of Technology Jet Propulsion Laboratory, anxiously waving a red file to get the attention of Professor Susan Denton, who was in the middle of giving a lecture on astrophysics. When she finally noticed what at first glance looked like a lunatic outside her classroom, she paused in mid-sentence, surprised to see a fellow doctoral candidate from her days at Berkeley.

Susan remembered him well, Marty having spent the better part of a school year trying to win her heart. Though they had gone to movies a couple of times and shared some laughs, she hadn't felt much chemistry between them, but they remained friends until they finished graduate school and then went their separate ways.

Now here he was out of the blue, five years later, fervently beckoning her into the hallway. She couldn't imagine what could possibly be so important.

"Excuse me for a second," Susan said to her class, and stepped out into the hall. She was five-six with red hair, freckles, her intensely expressive hazel eyes focused on this visitor from the past. "I'm in the middle of a class, Marty. So please make this quick."

"I need you to check some calculations for me," he said earnestly, offering the file.

"I'd be happy to," she said patiently. "But I need to finish class. Give me half an hour."

Susan turned back toward the room, but Marty impulsively grabbed for her elbow. She jerked away, suddenly wild-eyed. "Don't touch me!" she hissed acidly.

He stepped back, stunned by her uncharacteristic viciousness. "I'm sorry," he said, sensing that she had experienced something terrible since their last meeting. "I didn't mean to . . . it's just that . . . it's just that this will be the most significant . . . most *frightening* discovery in all of human history."

Susan went from angry to alarmed and intensely curious. In all the time she knew Marty, she had never seen him as melodramatic. If anything, he verged on being a classic academic bore.

"Well, God . . . what is it?"

"It's an NEO, Sue, and it's got our name on it." He gestured with the red file folder. "I've got all my calculations. I'd like you to review them before I take them over to JPL." Susan felt a sudden chill run through her. She knew Marty was an excellent astronomer and not someone prone to exaggeration. If he said the world was going to be struck by a near Earth object, chances were good to excellent it was going to happen.

"Well . . . how long do we have?"

"Counting today? Eighty-eight days."

She felt her knees weaken. "Jesus," she muttered. "Let me dismiss the class."

She returned to the classroom then. "Okay, everybody," she announced, I'm letting you go early today. We'll pick up right here on Wednesday."

The entire class sprang from their seats in a flurry of laptops and backpacks, and in less than thirty seconds the room was empty. Marty stepped in and closed the door, handing the folder to Susan.

She sat down at a student desk and skimmed through it, her almost savantlike mind checking Marty's computations on the fly. "This can't be right," she muttered, searching desperately for a miscalculation. "Marty, are you sure this isn't a comet? It's moving at over a hundred thousand miles an hour, for God's sake." She sat chewing the end of her hair as Marty had seen her do so many times in the past in the library at Berkeley. The idiosyncrasy was all the more endearing now.

"Why hasn't anyone else spotted this thing?" she wondered aloud.

Marty had gone to the window to gaze out over the Caltech campus two stories below.

"Because it's not coming from the asteroid belt," he said, referring to the asteroid field orbiting the sun between Mars and Jupiter, where the majority of NEOs were thought to begin their journey. "It's an ancient rogue, Sue. It came out of deep space, and it's probably been traveling half a billion years to get here, maybe longer."

"But at two miles across . . . it's huge. Somebody should've seen it sooner."

"Yeah," he said, turning around. "But remember, Jupiter was hit back in '09 by a comet so big that it left an impact scar in the Jovian atmosphere the size of the Pacific Ocean . . . and no one knew a thing about it until after it had happened. What's more . . . it was only an amateur astronomer who spotted the scar."

"How big was the comet that wiped out the dinosaurs?" she asked. "The one that hit the Yucatan."

"The Chicxulub bolide was nearly six miles across. It hit with an equivalent force of ten teratons of TNT and left a crater a hundred miles wide. This sucker's only a third the same mass but it's likely moving much faster."

"Jesus," she whispered. "Have you done the math on damage probabilities? Are we going out completely?"

He shrugged. "It's hard to quantify, but the sun will be obscured for at least of couple years, so you're talking about twenty-four months of freezing temperatures even at the equator . . . and with the ensuing famine? Mankind will likely survive it, but only barely. So at the very best, we're starting over."

"At least it's hitting land and not water, less acid in the atmosphere. There's no time left for anything, is there? Christ, Marty, I never even got married."

"*That's* not my fault," he said, smiling.

She couldn't help grinning back. "God knows."

She closed the file and stared off into space, thinking through his calculations. "No chance your observations are off?"

He shook his head with a frown. "Believe me, I've been over it a thousand times."

"You haven't told NASA?"

"Not yet, but I'm not sure it matters. It's right on top of us; even if they slam a nuke right into it, the damn thing's coming at us so fast it won't even blink. This is an M-class. Mostly iron, so it won't fragment much."

"Why do you suppose it's moving so fast?"

"Well, half a billion years gives it plenty of time to sling-shot around planets, stars, black holes . . ."

"Any chance Jupiter's gravity will pull it off course?"

"None. It's coming in at such a high cosine angle, Jupiter's gravity won't factor. Not even close."

She sighed. "Okay. How about I walk you over to JPL?" She got up and gave him the file. "Linda Creasey's a muckety-muck over there now."

"I know. I was headed to her next."

"So why even come to me? You knew there was nothing wrong with your math."

Marty held her gaze. "You know why, Sue."

"Still carrying that torch for me after all this time?" she said, slightly incredulous, but then softening. "It's very sweet, Marty, but you should have put it down by now and found someone else."

"Bollocks," he said with a smile. "I hardly ever leave

the observatory. I'm a total egghead. And besides . . ." He shrugged again, suddenly self-conscious.

"I'm listening."

"Well, it's selfish, I know, but I was hoping we could spend some time together these last few months . . . as friends."

"And then what?" she said quietly. "Imagine we survive the impact and the subsequent firestorm."

"I could take care of you," he offered, his voice thickening. "I could make sure you don't suffer."

Susan hadn't had time yet to think that far into it. "I'm sorry for the way I spoke to you in the hall."

"That's all right. I'm sorry for grabbing you. I wasn't thinking."

She shook her head. "No, I overreacted. I was attacked a year ago. Raped, actually. There's no way you could've . . . I've been jumpy as hell ever since."

"I'm sorry," he croaked, staggered by the news and hard-pressed to prevent it from showing on his face.

"He grabbed me from behind," she went on. "Pulled me down between some parked cars . . . had a knife. I've never told a soul." She looked him in the eyes then. "I can't believe how easily I just shared that."

Marty wasn't sure what to say. All he knew was that he wanted to hold her. "Anything you ever need, Sue, I'll be there."

She felt strangely touched by his devotion. "Can you promise you won't let it happen again? After things get bad . . ."

"I promise, Sue. I'll take care of us both if it gets to that point."

"Thank you," she said, amazed at how intimate the conversation had quickly become. "I'm not sure I could . . . in any event." She shook her head and forced a smile. "You know what?" she said, suddenly hopeful. "I'm so scared now that if you told me you made this all up just to get in my pants, I'd be so relieved I wouldn't even be mad."

He smiled sadly. "You know me, Sue. I'm not nearly clever enough to think up a scheme like that."

She touched his arm. "Let's go see Linda."

"Is she still her sweet self?"

Susan laughed. "Even sweeter."

WHEN LINDA CREASEY walked into Conference Room 2B on the far side of campus at the Jet Propulsion Laboratory, she was more than a little surprised to see Marty Chittenden sitting at the table beside Susan Denton. "Oh," she said, noticeably less than pleased. "Hello, Martin. I wasn't told you were here. It's been a while."

"A few years."

"I read your piece last year in *Astronomy Today*," she replied. "It wasn't bad . . . for supposition." She was an attractive yet somehow unpleasant-looking woman with a slender face and straight black hair that stopped at the base of her neck. "So what can I do for the two of you?"

Marty noted the increased air of superiority about her and sat forward in his chair. "I'm sorry to drop in unannounced, but I've got something very important to show you."

"Oh?" Linda said, taking a seat at the table. "What do you have?"

He pushed the red file folder over to her. She flipped it open and began to read. As she scanned the pages, her features visibly tightened. When she was finished, she closed the file and stared straight at Marty.

"How many others have seen this?"

At first Marty thought she was already plotting to steal his thunder, but there was a look about her that changed his mind, something more sinister. "No one," he replied cautiously.

"You're sure?"

"The only other person I've told is Susan."

"Well, these findings are huge," she said. "If accurate. What are your intentions?"

"To get the word out," he said. "People need to know so they can prepare."

"Of course," she said. "Let me make a few calls." She stood, keeping the file. "May I take this?"

"Just remember where you got it."

"You don't have to worry about that, Martin." She turned and quickly disappeared from the room.

Marty stared suspiciously after her. "What do you make of that?"

"Gut reaction? I think she already knew."

"Which means the government has to know, right?"

"Yep." Susan got up from the table and went to the door, peering down the hall. "This may create a problem for them."

"They're trying to keep it quiet," he realized. "Avoid mass panic."

"Will you do me a favor?"

"Sure."

"Get the hell out of here," she said. "I'll call you later—if I can."

"What are you talking about?" he said, rising.

"Think about it. How else could they keep this quiet? I mean it's *possible* you're the only astronomer to have spotted this, but what if you're not? What if there are others and they've got them locked up someplace?"

"That's a little paranoid, don't you think?"

"Give me your cell number and get out of here. I'm serious."

"What? But what about you?" he said, giving her his card.

"After you go public with it, they'll have to release me, won't they?"

"But she's got my file," he said. "And if you're right, they'll get to Mesa Station long before I do and seize my computers."

"True, but you can still tell someone where to look for this thing."

"Wait a second," he said, feeling suddenly silly. "Are you sure about this?"

"Linda's always been a cold fish, Marty, but I've never

seen her so calculated. Look, if you won't leave the building, then go wait in the ladies' room and stay there until I come get you."

"All right," he said, "but I'm going to feel pretty stupid if we're making a big deal over nothing." He left, entered an empty ladies' room just up the hall and slipped into a stall to wait.

Barely ten minutes later two men in dark suits appeared in the doorway of the conference room. "Are you Susan Denton?" the taller of the two asked.

"Yes," she said, her stomach fluttering. "Who are you?"

"Where is Martin Chittenden?"

"He had to step out. Who are you?"

"Check the men's room," the man said to his partner. "I'm Special Agent Paulis of the United States Secret Service." He presented his credentials. "Where did Mr. Chittenden say he was going?"

When she didn't answer, he repeated the question.

"I don't know."

The second agent reappeared, shook his head.

"Ms. Denton? I would strongly suggest that you answer my question."

"He got suspicious and left," she said, standing up. "Looks like he had good reason too."

Paulis took out his Nextel and pressed a button. "Looks like Chittenden smelled a rat and took off," he announced. "He's probably still on campus . . . Creasey says he's wearing jeans and a green shirt with short sleeves . . . and he's got rust-colored hair."

He put the phone back into his pocket. "Ms. Denton, I'm afraid I must ask you to come with us."

"Under whose authority?"

"The President of the United States," he said. "It's a matter of national security."

"I want to speak to Linda Creasey."

"In due time, but for now you'll have to come with us."

"This is unconstitutional!" she said louder than necessary

as they walked her past the ladies' room door. "Martin's done nothing wrong."

Barely breathing, Marty waited until he was sure they were gone, then quickly fled the building. He was threading his way through the lot to his rental car when he noticed two men in suits coming toward him. He bolted for the car and jumped in, but by the time he got it running, both agents were there.

"Get out of the car, Chittenden!" Paulis ordered, moving around to the driver side door, his partner remaining behind the car to prevent Marty from backing out.

Marty ignored the man's increasingly strident orders and slowly eased the car back out of the space. He knew he was taking a huge risk, but what the hell, the world was doomed anyhow.

Paulis produced a collapsible baton, used it to smash out Marty's window and lunged for the ignition key. Marty panicked and jabbed his finger into the man's eye. The agent swore and pulled back as Marty stomped on the accelerator. The car jumped back, and a pair of electrodes, fired from the second agent's Taser, bounced off the windshield. Marty hit the brakes, cut the wheel, shifted into drive and sped off.

Several minutes later, as he joined the traffic moving west, he had regained his composure and was mentally running through a list of astronomers he could call to help him, though now he wasn't entirely sure that was the best course of action. Was there any point in taking what he knew to the public? It would throw the nation into chaos, and in the end, there wasn't much most people could do to save themselves. By the time he reached the highway, however, he had made a decision. Freedom could be a dangerous thing, but the United States was still a democracy, and Americans reserved the right to control their own destiny to the very end.

As he pondered his next move, he knew he couldn't go back to his home or to Mesa Station. The airport was equally out of the question. The only thing he could think to do was ditch this car and rent another one along the way, buying himself some much needed time to get out of California. He knew of a retired, very sharp astronomer living in Idaho who would likely find this asteroid of particular interest, but she was up in her years and he had never actually made her acquaintance.

He thought about the agent then, and wondered if he had done any real damage to the man's eye. He hoped not, but he had broken no laws and was perfectly within his rights to defend himself. Just the same, he hoped he would never cross paths with the guy again.

# THREE

FORREST SWUNG HIS GREEN SURPLUS HUMVEE INTO THE truck stop and drove straight up to the fuel pumps. After he'd stuck the nozzle into the fuel port, he went inside to pick up some chips and beer for the guys back at the silo. They had all been working like mules turning the old military installation into an acceptable living environment. There was a lot of cleaning and painting left to do yet, but if worse came to worst, much of that could be done after they'd sealed themselves inside.

The most critical elements had to be dealt with first. They still needed to fill the old rocket propellant tanks with diesel oil to run the generators, and there was a lot of food yet to be bought and transported to the site. The ventilation intakes still had to be hardened against sabotage, and the lift elevator had jammed the night before. These repairs and supplies were going to be expensive and time-consuming, and Forrest expected to work up to the very last couple of days. All five of the men had taken out second mortgages on their homes and were in the process of maxing out the many credit cards they had picked up lately. They laughed about the huge amount of debt they would all have hanging over their heads if, by some miracle, NASA did manage to stop the asteroid. They knew this was the largest part of why the government had chosen to keep the rock a secret—if everyone took the measures they themselves were taking, the economy would almost certainly implode and total chaos would reign.

Forrest pondered this, along with many other grim realities, as he tugged a case of beer from the bottom shelf of the cooler. When he turned around he was abruptly shaken from these dreary reveries by the sight of a particularly beautiful woman standing in the potato chip aisle. She was slender, with bedroom eyes and long auburn hair full of lazy, natural curls. Wearing a brown halter top, shorts, and sandals, she had a fresh, lithe look about her.

"These are pretty good," he said, reaching to grab two bags of kettle-cooked potato chips.

She stole a glance at him. "Too much trans fat."

"You know, that's what I keep telling those guys," he said. "Way too much trans fat." He was looking directly at her now and smiling, the chips the furthest thing from his mind. "I'm Jack."

A slightly bemused smile spread across her face. "Does this often work for you, Jack?"

He chuckled. "Truthfully, I'm a little out of practice."

"I can see that," she said dryly.

"Okay," he said, feeling silly. "Safe travels."

"You too," she said, returning her attention to the task at hand. She heard him muttering to himself as he walked away—*My kingdom for some time!*—and couldn't help chuckling.

He stepped up to the counter and allowed the clerk to ring up the chips and beer. "How much do I owe you on pump nine?"

"It shut off at a dollar twelve," the clerk said. "You pretty much gotta hold the handle the whole time with those pumps. They're touchy."

"All right," Forrest said. "I'll pay for this stuff and come back after I fill up."

He was still waiting for the tank to fill when the woman came out with a bag in her hand and walked across the lot toward her car. He watched her for a moment then trotted off after her, unable to help himself.

"Excuse me! Miss?"

She turned as she was about to put her key into the door, looking annoyed. "I've got a boyfriend."

"Never doubted it for a second," he said, more business-like now, taking a pen from this pocket and writing his cell number down on the potato chip receipt. "Keep this number for a few months. I know this sounds like another stupid line," he admitted, "but you may hear something in the news soon, something that frightens you. If you do, I might be able to help."

She looked at him with a raised eyebrow. "I knew there was something odd about you. What am I supposed to hear that'll frighten me into calling a total stranger?"

"If I told you, you'd never believe me. And that's the truth. Just let the number float around the bottom of your purse. Throw it away in a few months. It can't hurt anything."

"How will I know if I'm hearing the right thing? I don't scare very easily."

She wasn't taking him seriously, but he didn't seem at all dangerous to her, and he was the most intriguing person she'd run into between Nebraska and South Carolina, where she'd been visiting her sister.

"Let me put it this way," he said. "If you have even the slightest doubt about it . . . that's not it."

She put the slip of paper into her purse. "Thanks . . . I guess."

"Drive careful," he said, and headed back to the Humvee.

Finding that the pump had shut off again, he mumbled an obscenity as he grabbed the handle and squeezed the trigger mechanism. He was watching the digits add up when the woman came walking over.

"Elizabeth never really said that, you know . . . 'Time. Time. My kingdom for some time.'"

He smiled at her, feeling butterflies. "Well then she should have."

"I know I've played right into your hands on this, but I need you to tell me what it is . . . this scary thing."

"Honestly, you won't believe me."

After considering the situation for a moment, she took the receipt from her purse and stuck it under the wiper blade of the Humvee. "I'm over it," she said, and turned to walk away.

"It's an asteroid," he blurted.

She turned back around. "A what?"

"A rogue asteroid. It's two miles wide and it's on a collision course with North America."

"You were right," she said, her eyes wide. "I don't believe you. Goodbye."

"In eighty-seven days it's going to slam into us somewhere between the Mexican border and the Yukon Territory at a hundred and ten thousand miles an hour."

She paused and stood looking at him.

"I'm told the resultant explosion and ensuing firestorm will kill every living creature aboveground out to a radius of eight or nine hundred miles. After that the sun's going to be obscured from the sky for an awfully long time." He plucked the number from under the blade and offered it back to her.

"Not that I believe you," she said, sticking the paper into her pocket, "but if this were true, why would I bother to call you about it?"

"My friends and I are preparing a shelter, a good one, and were hoping to save fifty people or so, mostly women and children."

"And why would I be so lucky?"

He shrugged. "Look in the mirror."

Her eyes narrowed.

"Hey, I know how that sounds, but you asked."

She studied him for the slightest hint of guile. "Well, you're either a damn good liar, or you're crazy enough to believe what you're saying."

"I'm going in to pay for my fuel," he said. "If you're still here when I get back, maybe we can talk some more."

When Forrest returned, the woman was back across the lot leaning against her car. He drove over and parked beside her. Getting out, he sat on the hood, popping the top from a beer bottle with a pocketknife.

The woman climbed up onto the hood and sat looking at him. "I'm normally a level-headed, common-sensical person. So why the hell should I believe you?"

"Beer?" he asked.

She shook her head.

"Maybe it's because a good friend of mine at the Pentagon broke about twenty different federal laws telling me what I just told you. Or maybe I just have an honest face," he added with a grin.

She couldn't help returning it, trusting him half for real and half for the fun of it. "Aren't they doing anything about it?"

"You've heard about those two high-tech satellites NASA's planning to launch into space?"

"I don't watch much television, but I'll take your word for it."

"The rockets are actually ICBMs, modified to look the part, but they're carrying nuclear payloads, not satellites."

"So they're going to blow it up?"

"The first warhead will try to blow it off course as it goes by," he said. "When that doesn't work, they'll park the second one in front of it and allow the asteroid to slam into it. Which isn't going to work either because it's coming too goddamn fast."

"Won't they ever tell us?"

"I expect it to leak, probably sooner than later." He took a drink from the beer. "But so far they've managed to keep it secret."

"And you're not lying to me?" she said. "You're not crazy?"

"Oh, well, I am a little crazy but I'm not lying."

"How'd you get that scar on your chin?"

"Rifle butt."

"Did it hurt?"

"I don't know. I was out cold."

She chuckled.

"If my buddy Wayne hadn't shot the guy off of me, I'd be dead."

"This really isn't funny, is it?" she said. "Assuming you're telling the truth, I mean."

"It's frightening as hell, if you ask me," he said, "but what good's pissing down our leg gonna do?"

"Not much. Where's this supposed shelter of yours? How big is it?"

"*That's* a secret. But it's not too far away and it's big enough." He explained to her how long they would have to live underground and why, and then he told her about his friends and some of the people who would be joining them. "We're not survival nuts. We're just five guys trying to save some extra people while we're busy saving our own asses."

"Have you given any thought to the psychological effects of living underground for eighteen months?" she asked. "I hope you've added a psychiatrist to the mix."

Forrest had never even considered it. "Damn, that's probably a good idea."

"Suppose you're telling the truth and I decide to take you up on your offer. Can I bring my boyfriend? Or do I belong to you in this little fantasy of yours?"

He laughed, liking her. "You sound like someone else I know. Yeah, you can bring him. So long as he's not prone to violence."

"What about our parents?"

He shook his head.

"Just like that?"

"I'm sorry but there's—"

"No," she said, cutting him off. "I get it. What you're saying makes perfect sense. I'm just seeing how deeply you've thought into this."

He looked at her. "What do you do? Are you a psychiatrist?"

"No, that's my boyfriend. I'm a sociologist," she said. "What you're proposing is really kind of fascinating. We discussed similar types of hypotheticals in school." She hopped down from the hood and shook her hair out with her hands, instinctively aware of how that would affect him and not minding. "I sure hope you're lying, but I'll hold onto your number."

"I'm Jack, by the way."

"It's been interesting, Jack." She walked around to the other side of her car.

"No name?" he asked.

"I'll tell you my name if we ever meet up again. How's that? Until then you're just some nut I ran into at the truck stop."

"Safe journey, beautiful lady."

"You too, Jack." She paused before getting into the car. "It's one of those old missile silos they've put up for sale out here, isn't it?"

He smiled. "I made it all up."

"Probably," she said.

He caught a glimpse of her license plate as she drove off: VERNICA. "Veronica," he said, jumping down from the hood. "That works."

# FOUR

**EVEN IN THE DARK MARTY CHITTENDEN COULD SEE THE TWO** agents in the gray sedan down the street from the home of Ester Thorn. He suspected they had probably tapped into her phone as well, so he was glad he hadn't called ahead. He had never met Mrs. Thorn, but he knew she had once been a highly respected astronomer at the Gemini Observatory in Hawaii. And he suspected the Secret Service had found her textbook on heavenly bodies in his office.

He took a brand new pay-as-you-go phone from his pocket and dialed Susan Denton's number, realizing he was taking a risk.

"Hello?" she answered.

"Hey, it's me," he said, relieved to hear her voice. "You okay?"

"Marty, where are you? You have to come back."

"No can do, Sue. I only called to make sure you were okay."

"I've signed a confidentiality agreement," she said. "Linda said you'll get the same deal if you come back."

He snorted. "Sure, I will. Listen, I gotta go. They might be listening. Talk to you soon."

"But Marty—"

He tucked it back into his pocket and moved off through

the shadows. Creeping along between the houses, he made his way through several backyards and over fences. In the night, no one noticed him except for a dog barking in a kennel. Arriving at Ester's back porch, he waited several moments to be sure no one was watching, then knocked at the door. A short time later the back porch light came on and Ester peered out the window. She was of medium height and wore her long gray hair in a single braid that came over her shoulder. Her grayish eyes were keen and alert, just like the photo on the back cover of her book, only older.

"Who the hell are you?" she said.

"My name is Martin Chittenden. I'm an astronomer with the Mesa Station Observatory in Flagstaff. I'm here because I need your help. I know you from your college textbook— *Heavenly Bodies and Their Origins.*"

Ester Thorn opened the inside door and stood leaning on her black lacquered cane. She looked him over and said, "Why the hell are you at my back door?"

"Because I don't want anyone to see me," he said. "Mrs. Thorn, I need to talk to you about an NEO that's going to collide with the Earth in eighty-six days."

"An NEO?" she said, visibly confused. "Why don't you want anyone to see you?"

"Because the government is trying to keep it a secret. Mrs. Thorn, if you'll just give me five minutes of your time, I can explain."

After deciding that Marty looked a little too soft to be a dangerous criminal, Ester unlocked the storm door and let him in. "You try anything, boy, and I'll crack you over the head with this thing." She gestured with the cane.

"No ma'am. I'm only here for your help. Honest."

She led him into the kitchen, where they sat at the table. Ester put on her glasses and took a hard look at him in the light. "Boy, you need some sun."

"Well, I burn easily," he said. "And I'm usually asleep during the day."

"Mm-hm. I remember those days well enough." She sat

back in her chair with her right hand propped on the cane. "I prefer sleeping nights now. It's better for my constitution."

"I'm sure it is," he said.

"Is Ben Stafford still down there at Mesa Station?"

Marty shook his head. "I've never heard that name. He must've left before I was hired."

"No, he didn't," she admitted. "I made him up."

Marty smiled.

"What about Ben Gardner?"

"Now that's a name I remember," he said. "He retired a year before I came on."

"So you drove all the way to Idaho just to see little old me, eh?"

"I sure did."

"Well, I don't know whether I can help you," she said. "There have been so many discoveries since I retired, I'm not sure I even speak the language these days."

"I'm sure you speak the language as well as ever, Mrs. Thorn. I've—"

"Call me Ester. Will Thorn died twenty-five years ago."

"Okay, Ester," he said, smiling. "So this might be a little hard to believe, but two months ago I spotted an asteroid that has turned out to be on a collision course with Earth. It's—"

"Which class?"

"M-class, mostly iron." He was glad she was still sharp-witted. "And after making sure that it was definitely going to hit us, I took my—"

"How big is it?"

"Three point two kilometers across at its widest point," he said patiently. "And it's tumbling on three different axes."

"All three, eh? It must've hit something pretty hard," she muttered. "When did you say it was due?"

"It's due to hit North America in eighty-six days."

"Velocity?"

"It's fast," he said. "Thirty miles a second."

Ester made a face. "That's pretty fast for an asteroid," she said thoughtfully. "It can't be coming from the belt."

"No," he said, shaking his head. "It's coming from the high north, almost straight down from the pole, not quite, but close."

"So it's coming from the Great Beyond, then," she said.

"I believe so," he said, recalling the term Great Beyond from her book.

"I'm not surprised so few have seen it, nor that the government wants to keep it a secret. How do you know they know?"

"Because there are two agents parked up the block watching your house."

Ester looked more taken aback over that than she had over the asteroid. "You're kidding."

"I wish I was. I took my findings over to JPL, and it turned out they already knew. Now they want to keep me quiet."

"So what do you want from me?"

"Advice."

"On what?"

"On how to take it public. The people have a right to know."

She looked at him. "Boy, do you know how stupid the people are?"

"I suppose I do, but they deserve a chance, don't they? I know it's going to create chaos, but chaos is inevitable. At least if the world is told beforehand, some people will be able to prepare."

"Oh, well, some people *are* preparing. You can safely believe that. The wealthiest passengers always get first crack at the lifeboats."

"I guess that's the part I don't like," he said. "The passengers in steerage deserve the same chance."

Ester smiled. "You do know that it won't much matter, don't you? Mankind is only barely going to survive this—and only the most barbaric of us at that. It's going to be a lot like starting over from the Bronze Age . . . only much less civilized."

"But if we can get word out now," he said in earnest,

"there are people out there with the resources to manage civilized attempts."

"And they'll be hunted by the barbarians," Ester persisted. "But you're right. A few pockets of civilized people might make it through if they're able to find a way to feed and defend themselves."

Marty grimaced. He had conjured a number of repugnant scenarios in his imagination over the past few weeks, but hadn't yet thought in terms of people hunting people.

"Do you know anyone we can go to?" he asked. "Someone with access to a telescope who can verify my findings and take them to the media? All of my personal colleagues are being watched."

"I know one or two old-timers still in the business, but that's not really the problem. The problem is how do I contact them without those government boys knowing about it? I'm an old woman, you know. If they see me suddenly driving off to the airport, they're going to know something is cooking."

"And they're probably tapped into your phone so you can't call anyone either. We need to think of a way to make them lose interest in you."

"Well, that's easy. Get caught."

"Get caught?" Marty asked doubtfully.

"Sure. After they've got you, they'll forget all about me, and I'll be able to go wherever I need to without them knowing anything at all."

"I wonder if they'd take me back to JPL or stick me in some secret government prison."

"Regardless," Ester said, "after the asteroid goes public, there won't be any reason for them to hold you."

"So you'll do it, then? If I let them catch me, you'll contact someone who can verify the story and take it to the media?"

"It's been a long time since I've taken a trip. And if you're right about this old rogue, it sounds like it might be now or never."

"So then we have to figure out a way for you to know when

I've been caught. I obviously can't just walk up to their car out there and turn myself in."

"It's almost that simple, though," she said. "I assume you've got a car around here someplace?"

Marty nodded.

She said, "Well, pull up to the curb across the street there and get out like you don't have a care in the world. I'm sure they'll put the old *habeas grabbus* on you before you can even make it to my front door."


**TWENTY MINUTES LATER** Marty drove past the Secret Service men and pulled to the curb in front of Ester's house. He shut off the engine and stole a glance in the rearview mirror. Summoning his courage, he got out and started across the street. A few seconds later he heard a pair of car doors open and shut and knew they were coming.

"Chittenden!" a man said. "United States Secret Service. Stop where you are!"

Marty turned to see the same two agents he had escaped from back at JPL marching toward him. He spun and bolted, but didn't make it more than a couple of steps before he felt a sharp sting between his shoulder blades and every muscle in his body was seized by a great electrical shock.

He crashed to the street, jerking spasmodically about on the asphalt. He was vaguely aware that he was screaming but couldn't control that either, and after eighteen agonizing seconds he lay on his face with drool running from the corner of his mouth. He had been Tasered and pissed his pants.

"Remember me, dickhead?" Agent Paulis said, kicking his foot. "I'm the guy you jabbed in the fucking eye." Paulis turned to his partner. "Juice him again, Bruce. He's trying to escape."

Agent Bruce pulled the trigger and subjected Marty to another eighteen agonizing seconds of electric shock. When it was finally over, Paulis knelt beside him on the walk and looked him in the face. "How do you like me now?"

Marty mumbled something unintelligible as the two men cuffed his hands behind his back and hauled him to his feet.

"You know, you might as well have drawn us a map," Paulis said they dragged him off to the car. "You left the old lady's book sitting right out on your desk. For a scientist, you're pretty fucking stupid."

Ester peered through the curtains and watched as they drove away. After she was fairly certain they wouldn't be coming back for her, she went into the bedroom and packed a small bag, which she took into the garage and put into the backseat of her car. Then she went upstairs to bed, wondering if anybody now working at the Gemini Observatory would even remember her.

# FIVE

VERONICA SAT UP IN BED AND TURNED ON THE LIGHT. IT WAS
two o'clock in the morning. "Michael, wake up."

Her boyfriend rolled over and squinted against the lamp
light. "What's wrong?"

"I need to talk to you about something."

He twisted onto his side. "Okay," he said sleepily.

"On the way back from Crissy's I met this guy at a truck
stop in Nebraska," she said. "And he . . . well, long story
short, he told me that an asteroid is going to hit the Earth in
like eighty days or something and that he and some friends
of his are going to try to save a bunch of women and children. I think they may've bought one of those old missile
silos the government's been selling."

Michael's face split into a grin. "Let me guess, he invited
you to help him repopulate the Earth."

"Something like that, yeah."

He chuckled and rolled back over. "That story could have
waited until breakfast. The man is obviously a paranoid de-
lusional."

She sat looking at him, a sinking feeling in her stomach.
She wasn't particularly close to her sister, but Michael had a
large extended family and they were very close.

"You don't want to hear what else he said?"

"Not particularly," he mumbled. "I talk to crazy people all day, honey."

"He was very convincing."

"Paranoids often are."

"He said that I could only bring you. No one else. Which means you'd have to leave your family."

He turned back over. "Are you telling me you're actually taking this goof seriously? Veronica, tell me you're not."

She sat looking at him, unblinking.

"Veronica, come on."

"He said he had a friend at the Pentagon who broke a bunch of laws even telling him about it."

"Now, hold on a second," he said, popping himself up on an elbow. "Since when do you suffer fools so lightly?"

"I like to think I never do."

"Then what's different about this one?"

She shrugged. "Like I said, he was very convincing."

Her body language was such that Michael had a sudden realization. "You were attracted to him." His tone was not quite accusatory.

"I wouldn't say that. But there was a very definite confidence about him."

"Which is another way of saying what I just said."

"I don't think that's fair, Michael. And so what if I was? You see women all the time you're attracted to."

"But it's not the same," he countered. "Men are chemically predisposed to chase after the opposite sex. For women it's different, it's cognitive."

"Oh, I'm so tired of that bullshit argument! Every time I catch you looking at another woman, it's the same crap."

He frowned, feeling only slightly guilty for not being able to help himself. "All I'm saying is that you were affected on an intellectual level."

"And don't you dare psychoanalyze me. I hate it when you do that."

He sighed and lay back, looking at the ceiling. "So have you talked to him since?"

"No. Are you going to listen to the story or not?"

He propped himself back up and smiled at her. "I'm all ears."

When she was finished, he took her hand and held it. "You're telling me you honestly believed all that?"

"I'm telling you that he was very convincing, and I don't appreciate being patronized."

"I'm not patronizing you. How's this . . . In the morning we'll Google the number and see what comes up."

"I've already done that, as a matter of fact, and nothing came up on that specific number, but I did discover that it's the same exact area code and prefix as the goddamn Pentagon."

A shadow crossed his brow. "Okay, that's odd," he admitted, "but it doesn't mean that's really his number."

"There's only one way to find out," she said, rolling out of bed.

"Honey, it's two A.M."

"He won't care if he's the sort of guy I read him to be," she said. "And if he was lying, so what if I wake him up?"

"But suppose you get the Pentagon?"

"Oops, wrong number!"

She fished the receipt from her purse and punched the number into her cell phone.

Then she pressed the send button and put the phone on speaker so Michael could hear.

"Hello!" Forrest answered in a shout. There was some sort of drill motor grinding away in the background.

"Is this Jack?" she asked, almost ashamed of the relief she'd felt upon hearing his voice.

"Yeah, who's speaking?"

"It's the woman from the truck stop."

"Veronica?"

"Yeah. How did you— Oh, you must've seen my plate."

"Hey, Linus," Forrest said to someone in the background. "Shut that fucking thing off a minute, I can't hear this girl. It sounds like the meteor may have gone public. Okay, Veronica, go ahead. Have they gone public already?"

She gave Michael a gotcha look, and he sat up a little straighter in bed. "No, Jack. No, they haven't gone public. At least not that I know of."

"Is something wrong, then?"

"Well, sort of," she replied. "I was wondering if you'd be willing to talk with Michael, my boyfriend. He doesn't believe your story."

Forrest laughed out loud. "Did you really expect him to? Put me on speaker."

"You already are."

"Okay, great. Mike, you there, man?"

"Yeah," Michael said.

"Listen, I'm sorry. The story was bullshit. I was just trying to get in her pants. You know how guys are."

"Yeah, I know how they are," Michael muttered.

Veronica turned off the speaker and put the phone to her ear. "You son of a bitch! You tell him what you told me, goddamnit! Don't make me look like an idiot!"

"Am I still on speaker?"

"No!"

"Veronica, listen to me." She sat in bed and leaned over so Michael could listen in. "Put yourself in his situation. The story's going to break soon enough. When it does, call me back."

"What was that drilling sound when you first answered?" she asked, hoping to garner some more telling information.

"Oh, that . . . well, we're busy with lots of arts and crafts right now." They could hear laughter in the background. "Listen, Veronica, I gotta go. Call me if you hear something."

"But wait!" she said. "What if it never goes public? What then?"

"Then I was obviously lying to you."

"No! I'm sorry but you've all but convinced me, so you're going to have to live up to the offer."

Michael gave her a look.

She could hear the sound of Forrest's Zippo lighter clicking open and then closed as he lit a cigarette.

"Okay," he said. "Tell you what. If it never goes public, I'll call you back at this number two days before the event, how's that?"

"Do you promise?"

"What the hell would a promise mean, Veronica? You don't even know me. Now try and get some sleep."

Forrest broke the connection.

"See?" she said, throwing the phone down between them in the counterpane. "See what I was talking about? Does he sound remotely nuts to you?"

Michael sat looking at her, realizing with mixed emotions that she had already made some kind of a connection with this mysterious Jack, who very definitely had a certain unmistakable *je ne sais quoi* about him even over the phone. "I'll admit that he seems to believe what he's saying. Beyond that . . . all we can do is wait and see."

"What do you think they were drilling?" she wondered, settling beneath the blankets. "You have to admit it's pretty late at night to be up working, and it's an hour later in Nebraska."

He chuckled as he reached across her to turn off the lamp. "For all we know, Ronny, the guy was drilling his way out of a prison cell in Guatemala."

# SIX

**AFTER AN EXHAUSTING ROUND TRIP TO NORTHERN MONTANA**
to visit his estranged wife, Monica, Forrest arrived back at
the silo a day later, tense and strung out on amphetamines.
He pulled up to a modest two-story house that had once been
used to house Air Force personnel during the Cold War. The
house had been built over the top of the silo entrance to
better disguise it from Soviet satellites.

Ulrich stood on the porch of the house watching as a giant
black German shepherd jumped out of the Humvee and ran
across the yard to pee on a fifty gallon drum of diesel oil that
was yet to be taken below.

"We running a kennel service now?"

Forrest gave no indication he'd heard Ulrich's dig as he
went about unloading the back of the Hummer, stacking
fifty-foot bundles of NM-B type wire and five-gallon buckets of latex paint neatly off to the side. Ulrich came down the
stairs and over to the truck.

"You expecting burglars or something? That's another
mouth to feed."

Forrest stopped and looked at him in the light of the cab.
"Are you intentionally being an asshole or do you really not
recognize him?"

Ulrich turned for another look at the German shepherd.

"You've been all the way to Montana and back? Jesus, you must've driven nonstop both ways."

"Yeah, well, Benzedrine's a wonderful thing," Forrest muttered, grabbing up two buckets of paint as if they weighed little more than a pair of barracks bags and heading for the house.

Because of his prosthetic foot, Ulrich grabbed a single bucket and followed him. They set the buckets down in the hall and went into the kitchen, where Forrest took a couple of beers from the fridge, knocking the caps off against the edge of the counter and handing one to Ulrich.

Forrest gestured at the dog with the bottle. "He eats a fifty-pound bag of dog food a month." He took a pull from the beer. "So we'll need at least twenty-four bags. And be sure to get Purina. Don't buy any of that generic shit. And get a bunch of those Milk Bones too. Fifty boxes or so."

"That's like six hundred pounds of dog shit somebody's gonna have to scoop up, and it sure as hell won't be me," Ulrich said.

"Nobody's asking you to," Forrest replied testily.

Ulrich glanced over his shoulder as the dog trotted through the house sniffing everything in sight. "How did you talk Monica into giving him up?"

"I didn't talk her into anything. She asked me if I wanted to save my son's dog and I said yes. Now, are you gonna pick up the food or do I have to go get it myself?"

Linus Danzig stepped into the doorway and stood looking at the wolflike dog trotting around the kitchen. He was a big country boy in his late twenties, wearing nothing but a pair of purple underwear.

"Fuck are you made up for?" Forrest asked irritably.

Danzig shook his head and disappeared back down the hall, realizing Forrest was in one of his moods.

Ulrich drank deeply from the beer and had a seat. "Wanna tell me about it?" He put his feet up on the table.

"Nothin' to tell," Forrest said, ripping the cellophane from a brand new pack of Camels. "She don't wanna live underground and she ain't gonna, but then I already knew that." He smacked a cigarette from the pack, lit it with the Zippo from his pocket and stood leaning against the sink staring at the floor.

"I can help you kidnap her," Ulrich said quietly.

Forrest looked at him, his eyes welling with tears. "I'd never do that to her. She'd kill herself belowground the first chance she got. Hell, if it wasn't for her horses, she'd have done it by now."

Ulrich sighed and rocked back, the wooden chair creaking beneath the strain. "There's a lot that's unsaid, Jack, but you know I think the world of that woman."

Forrest nodded, drawing pensively from the cigarette. "She's just so . . . full of anger, Wayne. She never shows it but it's there, right below the surface . . . Christ, that woman's angry."

"And she has every right. You guys lost your son. And who knows? Maybe if I hadn't talked you into that last mission—"

Forrest held up a finger, banishing the thought. "You never talked me into anything I didn't wanna do. Monica knows that. She's no more angry with you than she is me. Who she's really pissed at is him." He pointed up at the ceiling.

Ulrich looked at his boots. "Wanna cash it in?" he said suddenly. "We can give the silo to the trio and go to Montana. Erin will agree to it, Taylor too probably. Hell, those women were all thick as thieves at one time . . . and they miss Monica."

Forrest smiled wanly at his friend, knowing the offer was genuine. "Even if Monica wanted the company—which she doesn't—there's no way I'm letting any of your wives die if I don't have to. One's enough." He crushed out the cigarette in the sink. "I'm gonna go bring the rest of that shit in. I picked up some new office chairs too, by the way, since that request seems to have gone in one ear and out the other."

"Yeah, I don't have enough shit to buy without having to worry about your creature comforts."

"And there's a lot of assembly required," Forrest added with a chuckle, "so get the Dynamic Duo to put 'em together in the morning." He took Laddie outside with him, and the moment he was gone, Danzig reappeared in the kitchen doorway with Oscar Vasquez. Marcus Kane was asleep in the silo below.

"Is he okay?" Danzig asked.

Ulrich tipped his beer and looked at them. "You know who's gonna have to police up all that dog shit, don't you? He sure as hell isn't gonna do it."

Vasquez grinned. "And that dog's shit is gonna be *biiig*, *vato*."

Danzig laughed, both of them cracking up at the look appearing on Ulrich's face.

"Since you two dickheads are up," he said, dropping his feet to the floor, "we just got some new office chairs that need—"

Both Danzig and Vasquez vanished instantly.

"That's what I thought!" he called after them, taking another swig and muttering to himself. "Just what we need, the lingering odor of dog shit in those tunnels."

# SEVEN

HAROLD SHIPMAN CAME DOWN THE HALL OUTSIDE OF HIS office at the Gemini Observatory in Hawaii to find Ester Thorn seated in a chair against the wall, her hand propped on her cane, overnight bag on the floor beside her. "Ester?" he said. "My God, what a surprise! How have you been?"

Ester took his hand and used her cane to push herself to her feet. "I've been well enough," she said grimly, tired from her long flight over the Pacific. "But I'm afraid I come as a harbinger of bad things to come, Harold. May we talk privately?"

"Yes, of course," Shipman said, puzzled but amused to see that Ester had barely changed since the last time he'd seen her nearly ten years before, when she was his senior at the observatory. "You should've called, Ester. I could have made arrangements."

"There's time enough for arrangements," she muttered, watching him put his key into the door.

Shipman took up her bag and allowed her to precede him into the cluttered office that had once been hers, inviting her to sit across from him in one of the two chairs before his desk.

"So what in the world brings you all this way?" he asked.

"Thor's Hammer," she said, her old gray eyes unblinking as she allowed the silence to gather.

Shipman did not immediately respond, although he knew exactly what Ester meant, remembering well her vehement assertions that the industrialized governments of the world ignored the dangers of near Earth objects at the peril of all humankind. "Yes," he said. "Well, it's still out there somewhere, we all know that, but I'm afraid with all of the cutbacks and—"

"Would you like to see it, Harold?"

He went slack in the jaw. "Excuse me?"

"It's coming out of Ursa Minor," she said, referring to the northernmost constellation, often referred to as the Little Dipper.

Shipman turned in his chair, grabbing a chart of the heavens from a nearby table piled high with charts and texts. "Who's spotted it?"

"A young astronomer from Mesa Station. Martin Chittenden. Ever heard of him?"

"I recognize the name," he said, flipping through the chart. "I think I may have read something of his a while back in *Astronomy Today.* Something on deep space asteroids. Lots of conjecture. If I remember correctly, he thinks we're not paying enough attention to empty space."

"Turns out we haven't been," she said, her expression tightening along with the grip on her cane.

"Ester, what's going on? Are you telling me we're actually going to be hit?"

"We've got about eighty days to impact."

"Eighty days? How big is it?"

"Three point two kilometers."

"My God!"

"And it's coming at us so fast it'll make your eyeballs roll."

"But that just can't be," he said, scanning the same chart he'd seen thousands of times. "There's nothing out there, Ester. You know that."

"It's coming from the Great Beyond, and it's maybe as old as the Earth."

He turned the chart on the desk for her to see. "Show me where."

She used the tip of her cane to indicate the northernmost star in the sky. "The brightness of Polaris has probably helped to keep it hidden all these years. Like the Red Baron coming out of the sun."

"Thor's Hammer," he muttered. "I take it you've seen this creature for yourself?"

She shook her head.

"Well, then how do you know it's even—"

"The night he came to ask for my help in taking it public, he was abducted from my front lawn by two federal agents. They shot the boy in the back with a Taser gun, Harold."

"They're trying to keep it a secret, for Christ's sake? It'll never work!"

"That's not stopping the cowardly bastards from trying."

"Well, we sure as hell won't stand for that," Shipman said. "Not if this fellow knows what the devil he's talking about. I'll turn the dome tonight and we'll just have a look for ourselves. Though it could take weeks to come up with an orbital model that will prove our case."

"All we need are preliminary estimates," Ester said. "And those we can come up with in a few days, enough to get everyone on Earth with a telescope looking toward Polaris. Getting word out isn't going to be the problem. The problem will be in prepping these islands."

"Prepping the Hawaiians? For tsunamis? Where does Chittenden think it will hit?"

"North America. He's seems fairly certain of that. So it's not so much a tsunami of water I'm worried about. Once word gets out that the mainland is under the gun . . ."

"People will flock here by the thousands. We'll be overrun," Shipman concluded.

"That's right. So I think we need to get the governor's ear as quickly as possible. Do you know anyone in the local government?"

"I play golf with the mayor of Honolulu."

"Perfect. I think it's important that the Islands prepare to quarantine themselves. That might take some convincing at first, but once the insanity begins . . ." She shrugged. "Desperate times seem to precipitate their own desperate measures."

"This explains a few things," he muttered, sitting back in his chair and taking his pipe from a side drawer. "NASA's been cutting funding across the board and suggesting all sorts of odd things for everyone to look at out there. Even the GLAST telescope has been kept aimed in almost the opposite direction over the past five months or so."

"During my flight I was wondering about that new satellite program that was fast-tracked out of nowhere. The timing is too close. It has to be related. I'm even doubting they're satellites."

"You think they're trying for a shoot-down?"

Ester sucked her teeth. "It's all we've got, isn't it?"

Shipman shook his head, saying, "At two miles across, it won't work unless this thing's made of butter. What class is it? Did Chittenden say?"

"M-class."

"Well let's hope he's wrong, by God. Ester, you sure know how to wreck an old man's day."

"Oh, you're not even sixty yet," she said. "And look at it this way . . . neither of us has to worry about ending up in diapers now."

He tossed the chart back onto the table. "I'd also like to bring Sam Ash in on this. He knows a lot of people in cable news. That might expedite things once we've got some orbital models to offer."

"We have to keep this an absolute secret until we announce. And here's something else . . . when we do announce, we have to be ready to counter the skeptics and naysayers—all those same idiots who are still denying global warming."

"All right," he said. "We'll do our research, and then we'll get in touch with Sam. He's here on the island."

"The situation will deteriorate rapidly after impact," Ester went on. "First, it will be every state for itself. Then every city, every neighborhood, every block, and finally every man, woman, and child. This country's headed back to the Stone Age, Harold, and nothing can stop it."

"I'm afraid our immediate problems here will be of a somewhat different nature."

"Meaning?"

"Well, Pearl Harbor is home to the United States Pacific Fleet. That's a lot of permanently displaced sailors and marines. Who controls them after Washington goes out of business? What will the Admiralty decide to do about these islands? We could all too easily become a military state here."

"I hadn't thought of that," she said. "Obviously, the Navy possesses the facility to be either our saviors or the bane of our existence." She sat thinking for a short while. "Does President Hadrian still live here on the island?"

"He does."

President Barry Hadrian was a former president of the United States who had retired with his wife to his home state of Hawaii after two successful terms of office. He was in his fifties now and still very well respected.

"Perhaps your friend the mayor can talk to him," Ester suggested. "I doubt either of them would like to see us ruled by the military. Who's the governor these days?"

"Paola Reyes. A flimsy politician, to say the least. I don't see her standing up to the Navy once disaster has struck."

"Is she particularly popular among Hawaiians?"

Shipman shrugged. "Fifty-fifty. She goes where the smiles go, caters heavily to the tourists and local business."

"Then she'll not likely be missed," Ester decided. "But that's getting ahead of ourselves. The first thing we have to do is establish that Chittenden's NEO actually exists. After that we go on the offensive."

# EIGHT

**DR. MICHAEL PORTER WAS LYING ON THE SOFA WATCHING** CNN when a BREAKING NEWS bulletin suddenly interrupted the Nasdaq report. Aging anchor Wolf Blitzer appeared and tersely announced that a trio of astronomers from the Gemini Observatory in Hawaii was standing by to make a collective statement, concerning a large asteroid due to collide with the earth within the next few months.

"Fuck," Michael muttered, sitting up on the couch. "Hey, Ronny? You'd better come listen to this."

Veronica came quickly from the kitchen. "Is this it?"

He gestured at the television where Ester Thorn stood behind a podium between two much taller male astronomers. She spoke into a cluster of microphones. The caption in the upper right-hand corner of the screen read: LIVE.

" . . . and if these preliminary calculations are accurate," Ester Thorn said, reading from a prepared statement, "this object will collide with the Earth in sixty days. We are at this time still calculating the exact point of impact . . ."

"Holy shit!" Veronica whispered. "He was telling the truth." She felt a sudden surge of fear and sat down on the couch. Michael put his arm around her as they sat watching.

" . . . but we have determined with veritable certainty that we will be struck somewhere in or very close to North

America. The asteroid is coming toward us out of the northern sky at a velocity in excess of one hundred thousand miles an hour from the constellation Ursa Minor nearest the star we call Polaris. This means it is not coming from the asteroid belt within our solar system, and that it has very likely been traveling millions of years to get here.

"An asteroid of this size is on par with the object we believe ended the reign of the dinosaurs more than sixty-five million years ago. So, with that in mind, we believe it is essential for all nations to begin preparations at once. The time for denial has long since passed. We are a species with the means of preserving itself, but we must work together and we must begin today, this very hour. Thank you."

The reporters in front of the podium went nuts, shouting their questions, but neither Ester nor the men made an effort to answer as they walked back into the observatory.

"The government's been keeping it from us," Michael said. "Did you hear that bit about 'the time for denial has passed'? She was saying 'shame on you' to somebody."

"I wonder if they'll arrest her. If you think about it, this wasn't a very responsible way to tell us. People could well go nuts."

"That won't likely happen before the final week or so," he said. "At least not on a grand scale. Shock and denial have to run their course first. The biggest problem will be getting people to go to work, which is likely the reason we haven't been told. Anyhow, I doubt they'll arrest her. She's an old woman and that would only prove her point. If the government wants credibility, they'll have to offer us some kind of hope or solution."

As if on cue, Wolf Blitzer announced the President of the United States live from the White House.

"My fellow Americans," began the President, an elderly man with white hair, standing before a podium flanked by a pair of officials, "the time has come for me to share with you a discovery of great significance . . ."

When the President was finished, Veronica opened her

phone and selected Forrest's number, pressing the call button.

"Hello, Veronica," Forrest answered in a quiet voice a few moments later.

"Jack, the story broke ten minutes ago on CNN."

"Who broke it?"

"A group of astronomers in Hawaii. The President spoke right afterward."

"Did he speak live in front of reporters?"

"It was live from inside the White House. No reporters. He only spoke for about five minutes."

"Were there two other men in the shot with him?"

"You saw it?"

"No. It wasn't live. That announcement was taped weeks ago. Listen, pay close attention to whatever he says when he's live and in front of the media. Soon, he'll have to respond directly to whatever assertions are being made by these astronomers. The White House already has a battery of experts lined up to manage the public fear factor, but it's going to take a few hours to get them all to D.C. for a joint appearance. They're going to play it way down, make like it's just a matter of shooting it out of the sky, but every astronomer in the world will be weighing in over the next few weeks, and the facts will eventually override all their bullshit."

"How do you know all of this stuff?"

"I'd rather not get into that over the phone. But if you guys would like to meet, that's fine. We've got fifty-nine days."

"I think I'd like to meet sooner than later."

"Okay. Make it the day after tomorrow at the truck stop."

"Well, should we pack now? Do you need us to bring anything?"

Forrest laughed.

"What?" she said. "Don't laugh at me!"

"You can bring the chips and beer."

"I can't believe you're making fun of me."

"Veronica, I've had some time to come to terms with this. And you've had an entire month."

"Well, I've been hoping you were full of shit," she said.

"Oh, you knew goddamn well I was telling the truth. So, are you gonna ditch your old man now or what?"

"No!" she said indignantly. "Hold on . . ."

She turned to Michael, who was just hanging up with his father. "Honey, he says he can meet with us at the truck stop day after tomorrow. You okay with that?"

Michael crossed his arms and nodded. "Yeah, yeah we can do that."

"What time, Jack?"

"Make it nineteen hundred," Forrest said. "If anything comes up, call."

"Wait, what time is that?"

"That's seven P.M.," he answered with a chuckle.

"I'm glad you find this end-of-the-world stuff so funny."

"I don't find it funny at all. I think you're funny. See you then." He broke the connection.

Michael stood looking at her.

"How're your folks?" she asked.

"Dad's fine. You know him. But mom's already a wreck, worried about my sisters and all the grandkids." He put his hands in his pockets and laughed joylessly. "I'm not sure I believe this is happening, Ronny. It's worse than Pompeii. There's absolutely nowhere to run."

She shrugged. "That's why we dig . . . well, figuratively."

# NINE

FORREST TUCKED THE PHONE INTO HIS POCKET AND GRABBED
a pair of ammo cans filled with .223 caliber ammunition for
their M-4 carbines, short-barreled versions of the M-16 assault rifle. He carried the ammo into the house and waited
at the top of the basement stairwell for Ulrich to come up
and get it.

"Got a meeting with that girl from the truck stop day after
tomorrow," he said, handing the cans over. "Her boyfriend's
gonna be there, so I want you to come along."

"Suppose the guy's an asshole?"

"Hence the meeting, Wayne. That's what I'm looking to
find out."

"Just making sure, partner."

"The meteor's gone public, by the way."

Ulrich stopped as he turned to go down. "It's an asteroid,
Jack. Who broke the story?"

"A group of astronomers in Hawaii, I guess. You'd better
turn on the TV down there and find out what they're saying."

"I'll tell Linus to watch it," Ulrich said, heading down.
"He likes sitting on his ass."

After the ammo was stored belowground, Forrest took a
break in the house. He was smoking a cigarette on the couch
with Laddie at his feet when Ulrich and Vasquez came into

the living room and dropped onto a couple of chairs. The sun was setting and pretty soon the five of them would be gathering in the kitchen to make dinner.

"What are they saying on TV?" Forrest asked.

Ulrich rubbed his eyes, fatigued from lack of sleep. "Exactly what Jerry told us to expect—there's nothing to worry about, they're gonna shoot it down and the world will enter into an era of peace and prosperity."

Vasquez chuckled. "And the five of us will be asshole deep in debt for the rest of our lives."

"We should hope," Ulrich said.

Forrest pointed at Vasquez, his mind on forty things at once. "What are we going to do about your insulin habit in the long term?"

Vasquez shrugged. "I've got a lot of it down there on dry ice. If we keep it cold, it'll last a long time."

"But even if you've got enough for two years, there's a limit, Oscar. What do we do when you run out?"

"I guess you watch me slip into a coma and die, Homes. It won't hurt. I'll just go to sleep."

"I don't like that plan," Forrest said. "And neither will Maria or little Oscar. Is there a way we can manufacture it?"

"It's a hormone, dude. Shit, we may not even outlive my supply."

"For your information, *dude,* I plan to make it well beyond your goddamn supply, and if it's all the same to you, I'd like for you to be around when we come back up. Now what do you guys want to eat tonight? I say we grill some steaks and get completely pissed. This is going to be the last sane night on Earth."

"It's a damn good thing we've finished buying supplies," Ulrich said with relief. "They'll put the clamp-down on the food and fuel now. And ammo especially."

"Yeah, civilians won't be able to buy BBs after tomorrow," Vasquez added.

"Which is why we've saved the painting and the minor repairs down below for last," Forrest said. "I think I'll try getting in touch with Jerry at the Pentagon one last time before he's up to his ears in emergency protocol."

"Is there anything more he can do for us?"

"The way I see it, there's going to be a whole lot of shit being shipped all over hell's half acre by the government now, which means a logistical free-for-all . . ."

Marcus Kane came into the room and Laddie jumped up to greet him, wagging his tail. "I've seen enough of that bullshit on TV," he said, rubbing the dog's ears with both hands. "The President's calling for a worldwide prayer vigil."

"That'll help," Forrest said dryly. "Anyhow, Wayne, there's no reason Jerry can't cut some bullshit paperwork redesignating this site as a government installation long enough to ship us out a truckload of MREs. Maybe even some high-tech comm gear. We'll all be in uniform when they show up, and I'll wear my captain's bars . . . so long as there's an officer here to sign for the conveyance, no staff sergeant or even a shavetail lieutenant's gonna think anything of it. They'll figure there must still be a missile down there we're sitting on. G-3 will never catch the glitch before the meteor gets here."

"*Asteroid,*" Ulrich said.

"Heavens to mergatroids, if you ain't the most anal son of a bitch I ever met. What the hell does it matter what I call it?"

"Why can't you just call it what it is?"

"It can't have nothin' to do with wantin' a rise out of you," Kane said with a wink at the other two, and the three of them laughed.

"You three can kiss my ass," Ulrich said, getting up from the chair. "You'll *think* meteor when that big bastard slams into our atmosphere. It's gonna burn so hot that anybody within sight of it'll be vaporized before it even hits the ground."

"I got a book downstairs says not necessarily," Forrest lied easily.

"Well, you can stand up here and let us know then, Mr. Scientist. I'll pop the hatch and sweep your ashes up after it hits."

"Will you spread them on the ocean for me?"

"I'll flush 'em down the goddamn toilet," Ulrich said on his way into the kitchen. "You'll get there eventually."

# TEN

**JACK FORREST AND WAYNE ULRICH BOTH STOOD FROM THE**
table as Veronica Struan and Michael Porter entered the
truck-stop diner. Veronica smiled when she saw Forrest and
led Michael by the hand to the table. Introductions were
made and everyone shook hands before they sat down. A
waitress appeared and took their drink orders, then left them
to themselves in a nearly deserted section of the diner.

"Well, I'm sure you've got a ton of questions," Forrest said,
mostly to Michael. "So why don't we let you two begin?"

"Okay," Michael said, already somewhat relieved by the
professional, almost military bearing of the other two men.
"I'm still curious how you knew about this so much sooner
than everyone else. Do you really have a friend at the Pentagon?"

"Yes, I do," Forrest said. "And that's about as much as I
intend to say about him or her. Great risks were taken."

"I understand," Michael said. "So I guess my next question is why go to so much effort to save a bunch of total
strangers? It would be so much easier to save yourselves and
leave it at that."

Forrest deferred the question to Ulrich.

"Is it really so much different than a policeman risking his life to protect his community?" Ulrich asked. "Or a soldier risking his life to protect his nation?"

"Not diametrically, no," Michael said. "But in actual practice I believe that soldiers tend to fight for one another, rather than for king and country."

"Yes and no," Forrest said. "When we were in combat, sure, it was for the team. But it was for king and country that we volunteered in the first place."

"So you equate military service with what you're planning now?"

"Wayne, myself, and the other three men in our group have spent all of our adult lives defending people," Forrest explained. "Be they Americans or the innocents of some other country—which does not make us heroes. We're just particularly well trained for this kind of thing and we feel a certain amount of responsibility."

"Particularly well trained how?" Veronica asked.

"We're retired Green Berets," Ulrich said. "Special Forces operatives. And in the Special Forces we're trained to operate in small groups, as small as practical for any given operation. Which means that each man has to be as broadly trained as possible. The training can range widely, from foreign languages to the piloting of rotary winged aircraft."

"So you've been in combat?" Michael asked. "Shot people?"

The two soldiers glanced at one another.

"We've fired a few rounds in anger, yes," Forrest said dryly.

"I'm not trying to sound like an adolescent," Michael said. "I'm very curious about what sort of people you are, your backgrounds."

"Maybe we're a little unused to being questioned about certain things," Ulrich offered. "I suppose that's something we're going to have to get used to now that we'll be living among nonmilitary personnel."

"Do any of you have families?" Veronica asked.

"Most of us do," Ulrich said. "Only Jack and our buddy

Marcus are single. Though Jack's technically . . ." He looked at Forrest, unsure how to continue.

"What he means is that technically I still have a wife," Forrest explained. "But we've been separated for about eighteen months now and she won't be joining us."

Veronica was surprised and even a little disappointed to learn that Forrest was married, but she couldn't tell whether it was his decision for his wife not to join them or his wife's. So she asked.

"It's hers," he answered matter-of-factly, maintaining the military bearing. "I want very much for her to be with us, but after we lost our son she . . . well, she's very different now, and she has no desire to survive what's coming."

"I'm so sorry," Veronica said.

"I'm also very sorry," Michael said sincerely. "It's very difficult for a mother to lose a child. There's no way you might convince her?"

Forrest shook his head, his deadpan demeanor signaling a change of subject.

Veronica wasn't familiar with this all-business version of Jack Forrest, but she was pretty sure that he was being so soldierly now for Michael's benefit. The question was whether it was out of respect, or an attempt to convince Michael that he was capable of carrying off the task at hand.

"So you really think you can pull this off?" she asked.

"If we survive the impact, I'm confident that we can survive belowground for as long as the food holds out, which should be anywhere from eighteen months to two years, depending on how many join us. After that, I make no predictions or guarantees of any kind. What we're offering is a chance. Nothing more. And it's clearly not an option for everyone. It won't be easy living underground in such close quarters."

"How have you screened your candidates?" Michael asked. "Or haven't you?"

"I gave five hundred dollars to a social worker in the Lincoln area along with a list of criteria," Forrest answered. "I wanted reasonably intelligent, responsible, single mothers of healthy, underprivileged children between the ages of five and twelve. There were a few other stipulations, but those were the biggies."

"Because younger children eat less food?" Michael assumed.

"Correct. In all, we've tagged about fifty people in addition to our own families and friends."

"And you've contacted them all?"

"We've contacted none of them yet. We'll begin what we're calling the 'round-up' ten days prior to impact, and we obviously don't expect them all to accept the offer."

"No other men?"

"There are two," Ulrich said. "A surgeon and a dentist, along with their wives and children. Otherwise, no males older than ten."

"You can't risk having your hegemony challenged," Michael said.

"Bluntly put, that's exactly right," Forrest said.

"It makes good sense."

"Good to hear we have the psychiatrist's approval." Forrest said, grinning. "And you're a sociologist," he continued, pointing at Veronica.

"Yes," she said with a smile, glad to finally see his grin again.

"That's interesting," Ulrich said with an enthusiastic glance at Forrest. Up until this point he hadn't seen much advantage to their joining the group.

"And you don't think all this preparation is overkill?" Michael asked. "The government seems pretty confident they can stop this thing."

"It's a delaying action," Ulrich said. "They won't stop it. They know they're only buying time."

"Listen, I'll tell you how it's going to go," Forrest said, cutting to the chase. "That meteor—"

"Asteroid."

"That *rock* is going to smack into this planet traveling at something like thirty miles a second. After that, it's good night, Irene. Billions of tons of dirt and dust are going to smother the atmosphere, and much of this continent's going to catch on fire. So add all that smoke and ash to the mix as well. All of this brings on nuclear winter, and the government's strategic food reserves—those that survive the firestorm—are going to run out in less than a few months. Soon after that, people are going to be shooting one another over cans of Alpo. And by the time the civilized people have all been murdered or starved to death, the psychopathic alpha males are going to take over, creating their own little fiefdoms, deciding who to keep as enforcers, who to rape and who to eat. Our hope is to outlast those crazy bastards and try to find a way to grow some food through hydroponics and artificial lighting. We admit this last part's going to be dicey, but we feel a deep desire to at least give it a try."

"And if by some miracle we're wrong about how bad it's going to be," Ulrich chimed in, "we pop the hatch and go back to our lives. No harm, no foul."

Michael sat quietly mulling it over. "I know how naive it is," he admitted, "but it's still awfully hard to wrap my head around. You two talk about it as though you've already been through it."

"In a sense, we have been through it," Forrest said. "The only difference was the breadth and severity of the destruction. Large parts of Iraq and Afghanistan were literally obliterated, and cannibalism is about the only atrocity we haven't seen. Make no mistake—life's going to be a living nightmare for most of those who survive beyond the first few weeks."

"Would it be possible for us to see this place of yours?" Veronica asked. "You know, before we make our decision?"

"Most of our potential guests will to have to accept our offer sight unseen," Forrest said, "but if you two are willing to be blindfolded for the first fifty miles of the drive, I think it's doable. You'll have to stay the night with us belowground, however. I'm not making a second two-hundred-mile round trip tonight."

She looked at Michael and he looked at Forrest.

"What you're suggesting requires us to have a great deal of faith in what you've told us," he said. "Are the blindfolds really necessary?"

"Mike, if I plan to shoot you and take your woman out there in the middle of nowhere, is it really going to make a difference whether or not you're blindfolded?"

"We won't tell anyone where it's at."

"I know you won't," Forrest said. "But you certainly would if you knew where it was."

"I want to see it, Michael," Veronica said. "We'll probably be dead in two months anyhow. Let's take the chance."

Michael gave her a look.

"Listen, Mike," Ulrich said, "if it's any consolation, I don't care whether you join us or not. I mean, we could probably use your psychological expertise, but we've already got more names on the list than we can feed long-term, and my biggest fear is that the majority of them are going to accept our offer."

"Then why ask so many?" Veronica said.

Ulrich thumbed toward Forrest. "Because he won't listen to reason."

Michael had paid very close attention to the way Ulrich and Forrest comported themselves from the moment he set eyes on them, and so far neither one had said or done anything to make him believe they were being deceptive.

"Okay," he said at length. "I guess we'll take the chance."


**THE RIDE TO** the silo was long and uneventful, and Ulrich allowed them to remove their blindfolds after they'd gotten off the interstate. In the dark, one cornfield looked exactly like another, and there were no signs along the way to betray their location because they had been removed weeks earlier under cover darkness in case it ever became necessary to show someone the installation, as they were doing now, without betraying its location. There was no point in taking chances, and the last thing the authorities were worried about at the moment was missing road signs.

"Oh, he's beautiful," Veronica said, seeing Laddie looking back at her from the front passenger seat. She was seated between Michael and Ulrich.

"I thought I smelled a dog," Michael said.

"See?" said Ulrich, annoyed that he had been displaced by a dog and forced to sit in the back, though he was enjoying the proximity with Veronica, who smelled like flowers. "I told you he needs a goddamn bath."

"He hates baths," Forrest said, pulling a cigarette from its pack with his lips. "He fights so hard it's not worth the trouble." He lit the cigarette and winked at the dog.

A mile from the site, Ulrich asked them to put the blindfolds back on. After they had walked both of them into the house and down the stairs to the main blast door, Veronica and Michael were allowed to remove them.

"So there's a house above us?" Veronica asked, looking around the basement.

"It wasn't common practice," Ulrich explained, "but we're so far away from Tinker Air Force Base out here that they built an off-duty quarters for the aboveground security personnel."

"This is blast door number one," Forrest said. "It's ten inches of solid steel and weighs one ton. This door alone should be more than enough to keep out anyone trying to get in, but there's a second door just like it twenty feet down the concrete security vestibule. Remember, these installations were designed to survive a nuclear attack, not a direct hit, but anything in excess of three miles would probably have failed to disable the missiles that were installed here."

He sealed door number one behind them and led them down the lighted tunnel to number two, lifting an eight-pound sledgehammer from the floor in the corner and banging out a code against the door.

"We'll have to remember to change that code now," Ulrich said with a smile.

"Whatever," Veronica laughed. "Like either of us knows Morse code. Doesn't the intercom work?"

"Not at the moment," Forrest said. "There's a short somewhere inside the conduit and we haven't gotten around to running a new wire yet. We'll also be installing a number of small fiber-optic cameras. We've had more time-sensitive issues to deal with up to now. Like stocking up on food."

The door opened a minute later and there stood Marcus Kane, a look of surprise on his face. "Already?"

"This is just a tour," Forrest said. "These are the prospective guests we met earlier tonight. Where are the gamers?"

"Playing Xbox down in Launch Control," Kane said. "Where else?"

"Launch Control? I thought you said the missiles were gone," Veronica said.

"We still refer to the chambers by their old names," Forrest said as he led the way down five flights of stairs spanning three stories. "This way to silo number one."

The thirty-foot steel tunnel was suspended from vibration dampeners made of coiled steel shock absorbers. The walkway itself was covered with steel grating.

"This is blast tunnel number one," he said. "It seals at both ends to keep out the exhaust during launch." He opened the blast door and led them into the actual missile silo. "Be careful on the catwalk," he warned. "It's a ten-story drop to the bottom."

"Holy cow!" Michael said, looking around. "This thing is huge."

"It had to be to hold a rocket, Michael," Veronica said.

"I'm sorry, honey. I forgot you knew all about missile silos. Perhaps you'd like to give the tour?"

"Shut up," she said, looking over the railing to the bottom, where she saw a veritable pyramid of cardboard boxes. "Is that all food down there?"

"Most of it," Ulrich said, peering over. "Be careful of these railings. We've rewelded them, but some are pretty badly rusted, so don't be overly confident."

"Is all that food as well?" Michael asked, gesturing at the boxes and crates stacked all around the silo's many levels, levels originally used to allow Air Force personnel access to the missile's many systems. There were nine levels, three above where they stood and five more below.

"Most of it," Ulrich repeated, not being overly informative.

"My God, you guys have been busy," Michael said. "It's like a warehouse."

"That's the idea," Forrest said. "Let's head to Launch Control."

In Launch Control—a perfectly round room full of steel shelves filled with everything from foam cups to ammunition—they found Kane, Oscar Vasquez, and Linus Danzig all sitting in expensive office chairs before a large-screen television, playing *Halo*.

Forrest introduced the men around and everyone shook hands.

"This was the brains of the installation and remains so today," Ulrich explained, showing them the main console. "Once the aboveground cameras are installed, we'll be able to see what's going on up there at all times, both inside and outside the house. These three monitors will run on battery power most of the time. There are large dry cell batteries down those spiral stairs, which will be kept charged by bicycle generators. So the more people we have down here, the fewer turns we'll have to take at riding the bicycles."

"And suppose the asteroid hits close enough to destroy your cameras?" Michael said. "What then?"

"We'll be blind as bats down here until we're able to go up and replace them. Which could be anywhere from days to months after impact."

"What about fresh air?"

"There are two ventilator shafts with filtration systems," Forrest said, "but to be honest, those are this facility's one vulnerability. Fifty people suck a lot of air, and if those systems are compromised, we'll have to take steps."

"Steps?"

"Drastic measures. Like lowering the lift elevator or opening the main entrance in order to allow in new air, which may well be contaminated. The blast tunnels, however, will remain sealed at all times, which will allow both silos to stand as fresh air reservoirs in case there is ever a problem with ventilation. They'll buy us a few days, at least."

"So someone up there could sabotage the ventilation shafts?" Michael said.

"Potentially, yes. If they find us and if they know what to look for."

"But it's not like we have to sit down here and just let them do it either," Ulrich said. "If they can move around up there, so can we, and with our NBC suits—that's for nuclear, biological, and chemical—we'll be a lot less vulnerable to whatever contaminants there may be. And unless we're vastly outgunned, we're confident we'll be able to reduce any such threat without a great deal of trouble."

"I like the term 'reduce,'" Veronica said with a smile. "It's got a such gentle feel about it."

"We'll be anything but gentle if and when the time comes," Danzig remarked, rocking back in his chair and squirting a large glob of Cheez Whiz into his mouth. "You can believe that."

"So you do have weapons, then?" Michael said.

"Absolutely," Forrest replied. "Like I said, it's our intention to survive this thing. Have no illusions. Cruel times are headed this way and in order to live through them we may well be forced to make some heartless and selfish decisions."

"Like ignoring starving children at the gate?" Veronica said.

"Once we seal door number one behind the last guest, it doesn't open again until after impact, and then only if it's absolutely imperative in order to protect the integrity of the installation. I don't care if fifty starving children come scratching at the door."

Veronica looked at Michael. "How's that for a reality check?"

Michael shrugged his shoulders. "Unfortunately, they're right. That's why it's called a holocaust. You can't possibly save everyone who deserves to be saved."

Ulrich smiled. "I think you and I might get along, Doc."

Forrest chuckled. "Two bloodless bastards." He led them down the hall to the adjoining living and sleeping quarters, each about the size of a classroom, explaining that by day the bedding would be rolled up and stored along the walls.

"It's going to be a bit cramped," he conceded, "but I think we'll manage okay."

"I don't think white's a good color for these walls," Michael said at once. "Professionally speaking, that is. You might want to consider a bright yellow or a lime green like you've used in the tunnels, something to cheer up the environment. White is too stark. And stay away from orange and red. Especially orange. They're inflammatory colors."

Forrest and Ulrich exchanged glances.

"Can you think of anything else?" Ulrich asked, interested.

"Well, what do you have planned for recreation?" Michael asked. "Aside from the bike riding."

"We've got a huge selection of DVDs and video games," Ulrich said. "Lots of books, music CDs."

"What else?"

The soldiers looked at each other again.

"That's not enough?"

Now it was Michael and Veronica's turn to exchange glances. Veronica even laughed.

"Um, no," Michael said. "Not unless you want these people going stir crazy down here and slitting their wrists after six weeks. You're talking about twenty-four months of virtual sensory deprivation, and a total lack of sunlight. They're going to need real stimulation, the opportunity to create, to use their imaginations. Distraction."

"Hey, Mike, this isn't a theme park," Forrest said. "It's a

bomb shelter, man. Nobody said it was going to be fun down here. There's only so much we can do for good times. Maybe they can get creative in the kitchen or something."

Veronica laughed again. "I think you guys have been blowing things up for too long. These people aren't soldiers, Jack. They're women and children. You know, *civilians*."

"So what do you suggest?"

"Look, it's really not that difficult," Michael explained. "Go buy one of every board game you can find. They won't take up that much room. You can store them in the silo. And get lots of jigsaw puzzles. Word books, puzzle books. And for God's sake get some toys down here! Building blocks, Legos, little cars. Some of those plastic army men even. I assume you were kids once yourselves."

"You might even bring some musical instruments down," Veronica suggested. "Let some of the kids teach themselves how to play. A few of them are bound to have some natural talent. And what about some puppets? They can put on puppet shows for each other. Little kids love that stuff. Things they can apply their imaginations to."

Forrest looked at Ulrich. "You getting all this?"

"I'll send the Dynamic Duo out tomorrow," Ulrich said. "But I'm drawing the line at musical instruments. I'm not listening to that goddamn racket."

Forrest chuckled sardonically. "As you might imagine, he's great with kids."

"Next up is the kitchen and the mess facilities," Ulrich said, leading the way. "Both of which are equally cramped . . ."

When the tour was finished and after the sleeping arrangements had been made for the night, Michael and Veronica sat down in Launch Control with all of five of the men.

"I have to be honest with you," Michael said. "I think fifty is a bridge too far. I think you should cut that number in half. Tinkertoys and puppet shows not withstanding, it's going to be very crowded down here. Tempers are bound to flare even if things are going well, and I don't think you should count on them going well. It's human nature to complain."

"You're starting to sound like him," Forrest said with a nod toward Ulrich. "Nobody said this was going to be easy or fun."

"But why not increase your chances for success?" Veronica asked, stroking Laddie's head as he stood panting alongside her. "It's better to save twenty or thirty than to *almost* save fifty. Wouldn't you agree?"

"You're beating a dead horse," Ulrich said. "He's intent."

"I reiterate," Forrest said. "I do not believe that everyone's going to accept our offer."

"So you're the supreme commander here?" Veronica said, purposefully asking a potentially provocative question in front of the other four.

"I'm in command, yes," he replied without blinking. "I was their commanding officer in the Army, but now we're all friends of equal standing and it's been agreed that I'm to lead. Only a vote of four-to-one can overrule one of my decisions."

"And what about your civilians?" she asked. "Do they get a vote?"

"No."

"Is that fair?"

"Do I strike you as a tyrant?" he asked, digging the pack of cigarettes from his shirt pocket. "I'm not in this because I get my rocks off telling people what to do. Authority comes with a lot of responsibility, and the fewer orders you have to give, the better."

Michael did not fail to notice that Forrest was smoking a lot, and that he was obviously under a lot of stress. "Do you plan to smoke down here after the civilians arrive?"

"I'll do my smoking in the cargo bay," he said. "That's where the lift elevator is located. There are two blast doors separating the bay from the main complex."

"I take it you've stocked up on cigarettes?"

"I've been smoking for a long time. I intend to cut back, maybe even quit, but now is clearly not the time for me to attempt to do that."

"No, of course not," Michael said. "Only curious."

"You're analyzing me," Forrest said. "I get that. You're a shrink and it's probably to be expected. So what's your evaluation so far?"

"Well, we could talk about that later if you—"

"Lay it on me, Doc. I don't keep secrets from these guys. Do you think I'm a narcissist?"

"Not at all. But at the risk of offending you, I will say that I think the loss of your family has—"

"Michael . . ."

"He asked, honey, so I'm telling him . . . I think the loss of your family has clouded your better judgment in terms of how many people you should try to save. Beyond that, this seems like an entirely worthwhile endeavor to me, considering what's to come. And you seem to me a capable group of men."

Ulrich exchanged glances with the others, none of them exactly disagreeing with Michael's observation about Forrest, though they had not considered the point before. Forrest had always been their leader, and soldiers weren't generally in the business of questioning their officers' motivations, though Special Forces operatives were typically allowed a higher level of input than members of the regular rank and file.

"How about you?" Forrest asked Veronica. "What do you think?"

"You know," Michael said, "I'm not sure she's entirely capable of offering an unbiased opinion where you're concerned. She's attracted to you."

"Michael!" Veronica nearly shouted. "That's not funny!"

"I think thou dost protest too much. Are you going to deny there's chemistry between the two of you? If you are, then there's really no sense in my being a part of this equation . . . is there?"

She sat staring at him, her eyes angry and embarrassed. The other men stifled grins.

Forrest, however, admired Michael for bringing it out into

the open. It forced them to acknowledge a reality that had been an eight hundred pound gorilla in the room.

"It's not anything to be ashamed of," Michael said easily. "Nor is it something to be denied. Not if we're considering living among these men and so many others in such a confined space for such an extended period of time. Because now we're getting into your area of study, and you understand the social dynamics involved here even better than I."

She crossed her arms, painfully aware that her body language, as usual, was confirming what Michael already knew. "This could have waited," she said thinly.

"I don't think so," Forrest butted in. "Not from Mike's point of view, it couldn't." He turned his attention to Michael. "I think Veronica's one of the most attractive women I've ever seen," he admitted. "It's why I told her about our little project here. But the truth is that she reminds me of the way my wife Monica used to be. So do I enjoy her company? Absolutely. Is it my intention to try and steal her away from you? No. And for the record, I don't feel that I could if I tried."

Veronica realized that this was very probably only the beginning of the gender dilemmas they would all be facing if they chose to continue with this attempt. Women were going to be commoditized the world over; there would be no forestalling that phenomenon after the asteroid hit. Females enjoyed parity with males only as a result of law and order, and while this concept was fascinating to her from a sociological perspective, as a woman she was frightened by it. This was not some collegiate hypothetical case study. Humanity was on the very brink of being thrust into a world where the strong would hold absolute dominion over the weak.

"May I assume that I'm to have at least some say over who I do and do not choose to be with?" she said, looking between the two of them.

Forrest grinned. "I was merely stating my opinion."

"Well, for everyone's general knowledge here," she said, looking at all the men, "I love Michael and—unlike most *men*—I'm quite capable of controlling myself, even if I happen to find someone other than my mate attractive. So to answer the question, yes, there is chemistry between Jack and I, but it's not an issue for me. Nor do I believe it will be for him."

"Well, I have a more important question for you," Kane said to her.

She looked at him. "Yes?"

"Do you have a sister?"

Everyone laughed.

"I do," she said, smiling, "but I'm sorry. She's married with two kids and lives on the East Coast. Now, if no one minds, I'd like to clean up before we turn in. Is there hot water in the shower room?"

"Yes," Ulrich said. "We're tapped into a natural gas line and we have our own well, so there will always be plenty of hot water."

"Excellent," she said getting up. "This feels a little like being away at camp."

When she was gone, the trio went back to playing *Halo* and Forrest turned to Michael, asking, "Does she fully understand what's going to happen? It's the 'camp' remark that makes me ask."

"She understands as well as I do," Michael said. "But then I'm no less a stranger to death and destruction than she is. Regardless of how much we prepare ourselves, it's still going to be an incredible shock if and when it finally happens."

"I understand you've got a big family."

"I do."

"It won't be easy to leave them," Ulrich said. "How does Veronica feel about leaving hers?"

"She's not really close with her sister," Michael said. "She's all for this, so if we choose to pass on your offer, it will be because of me."

"I feel I should apologize for the way this has played out," Forrest said. "It was purely on a lark that I said anything to her that day."

"And I appreciate that. But it is what it is. Had you not found her attractive, and vice versa, I wouldn't be sitting here trying to decide whether I want to take advantage of such an opportunity. And maybe that would be a good thing . . . I don't know. But I guess the truth is that hundreds of thousands of people might soon find themselves wishing they'd had such a decision to wrestle with."

Ulrich leaned over to put a hand on Michael's shoulder. "There is no 'might' in this equation, Doc. The four horsemen are right over the hill . . . and they're riding hard."

# ELEVEN

**MICHAEL STOOD IN HIS PARENTS' BACKYARD LOOKING NORTH** into the night sky, a glass of wine in his hand, listening to his brothers and sisters and their families visiting inside the house. He'd been drinking a lot of wine lately. Many of them had. There were dozens of bottles in his father's cellar, and there was no point in letting so much expensive wine go to waste. No one knew exactly where the asteroid was going to strike, but Phoenix was almost certainly within the danger zone.

He felt his father's reassuring hand on his shoulder and turned to give him a smile. "Hey, Dad."

"Can you see it?" his father asked, looking up with him.

"No, but it's hard not to look."

"And even harder to believe," his father said. "It looks so peaceful up there. But it's actually a very violent place." Robert Porter was a retired vascular surgeon in good health, with a head of thick white hair and discerning eyes. He had always been well respected by his friends and neighbors.

"Did you hear about the food riots in L.A.?" Michael asked.

"Yes, I did."

"And they're hijacking trucks along the interstate now."

"It's only going to get worse," his father said. "Wait until the food actually runs low. The riots will be ten times as big, and the Army will be shooting people in the streets."

"There are police in every supermarket now," Michael said. "To keep people from hoarding. Nobody's allowed to buy more than fifty dollars worth of groceries at a time."

"Your mother tried to withdraw a thousand dollars from the bank this morning. There's a two-hundred-dollar-a-day limit on withdrawals now. People have stopped paying their bills. By this time next month, the banks will probably be busted. First the economy collapses, then society itself. Rome fell in the same order."

"Yeah, but the Romans only had to deal with the Huns." Michael took a sip of his wine and looked back up at the sky.

"I understand that you and Ronny have received a rather interesting offer."

Michael was startled. "She wasn't supposed to tell you about that."

"She didn't say anything to me. She told your mother. And you know how good your mother is at keeping secrets."

"I didn't want her upsetting you guys," Michael said, glancing back at the house for a glimpse at Veronica. He could see the rest of the family talking. His mother was going on about the importance of the prayer vigil again, insisting that God couldn't possibly refuse to save them if the entire world was joined in prayer.

"We're not upset," his father said easily. "How do these people seem to you? Do you think they know what they're doing?"

Michael shrugged. "I'm not a survivalist, Dad. I don't know."

"I'm not asking what you know. I'm asking what you think."

Michael took another drink and mulled it over a moment. "Yeah," he said finally. "I'd have to say they do."

"It's a pretty generous offer."

"Hell, the guy made the offer to Veronica, not me. If he'd known I was in the picture he'd never have said anything."

"She's a beautiful woman."

"Well, there you go."

A few of the youngest grandchildren came scampering out the door, chasing after a golden retriever with a tennis ball in its mouth. The dog was up in his years, but his spirit was willing and he did a good job of keeping the ball for himself. There was a lot of squealing and laughter, and Michael observed his father closely as he watched his grandchildren. From the smile on the man's face, one would never have guessed the world as they knew it was coming to an end.

"Pa Pa!" said one of the little girls, running over to him. "Chance can catch the ball from way up high even!"

"Yes, he can!" the older man replied. "He's an excellent ballplayer, isn't he?"

"Yeah, and do you know what?"

"What, baby doll?"

"My mom said we can get a dog too when I get older."

"Just a couple more years, honey."

The children romped about for a while longer and eventually led the dog back into the house.

"That's the best damn dog I ever had," his father remarked.

"He's good with the kids, that's for sure."

"So what about these guys?" his father said. "Do you think they'd kill you and take Ronny for themselves?"

Michael shook his head. "No, I don't. I believe they're good men trying to do a good thing. They were all in the military, and I got the distinct impression they're no strangers to violence. They say they were Green Berets."

"So they can handle themselves?"

"I'd say so, yeah."

"Hmm. If you ask me, son, I think you and Ronny would make a unique and valuable addition to a group like that."

Michael stopped short before taking a sip of wine. "What are you saying?"

"I'm saying I think things happen for a reason," his father replied. "I always have, you know that. And this is one of those rare times in life when I think I can actually see the reasoning."

"To what?"

"Well, there probably weren't a handful of men in this entire country who knew about that . . . that ball of fire out there. And one of them just happened to bump into Ronny at a truck stop in the middle of nowhere? A woman who just happens to be a sociologist who just happens to be shacked up with a psychiatrist?"

Michael couldn't help grinning. His father always referred to his and Veronica's living together as being "shacked up."

"But what about mom?" he asked.

"She would adjust. You've got five brothers and sisters in there who will be more than glad to gobble up your share of her attention. Not to mention nine nieces and nephews. You've always needed less than the others. You're the loner. And you're the only one who isn't married with a family."

"This is my family, Dad. I'm not going anywhere."

"And I'm not telling you to," his father said equably. "I'm just saying you should consider it."

Michael stood looking at him, the gears slow to mesh.

"Son, I'm sixty-five years old. And these past few days I find myself thinking in terms I never imagined possible. Do you realize that I may actually have to take your mother's life at some point within the next year, depending on how things go?"

Michael whirled the wine around in his glass. "I try not to think about it, actually."

"Now, as for my daughters and my daughters-in-law," his father went on. "Those decisions will be up to my sons and my sons-in-law. Your mother is my only concern. She's the one person I have to look after, my sole responsibility. The rest of you are adults and you're responsible for your own families, though I expect us all to be together until the end. But who knows when that will be? Or how much of a living hell we'll have to endure just to get to it? I won't watch your mother starve to death or be violated. I won't allow her dignity to be taken away from her. And to be perfectly honest with you, I'd much prefer it if at least one of my children was someplace safe when that ghastly type of decision is being made."

The gravity of his father's point was not lost on Michael, and he told him so. "But I'd feel like I was running out on you guys, Dad."

"That's because you're still looking at the world as it is, son. Not as it's going to be." He pointed into the sky. "That thing is coming, and by this time next year, ninety percent of this country's population will be dead of starvation. But! During the months leading up to that, do you think your brothers and sisters are going to be taking food from their kids' mouths and giving it to their nieces and nephews?"

"Dad, come on. My God."

His father looked at him with one of those fatherly expressions. "Now who's in denial, Doctor?"

"I hope you don't start talking like this to any of them," Michael said. "Jesus Christ."

"Frankly speaking, son, they're not equipped to handle the truth. You are. And that's why I don't believe it was simply a matter of chance that Ronny ran into that guy. She'll stay here and die with you, if that's what you want, because she loves you, but I don't think that's a responsible thing for a man to ask of a woman, particularly of a woman so willing. It's a betrayal of her faith."

Michael again looked thoughtfully into the wineglass. "And she'd never say so, but I know she feels that way, at least on some level."

"If you don't take her, I'll tell her to go without you. She won't listen, but I will tell her."

Michael was ashamed of himself for it, but he was grateful that his father had given him this reprieve. "Okay," he said quietly.

"And you might want to talk to your brother Stephen about taking your niece along," his father added.

"Which one?"

"Well, the twins are both a little young, wouldn't you say?"

"Melissa?"

"She's as bright as a light," his father said. "And her future was equally bright until that rock up there happened along. And she's the most like you of all the others; she lives in her own head. She'd have a lot to offer a new society. Provided that guy will let you bring her."

"He probably would, but there's no guarantee that—"

"There are never any guarantees, Michael. It's a chance—that's all—but it's more of a chance than ninety-nine percent of the rest of the world has. And she's worthy of it."

"She's your favorite," Michael said, taking a sip.

"All the more reason," his father admitted. "I make no apologies for how I feel about any of you. I'm the founder of the feast."

**It was one** o'clock in morning before Michael and Veronica were able to discreetly lure Stephen into the garage, and by the time they finished telling him of their intentions, he was looking at them as if they'd lost their minds.

"What's with you two?" he said, adding: "And what's up with the old man?"

"It's just something to think about, Stephen," Veronica said. "If nothing bad happens, we'll come back. But if it does—"

"Ronny, no," Stephen said. "My daughter's staying here with us. I can't believe Dad would even suggest something like that. It had to be the wine."

"He wasn't drinking tonight," Michael said.

"Well, then he shoulda been!"

Veronica gave Michael a look, signaling she thought the time had come for them to play dirty.

"Well, that's not the worst of what Dad's got on his mind," Michael said.

"I can imagine."

"I doubt it," Michael said. "Have you thought about what will happen after the food runs out? You do realize people are going to start killing one another."

"And eventually," Veronica tossed in, "they'll be eating one another."

"Stop it!" Stephen insisted. "You two are insane!"

"Then what do *you* think is going to happen?" Michael asked again.

"I don't know, but not that! Christ Almighty. This isn't Thunder Dome."

"So where is the food going to come from?" Veronica wanted to know.

"The government. Where else?"

"Stephen, there isn't going to be any goddamn government," Michael argued. "That rock is going to *obliterate* this country. Millions are going to die. Millions."

"Okay, fine," Stephen said. "Then we die together. Just like we were all talking about earlier."

"Suppose we survive the blast?" Michael ventured. "Then what?"

Stephen's mind was searching, trying to form a counterargument, but he couldn't come up with anything. "We do what we have to do," he said. "How's that?"

"Just like everyone else," Michael said. "And what happens to Melissa if you get killed by some psychopath over a can of dog food? We're not talking about a temporary downturn in the economy. We're talking about the end of society—and it's going to happen."

Stephen stood leaning against the fender of their father's car and didn't respond.

"You don't have to decide tonight," Michael said. "There's time. But consider this . . . If the time comes and you find yourself watching your children starve to death—or worse—don't you think you might end up wishing you'd let Melissa come with us? Just maybe?"

For the first time, it seemed that Stephen had heard him. He came off the fender and went to the garage door, looking out through a window. "Do you really think it's going to be like that?"

"How else could it be?" Michael said. "This is precisely

the same kind of event that wiped out the dinosaurs. I know it's hard to accept but you need to try."

Stephen turned around. "This is why you're the doctor and I'm the pipe fitter. I'm too . . . I don't know. Simple-minded."

"You are not," Michael said. "And this was Dad's argument, not mine. I'm only just now coming to grips with it myself."

"And you'll bring her back if things aren't too bad?"

"Of course."

"I don't know if we'll be able to get Cindy to go along with this," Stephen said. "You're going to have to really scare the shit out of her—I can't be the one to do it."

"Melissa will probably decide to stay anyhow," Michael said. "But it makes—"

"No," Stephen said. "She'll go. She's smarter than Cindy and I put together. She's always talking to me about things I don't even understand." He stood chewing his knuckle, a nervous habit he'd had all his life. "She's Dad's favorite, you know."

Michael grinned. "Everybody knows. Hell, she's mine too."

"That's because she's exactly like you two," Stephen said. "I just wish I understood her better." And without warning, he broke down and began to cry. "Now it looks like I never will, goddamnit."

Veronica went to Stephen and put her arms around him. She knew that scenes all too similar to this one were playing out all across the planet, and she couldn't help feeling slightly detached from it all. Perhaps it was because she had never been close with her own family, but she found the idea of having a front-row seat to the end of civilization morbidly fascinating. And now that Michael had decided they would join Jack and the others after all, she found herself feeling almost excited. This was going to be the ultimate sociological paradigm.

"It's not fair!" Stephen was moaning. "I have to give my baby away. I can't fucking believe this is happening . . ."

# TWELVE

THE ASTEROID WASN'T DUE TO STRIKE FOR FOURTEEN MORE days, but Forrest had asked Veronica if she and Michael would be willing to come early in order help them with the final preparations. There were still certain items that needed to be purchased, like batteries, deodorant, toilet paper—which was bound to run out no matter how much they stocked—and other miscellanea. There was also still a lot of organizing to be done belowground.

Forrest arranged to meet them at the same truck stop where he had met Veronica. Right on time, a black Volvo station wagon pulled into the lot and drove straight over to the Humvee, where he sat behind the wheel smoking a cigarette. The unexpected sight of the pretty teen with curly brown hair in the backseat should have annoyed him, but it didn't.

"Hang tight, champ," he said to Laddie and got out, crushing the cigarette on the fender.

"Now before you go off the deep end," Veronica said, getting out on the driver's side, "give me a second to explain."

"Off the deep end?" he said with a grin. "Do I strike you as an off-the-deep-end kind of guy? If I don't like her, she's not coming. It's that simple."

He smiled at Melissa as she was getting out.

"How ya doin', Doc?" he said to Michael.

"Not bad," Michael said, still nervous about the situation. "You?"

"Hello," Forrest said to Melissa. "I'm Jack. I hope these two haven't told you what an asshole I am."

Melissa smiled shyly. She was fair-skinned with an unblemished complexion and light brown eyes.

"What's your name, sweetheart?"

"Melissa."

"Nice to meet you," he said, offering his hand.

"We only brought her because—"

"Do you mind?" Forrest said. "I'm talking to the kid here."

Veronica pulled her shoulders back, looking at Michael as he came around the back of the car.

"How did you *ever* get hooked up with these two?" Forrest asked the girl.

"Michael's my uncle," she said, grinning.

"Have they told you about my master plan to take over the universe?"

"Yeah," she answered, laughing softly.

"And you're sure you want to join us?"

"Yes," she said, "but I have a question."

"Only one?"

"Will I be able to call my parents every day until . . ."

"Until what?"

Veronica spoke up, "Until the—"

"I'm not talking to you . . ." he said in a singsong voice. Melissa giggled.

"Until what, honey?"

"Until the asteroid comes," she said, her eyes smiling.

"I'm making sure you understand the gravity of the situation," he told her. "I'm not trying to be a jerk."

She nodded. "I understand."

"Okay. And you know there's no guarantee we're going to survive?"

"I know that," she said. "But somebody needs to try."

"I agree," he said, deciding he liked her. "And yes, you can call your parents as much as you like until the meteor comes."

"I thought it was an asteroid."

Forrest chuckled. "I stand corrected."

He at last turned his attention to the adults, noting the station wagon was full of boxes. "Bring enough shit?"

"Most of it's books," Michael explained. "You know, for helping to pass the time."

"All right," Forrest said. "Let's get the boxes loaded into the Humvee. Your bags you can tie to the roof rack."

"You mean we can't take my car?" Veronica said.

"Nope. Can't leave anything parked above the site to give the impression anyone lives in the house. It needs to look deserted."

"I told you," Michael said.

Veronica gave him a look. "Fine," she said, tossing her hair over her shoulder and turning to open the back door. "This is the first car I ever bought new."

Forrest exchanged grins with Michael, asking, "Were you planning on driving it around down in the silo?"

"Shut up, Jack!" she said, wrestling a box from the seat.

"I brought all sorts of books," Michael said.

"Fine. Come on, kid. Let's go get something to drink while these college pukes do the lifting."

"Okay," Melissa, following him off toward the station.

Veronica stood with the box in her arms watching them. "Did you see that? He didn't complain one bit over her."

"Did you really expect him to?" Michael asked, pulling another box of books from the rear compartment. "She's a pretty girl."

"She's fifteen, Michael."

"Oh, for God sakes, Veronica, that's not what I meant. Melissa affects everybody that way."

"She likes him too, I can tell."

"What, are you jealous?" he asked, chuckling.

"Shut up," she said. "I was just commenting."

Inside, Forrest picked up an empty cardboard box the clerks had left on the floor and gave it to Melissa. "Load that up with whatever you want. I have to use the restroom."

"You mean just for me?" she asked, confused.

"Does *you* mean something different out there in Colorado?"

"No," she said bashfully.

"I haven't bought anything for a kid in a long time," he said, his smile waning. "I've got some catching up to do."

"What do you like?" she asked, glancing around. There were bare spots on many of the shelves but the candy was still plentiful.

"Camels," he said. "Filterless."

She laughed. "I'm not old enough to buy cigarettes."

"Looks like I lose," he said, heading for the restroom.

Veronica and Michael were standing beside the Humvee waiting when Forrest and Melissa finally came out. All the boxes were loaded and their bags lashed to the roof rack.

Melissa was carrying her box full of snacks.

"Who's all that for?" Veronica asked.

"It's for the kid," Forrest said. "So don't let me catch your fingers in the box."

Melissa laughed. "You can have some, Ronny."

"You're too easy," he said, walking around to the driver's side. "Load 'em up."

"Didn't take her long to get you wrapped around her finger," Veronica said, loud enough for only Forrest to hear.

"You're just jealous," he muttered, brushing by her.

"Jack?"

He turned. "Yes?"

"Fuck you."

He laughed and jumped in to see that Michael was afraid to get in on the other side with Laddie staring him in the face. "Get in back, buddy." The dog responded immediately, taking up station in the backseat between the two women.

Michael got in and shut the door.

Laddie suddenly started barking at Michael, causing the

man to flinch and cower against the door. The dog settled a few moments later and seemed to relax.

"What did I do?" he asked, unsure whether it was safe to move.

Forrest glanced back at the dog to satisfy himself there was no danger and then grinned at Michael and shrugged. "I guess the dog's a judge of character."

Veronica laughed, petting Laddie.

"No, seriously. Should I be afraid?"

Melissa said, "He was just letting you know he didn't like you taking his seat."

Forrest gave her a wink.

"Is he pissed?" Michael asked. "Because I can sit in the back."

"He's said his piece," Forrest said. "Okay, everyone remember to keep your hands and feet inside the ride at all times until the ride comes to a complete and final stop. Remember that Captain Jack Forrest is not responsible for any lost or stolen articles while en route to the secret Army base. And as always," he added with a quick glance into the back, "enjoy your day at Cedar Point." Then he tromped the accelerator and wheeled hard around, roaring out of the lot and onto the highway.

# THIRTEEN

**MAJOR BENJAMIN MORIARTY, U.S. AIR FORCE, STILL HAD** no idea why he had been ordered to deliver two truckloads of MREs to a decommissioned Titan missile installation, but he sure as hell intended to find out. If NASA failed to stop that goddamned asteroid from hitting the planet, MREs were going to be worth a thousand times their weight in gold. And no way was he giving away so much of his garrison's food without a damned good reason—regardless of what some chair shiner back at the Pentagon had to say about it.

"What the fuck is *this* now?" he cursed from the passenger seat of the Hummer.

"I'm not sure, Major," said Lieutenant Ford, slowing the vehicle. "They look like dog faces."

"See?" Moriarty said. "This is what I'm talking about. They're not even Air Force personnel."

"Looks like they're Green Berets," Ford said, pulling into the gravel lot just inside the old hurricane fence still enclosing the site.

"I don't give a damn what they are," Moriarty said, throwing open the door and stepping out into the gravel. "They're not getting our rations without an explanation."

Forrest stood waiting with Ulrich and Danzig near the house, all three of them with M-4 carbines hanging from their shoulders.

"Aw, piss," muttered Danzig, spitting a wad of tobacco juice into the gravel. "They sent a goddamn major."

"Easy," Forrest said.

All four men were wearing open mikes so they could communicate with Kane, who was positioned in the upstairs window of the house with an M-21 sniper rifle.

"Looks a little salty, doesn't he?" Ulrich observed.

They snapped to attention and saluted as Major Moriarty came stalking up to them, armed only with a 9mm Beretta that hung from his hip in a green nylon holster.

"Who's in command here, Captain?" Moriarty demanded.

"That would be me at the moment, sir," Forrest replied.

"Define 'at the moment.'"

"Well, sir, Colonel Vasquez is away at the moment. Are those the MREs we were told to expect, sir?"

"They are, but I'm going to need a good explanation before I leave them."

"Explanation, sir?"

"Who are they intended for, Captain? This installation is no longer active."

"I wasn't told who they were intended for, sir. I was simply given orders to receive them and to secure them, awaiting Colonel Vasquez's arrival."

"Which will be when?"

"I was told sometime within the next twenty-four hours, sir."

"Well, when the colonel arrives, Captain, you can tell him to give Colonel Wells at Tinker Air Force Base a call. I'm not giving up these MREs to an Army captain in the middle of nowhere. I don't care if he is Special Forces."

"I was told your orders came straight from the Pentagon, Major."

Moriarty stiffened, noting that Forrest had addressed him as *Major* this time, rather than *sir,* which was acceptable, but it put the two of them on a more equal footing, a nuance that Moriarty did not especially appreciate.

"Captain, exactly what is this installation being used for now?"

"I'm not at liberty to say, Major. It's classified."

Moriarty stood mulling it over. "I'll just have a look below, then."

"I'm afraid I can't allow that, sir," Forrest said, neither he nor either of his men so much as twitching a muscle.

"Excuse me, Captain?"

"I said I cannot allow that, Major. My orders are very specific in that regard."

"Do you mean to imply you intend to open fire on me if I attempt to go below?"

"It means, Major, that my men and I will do whatever is necessary to carry out our orders." Forrest could see that Moriarty was considering whether to call his bluff, so he added: "I should also like to inform the major that he is being covered by a sniper positioned in the upstairs window of the structure behind me and to my left."

Moriarty shifted his gaze to the upper windows of the house, and though he couldn't see inside, he didn't doubt Forrest's word. Green Berets were touchy bastards, the lot.

"Well, then as far as I'm concerned, Captain, this is a typical example of Special Forces trying to avoid protocol, and I don't intend to subsidize this kind of bullshit. So have your colonel give my colonel a call, and we'll see which has the bigger dick."

With that, Moriarty turned and headed back toward the Humvee.

Kane spoke into Forrest's ear from the upstairs window: *Do you want me to take 'em out? I can hit all four of them from here.*

"No," Forrest said quietly. "We'd have to go belowground today and lock the door. These MREs were only a bonus."

Just then an Army green Humvee came into view at the bottom of the hill and started up the gravel drive.

"Shit," Ulrich muttered. "This might force our hand."

"Kane, be ready to fire on my word," Forrest said.

"Roger that."

"**ARE YOU SURE** about this?" Michael was asking, sitting nervously in the passenger seat beside Vasquez.

"Relax," Vasquez replied, pressing the Velcro-backed black eagle insignia of a full colonel onto the front of his Army combat uniform. "But be ready to hit the deck."

"Oh, great!" Michael moaned. "I'm shitting my pants over here, Oscar."

Vasquez shifted into low gear, climbing the grade. "Get ready to look your part." He drove up, stopped alongside the nearest truck, and got out smiling.

"Excellent!" he said, loud enough for Moriarty to hear, but pretending not to notice him as he glanced into the back of the deuce-and-a-half at the load of MREs. "Well, what do you think, Congressman?" he went on, gesturing at the compound. "We probably won't need to utilize the place, but as you can see, there's no indication of what lies beneath, and I think your colleagues will find the accommodations acceptable."

Moriarty heard this as he approached, saluting Colonel Vasquez and introducing himself. Vasquez looked a little young for a full bird, but Special Forces personnel tended to hold rank at younger ages than the regular Army, another fact Moriarty resented.

Vasquez shook Moriarty's hand. "I appreciate you making the trip on such short notice, Major. Please be sure to thank Colonel Wells for his consideration."

He could see that Forrest was watching him intently from fifty feet away and heard him speak into his ear: *"Don't lay it on too thick, numb nuts."*

"Wouldn't dream of it," Vasquez muttered, keeping up his smile. "Major, this is Congressman Ted Strong of Nebraska. He's one of the congressmen who will be taking shelter here in the unlikely event that NASA fails to stop the asteroid."

Michael shook hands with Moriarty, trying to appear casually official.

"Pleasure to meet you, sir," Moriarty said. "I wasn't aware that this installation had been recommissioned. Most of these old silos have been sold off privately."

"So was this one," Vasquez said, "as far as anyone knows. Is that understood?"

"Yes, sir," Moriarty said.

"Good. Well, I think these trucks will be fine right where they are," Vasquez continued. "We'll be sure to get them back to Tinker within ten days or so. There's no sense unloading all these damn cases if they're only going be driven back after we stop the asteroid. The four of you will fit comfortably enough into your Humvee, won't you?"

"Uh, yes, sir," Moriarty said.

"Great," Vasquez said. "That will be all then, Major, you're dismissed. And don't forget to give Colonel Wells my regards."

"I won't, sir," Moriarty said, turning for the Humvee.

"Oh, and Major?"

Moriarty turned back around. "Sir?"

"I don't think it'll be necessary for the colonel and I to compare penises, do you?"

Moriarty flushed. "Um, no, sir. And please allow me to apologize for that remark, sir. I wasn't aware you were on a network, sir."

*"That's enough!"* Forrest was hissing into Vasquez's ear. *"Just let the son of a bitch leave!"*

Vasquez smiled and gave Major Moriarty a casual salute. *"Vaya con dios,* Major."

"Sir!" Moriarty said, and hustled his men into the Humvee. Within a minute they were down the road, headed out of sight.

Forrest walked over and gave Vasquez a shove. "I told you not to ham it up!"

Vasquez laughed. "He won't say shit when he gets back to Tinker now."

"You did okay there, Doc," Forrest said, lighting up a smoke. "Congratulations. You just helped us pull off a federal crime."

"Wonderful," Michael said, feeling slightly sick to his stomach. "And I didn't even get to carry a machine gun."

# FOURTEEN

FORREST KNOCKED AT ANDIE TATUM'S DOOR TWO SUNDAYS
before the asteroid was due to strike. Her name was not on
the list he had purchased from the Lincoln social worker.
She was a widowed mother whose acquaintance he had
made months earlier in a health food store, when she saw
him rake an entire shelf of vitamins into his cart as she led
her six-year-old daughter past him down the aisle by the
hand.

"Someone must be pretty sick," she had remarked.

Forrest smiled. "I'm an obsessive compulsive. I have to
buy every bottle of vitamins I see."

Andie laughed. "May I ask what they're really for?"

"You wouldn't believe if me I told you."

"I might," she said. "I'm a kindergarten teacher. I hear a
lot of creative stories."

She had not been wearing a wedding band, and at that
point Forrest sensed that she found him attractive. "I deal in
black-market vitamins."

"No, really," she said, laughing. "There's has to be an interesting explanation."

"To be completely honest," he said, suddenly serious, "it's
a secret."

With that, the conversation trailed off, but Forrest had

written her license plate number down in the parking lot. Hers was the last name he added to the roster, aside from Veronica's.

Andie answered the door, and though she was at first confused by his uniform, she did recognize him, putting her hand on her hip and shifting her weight to one leg. "You're the vitamin guy."

"Yes, ma'am, that's me," he said with a smile. "My name's Jack Forrest. And you're Andie Tatum, correct? Widowed mother of a six-year-old daughter named Trinity Marie Tatum?"

"Yeah," she said, a little intimidated. "What's the Army want from me now?"

"I'm actually U.S. Army, retired. The uniform is just to instill some confidence."

"Confidence in what?"

"In the offer I've come to make you. May I come in?"

She stood thinking it over. "I suppose."

He stepped inside and took the green beret from his head. "This won't take long."

"Have a seat."

They sat across from one another in the living room.

"Is Trinity home?"

"She's at my sister's playing with her cousins," Andie said. "This has something to do with the asteroid, doesn't it . . . and all those damn vitamins?"

"It does," he replied. "Myself and four friends have prepared a large underground shelter here in Nebraska and stocked it with enough food for at least eighteen months, depending on how many people decide to join us. We've accommodations for a maximum of fifty."

"And you're asking me?"

"I am."

"Well . . . why?"

"Because I liked you immediately," he said frankly. "Aside from a few friends and family, everyone else we're asking has been selected according to certain criteria. The location is a complete secret, so you'll have to accept the offer sight unseen, should you choose to join us."

Andie sat back in the sofa. "You're serious?"

"Yes, ma'am. I'm as legitimate as the asteroid itself."

"But I don't understand why anybody would . . . people don't just do this for strangers out of the kindness of their hearts."

Forrest shrugged. "We do."

"Well . . . how do I know that this is for real? I mean, you could be anyone."

"That's true," he said. "You'd be taking a complete leap of faith. But if you do decide to take it, you'll be taking it for your daughter. She's the future."

"So there will be other children?"

"Yes. A couple of single mothers have accepted our offer so far, but most have declined—as expected. There are only a few women left to visit."

"And the government has nothing to do with this?"

"Nothing at all. If they knew, I'm sure they'd try to shut us down. Hoarding food is a federal offense now, as I'm sure you've heard."

"But you started hoarding a long time ago, didn't you? Buying all those vitamins. That was months before anyone else even knew . . . which means you're connected."

"After a fashion, yes."

"So you don't think NASA can stop it?"

"The shoot-down hasn't a chance in hell of working," he said. "That's just propaganda to try and preserve law and order."

"Can I bring my sister and her family?"

"No, ma'am. Yours was the last name I added to the list."

"But you just said some have refused your offer."

"I made a long list because I knew most wouldn't accept. It is a hard story to swallow."

He went on to explain the setup in the silo in greater detail, and at length Andie got up from the sofa and slowly paced the room. "I don't have any idea what to do," she admitted finally. "How long do I have to decide?"

He looked at his watch. "What time will Trinity be home?"

"You mean I have to decide right now?"

"No, but before sunset would be helpful."

"You said your name is Jack?"

"Right."

"Jack, I can't just leave my sister and my nephews. My brother-in-law's a goof but he's a nice guy. He wouldn't cause you any trouble."

"If you decide to stay with them," he said, getting to his feet, "you're going to die with them . . . but I understand that some would prefer it that way." He took a slip of paper from his pocket. "This is my number. Call me if you decide to accept our offer. Again, sooner would be better."

"But wait. That's it? I can't bargain?"

He looked at her, his face set. "Your husband was a soldier. What would he want you to do?"

"That's not fair," she said. "You know all about me and I know nothing about you, about any of you."

"You know we've got plenty of vitamins."

She couldn't help smiling. "You know, I was trying to flirt with you that day, and you were rude to me. I never flirt with men in front of my daughter—ever."

"Would you have believed me had I told you the truth?"

She pushed her dark hair away from her eyes and looked at him. "No, I'd have thought you were being a smartass—and you are a smartass. That uniform doesn't hide anything from me. I was a camp follower for too long."

"One suitcase for each of you," he said, turning for the door. "No more. A bag of Trinity's favorite toys if she likes—but that's it. We've toiletries aplenty."

"Did you know Kevin?" she asked suddenly. "Is that why you're really here? Did he ask you to look after us?"

"I would love for that to be so," he said with a sad smile. "That would be a beautiful story. But I never had the honor of meeting your husband. I do know, however, that Sergeant Tatum was killed three years ago in Afghanistan and that he was a brave man. I would be honored to save his family from what is coming."

The unholy image of her daughter dying of starvation flashed through her mind, and she recalled the deep timbre of her husband's voice. This man Forrest's voice had that same quality.

"Don't give our place to anyone else," she said, her eyes abruptly filling with tears. "I just don't know what to tell my sister."

"Some aren't saying anything," he offered by way of suggestion.

"I can't do it that way," she said. "Don't take this wrong, but I think I wish you hadn't come."

"We've heard that from others," he said gently. "But I think that Trinity should make your final decision something of a no-brainer. At least she would for me."

"But what happens in two years?"

"Ask me in two years." He grinned. "I'll wait to hear from you, Andie."

"Are you married?" she blurted. "Are you bringing anyone?"

His grin grew broader as he reached for the knob. "No, ma'am. And all flirtations aside, I do hope you'll accept our offer. We've busted our asses getting this place ready. It would be a shame if the only teacher on our list stayed behind."


**WHEN FORREST ARRIVED** back at the silo, Dr. Sean West and his wife Taylor were standing on the porch talking with Dr. Price Wilmington, DDS, and his wife Lynette. Both doctors and their wives were old friends, and they had been in on Forrest's plan from its inception; the doctors were former military men as well.

"Good to see you, Jack," Dr. West said, shaking hands. He

was a thick, barrel-chested man with dark eyes and hair, and stood beside his slender wife Taylor, who had short blond hair and a kind face.

Forrest shook his hand and turned to Dr. Wilmington. "Price, how was the trip?"

Dr. Wilmington was African American, a little shorter in stature than the other men, and had short-cropped hair. His wife Lynette was white and taller than her husband, with long blond hair and bright blue eyes. She was a gossip with an innate sense of bad timing.

"When's Monica getting here?" she asked before her husband could even respond to Forrest's question.

"She's not," Forrest said, not quite blowing her off, though almost. "How was the drive, Price?"

"Long!" Price said with a smile. "And you know, Jack, I'm not sure we'd have made it all the way across if we had waited another couple days. They're imposing travel restrictions now."

"See how the bastards talk from both sides of their mouth?" Ulrich said, stepping onto the porch. "If NASA's going to stop the rock, why the travel restrictions?"

"I think NASA's story is losing credibility pretty quickly now," West said. "Those astronomers from Hawaii were on CNN again last night. They said unequivocally that NASA's crazy if they think they can stop this thing. Even the B612 Foundation is finally speaking out against the attempt."

The B612 Foundation had been founded by a group of former astronauts years earlier, dedicated to protecting the planet from near Earth objects. To this point they had been strangely silent on the subject of the shoot-down plan, and it was suspected the government had threatened them.

"The European Space Agency has announced they're going to fire their kinetic impactor at it," Price volunteered with a dry smile, sipping from a glass of wine.

"Which will be about as effective as throwing an iPod at a speeding truck," Ulrich remarked.

Forrest excused himself and slipped inside to get out of his uniform and find a beer. Taylor West followed him, asking, "Jack, why isn't Monica coming?"

He turned and frowned. "She's committing suicide without committing suicide."

Taylor's eyes filled with tears. "There's no way . . . ?"

Forrest shook his head and went below, pretending not to notice Veronica watching him from the kitchen doorway.

Back outside, Lynette said to Ulrich, "Wayne, why isn't Monica here?"

"She doesn't want to live underground," Ulrich said. "And it's probably best not to bring her up around Jack."

"Well, he should have kidnapped her if that's what it took," Lynette insisted. "My God!"

"I hardly think that would have been appropriate," Price told her, knowing that Ulrich was not Lynette's greatest fan.

"Price, you'd never leave *me* to die. It's Jack's responsibility to save that woman from herself!"

Ulrich had never cared for Lynette, having always secretly suspected she had married Price for his money. And there was no time like the present to set her straight on Monica. "Lynette . . ." he said, noticeably stern.

All eyes went to Ulrich.

"Whatever you've got to say on the subject, get it said before Jack comes back upstairs. After that, I don't want to hear another word about Monica for the next two years."

Lynette grew red in the face. She had always been a little afraid of Ulrich, because unlike most men, he wasn't dazzled by her fake tits and long legs. "Wayne, I was only saying—"

"I don't care what you were you saying," he said, cutting her off. "You've got no idea what the hell you're even talking about."

"Jesus Christ, Wayne. Relax!"

Ulrich took a step forward, his gaze cutting into her. "Did you understand what I just said?"

The tension in the air was suddenly thick enough to cut with a knife, and Ulrich could see Lynette looking to her husband for support, but Ulrich didn't care. He wasn't about to have their hegemony challenged by this cunt while there was still time to find another pair of doctors.

To his surprise, neither doctor said a word. Apparently, Lynette was on her own.

"Yes," she said, trying to appear dignified. "I understood you very well."

He turned to go inside, muttering, "Excuse me," as he slipped between the pair of doctors.

"Price, you didn't even *try* to defend me!" Lynette hissed.

"Honey, I've told you before that Wayne's no one to trifle with," Price said. "He and Jack are polar opposites. And I warned you about the arrangements here."

Inside the house, Ulrich saw that Veronica had heard the exchange through the screen door. She was grinning as she followed him into the basement.

"I take it you were nipping that flower in the bud?" she asked.

"Price should have divorced her ass years ago," Ulrich said. "She's a fourteen carat bitch. All I can figure is that she's a dynamo in the rack."

Veronica smiled. "There's one in every group, Wayne. If we got rid of her, another would just pop up in her place. Sometimes it's best to keep the devil you know."

# FIFTEEN

ESTER THORN STOOD LEANING AGAINST HER CANE, HER TIRED eyes fixed on the television screen at the Hotel Sheraton in Hawaii where she and a number of other astronomers were staying. Harold Shipman stood beside her, teething the stem of a pipe. Their colleagues were seated around them in the conference hall, everyone nervously awaiting the results of the imminent atomic blast meant to push the asteroid off course.

In the preceding weeks, a few halfhearted attempts had been made by the federal government to muzzle Ester and her colleagues, but the Hawaiian governor intervened on their behalf.

"Damn fools," Ester muttered. "Why don't they just let it alone? They're going to push it into the Pacific, Harold. You wait and see. Then there's going to be some real devastation."

"Not the least of which will be to the Hawaiian Islands," Shipman said. "The mega-tsunami will wash every one of us out sea. My God, the wave will be thousands of feet high. Can you imagine it?"

"I half expect them to lie and tell us it worked."

"No, there are too many watching now. The time for lies has passed."

Wolf Blitzer was adroitly explaining the many facets of rocket guidance and atomic yield, seemingly detached from the reality that he, along with everyone else at CNN, would likely be dead in the near future.

"The very fate of our world hangs in the balance," he commented gravely, determined to remain theatrical to the last.

"Which species do you suppose will take over?" Shipman wondered.

"Oh, it'll likely be the rodents again," Ester said with a sigh. "I wonder if we'll do a better job next time around."

"Wouldn't it be something if we humans evolved all over again?" he said with a cynical laugh.

"I don't see why we wouldn't," she said. "In some form or another. Nature will be starting over from nearly the same slate as sixty-five million years ago. Primates are bound to reevolve at some point down the line."

"It can't happen the same way twice, Ester. There are too many variables to contend with . . . climatic, geological, evolutionary . . . the list goes on and on."

"All of which were dealt with before," she said obstinately, "and we still found a way. Though it's too bad we'll never know."

"Well, we're not extinct yet," Shipman said. "Some of us may survive."

"I wouldn't hold my breath," Ester said. "A few thousand of us survived the Younger Dryas impact, but I don't know if modern man is up to the task."

"Did Marty Chittenden ever call?"

She shook her head. "They've probably still got the boy under lock and key someplace."

"I wonder if he regrets his decision."

"I doubt it," Ester said. "He was committed."

Then Wolf Blitzer appeared on the screen, looking almost ill.

"Ladies and gentlemen, we have just received word from NASA and the Jet Propulsion Laboratory that the nuclear warhead intended to knock the asteroid off course has detonated successfully but failed to affect the asteroid's trajectory. Preliminary calculations indicate that the detonation occurred a half second too late for the explosion to have its maximum effect . . ."

"Well, that's that," Ester said, tamping her cane twice against the carpet. "So much for world prayer."

"There's still the kinetic impactor," Shipman said with a dry smile.

"Yes, perhaps our European colleagues will manage to chip its tooth," she said. "I'm going to my room to lie down for a while, Harold. I'm exhausted."

"Okay, Ester. I'll wake you if there's trouble on the island."

"I don't know what I'd be able to do about it," she muttered.

Shipman chuckled. Ester's dour sense of humor had always tickled him. Now he would have to go get his wife and aged mother-in-law to move them into the observatory with him; he didn't want them living in town now with the Earth officially doomed.

He took some limited comfort, however, in the fact that the Hawaiian Islands had remained relatively calm throughout the crisis, the general consensus among the islanders being that they stood a better chance of surviving in the long term than anyone else in the United States and perhaps even the world. And since all flights to the Islands had been canceled a month earlier, the largest increase in population was likely to be at Pearl Harbor once the U.S. naval fleet began to arrive in port.

The entire Pacific Fleet had sortied the week before against the eventuality of an oceanic impact, which would almost certainly have resulted in a mega-tsunami that would have devastated both the Hawaiian Islands and the entire west coast of North America for dozens of miles inland. But with the asteroid still on course, that was no longer a concern, and Dr. Harold Shipman found himself feeling terribly disappointed. A mega-tsunami would have made their deaths quick and painless, and would have been an utterly breathtaking sight to behold in their final moments.

# SIXTEEN

AFTER MARTY CHITTENDEN'S APPREHENSION BY THE SECRET
Service, Agent Paulis had requested clearance to keep him
detained and out of sight on campus at the California Institute of Technology, much in the same manner as two other
astronomers who had spotted the asteroid. They were being
illegally detained elsewhere in the U.S., one under house
arrest in New Mexico, the other involuntarily committed to
a mental hospital in Washington, D.C.

Susan Denton had been allowed to visit Marty and bring
him food during his detention, and she came to truly detest
Agent Paulis, who seemed to take personal enjoyment in
keeping Marty locked in a tiny room on the top floor of a
deserted dormitory across campus.

Now, she stepped off the elevator and walked briskly
down the hall toward a pair of Secret Service agents standing guard outside the room. "Okay, guys, you can let him
out. The nuclear warhead didn't work, so we're all as good
as dead."

"Are you sure?" one of the men said, strangely surprised.

"Yeah. Call Agent Paulis if you don't believe me."

He tried reaching Paulis on the phone but all he got was
voice mail. "That's odd."

"See? He's obviously abandoned you guys. Don't you think it's about time you started thinking for yourselves?"

A minute later the Secret Service agent was able to reach someone on the phone to confirm that the warhead had failed to divert the asteroid and that most government employees were fleeing D.C.

"The government's already shutting down," the agent said, tucking the phone away. "I'm trying for Seattle. My sister lives there."

"You'll never make it," the other said. "The interstate's going to be total gridlock."

"I'll steal a fucking motorcycle if I have to. What about you?"

"I'll go to Camp Pendleton. I've got some friends in the Corps who'll let me in."

"And what about Marty?" Susan asked.

One of them gave her the key to Marty's room. "Good luck to you. Be damn sure you're off the streets before dark. And tell Chittenden it was nothing personal."

The men headed for the elevator, and Susan keyed into Marty's room. "Hey, you."

Marty was sitting on his bed against the wall, reading a book. "What's happened?"

"The first rocket failed to push the asteroid off course, and the second never even made it off the ground. The Secret Service guys took off, so you're free."

"Then we have to get the hell out of here," he said, getting up, then leading her out of the room by the hand. "We'll go to my place. I've already stocked up on food."

She hurried along beside him and they road the elevator to the ground floor. "Marty, we'll never make it to your place. The highways are jammed."

The elevator doors opened and they moved quickly toward the parking lot.

"We have to get out of town," he said.

Her car was nearly the only one left in the lot.

"You'd better drive," she said, giving him the keys. "I don't handle heavy traffic well."

"We'll stick to the side streets," he said, getting in and starting the motor.

"We should just go to my house. We'll never make it to Mesa."

"We'll starve in California, Sue. Do you know how many people are here? The food won't last a month. Nothing's being produced now."

"We'll starve in Arizona too," she argued. "That's if we survive the blast."

Traffic thickened up a mile from campus, but it was moving, and so far motorists were still obeying the traffic signals.

"Okay, we'll stay at your place tonight," he conceded. "That will give all these people a chance to get home to their families. Tomorrow it won't be as bad and we can get out of town."

She suddenly had a frightening thought and grabbed his arm. "You're not going to ditch me if things get bad, are you? If I start to slow you down?"

He looked at her. "Susan, no." He paused and continued, "In case you hadn't noticed, I'm still in love with you."

She looked down. "I'm sorry I've never felt the same. I feel responsible for you being stranded so far from home."

"Hey, so long as I'm with you, I don't care where I am. All I'm worried about is not being able to protect you."

She opened the glove box, took out a Walther PPK .380 pistol, and gave it to him. "Will that help?"

He looked at the pistol in his hand. "I've never fired one."

"I bought it after I was attacked," she said. "If I can shoot it, anybody can."

# SEVENTEEN

IT WAS THE DAY AFTER THE FAILURE OF THE SHOOT-DOWN, and Forrest was standing over the grill cooking hamburgers and hot dogs, drinking a bottle of Corona and smoking a cigarette. The sun was shining and there wasn't a cloud in the sky, a perfect summer day in June. The children were chasing each other around in the tall grass, and their mothers were busy setting the tables.

"You do know," Ulrich said, "that if the government shows up, it's going to be tough getting everybody belowground."

Laddie came trotting over and dropped a tennis ball at Forrest's feet. He threw the ball as far as he could out into the field and the dog tore off after it. "The world ends in sixteen hours, Wayne. We're the last thing on the government's to-do list."

Ulrich tipped his beer, watching the dog search the grass for his ball. "I hope you're right."

Across the yard, Veronica and Melissa were watching everyone from where they sat in the grass. Veronica was in a detached state of mind, only half present, observing the entire group with an analytical eye. She spotted Michael helping a woman named Karen Schott set the table, and wondered what they were talking about, having noticed with little jealousy the chemistry between them on the day of Karen's arrival three days earlier. The two West children were playing in the backyard with a little boy named Steven, who Marcus had rescued along with Steven's mother Tonya from her abusive boyfriend a few days ago.

She could also plainly see that Tonya had the hots for Kane, and that another invitee, Maria Mendoza, did as well. This Maria would be called Maria two to distinguish her from Oscar's wife, Maria Vasquez.

In the end, only eight women had accepted the offer to join the silo population, bringing nine children along with them, which brought the group's grand total to thirty-six: fourteen women, eight men, one teenage girl, and a noisy band of thirteen children—six boys and seven girls.

Ulrich was satisfied with the final tally, and Veronica and Michael both were encouraged by the blend of personalities. Tonya was still a little bit withdrawn, but she would likely warm up as time went on. The dentist's wife, Lynette, was the only obvious phony in the lot and she would be easy enough to deal with.

Besides Tonya, Karen, and Maria two, the women included Andie Tatum—the brunette Forrest had met at the health food store—Joann Parker, a tall, sexy black woman; Jenny Brennan, a redhead with lots of freckles; Michelle Freeman, a bubbly blonde; and Renee Letterman, a less than bubbly blonde.

Michael came over from the table and sat in the grass with Veronica and Melissa.

"Karen's little girl is a cutie, isn't she?" Veronica said, unable to help testing the water.

"Which?" he said. "Oh, Karen's little girl. I forget her name. Yeah, she's a cutie."

That was when Veronica felt her first real spark of jealousy. If Michael was pretending to forget the daughter's name—and he was—it meant he liked the mother more than he wanted her to know. "I think her name's Terri," she said helpfully.

"That's right. Terri. Have you guys tried the potato salad?"

"Not yet," Melissa said. Seeing Forrest, she got up and walked over.

"She really likes him," Veronica said.

"He's a good father figure for her," Michael said, glancing toward the grill. "Better than me for sure."

"Don't say that. That's ridiculous."

"Well, what I mean is, Jack's a lot more like Stephen than I am."

"Tell me something."

"What?" He suspected he knew what she was going to ask.

"Are you attracted to Karen?"

He fell back on his arms with an audible sigh. "No more than you are to Jack."

She looked down into her lap. "I suppose that's a fair reply."

"Baby, I love you. You know that."

"I love you too," she said, pulling at the grass. "Michael, I'm scared to death."

"We all are. How could anyone possibly not be?"

"What if I crack? What if I make a complete ass out of myself down there?"

"You won't. You'll be too busy comforting everyone else."

Erin Ulrich and Taylor West came walking up holding two wineglasses each. "No serious faces allowed today," Erin said.

"You caught us!" Michael laughed.

The women sat down cross-legged in the grass, each offering a glass of wine.

"You know, we really couldn't be in better hands," Taylor said, touching glasses with them. "Erin's husband and the others are as good as they come."

"And Taylor's husband is an excellent doctor," Erin added. "For that matter, so is Price. He's actually an oral surgeon."

"Have you known Price's wife very long?" Veronica asked.

Erin and Taylor exchanged grins, everyone glancing

across the yard to where Lynette stood talking with some of the mothers. She was dressed in a skimpy top and tight-fitting jeans with heels.

"How does one explain Lynette?" Erin said with a giggle, having finished off a glass of wine already. "Yes, we've known her for about five years."

"Does she plan to dress like that down below?" Michael wondered.

"Probably," Erin said, sharing another laugh with Taylor.

"She's really very sweet, though," Taylor added.

"I wouldn't go that far," Erin said. "But she tries. I'll give her that."

"Your husband doesn't seem to care for her," Veronica said.

Erin looked at Taylor and they both started laughing. "Actually, Wayne can't stand her."

"Boy, I need to get caught up here," Michael said, taking a large sip from his glass. "You two are having a great time."

"Damn right," Erin said, touching glasses again with Taylor. "This may be the last fun we ever have."

"I just wish Monica had come," Taylor said, suddenly glum.

"Hey, no sad faces," Michael reminded her.

"You're right!" Taylor said, brightening quickly.

"Do you two know her well?" Veronica asked, provoking a discreet but disapproving look from Michael.

"We used to be a trio," Erin said. "But after their son Daniel was killed, the whole world changed. Monica withdrew from everyone . . . even Jack."

"How did he die?"

"His den mother was driving him home from a Cub Scout meeting," Taylor said. "Some drunken teenagers ran a red light. Jack and Wayne were both overseas when it happened. It was an absolute nightmare for Monica . . . for all of us, really."

"My God," Veronica said. "No wonder he's so intent on saving the rest of us."

"Jack doesn't even understand the *concept* of quit," Erin said. "He drives my husband crazy. But they have a bond I'll never begin to understand."

**ACROSS THE YARD**, Andie walked up to the grill and stood quietly listening as Melissa explained to Forrest the nuances of quantum theory and quantum mechanics.

"Okay," Forrest said. "So basically quantum theory was the big deal until quantum mechanics came along?"

"Yeah," she said, throwing the ball for Laddie. "But now they're the same thing . . . sort of. I wish I could it explain it better. I can see it my head but it's tough to put into words."

"No," he said. "You explained it very well. I'm just too dumb to absorb it."

"You're not dumb. If you studied it, you'd get it."

"I doubt that," he said, glancing at Andie. "This girl's a genius."

Andie smiled at the younger woman. "You learned all that on your own, Melissa?"

"It's just a hobby," she said. "They don't teach it to sophomores."

"Well, I know who I want for my assistant teacher," Andie said.

Melissa smiled, concealing her disappointment at losing Forrest's undivided attention.

"How's the wine?" Forrest asked.

"Very good," Andie replied.

"How's Trinity getting along?" The kids were playing on the swings.

"They're all wonderful children," Andie said. "I don't know how you've managed to pull this off, Jack, but you've done quite a job."

"I only get a fifth of the credit . . . and we're a long way from pulling this off."

He turned to see Melissa walking toward the house. "Hey, kiddo!"

She turned around quickly.

"We're gonna talk some more, right?"

She smiled big and nodded, then trotted toward the house.

"I think I chased her off," Andie said. "I didn't mean to."

"No, she's fine," he said, taking the ball from Laddie and throwing it.

"That dog loves to play fetch!"

"My son and he used to play for hours," he said, turning the burgers. "And Danny was always the first to get tired."

"Where's Danny now, with your ex?"

"No, he was killed in a car crash two years ago." He set his beer aside and started to remove a batch of hot dogs from the grill. "Laddie's all that's left of him."

"I'm sorry, Jack. I had no idea."

"It's okay. I've dealt with it, for the most part."

"Is that what . . . what ended your marriage?"

"In a nutshell . . . but the life of an army wife isn't easy. You know that."

"No, it isn't," she said. "But I understood that Kevin had a job to do."

"Monica did too."

"Is it soup yet?" Veronica asked, coming up from behind with her empty wineglass, touching him on the shoulder.

"Just about done," he said, giving her a smile.

Andie saw the look and realized at once that Veronica had a very definite lead. Oh well, she thought. There's time, hopefully. "Excuse me. I'm going to go and get the kids ready to eat."

"If you need help rounding them up," Veronica said, "give me a shout."

"Will do," Andie said.

"So what's up?" Veronica asked, looking Forrest in the eyes.

"Dunno," he said, taking the ball from Laddie and hurling it back out into the grass. "What's up?"

"You've been avoiding me today. How come?"

"Just keeping things in perspective."

"Have I done something wrong?"

"Nope."

"Have you called Monica?"

He looked at her. "Veronica . . . please."

"You should at least call her."

"With respect . . . you need to mind your own business."

"You'll regret it if you don't, Jack."

"Are you going to press this until I say something rude?"

She set the glass down. "I won't say any more." She stood for a moment with her hands in her pockets. "I think Michael's found a girlfriend."

"What the hell's that supposed to mean?"

"He's bonding with Karen."

"Oh, Christ."

"Well, I'm just saying . . . I can't really help being fascinated by this dynamic."

He took a moment to light up a Camel, tucking the Zippo back into his pocket. "Yeah, well don't forget that you're a part of this dynamic too. How are you getting along with your new friends over there?" He pointed over his shoulder with the tongs at Erin and Taylor. Taylor was lying on her back now with her head in Erin's lap, looking up at the sky, and they were laughing themselves silly over who knew what.

"I like them," she said warmly. "They're . . . real."

"They always have been." He took the burgers from the grill and stacked them one at a time on the tray. "Did they fill you on all of my juicy gossip?"

"They care about you and Monica very much."

"Yes, they do," he agreed, offering her the tray of hamburgers. "Mind taking these over to the table for me?"

She paused before accepting the tray. "It's going to be a long two years, isn't it?"

He grinned. "Yes, ma'am, it is . . ."

# EIGHTEEN

"OH, MY GOD, LOOK AT THAT!" SUSAN GASPED, POINTING out the windshield at a mob trying to overturn a school bus. "That's a dead cop in the road, Marty!"

"I see him," he said, making a sharp right turn down a side street.

They had made it almost as far south as San Diego by noon on the day after his release, and this was the most trouble they had seen so far.

"It's all coming unraveled now." He made a left and continued parallel to the street they had just turned off of, both of them glimpsing the mob down the side streets as they passed. They couldn't tell what started the riot, but the mob was comprised of men and women of various races.

"What do they hope to accomplish?" she wondered in dismay.

"Nothing," he said. "They're angry and afraid and they don't know what else to do. They've been lied to and they know it." He swerved around an empty delivery van sitting in the road, then had to slam on the brakes to avoid running over a man pushing a shopping cart filled with bags of dog food.

"Watch where the fuck you're goin', muthafucker!" the man shouted, aiming a revolver at them.

"I'm sorry!" Marty said. Then he pointed behind the man. "Look out!"

Another man hit the dog food man in the back of the head with a pipe and snatched the revolver from the pavement, running off down the street with it.

"Jesus Christ, Marty, get us out of here!"

He had to drive up onto the sidewalk to get around the dog food man who was now lying in the street with his skull cracked open. Someone else grabbed the front of the shopping cart and ran off in the other direction. The street was blocked up ahead by a burning police car, and there were hundreds of National Guard troops marching in echelon past the flames. It was unclear where they were headed, but their rifles were fixed with bayonets and ready to fire on anyone attempting to impede their progress. Marty made another right turn, driving up onto the sidewalk once again to get around more deserted cars blocking the side street.

"We're never going to get out of the city," she whined. "We should have stayed at my place."

"We'll find a way through, Susan. There's lots of road."

The next street over was passable, with half a dozen cars racing east toward the highway, ignoring traffic lights all the way. Marty pulled out behind them and drove as fast as he dared, trying to keep up with them, an uncertain herd mentality telling him there was safety in numbers. The cars at the front of the pack mowed down any pedestrians audacious or careless enough to cross the street in front of them, and the sound of the bodies thudding against the bottom of the car—as Marty was forced to run them over as well— made Susan sick to her stomach.

"Marty, I'm going to throw up."

"Roll down the window or use the backseat, honey. If I stop now, they'll kill us!"

She powered down the window and leaned her head over the passing pavement, holding her hair and retching twice into the wind at sixty mph. She pulled her head back in and grabbed a bottle of water from the backseat, rinsing her mouth and spitting it out the window.

Marty followed the car ahead of him up the on-ramp to the highway and merged with the speeding traffic. "Well that was definitely surreal," he said, relieved to be in traffic for the first time in his life.

"You scared the piss out of me!" she said, hitting him.

"But I got us through."

"You also called me honey. Don't think I didn't notice."

He caught her thin smile from the corner of his eye and felt warmth spread through his loins. "It was a figure of speech."

"Mm-hm," she said, watching the cityscape passing by. "We've got a long way to go. We'll need to stop for gas again before we get there."

"We'll find a place."

Five miles up the highway they got a flat tire.

"Son of a bitch," he said, crossing the lanes to the berm. "Can we catch a break?"

"There's a spare," she said, watching fearfully out the back window to see if anyone was going to stop and hassle them.

He got out and opened the back hatch, lifting the cover to the spare tire compartment to find a doughnut-sized space saver tire. "Just what I thought."

"We must have hit something in the road," she said, joining him at the back of the car, her red hair blowing in the wind.

He looked at her askance, wondering if she'd already forgotten the bodies.

Halfway through changing the right rear tire, a car pulled off the road with two large men inside.

"Oh, crap," Marty said.

"Need some help?" the passenger asked as he climbed from the car.

"No, we're fine," Marty said. "Thanks anyway, man."

Both men were covered with jailhouse tattoos, and they were watching Susan too closely for comfort.

"Why don't you let us give you a hand?" the passenger said, coming close. "You gotta make sure you get those lug nuts good and tight."

"*Good* and tight," the driver echoed.

Marty took the pistol from his pocket and pointed at them. "I said no thanks."

They stopped short but didn't appear afraid. The passenger looked at his buddy. "I don't think he's got the cojones."

There was a sharp crack and the man grabbed his thigh, stumbling backward. "You motherfucker!" he screamed, his face twisted in anguish, blood quickly gushing through his fingers.

"Chill the fuck out, man!" the driver shouted, pointing at Marty. "All we wanted to do was help, you son of a bitch!"

"Get lost!" Marty shouted, taking a step forward.

"Marty, let them go."

"Move it!"

The driver helped his bleeding friend back into the car and got behind the wheel, speeding off with the wounded man giving them a bloody finger.

"I don't think he'll live long," Marty said, going quickly back to his work. "Did you see how bad he was bleeding? I must have hit the femoral artery."

"Do you think they were really . . ."

"Gonna take you?"

She nodded.

"I'm positive."

Two hours later, just across the border into Arizona, they began to run low on fuel and started looking for an acceptable gas station. Every station they passed for thirty miles was swarming with motorists, and many of the stations appeared to be more or less under siege. One they passed was fully engulfed in flames.

They finally spotted a Shell station with only a few cars at the pumps. People were running in and out, picking the place clean, but Marty decided to give it a try.

They pulled up to one of the pumps and he got out and

swiped his card. To his immense relief, the card was authorized and he grabbed the nozzle from its slot and stuck it into the fuel port.

"Hey, buddy?" a man said, poking his head around the pump. "Do you suppose we could use your card? There's nobody working in there and all we got is cash."

Marty glanced into the man's car to see that he was traveling with a wife and two children.

"I'll pay you double," the man said.

"You can owe me," Marty said, lending him the card. "Pump as much as you need."

"Thanks a lot." The man ducked back around.

When Marty was putting the nozzle back into the slot, the man stepped back from around the pump, and even as Marty was reaching for his card, the man jammed a .357 Magnum into his face.

"Sorry, buddy," the guy said, "but we got a dead battery. Tell your old lady to get out of the car."

"Hey, whoa!" Marty said, stepping back. "We're more than willing to give you a jump, man."

"Get her the fuck outta the car!" the man ordered.

"Bill!" the man's wife shouted. "Let them give us a jump!"

"We don't have any fucking cables!"

Marty pointed at the station. "They'll have some inside!"

The man pointed the weapon at Susan. "If I have to tell you one more time, I'll shoot her. I swear to Christ!"

Susan got quickly out of the car. "Let them have it, Marty."

The man trained the gun on Marty as his family loaded into their car. The woman offered to let Susan get their bags of food from the back.

"Don't let them take a fucking thing!" her husband ordered, never taking his eyes off Marty.

That's when Marty first noticed the gold star on the man's belt.

"Protect and serve, huh?"

"Fuck you," the man said, getting into their car, keeping the gun trained on him. "I got a family to take care of. Get over there where I can see you and keep your hands up. I see the gun in your pocket."

Marty stepped back and kept his hands up as the man drove away with their car and all of their supplies.

Susan jumped into the cop's car and turned the key. There was a clicking noise under the hood but that was it. In the backseat there were a few meager rations and two bottles of Gatorade. "At least they left us something," she said. "Maybe we can get somebody to give us a jump."

During the confrontation, the looters had cut the pump island a wide berth, not wanting to risk getting shot, but now that the maniac with the gun was gone, a large group of teenage Latino males were taking notice of Susan, loitering about and smoking cigarettes they had stolen, talking furtively among themselves. A few of them were marked with gang tats and had moco rags tied on their heads.

"We'd better just get moving," he said.

"Okay, yeah," Susan replied, taking his meaning.

They took the supplies from the back of the car and started off on foot toward the highway. Marty had no idea what they were going to do now, but they needed to get away from the gang because there were more of them than there were bullets in the gun.

"Shit," he said with a glance over his shoulder. "They're following us."

"I'm scared," she said, grabbing his hand.

Marty could feel her trembling, and his bladder filled with ice.

"Don't run before they make their move," he said, spotting half a dozen or so civilized-looking men standing across the street in front of a doughnut shop. "Maybe we can get some help from those guys over there."

The gang started trotting after them.

"They're coming!" she said in panic.

"Don't run!" he hissed, gripping her hand tighter.

The group caught up and encircled them. "Hey, *mama-sita*!" the apparent leader said with a heavy Chilango accent, flicking his cigarette away and grabbing at Susan's T-shirt. "Let's see what you got under the hood, *esa*."

The others laughed, making exaggerated gestures as they flicked the ashes from their cigarettes or swaggered along combing their hair.

Susan fended off the advance and kept walking, squeezing Marty's hand.

"What's the matter, mama, you don't like young dick or what, eh? We'll show you a good time."

They kept walking, but as they drew closer to the doughnut shop, the men on the sidewalk filed inside, and that's when Marty knew they were in deep shit. The gang knew it too, of course, also watching to see what the doughnut men were going to do. Now confident, one of them grabbed Susan by the hair from behind and another tore at her T-shirt, exposing her bra.

Marty shot the leader in the face at nearly point-blank range, blowing his teeth out the opposite side of his face. Someone stabbed him a glancing blow to the shoulder from behind and he spun around, shooting the youth in the belly as the rest of them dragged Susan off at the run. She screamed for help as they lifted off her the ground and Marty ran after them, shooting two of them in the back before the gun jammed.

Three of the teens turned on him immediately and began to assault him in a flurry of fists and feet, beating him quickly to the ground and stomping him. Marty blacked out, and they left him where he lay on the pavement.

Susan was shrieking now, clawing at her young assailants as they hauled her off toward an alley, kicking furiously in a futile attempt to get her feet back on the ground.

A rescue-green Jeep Rubicon suddenly came streaking into the lot and mowed four of the teens over in one blow. The driver hit the brake and cut the wheel hard, gunning for the rest of them. The gang panicked, dropping Susan to the ground and running for their lives from the Jeep.

The driver stopped and jumped out, firing a single shot after them to keep them running.

"Are you okay?" he asked, offering Susan a bloody hand to help her to her feet.

She was sobbing and trying to remake her shirt and bra in order to cover her exposed breast.

"Come on," the man said, walking her toward the Jeep. "We need to go."

"Marty!" she said. "Where's Marty?"

"That him over there?"

She saw Marty getting to his feet, staggering and bleeding from a gash in his head, and she ran to him, grabbing him and bawling.

"I'm okay," he said hazily, seeing their dark-haired rescuer walking up in black jeans and a blue denim jacket, his cowboy boots spattered with droplets of wet blood.

"You gave a good account of yourself, partner."

"Thanks," Marty said, holding his head.

The cowboy cut the men in the doughnut shop a hard look and they turned away from the windows. "Don't mention it," he said. "You two had better mount up. We can't get caught flat-footed in the open."

The Jeep had a hard-top cover, and there were four red five-gallon fuel cans strapped to the roof.

Susan climbed into the backseat on the driver's side and Marty rode shotgun. The cowboy belted himself in and wheeled the Jeep around toward the highway, where the traffic now headed into the desert wasn't a great deal busier than it would normally have been at that time of year.

"Where ya headed?"

"Mesa."

"Well you're in luck," the cowboy said. "There's enough gas for the run. My name's Joe."

"Where are you going?" Marty asked.

"Down the road a ways," Joe said, shaking a smoke from

a pack of Marlboros and lighting it with the lighter from the ashtray.

Marty glanced into the backseat at Susan. She shrugged her shoulders. There was an M-1 carbine on the seat next to her along with a green bandolier of extra magazines.

"What's down the road a ways?" Marty asked.

"More desert," the cowboy said, exhaling a large cloud of smoke, which was blown quickly away by the wind.

"More desert?"

The cowboy stuck the cigarette between his teeth. "Here," he said, taking his .45 automatic from the small of his back and giving it to Marty. "Better acquaint yourself with that. You'll likely need it."

"I don't understand," he said, glancing again at Susan.

"The magazine holds seven shots," Joe went on. "You pull back on the slide to load a round into battery. There's a slide lock on the side there. It's like a safety. It kicks some but you and your girl can handle it. The carbine in the back is easy too. I'll show you how to use that in a bit. Right now we just need to put some real estate behind us. I've got some pretty bad hombres after me, and if they ask around back there, somebody's bound to tell 'em which way we went."

"Why are they after you?" Susan asked.

Joe dragged deeply from the Marlboro. "Well, let's just say I gave 'em a good dose of the same medicine I gave those spics back there."

"Were they trying to rape somebody?" She couldn't help asking.

"No, they'd done raped her already," Joe answered quietly. "I killed all seven of 'em, but I didn't know the bar was full of their friends. It was a Mongol bar."

Susan gasped. "My God, they were Chinese?"

"The Mongols are a biker gang, Suc."

"Outlaw biker gang," Joe added. "And they're already rapin' and pillagin' their asses off."

"They raped a woman outside a bar?" Susan said, quietly aghast.

"In the back of a pickup."

"About how many bikers are after you?" Marty asked, looking into the side rearview mirror, half expecting the horizon to be filled with motorcycles.

"A lot," Joe said. "But don't worry about it. Where this Jeep can go, their Harleys can't follow."

Marty could see Susan sitting forward now with her head in her hands, and he wanted badly to climb into the backseat and hold her, but he didn't want to do it in front of Joe.

"Where's the woman now? Did you have to leave her behind?"

"She's dead. She needed a hospital bad and there just wasn't one to be found."

"You mean you had to . . ."

Joe nodded. "That's what I mean."

Ten miles farther on, Joe pulled off the highway, drove right through a fence onto a dirt road and then down into a dry arroyo where they couldn't be seen from the road.

"End of the line," he said, climbing out.

Marty looked at Susan and then noticed that Joe's seat was soaked with blood.

"Oh, no," he muttered, and got out to find Joe sitting in the dirt behind the Jeep, against a rock.

"Get me that carbine outta there, partner. I need to show you how to work it."

"How bad are you?" Susan asked, getting out of the Jeep with the carbine.

"Bad enough, darlin'. Lemme see that."

He made sure they knew how to operate both weapons and had them each take a few practice shots.

"Okay," he said, lighting up another cigarette, this time with a disposable lighter from his jacket. "Off you go now."

"No," Susan said, "we'll stay with you."

"Get on," Joe said. "I need time to talk with my wife before I die."

"The phones aren't working," Marty said. "There's too many people making calls."

"I don't need a phone to talk to the dead. Get on now. And ride parallel to the highway whenever you can. Most road warriors won't be able to follow you off road. Those that can, you just shoot 'em with the carbine."

Susan knelt beside him in the dirt and gave him a hug. "We'll never forget you."

"I don't envy either of you what lies ahead, honey."

Marty offered Joe his hand and then he and Susan reluctantly got into the Jeep.

"Hey, partner! Come back here a second."

Marty got back out. "What do you need?"

"Don't you let that girl be taken alive again, hear?"

"It was your wife back there, wasn't it?" Marty said, his eyes filling with tears, his voice thick. "They shot you and took her, didn't they?"

"Biggest mistake they ever made was not killin' me," Joe said. "Love her long as you can, partner, but don't you be afraid to do what needs done. Hear?"

"I won't," Marty said, wiping his eyes with the tail of his tattered shirt and turning to get back into the Jeep.

"Why are you crying?" Susan asked. She looked out the back window to see Joe resting his head against the rock, eyes closed. "What did he say?"

"Nothing," Marty said, starting the motor. "He died."

He drove up out of the wash, back through the hole in the fence, and sped off down the highway, both of them listening to the tires humming against the asphalt. Susan tried the radio. There was no music, just a lot of news. Bad news about civil unrest and the state government's inability to do much of anything about it. People were being urged to stay in their homes and off the highways.

# NINETEEN

**THEY HADN'T DRIVEN VERY FAR BEFORE MARTY SPOTTED THE** first of the motorcycles coming over the horizon in the rearview mirror. They were still a few miles back but gaining.

"This isn't our day, Sue."

"What?" she said, whipping her head around. "Mongols?"

"Gotta be," he said, hitting the brakes and pulling quickly off the highway.

"What are you doing, for God's sake?"

He climbed into the back. "Drive, Sue! Drive as fast you feel safe."

"But . . . Marty!" She climbed behind the wheel and shifted into drive, pulling back onto the highway as he prepared to fire the carbine out through the back window. "Marty, I don't know if I can do this!"

"We'll talk about it later!"

He watched the Harleys closing on them gradually, dodging in and out of the traffic. They flew past a stopped state trooper's car. The red and blue strobes on the roof were flashing wildly but there was no trooper to be seen anywhere.

"Marty, they're getting closer."

"I'm watching them," he said, holding the lead driver in the sights of the carbine. "I have to let them get close enough to hit them."

"I think they've got guns!"

"Of course they've got guns!" he said, unable to help laughing at the pure insanity of the moment. " 'I think they've got guns.' "

"Shut up, Marty! Who are you, Mel Gibson now?"

"Don't make me laugh, Susan. I have to shoot these guys and I'm trying not to piss my pants back here."

She swerved wildly to miss a stalled car in the fast lane. "Holy Christ!" she said in terror. "I almost plowed right into that fucking thing!"

"Watch the road, not the mirror!"

There were about forty bikes behind them now, and Marty was aiming for the belly of the lead rider. The guy wasn't a fat, sweaty, bearded hog as he had expected most of them to be. He looked more like Arnold Schwarzenegger from one of the Terminator movies, and he was driving one-handed, gripping a shotgun like a cowboy on horseback.

Marty fired the first round, shattering the rear window and causing Susan to scream and swerve inside the lane.

The biker began weaving to throw off Marty's aim, blasting off a round of buckshot that was ineffective at that range. Marty fired again and shattered the headlight. His third shot struck the biker in the chest and the man lost control immediately, dropping the shotgun and fighting to keep from crashing, but he was doomed. The bike went down and flipped over on top of him. One of the bikes coming up ran him over and crashed. Another rider tried to dodge the first bike but clipped the handlebars and flipped over, his bike virtually disintegrating as it slammed into a bridge abutment.

"Got three in one shot!" Marty said.

"I heard three shots," Susan muttered, checking her speed, not trusting herself to drive much over seventy.

Surprised to discover a gunner in the Jeep, the rest of the Mongols dropped back, shouting back and forth, trying to decide how best to handle this new development.

Marty fired again and hit one of them in the head. A

lucky shot, but the rider flew right off the back and his bike continued on for nearly fifty feet without him before heading down into the median and flipping over. The rest of the riders slowed way down after that and allowed the distance between them and the Jeep to increase greatly.

"They're letting us go. You did it, Marty!"

"I doubt it," he said, sensing what they were up to. "They're not turning back. They'll probably try to shadow us all the way to Mesa."

"So what do we do?"

"Find a place to get off the highway. Drive cross-country through the desert like Joe told us."

"I don't know. What if we get stuck or have a breakdown?"

"And what if these maniacs follow us all the way to my house?"

They continued for another ten miles, the bikers hanging back about a mile or so in the slow lane, letting the faster traffic pass them on the left. Another state trooper streaked by going the other way, lights flashing, but they didn't think for a minute that he would be any help, and the bikers certainly didn't seem too shaken up over him.

"Okay," Marty said, remaining in the backseat. "I know this area. About five miles ahead there's a rest stop. Pull in and we'll switch."

"They'll be right on top of us by the time we get back on the road."

"We're not getting back on the road," he said. "We're going over land where those bikes won't be able to stay with us."

They passed the sign for the rest stop and a mile later exited the highway. Susan sped up the ramp into an area where military vehicles were gathered. There were armed soldiers wandering all over the place, and a bunch of them aimed their rifles at the Jeep, ready to blast it apart.

"Oh, shit!" she said, getting on the brakes and slowing just in time. She cut the wheel and rolled into a parking spot, then got out and ran toward the soldiers, who were watching her as if she were crazy.

"We're being chased!" she shouted, pointing back at the ramp. "Bikers are trying to kill us!"

The soldiers looked toward the ramp and stood waiting to see. Within fifty seconds the Mongols came rolling into the rest area smelling blood, but the moment they saw the soldiers they put the coal to the fire and roared right on through toward the exit.

"Shoot them!" Susan was shouting. "You're letting them get away!"

The troops watched as the last of the bikes rumbled through, and then stood looking at her.

"Why didn't you shoot them, for Christ's sake? You could've gotten every damn one of them!"

Marty took her by the arm and walked her back to the Jeep. "Sorry, guys," he said over his shoulder. "It's been a rough day." Then to Susan, in a lower voice, "Your breast is showing!"

"Oh, shit," she said, grabbing at the shirt to cover herself.

"We'll just hang here for a minute," he said. "I can get us to Mesa without the highway now."

"Maybe we can get these guys to escort us," she said, getting back into the Jeep on the passenger side.

"Susan, they're not our personal bodyguard. They're men with guns and they just got a pretty good look at your tit."

"It's not a 'tit,'" she said thinly. "It's a breast."

He chuckled wearily. "Do you know how stupid you sound?"

A couple of troops came up to the Jeep.

"What's going on?" a tall sergeant asked. His name tag read FLYNN.

"We were attacked on the road," Marty said, wishing he'd hidden the carbine lying across the backseat. "Those bikers murdered our friend and his wife earlier today. They just tried to do the same to us."

The sergeant stood looking at him, noticing the weapon in the back. "Where did you get that?"

"It belonged to a friend," Susan said. "This is his Jeep."

The sergeant stooped so he could get a better look at her. "Are you injured?"

"No, but Marty is. He's got a stab wound in his shoulder and a gash to his head."

"It'll be okay," Marty said, wishing she would shut up. "We're going to get going in a minute."

"Get a medic over here," Flynn said to the other soldier. He turned his attention back to Marty. "Is that the only weapon you've got?"

Marty considered lying but thought better of it, since the pistol was concealed under his shirt, rather than under the seat. He knew he should have thought to stash it there, but Susan had jumped from the Jeep so fast he hadn't had time to think.

"No, I've got a pistol too."

The sergeant stood looking at him, waiting for the medic. "Where is it?"

"Under my shirt."

"I'm going to ask you to leave it in the Jeep while you're being treated," Flynn said.

"That's fine," Marty replied, the feeling of sweet relief spreading through his veins.

A woman in uniform, complete with helmet, appeared at the sergeant's side with a large green bag over her shoulder. "Who's injured?"

"This man has a stab wound to the shoulder and a gash to the head," Flynn said. "See what you can do for him."

He stood by while Marty stashed the .45 in the glove box, then walked off to join the other troops as the medic began to probe Marty's wounds.

"Thank God you guys were here," Susan said to her. "Those maniacs were trying to kill us."

"If I might make a suggestion," the medic said. "Woman-to-woman. You need to start making yourself less notice-able."

Susan self-consciously doubled her grip on the shirt. "I was a little freaked out . . . but that's good advice. Thank you."

"Where are you two headed?" the medic asked, pouring peroxide onto Marty's head wound and sopping at it with a wad of cotton.

"Mesa," he answered, wincing slightly.

"Married?"

"We're just friends," Susan said.

"Are you prepared to die for her?" the medic asked, her tone very frank.

"He's almost done that a couple of times already," Susan said, sounding oddly proud.

"The way you prance around in front of men," the medic said flatly, "I believe it."

"She was just freaked out," Marty said.

For a fellow woman, the medic didn't seem to have an ounce of sympathy. "You endanger us all by drawing attention. You understand?"

Susan looked down at the pavement. "Yeah."

The medic opened a foil pack of sutures. "I'm going to sew these up."

"I appreciate it," Marty said.

The sergeant came back across the lot and offered a digital ACU jacket to Susan. "Put that on and keep it zipped."

"Thank you," she said quietly, never having felt so much like a tramp in her life. Didn't these people realize she was a victim, for God's sake?

"I put out a call on those bikers," Flynn said. "But I wouldn't count on anything being done. When you get back out on the highway, you'd better keep your eyes peeled."

"Actually, we're going right out the back of the rest stop," Marty said. "We're going to try keeping off the highway."

"Might not be a bad idea," the sergeant said, and walked off again.

"Where are you guys going from here?" Marty asked the medic, whose name tag identified her as Emory.

"No idea," Emory said. "We're waiting to decide."

"You don't have any orders?" Susan asked.

"After that asteroid hits, our orders aren't going to mean

shit. We just plan on getting as far away from the impact area as possible."

"Call your sergeant back over here," Marty said.

"Why?"

"I might be able to help you decide which way to go."

Emory got on her radio and called the sergeant back over.

"What do you need?" he asked.

"Sergeant, believe it or not, I'm the astronomer who took the asteroid public."

"That so?" the sergeant said, not entirely convinced.

"It is, and I might be able to offer you a suggestion as to where you don't want to be tomorrow morning."

"How's that?"

"Because I work at Mesa Station, and I've actually seen this beast with my own eyes. Most of my calculations have it hitting in the tristate area of Wyoming, Montana, and South Dakota. I formed a couple of orbital models that predicted it would hit farther north, but none of them predicted that it would hit any farther south than Wyoming. There's the remotest possibility of it hitting in the Great Lakes, but that's it."

"Washington says it could it hit anywhere between Central America and the North Pole."

"Well, Washington is wrong. If I were you guys, I'd head due south. This thing's blast radius could be anywhere from five hundred to a thousand miles, and nothing within that distance is going to survive unless it's deep underground."

"Washington says closer to five hundred miles."

"That was before their nuclear blast may have given the damn thing a boost."

"I'll talk to the lieutenant," the sergeant said, turning away. "Appreciate the information."

"Maybe we could go with you guys?" Marty said to Emory.

She glanced over her shoulder to see if any of the men were within earshot. "You don't want to come with us, regardless of where we go."

"What's that mean?" Susan said.

"There are eleven women in this unit," Emory said. "And as soon as it gets dark tonight, we're hauling ass down the highway."

"But you're in the Army . . . aren't you all like family?"

Emory drew the needle through the flap in Marty's shoulder wound. "Where did you find her?"

Marty smiled at Susan. "She's actually a genius in her field."

"Which is what? Home decorating?"

"Hey!" Susan said. "I'll have you know I'm a professor of astrophysics."

Emory drew another stitch through the wound. "That explains it."

"Well, we can't all wear camouflage for a living," Susan snapped.

"Please don't shoot her," Marty said. "I know she's a little mouthy, but she's the only woman I've ever loved."

Emory finally cracked a smile. "Lucky you."

Susan shook her head and went to sit in the Jeep.

"She's pretty," Emory said quietly. "I'd jump 'er."

Marty looked over his shoulder at her and grinned. "What happened to 'don't ask, don't tell'?"

"Maybe I meant I'd like to beat her up."

"Maybe it's both," he said with a chuckle.

Emory finished stitching and dressing his wounds and turned to close up her bag.

"Are you really in that much danger here?" he asked her.

"Fifty horny guys with M-16s? No law and order? What do you think?"

"They can't all be animals, can they?"

"No, but we're not hanging around to find out who is and who isn't. We've got rifles too, and we're splitting before they're taken away from us." She gave him back his shirt. "You're good to go. Take these antibiotics with you."

"Thanks," he said, shaking her hand. "Should I say anything to the sergeant before we go?"

Emory shook her head. "Just go."

"Want to jump in and go with us?" he asked as she walked with him toward the Jeep.

"I can't bail on my friends, but thanks for the offer. Look after the princess."

"I'll try," Marty said, opening the door and getting in. "I'm Marty, by the way."

"I'm Shannon."

"Good luck, Shannon."

"Shit, we're all fucked, Marty." She shut his door and stepped back as he started the motor, then watched him drive off and crash through the fence at the back of the rest area.

The sergeant and another female soldier came walking over as the Jeep rolled away over the terrain.

"We're on for eleven-thirty," Sergeant Flynn said.

"Roger that," said Emory. "What did you tell the lieutenant?"

"What do you think I told him? I told him the astronomer said we should roll due north."

**AS THEY DROVE** along over the rugged terrain, Susan was grinning at Marty.

"What?"

"You liked her."

He laughed. "Well, guess which one of us *she* liked."

Susan's smile disappeared. "You're making that up."

"No," he said. "Her exact words were: 'She's pretty, I'd jump 'er.'"

"That's disgusting," she said, crossing her arms and looking out the window.

He laughed some more.

"It's not that funny, Martin."

"Well, considering what we've been through today, Susan, I'd say it's just that funny."

# TWENTY

THE SUN WAS GOING DOWN, AND THOUGH MOST OF THE
adults in Forrest's flock were fairly inebriated, it was a so-
bering moment as each reflected that this could be the last
sunset they ever saw. They sat watching it, the foundation of
all their sunny days and brightest memories, shading their
eyes as it faded to a darker orange, many of them whispering for it not to go. Even the youngest children seemed to be
experiencing an instinctive sense of loss.

After it disappeared, the mothers gathered their children into their arms and held them tight, telling them how
much they loved them and pledging that nothing would ever
change that, no matter what the future held. Forrest stood
watching over them all with Laddie at his side, a carbine
slung across his back: a lethal talisman to ward off whatever
evils might come to pass in the following months.

"By the time it gets dark," Ulrich announced to the group,
"we'd like everyone to be inside the house, but feel free to
remain aboveground until midnight."

"I guess it's time we started moving this party inside, then,"
Erin said, forcing herself to cheer up. "Who wants coffee?"

"I'll help you make some," Andie said, her gaze on Forrest for a long moment as she joined Erin on her way to the
house.

Forrest watched as Joann Parker came strolling gracefully up to him, looking very solemn, leading her five-year-old daughter Beyonce by the hand.

"Is everything okay?" he asked.

"We're fine," she said. "I'd just like to thank you for today. The rest of the world is suffering so badly right now . . . but you've managed to make today special."

"It's my privilege," he said, kneeling to talk to her daughter. "How are you, beautiful? Did you have fun with Laddie today?"

"Yes," she said, smiling and petting the dog's ears. "Mommy says you're an army man. That's why you have a gun."

"Well, I'm sort of an army man, yeah. But I only have a gun in case some bears come around and try to eat up all our food."

"Bears?" she said incredulously, as if the idea of a bear in Nebraska was the craziest thing she had ever heard.

He laughed as he stood up. "Your daughter is apparently unaware of the growing bear population here in the Great Plains."

Joann laughed, and for a moment she looked as though she wanted to say something more, but she excused herself instead and led Beyonce off toward the house.

Ulrich came over and stood at Forrest's side. "Did you touch base with Jerry one last time?"

Forrest nodded. "He wishes us luck. He's back in Havana now."

They went inside, and the house was crowded even with everyone spread more or less evenly throughout the five rooms.

"Where's Melissa?" Forrest asked Veronica.

"She's out on the porch . . . she's upset, Jack. It's been two days, and she hasn't been able to reach her parents with all the cell phone usage."

He crossed the house and stepped out onto the porch where Melissa was sitting in a chair. Laddie was beside her, watching the night.

"What's got you down?" he asked, taking the chair beside her and resting the carbine barrel-up against the railing.

"Can I see that?"

"Not right now. What's got you down?"

"You know what it is," she said, petting the dog.

He flicked his cigarette out into the yard.

"You should quit smoking."

He took the pack from his pocket and set it on the windowsill. "How's that?"

She rolled her eyes. "You've got like ninety cartons downstairs."

"So when's the last time you talked to your parents?"

"The day before yesterday."

"Come on," he said, taking her hand and grabbing the carbine.

Veronica saw them headed for the basement and started to follow, but Michael stepped in front of her.

"Where are you going?"

She pointed after them.

"You don't have to be in on every little thing," he said. "Let her have some time with him."

"Why aren't you talking to your girlfriend?"

"I thought I was."

"I don't want to dance around this," she said, suddenly frustrated. "Let me know if you decide to get to know her better."

"I hardly think you've got room to criticize."

**DOWN BELOW IN** Launch Control, Forrest sat down beside Melissa, switched on the satellite phone and typed in a number from memory.

"But I thought you couldn't—"

"Shh!"

The phone rang only twice.

"Jack, is that you?" someone answered over the speaker.

"Yeah, Jerry, it's me. Thanks for picking up."

"Has something gone wrong?" Jerry asked. "I didn't think we were supposed to talk again."

"I need a favor, Jerry."

"Another one? Jesus Christ, Jack!"

"Hey, this one's easy," Forrest said. "I need you to patch me through to a specific cell phone number."

"We're on a military satellite, Jack. There are certain risks involved here."

"What are they going to do, Jerry? Come and get you down in Havana after the meteor hits?"

"Give me the fucking number, you greedy pain in the ass."

Forrest gave him the number. "Thanks, Jerry. Godspeed."

"Same to you, old friend."

A minute later the line was ringing.

"Hello?"

"Mom!" Melissa blurted.

"Oh, my God, baby! Are you okay? Stephen, it's Melissa! Baby, we've been going crazy trying to reach you! Are you okay?"

"I'm fine," Melissa said, her voice cracking as she began to cry.

"Take all the time you need," Forrest whispered, touching her on the head and leaving her alone in Launch Control, signaling Laddie to stay with her. He went back upstairs and out into the backyard, and half an hour later Melissa reappeared to find him at the picnic table smoking a cigarette.

"I thought you quit," she said, sitting down beside him.

"I started up again."

She leaned against him and rested her head on his shoulder. "We got cut off."

"Military satellites will do that," he said. "They prioritize every thirty minutes. I should've warned you."

"At least I got to talk to them. Thank you."

"You bet."

She was silent for a moment. "We're all going to die, aren't we?"

He smiled in the porch light. "Eventually."

"That's not what I mean."

"This has happened before, and mankind snapped right back." He pushed a curl away from her sad eyes. "There's no reason to assume we won't make it."

"Man hasn't recovered from something like this."

"No? Well, I've got a book downstairs written by that Ester Thorn lady on CNN. She says an asteroid hit a glacier on this very continent about thirteen thousand years ago during the last ice age—the Younger Dryas, she calls it. She says that's what killed off the woolly mammoth and the saber-toothed tiger."

"Well, cavemen were a lot tougher than we are."

"They weren't tougher than me," he said. "I'd kick a caveman's ass."

She laughed softly, as Kane stepped out onto the back porch.

"Jack! You might want to come down and have a look at the news. Things are really going to shit in a hurry. Federal troops are firing on civilians in New York and D.C. . . . and it sounds like China just invaded eastern Russia."

# TWENTY-ONE

ESTER THORN TOOK HER EYE AWAY FROM THE TELESCOPE AT the Gemini Observatory and looked at Harold Shipman. "It's so damn close now, just seeing it is enough to curdle an old woman's blood."

Shipman helped her to step aside so his friend from the local television network, Sam Ash, could have a look at the asteroid for himself.

When Ash peered through the eyepiece, what he saw reminded him somewhat of looking head-on at a spiraling football. If he blinked his eye, he could capture the briefest glimpse of a rocky-looking surface illuminated by the sun, but not much more. "It's spinning wildly, isn't it?"

"On a number of different axes," Shipman said, "coming right at us at a hundred thousand miles an hour, made of almost solid iron . . . like an artillery shell."

"An artillery shell as big as a town," Ester grumbled, ambling off toward the office.

Ash followed them down the corridor. "Why do you suppose no one ever named it?"

"I suppose because why bother?" Shipman said. "No one knows who was the first to spot it, and that's who typically names these things."

"It's the Chittenden Bolide," insisted Ester, stopping in

the office doorway and turning to rest on her cane. "But the world doesn't need to hear that. Marty wasn't looking for fame. He was looking to save lives. That's why we've called you, Sam. We need your help with the media again."

"You've got it. What do you need me to do?"

"We need a propagandist." She smiled mirthlessly. "Up for it?"

"Well, I guess that depends," he said with a glance at Shipman. "What am I propagandizing?"

"Opportunity!" she said. "In less than twelve hours the United States will be dead, and that's going to leave us all alone out here on the ocean."

"Where exactly is the opportunity in that?"

"In the Earth and its resources, primarily these islands and their waters. I don't want to get all preachy with you, Sam, and I certainly don't think we should get preachy with the people, but we've got a chance to get it right this time, and I'm willing to cheat to make that happen."

Again Ash glanced briefly at Shipman. "Well, maybe you need to get a little preachy with me, Ester, because I'm not sure I follow you."

"All right," she began. "This has been a profit-based society for the last two hundred years, and that's why we're all about to die. Had this been a resource-based society . . . we would have stopped that asteroid a month ago—or even two months ago—because we'd have been prepared. So tonight we need you to go on TV and stress that very point. You accuse the government of allowing corporate greed to kill the Earth. You get the people angry, and by getting them angry you get them motivated to take action . . . Then you offer them a course of action to take.

"You tell them we'll defy the failures of the past by working together to build a sustainable future this time, a future based on a partnership with this planet instead of endless exploitation. It won't be an easy task, hell no, but nothing worthwhile ever is. Our inexcusable failure to stop this asteroid is testament enough to that."

She tamped her cane once against the floor and stood looking sternly between the two men. "What do you say to that, Sam?"

Ash was thoughtful for a long moment. He rubbed his chin, then he cast his gaze back to Ester. "I can't do it."

"What do you mean, you can't do it?" she demanded. "You're in charge of the network! You're saying you disagree?"

"I'm saying I can't sell it."

"Hogwash! All you have to do is put some passion behind it!"

Ash looked at Shipman and smiled. "Honestly, Harold, am I the person to sell this . . . 'opportunity'?"

Shipman smiled back, shifting his weight. "No. No, I don't think you are, after all."

Ester turned on him angrily. "What's that supposed to mean?"

"We mean, Ester, that it's got to be you. You're the one who brought us this far, and I'm sorry, but you're the one who's going to have to take us the rest of the way." Shipman looked at Ash. "How soon can you get her on the air?"

Ash shrugged. "Within the hour if we leave now."

"Now, wait just a minute!" Ester protested as Ash stepped toward her. "I'm an old woman. I can't start a movement. I don't have the energy for it!"

Ash put his arm around her shoulder, preparing to lead her down the corridor. "Ester, forgive me for saying so, but that's bullshit. You've already started it, and I'm afraid you're just going to have to finish it."

"I didn't start a goddamn thing," she griped, taking a reluctant step forward. "It was Marty Chittenden who started it, by God, and now I'm the one left holding the bag!"

# TWENTY-TWO

**DURING THE FINAL LEG INTO MESA, MARTY KEPT THE JEEP** off the road. He drove parallel to the highway until the Mongols spotted them, then veered deep inland and southeast to terrain that was too rugged for the Harleys. By the time they got into town it was nearly dark, and judging by the loud music blaring from most of the houses, it seemed that the people in his neighborhood either didn't believe the world was about to end or had decided to go out partying. People were drinking and carrying on, and a few were dancing naked in the middle of the street.

"Wow," Susan said. "It's like a rave."

"It's nice to see we've still got power." He parked the car on the concrete drive and took the guns inside.

"I need a shower," she said, dropping down on the couch.

"You're in luck. I've got an electric water heater, but you'd better hurry because the power could go at any time."

She stepped into the bedroom and crossed to the master bath, closing the door behind her. Marty heated them some canned soup, since the perishable food in the fridge had gone bad during his extended stay in California. She came from the bath a little while later and sat at the table in his robe, eating her soup. Her wet hair was wrapped in a towel, and he thought she looked so amazingly sexy sitting there in his robe that his throat tightened and it was difficult for him to swallow. He was about to compliment her but didn't trust himself to conceal the intensity of his attraction, so he tried not to look at her as he ate.

"The water's still hot," she said, pulling the towel from her head and buffing her hair dry.

"Okay," he said, his voice throaty. "Thanks." He was recalling the sight of her naked breast at the rest stop earlier that day, the strawberry nipple, and was looking forward to getting a shower of his own. He got up and took the guns from the table with him into the bedroom, where he set them down on the dresser.

Susan followed him in and sat down on the bed. "Would you mind leaving the bathroom door open so we can talk? I'm still a little scared."

"Um, yeah . . . okay," he said, disappointed; now it would be almost impossible for him to jerk off without her realizing it. He undressed, turned on the shower, and stepped in beneath the water, closing the door to the stall.

"Are you in?" she called.

"Uh, yeah."

"I need to brush my teeth," she said, coming into the bathroom. "I found a new brush in the drawer. Can I use it?"

"Absolutely." He stood in the shower willing his erection to go away, but it wouldn't. Maybe if he soaped it up and was quiet about it, he could manage without her knowing.

"I wonder if they'll party all night," she said, brushing her teeth in the mirror.

"I don't know," he said. He loved her company, but she was making this difficult.

She handed his toothbrush and toothpaste over the top of the shower wall. "Here you go."

"Uh . . . thanks."

"You're not masturbating in there, are you?"

"No!"

"You'd better not be. That would be disgusting."

"Shut up, Sue." He began to wither after that, so he went

ahead and brushed his teeth, careful to keep his head and shoulder wounds out of the water.

"Hurry up and get out of there," she said. "I've got an idea."

He made a face at her from behind the smoked glass and waited for her to leave the room, turning off the water and yanking a towel from the ring on the wall as he stepped out. He dried himself and wrapped the robe around his waist before going into the bedroom, where Susan sat on the edge of the bed with the covers turned down.

"If we're going to do this," she said, "there have to be some rules."

"Do what?" he asked in shock, his erection suddenly back on the move.

"Duh, Marty! What do you think?"

"You're not serious!"

She couldn't help snickering at him. "Well, if you're not interested . . ."

"I'm interested! I just can't believe it. Susan, you're—"

"No kissing and no oral," she said, holding up a finger to cut him off. "And no dirty words."

"Okay," he croaked, his throat constricting with the realization that it was really going to happen.

"And you have to promise not to come in me . . . I can't believe you don't have any condoms stashed, Marty. What kind of guy doesn't have at least one condom in his bedroom?"

"The kind who never gets laid," he retorted.

"Well, that's what you get for wasting your time waiting for me."

"But it wasn't a waste of time, Sue . . . you're here."

She couldn't help feeling touched, and was damned if she couldn't feel herself blushing as well. "Well . . . get that towel off and let's have a look at you."

When he took off the towel, she was startled by the size of his erection. "Oh, Lord," she said with a laugh, covering her mouth.

He covered himself quickly, turning red. "What's the matter?"

"It's . . . it's huge, Marty. I had no idea you were so well endowed."

"Does that mean the deal's off?"

"No," she said, secretly thrilled. "But you have to promise to be gentle."

"Of course!"

"And not just because of your size . . . you know?"

"I know," he said quietly, remembering her secret.

She stood up and slipped out of the robe, letting it fall to the floor. Marty went to her and held her tenderly in his arms. "You're so beautiful," he whispered.

"Do you mind if we start with me on top?" she asked, timid now.

"Anything you want, Susan."

They got into bed and somewhat clumsily found their positions, Marty flat his on back and her straddling his waist, trying without success to mount him.

"I'm sorry," he said self-consciously. "I'm too big, aren't I?"

"No," she said. "I'm just a bit . . . would you mind going down on me?"

He laughed. "Are you crazy?"

A few minutes later she mounted him again and this time there was no trouble at all.

"God, that feels good," she said with a sigh. Then she giggled the way a teenager might. "You should've told me you were built like this years ago."

"Yeah, sure. Like that would've helped."

She smiled, closing her eyes and putting her head back as she began to move with him.

It was all Marty could do to hold off. He thought about the asteroid, naked old women, dogs crapping on the sidewalk, even quadruple amputees . . . anything but how beautiful she was or how much he loved her. He could tell that she was probably thinking of someone else, and while that did hurt a little, it didn't spoil the experience. She was his fantasy come to life.

It took her quite a while, but he continued to control himself, even as Susan began to moan and to squeeze him with her thighs, rocking with more urgency and starting to shudder deep within, her breath coming in staggered little girlish gasps. Finally she sighed and rolled off, laid her head on the pillow and smiled at him.

"You feel really, really good," she said happily. "I'm sorry that took so long."

"You can do that forever if you like," he said softly. "I know it can't be easy with someone you're not attracted to."

"It wasn't that," she said, touching his face. "I wasn't imagining you were someone else or anything. It's just that this was the first time I've been with anyone since . . ."

"I understand," he said, feeling warmth spreading over him. "So, is it my turn?"

"Yep. You've earned it."

He moved between her thighs and she smiled up at him as he entered her. "You can forget the coitus interruptus," she said bashfully.

"But what about a baby?"

"Marty, we're not even going to be alive nine months from now. And it wouldn't keep me from getting pregnant anyway . . . we might as well enjoy this."

He began moving slowly, but after a couple of minutes he couldn't help gasping and touching her face. "Please, Susan," he finally said. "Can I kiss you just once?"

She took his shoulders and pulled him down to her, kissing him lustfully and causing him to explode inside. She gasped as the startling sensation triggered a second climax, which was so unexpected that she laughed aloud and wrapped herself tightly around him as he groaned like a man put to the rack.

"Marty, that was amazing!" she said after he collapsed beside her, his chest heaving. "Is there always so much of it? My God! You were in the wrong business!" She cackled with delight at her own joke, almost giddy from the release.

He was still catching his breath. "Oh, sweet Christ, Susan. I love you so fucking much!"

She felt between her legs with her fingers and brought them away, looking at them. "Damn," she said in awe. "I'm amazed."

He kissed her breast. "Thank you."

"We're gonna have to do this again, honey."

"Honey?" he said in disbelief. "Do you mean that?"

"You know," she said with a melancholy smile, "it may have taken the end of the world . . . but I think you may have finally won me over, Marty. This was really something unexpected."

The smile that came to him was so big that he thought his face might crack. "Was it my gunplay out on the highway?"

"No," she chuckled. "I'm pretty sure it was your gunplay right here in bed."

"You've got no idea how much I love you, Susan."

She held up her fingers and giggled. "Actually, I've got a pretty *good* idea."


**NEITHER OF THEM** noticed a tall man in a dark suit stride into the bedroom holding a pistol, until he spoke aloud. "That was quite a show."

"What the fuck are *you* doing here!" Marty bolted upright. "Get the fuck outta my house!"

Agent Paulis laughed. "It's not your house anymore, asshole. It's been mine for days. And I'd like to thank you for stocking my basement with food."

Marty knew he was a dead man, that he'd never be able to protect Susan now. "You've been living down there?" he said, aghast.

"Get out of my bed," Paulis said, gesturing with the weapon. "The little lady and I don't want your blood all over the mattress."

Without warning, three loud cracks rang out. Hit in the

chest, Paulis stumbled backward into the wall and slid to the floor. Quickly, Susan pulled the pistol from beneath the sheet and tried to shoot him again, but the Walther jammed just like it had for Marty earlier that day. Paulis made an odd strangled sound and struggled to lift his weapon, but Marty sprang from the bed and threw the lamp at him, then rushed at Paulis and kicked him in the chin with his bare foot.

Paulis slumped over and continued to make the grotesque gurgling sound for almost a minute before falling silent. He still wasn't quite dead, but Marty didn't waste any more time. He wrapped the agent in a sheet and dragged him from the room, down the tiled hallway and out the back door, where he stashed the dying man under his deck.

When he returned to the room, Susan was still sitting in bed, staring in disbelief at the jammed Walther in her hand with the empty shell casing stove-piped in the receiver.

She looked up at him disgustedly. "I don't believe it."

"Believe what, honey?"

"Those guys at the gun store sold me a piece of shit!"

# TWENTY-THREE

PRIVATE SHANNON EMORY RAN AROUND TO THE OTHER SIDE of her overturned Humvee and dragged Sergeant Flynn out through the window. The four female troopers in back were either dead or so close to death that it didn't matter, doomed the minute the rear window of the vehicle had been struck by a 66mm LAW rocket fired by their male counterparts from within the company.

The six women crammed into the lead Humvee had stopped to come back in support, the roof gunner firing the .50 cal machine gun. Orange tracers streaked through darkness as the heavy, half-inch rounds easily pierced the hulls of the lighter armored Humvees driven by the men. The female gunner killed the driver of the closest vehicle, setting it on fire and forcing the other two pursuing Humvees to retreat back down the highway. "How bad are you, Sarge?" Emory said, collecting their carbines from inside the Hummer.

The machine gunner opened up again with a long burst, spotting three survivors from the burning Humvee as they advanced up the median. Their bodies virtually exploded from the hydrostatic shock of the .50 cal rounds.

"Shannon, let's go!" the gunner screamed. "Before they bring up the javelin!"

"Can you walk?" Emory said to the sergeant.

He held onto her shoulder, putting one foot forward. "I'm okay."

They packed themselves into the armored Humvee with the remaining six female troops, and the driver sped off down the highway.

"Take the first exit," Sergeant Flynn said. "We can't outrun them. We'll have to lose them." He smacked the gunner on her leg, and she ducked down inside to see what he wanted.

"Be careful with that barrel. It only takes a four-second burst to warp it!"

"Hooah!" the gunner said, and stood back up to cover the rear.

The driver raced along in the night at fifty mph in the fast lane, where there seemed to be fewer cars out of gas. Two travelers tried to flag her down by stepping right out in front of her, and got themselves run over for their efforts.

"What the hell was that, Sheree?" someone asked from the back.

"Muthafuckers in the road, girl." Sheree was weaving in and out of the stopped cars, trying to keep her speed up.

"I guess Lieutenant Boyle didn't like us taking the only two armored Humvees," Flynn said.

"Fuck 'em!" Sheree said. "We know what they was plannin'." She slowed down as she pulled off the highway and drove up the exit ramp. "Which way we goin', Sarge?"

"South. That's all I know to do."

"*Contact!*" the gunner screamed from above, and the .50 cal began to hammer away once again.

The others craned their necks to see out the thick back window, but all they could see were the tracers streaking off to the rear and to the left. Suddenly, a brilliant fireball behind them illuminated the countryside, revealing half a dozen civilian silhouettes near the road with hunting rifles and shotguns.

"Roadblock!" Sheree shouted, hitting the brakes and cutting the wheel to skirt a number of cars parked across the road.

The gunner collapsed and fell down inside on top of them, a bullet through her head.

"Goddamnit!" Emory swore, feeling the dead gunner's brain oozing into her hands. "She's gone, guys."

Sergeant Flynn took a helmet from one of the women and stood up to man the gun. "This mission sure went to shit in a hurry."

Emory opened the back door and allowed the woman's body to fall out as they sped along. "Sorry, Carmen, we'll see you soon."

From the turret above, Flynn scanned the countryside through a night vision device attached to the front of his helmet. There wasn't much to see except empty terrain. Thirty miles later they came across an abandoned silver mine, and Sheree pulled off the road and drove up the hill, shining the lights on the gate. There were close to twenty motorcycles parked outside the entrance to the mine.

"Shit, I know who that is!" Emory said. "Get us out of here, Sheree!"

There was a rifleshot, and Sergeant Flynn fell down into the Humvee, hit in the neck. Blood was spurting from his carotid artery, and Emory clamped her hand over the wound as Sheree jammed the vehicle into reverse. The other women in the Humvee shouted an instant before they were rammed in the front right by a black Dodge van. The steering wheel spun wildly in Sheree's hands as the vehicle whipped around, catching her thumb with the cross bar and snapping her wrist.

"Dismount!" shouted the soldier in the passenger seat, deciding their only chance now was to fight it out.

"Don't!" Emory warned, but it was too late, the others were already piling out on either side of the vehicle. She covered Flynn's body with her own as the bullets began to fly, the staccato sound of their M-4s met with a fusillade of shotgun blasts at close range. Her comrades screamed as they fell, and moments later there was no sound except for the idling engine. As Sergeant Flynn died under her, Emory grabbed for her weapon, but someone caught her ankle and jerked her out the back door. She landed hard on her chin and saw stars as she rolled to her back, trying to kick away the hairy blond man dragging her across the gravel toward the entrance to the mine.

A biker chick swore at her viciously and kicked her in the side of the head, and the lights went out.

# TWENTY-FOUR

"SEALING BLAST DOOR NUMBER ONE," FORREST ANNOUNCED over the radio, pushing the door shut, pulling the lever hard to seal it tight, and turning the bright red wheel to extend the sixteen three-inch steel pins around the entire jamb. "Door one sealed."

"Roger that," Ulrich answered from Launch Control, watching him on the monitor.

Forrest then withdrew twenty feet to the second blast door, holding the barrel of his slung carbine with his hand to prevent it from scraping against the wall. He stepped into the stairwell and allowed Kane to push the door closed and seal it.

"We're a hundred percent," Forrest announced. "How do we look above?"

"No contacts . . . everything's nominal."

"Welcome home, gentlemen, and congratulations. Phase one is finally complete."

"Hooah!" came the unanimous reply.

Forrest and Kane made their way to Launch Control, where they stashed the carbines in a locked steel cabinet, hopefully never to need them again. Each man had a key to the cabinet, which he would wear on a chain with his dog tags twenty-four hours a day for the next two years.

"I imagine the ladies are all glued to the televisions?" Forrest said.

Ulrich confirmed this. There was a TV in Launch Control too, but the volume was down. Forrest and the others had seen so much violence in their days overseas that watching it on television held no special appeal for them. They were interested in updates, but the endless repetition only annoyed them.

"Well, that should hold their attention for a while," Forrest said. "How long do you think before the power grid begins to fail?"

"So far they seem to be keeping the fires stoked up there," Ulrich said. "There haven't been any blackouts reported yet, which I find remarkable. But after tomorrow's impact I expect the entire grid to fail in a cascade effect all the way to the eastern seaboard. There's no way it's going to be able to sustain itself after such a large part of it is blasted out of existence."

"I hope the aboveground cameras survive," Vasquez said. "I don't like the idea of being blind down here."

"After the fires go out, we can go up and replace them," Danzig said.

"I'm not too keen on that idea either. What if that nuclear blast of theirs radiated the whole damned asteroid?"

"That's what the NBC suits are for," Forrest said. "What time do you plan to lower the antenna array, Wayne?"

"Just before sunrise. I'd like to leave it up right to the end, but in case the damn thing jams again I want to leave some time for us to go up and fix it."

"That's what we'll do, then." Forrest checked his watch against the clock in the console: 0505 hours. "Almost exactly four hours to go. Are the kids asleep?"

"The women put them to bed in the cafeteria for tonight," Danzig said.

Dr. West came into Launch Control and gave them each a time-released Benzedrine capsule. Forrest wanted them all as alert as possible, and after a day and a night of drinking, amphetamines were the only solution. They had all used amphetamines numerous times during special operations overseas and were aware of the sleep debt they were accumulating, but there would be plenty of time to repay that debt in the coming days. For now, they were on a war footing and needed to remain sharp.

"Doc, talk to you a minute?" Forrest said, beckoning him into the blast tunnel.

West followed him in and pulled the door closed.

"Is there anything going on with Lynette I should know about?" Forrest asked. "Has Price said anything to you?"

West frowned. "I think Price is worried she may not handle this very well. I've already talked to Mike about her. I told him I'm more than willing to let him treat any mental health issues that arise. Hey, are you . . . well, you and Veronica seem—"

"Nothing's going on. Why, are people talking already?"

West smiled. "This place is wall-to-wall with women. What do you think?"

Forrest laughed sardonically. "And this looked so easy on paper."

"Who I'm worried about is Oscar," West said. "When his insulin finally runs out, he's done for. You know that, right?"

"Yeah, I do," Forrest said heavily. He had been there when Vasquez was shot during a mission in Afghanistan, losing part of his pancreas. "One day at time, Doc."

Forrest patted him on the shoulder and made his way to the common chamber where the rest of the adults were watching two different news channels on two different televisions. All were absorbed, and a few looked downright frightened. Joann was holding Renee's hand. At the age of twenty-three, she was the youngest mother in the group, and she looked petrified.

Lynette was the oldest woman at thirty-eight, and she appeared on the verge of tears as well. Forrest caught her attention and gestured for her to join him.

"Is something wrong?" she asked, expecting to be in trouble for something.

"Hey, Lynette, would you keep an eye on Michelle for me? She looks terrified."

"Me?" she asked in surprise.

"You'd rather not?"

"No . . . I mean, sure, I—"

"I'd go over and sit with her myself," he went on, "but I'm going to be moving all around the installation during the hour building up to impact."

"No, no," she said, suddenly finding confidence. "I don't mind at all."

"Thanks," he said. "She's one of the younger mothers, and you wives have all known each other so long . . ."

"No, I understand. It's no trouble. Thanks, Jack."

Price winked at Forrest from across the room as Lynette went to Michelle. Forrest smiled back and slipped into the cafeteria for a peek at the children, all nestled in their sleeping bags in orderly rows on the floor. Laddie stood up from the floor, where he'd been keeping guard among them.

"You're fine," he said quietly, and the dog settled himself back in.

Melissa was in the cafeteria as well, but she wasn't asleep. She sat at one of the tables reading a book.

He sat down and offered her a stick of gum.

"Thanks," she said. "How much longer now?"

"About four hours."

"Do you think there will be earthquakes?"

"There sure could be," he said. "Some of them might even be pretty big, but they won't hurt the silo. We might jiggle around in here, but this installation is resting on giant steel springs."

"What if the asteroid hits nearby, though?"

"Well, either everything's going to be just fine . . . or we won't know what hit us."

"But what if we're right on the edge of the crater or whatever?"

He couldn't help chuckling. "Then this place will probably

crack in half, and we'll be looking out that wall over there at the biggest hole in the ground any of us has ever seen."

She smiled. "I'll bet you were a good dad."

And just like that, his eyes flooded with tears. "That's a nice thing for you to say," he said thickly. "I don't know if I was or not."

"You were. Taylor said so."

"Okay," he said, blinking the tears away. "How about we stick to earthquakes?"

She looked over at Laddie and patted her leg. The dog jumped up and immediately came over to her. "Do you think maybe you could be my stepdad?"

Forrest was so overcome that he excused himself. He went straight to the lavatory and splashed water on his face at the sink, drawing a deep breath as he looked at himself in the mirror. "Well, you're a fine figure of leadership."

When he stepped out, Melissa was there waiting, a worried look on her face.

"Come here," he said, giving her a hug. "Don't worry. It caught me off guard. I'd be happy to."

She hugged him tighter. "I asked Uncle Michael if he minded and he said no."

"Well, I'll have to be sure to thank old Uncle Mike," he said quietly.

"You're not mad at him, are you?" she asked, looking up at him. "I asked him not to say anything until I was sure I wanted to ask you."

"No, no," he said. "I'm very flattered. Thank you for asking. But you've only known me a couple of weeks. You may change your mind later."

She stood back and shook her head with a smile. "I know I'm a kid, but kids know a good dad when they see one."

He choked up again. "You're going to have to stop that," he said softly.

She stepped forward and lifted herself up onto her toes, giving him a kiss on the cheek. "Thank you."

On his way back to Launch Control, Forrest passed Michael in the corridor. "Thanks for the heads up, *fucker*."

Michael stopped and turned. "You didn't tell her no, did you?"

"Yeah, douche bag," he said without looking back. "I told her no."

Michael chuckled and stood watching as Forrest turned the corner. "Sorry, Jack, but you brought this on yourself."

# TWENTY-FIVE

WHEN THE ASTEROID STRUCK THE EARTH'S ATMOSPHERE, IT was traveling at nearly a hundred thousand miles an hour and burning at nearly one million degrees Fahrenheit. Jack's wife and the horse ranch were vaporized before they were ever aware of its arrival. It struck near the Montana-Canada border with a force three-quarters of a million times more powerful than the Soviet Emperor bomb, the most powerful man-made bomb ever detonated. It blasted a crater nearly a mile deep and fifty miles wide in the Earth's crust, hurling millions of tons of dust and rock into the atmosphere and sending out a blast wave hot enough to kill every living creature aboveground for six hundred miles. Winds traveling at thousands of miles an hour flattened trees and buildings for at least half that distance, pulverizing them. A massive heat wave spread out from there, setting fire to large swaths of land within a radius of fifteen hundred miles.

All of which took place in seconds.

Within the next few seconds massive earthquakes emanated from the epicenter for a thousand miles, triggering lesser quakes all across North America and down into Mexico. Massive cracks appeared in the Earth's crust over Yellowstone National Park, and the geysers there shot giant plumes of boiling water hundreds of feet into the air even as the park was devoured in flames. Rivers shifted and changed direction, giant landslides occurred all across the northern Rockies, and a dark cloud of smoke and dust began to envelop the continent, fed by the ash borne up from flame-driven winds.

The continental power grid began to fail immediately, and a massive blackout spread across both the United States and Canada in all directions, killing the power to every city within minutes after impact. Cities at the outer edges of the blast zone were set ablaze, and rescue workers were hard-pressed to even breathe in the heat, much less fight the fires. Three hundred million Americans and Canadians were dead within sixty seconds of the asteroid hitting the atmosphere, at least half of whom had been obliterated by the initial blast.

Tremors were felt the world over within the first half an hour, and though the asteroid did not strike the sea, tsunamis occurred as fault lines along the ocean floor shifted and distorted the water depths to send twenty-foot waves across the ocean surface, swamping the coasts of Europe, Africa, and Asia within the first few hours.

Horrifying satellite images were beamed down all across Europe, the Middle East, Asia, Australia, and South America as the ring of destruction spread across North America, and the continent was blotted out over the first couple of hours. Everyone watching now understood with absolute certainty that the shroud of darkness would soon blanket the world. Theirs would be a less cataclysmic end, a slow and methodical procession of starvation and disease, a horrific return to the Dark Ages on a global scale.

The long winter had not quite begun, but it was coming.

# TWENTY-SIX

**MARTY AND SUSAN WERE IN THE BASEMENT MAKING LOVE,** wrapped in one another's arms at the moment of impact, but they felt a sudden tremor in the concrete floor, vibrating as if an eighteen-wheeler had been dropped in the street right in front of the house from twenty stories.

"Sweet Jesus!" Susan said, sitting up.

"We're still here," Marty said. "Holy shit, we're still here!" He scooted across the mattress to turn on the television, but there was only static, and a few seconds later the power went out.

"That's it, Marty. We're dead in the water."

The wind began to pick up outside the house, and soon it sounded as though a storm had blown in. When they heard a cannonade of massive thunderclaps, they quickly dressed and went upstairs to see a raging dust storm outside the kitchen window. In the living room, they peeked through the curtains, and the houses across the street were completely obscured, the wind now howling like a freight train. They watched in fascination as the dust continued to blow past the house, all sorts of debris soaring by.

"We'd better be careful of the windows," he warned.

"How long will it blow like that?"

He laughed. "I've got no idea," he said, lifting his arms

and letting them fall. "Think of it, Sue. This is what killed the dinosaurs!"

"I am thinking of it, Marty. It's why I'm ready to shit a brick!"

He put his arms around her. "Don't worry, I am too."

A softball-sized meteor struck the roof and shattered the clay tiles.

"What was that?" He looked back outside and saw stone-sized meteors striking down all across the neighborhood. "Oh, shit! The ejecta's coming down. Let's get back to the basement."

After half an hour the worst of the meteor shower seemed to have passed and the winds at last began to abate, but the dust in the air took hours to settle, and by then the sun had begun to vanish behind the veil of smoke and dust in the upper atmosphere. They went back upstairs and watched as the neighborhood was slowly revealed, everything coated in fine brown dust.

"I don't suppose there's any point in going outside," she said.

"We'd only leave footprints to show that we're in here."

"So what now?"

He stood looking at her. "This is it, honey. I'm sorry."

"Damn." She sat on the couch and peered through a gap in the curtains. "I thought I was ready for this, but I'm not."

He sat down and took her hand. "How could anybody be?"

"Look at you. You're calm as a cucumber."

"I'm only being calm for you. Inside I'm shitting bricks too, believe me."

She touched his face and tears formed in her eyes. "I don't really deserve you."

He shook his head. "Not true. That's my decision."

"But . . ." She sat looking at her hand in his. "You deserve to be with someone who loved you . . . who loved you before this."

"Hey, if you love me now even a little bit, I'm a happy guy."

"I do," she said with a smile. Then she took his hand in both of hers. "I want to tell you something, and then I don't want to talk about it ever again. Okay?"

He nodded.

"It's up to you," she told him. "It's up to when we . . . when we quit."

"Susan, it's too soon to be—"

"Shush! Sometime between now and when the food runs out—*before* it runs out, Marty, because I don't want to see it coming—I want you to take care of it. That means from this moment on, whenever you decide is fine. I just don't want to know when it's coming. I know that's a lot to ask because I know how much you love me, but I'm asking you to promise me."

His eyes started to water. "Susan, I can't promise that, not like that. There may—"

"You have to!" she insisted. "Because all I want to do from here on is eat, sleep, and make love. That's it. And I won't be able to enjoy our time together unless I know you're going to take care of it when the time comes. Promise me, Marty. Please. If you love me like you say you do, promise me."

"Okay," he said reluctantly, knowing that it would be an extremely difficult promise for him to keep, and that he might well end up reneging when the time came.

"Thank you," she said, and she kissed him. "You don't know how much better that makes me feel."

He was tempted to say that he knew exactly how much better it made her feel because he now felt that much worse . . . but it was his responsibility to take care of her, and her peace of mind was every bit as important to him as her physical safety. "So what do you want to do?"

"Let's watch outside for a little while and then go finish making love."

"I wonder how long before anyone else will come out."

"They're probably all thinking like we are," she said. "Party time is definitely over."

"Hey, speak of the devil," he said, pointing.

A few young men were coming out of the house across the street and getting into a van. They were toting shotguns and carrying packs over their shoulders.

"Do you know them?"

"It's the Gilberts," he said. "They're cousins. Normally pretty nice guys, but it's a different world now."

"Where do you think they're going?"

He shrugged. "I'm curious as hell, but I'm not going to ask."

"I wish we could. Normally I'm pretty withdrawn, but right now I really feel like being around people."

"How about a shot of tequila instead?"

She smiled then. "That's what I like about you." She got up from the couch and began to unbutton the shirt he had given her. "You're always thinking."

# TWENTY-SEVEN

**ULRICH SAT AT THE CONSOLE IN LAUNCH CONTROL WITH ERIN** in his lap, counting down the time to impact. Taylor and Dr. West sat beside them in the light of an electric lamp. They had shut down all the generators and disconnected all of the main batteries against the possibility of damage to the silo, wanting to mitigate any chance of fire.

"T-minus sixty seconds," Ulrich said into the intercom.

Erin hid her face in his neck and he rubbed her back. "We'll be okay, baby."

"I'm fucking terrified," she whispered. "I'm so glad we never had kids, Wayne."

"Shhh," he said softly.

In the common chamber, Forrest stood against the wall with his hands clasped in front of him, smiling calmly in the lamplight as the women sat in the center of the room holding their children. Melissa sat against the wall near Forrest, with Laddie between them, and Veronica sat across the room with her back against Michael's chest. Forrest was mindful not to make eye contact with her.

He did notice that Andie was looking in his direction more than any of the others, so he gave her a wink that brought a smile to her otherwise frightened visage.

Lynette was sitting with her husband, Price, on the floor beside Michelle, as he had asked her to.

Kane was sitting behind Tonya, who sat holding Steven in her lap; it was the first time Forrest had noticed them showing any affection. Vasquez and Danzig sat beside them with their wives and children.

Forrest's original plan had been to let the children sleep through the impact, but the mothers vetoed that idea unanimously, wanting their children in their arms at the moment everyone they knew and loved was blasted out of existence.

"I've made a mistake," Karen said in a sudden panic. "I should be with my sister where I belong." She pulled her daughter close and began to weep.

Veronica felt Michael tense up, and felt that her suspicions were confirmed.

Forrest continued to smile calmly, very pleased with how they were all doing so far, Karen's little outburst having been the least of what he was prepared to deal with.

"Okay, kids," he said happily. "Everyone get ready to hold your noses like we practiced earlier."

All of the children and their mothers held their noses.

"Now, when I say, everyone pinch your nose and blow gently until your ears pop."

Dr. West had suggested this as a precaution against a sudden increase in air pressure within the silo—which no one expected, but then again no one had ever experienced a six teraton explosion before.

"T-minus thirty seconds," Ulrich said.

All of the mothers told their children how much they loved them.

"T-minus ten . . . nine . . . eight . . . seven . . . six . . . five . . . four . . ."

"Everyone blow," Forrest said gently.

"Two . . . one . . . impact."

A few seconds later the earth shuddered deep within and all around them, groaning as if stricken a mortal wound.

There was no change in air pressure, and no sense that the silo was being squeezed or in danger of implosion.

Almost everyone held their breath, waiting.

"Sounds like it hit pretty far away," Kane said, looking up at the ceiling.

Forrest winked at him and held up his *one second* finger. Then, as if on cue, the entire complex shook violently as the shock wave passed through the earth's crust. Forrest pressed hard against the wall, bracing his feet against the floor as the room jiggled back, forth, and up and down on its shock absorbers. The women and the children screamed in terror, all of them covering their heads, but nothing fell and no cracks appeared in the walls, the entire installation having been purposefully built to absorb this very kind of shock wave. Within a few seconds the earth stopped shaking and everything grew silent.

"Well, they apparently knew what they were doing when they built this place," Forrest said.

"Is it over?" Joann asked, lifting her head.

Lynette and Michelle were crying in one another's arms, and a few of the children were crying as well, but everyone else was reasonably well composed, considering the circumstances.

"Expect aftershocks," Forrest replied, "but I think we've felt the worst of it."

He looked down to see Melissa looking up at him, her arm around Laddie's shoulders. The dog seemed more curious than disquieted. "You okay?"

"No crater," she said with a smile.

"That should be about a thousand miles north of here." He tweaked her nose and went about checking to make sure everyone else was all right, asking if anyone felt like they were going to be sick. When everyone said they were okay, he asked one of the men to go below and reconnect the batteries. Then he stepped into Launch Control.

"What do you think, Wayne?"

Erin stood and took Taylor by the hand. "We'll go sit with the others now."

The women kissed their husbands and left the room.

"We should be feeling an earthquake any time," Ulrich said.

Ten minutes later they felt their first real tremor, but it was nothing compared with the shock wave.

"Switch on the cameras," Forrest said. "See if we're blind."

Ulrich turned on the monitor and they were all surprised to see that the house wasn't yet in flames. When he switched to the outside feeds, however, it was an altogether different scene. The grasslands all around the house were burning.

"Good thing we mowed back all that grass," Ulrich said. "We may get to keep the house."

"Is it raining fire?" West asked.

"Sure as hell is," Forrest said. "The asteroid blasted millions of tons of rock into the outer atmosphere."

"Then we'll be lucky to keep the house," Ulrich said, drumming his fingers.

"The house was always a bonus," Forrest said. "So were the cameras."

Taylor came back into the room and said to her husband, "Honey, Lynette's hyperventilating. Price and Michael have taken her to Medical."

West looked at Forrest and smiled. "And so it begins."

Forrest patted him on the shoulder as he passed. "Take good care of her, Doc. She's the life of the party."

"Shame on you, Jack Forrest," Taylor said.

Forrest followed them out on his way to check the missile silos for damage. He went to the end of blast tunnel number one and slowly cracked the blast door, shining a flashlight into the chasm before stepping in. When he turned on the lights, everything seemed to be in order, but he walked every level to make sure, seeing that a few boxes of food had fallen over but nothing more. As he was about to leave the silo, the door opened and Veronica stepped onto the deck, pushing the door closed behind her but not sealing it.

"Is something wrong?" he asked.

She stepped into him and began to kiss him. Forrest allowed himself to be backed up against a stack of boxes and sank his fingers into her hair, opening his mouth to let their tongues intertwine as they sucked hungrily at one another. He turned her around and pressed her up against the boxes, giving her one last long kiss and backing away.

"Okay!" he said, breathing deep and straightening his shirt. "Now that we've both gotten that out of our systems . . ."

"You didn't look at me once the entire time!"

"What did you want me to do, shout, 'Baby, I love you?' "

She looked at him and put her hands on her hips. "What are we going to do?"

"What are you talking about?"

"About us?"

"What us?"

"Jack, you're not funny."

"Hey, you know what?" he said. "The fucking world hasn't even been dead half an hour. Let's see if we can get through the first twenty-four before we start acting like we've lost our goddamn minds."

"I need to know if you want me."

"We're not having this conversation right now."

"Why not?"

"Because my wife was just killed by a fucking meteor! How's that for starters?"

"Oh, Christ," she said quietly. "I'm sorry, Jack. You're right. I didn't even . . ." She covered her mouth. "I'm sorry. I'm so sorry."

"Aw, shit." He jacked one leg back against the wall and fired up a cigarette. "This mission already isn't going according to plan."

"I disagree," she said quietly. "But you're right. We should wait and talk about this later. I'm sorry I've made you angry."

"You haven't made me angry, Veronica. I'm hopped up on Benzedrine."

"I didn't know that."

"We all are, in case there's an emergency." He took a long drag from the cigarette. "And what do you mean you disagree? You can't tell me we just acted normally."

"This is by no means a normal social dynamic. The world just ended. I think we're entitled to let our inhibitions drop for a minute."

"You are, but I'm not," he replied. "What's Michael going to think about you being gone?"

"Honestly? He's probably talking to Karen."

"Oh, okay. So that's what sent you chasing after—"

"I didn't chase you anyplace, Jack! You chased me, remember?"

Forrest took another drag and smiled. "Yes, I do."

"So what happens if I choose wrong?" she wanted to know. "Suppose Michael decides he loves Karen a few weeks from now—which will be my fault, admittedly. Andie is hot on your butt! I could end up alone in this brave new world of ours."

"Take the time to figure out what *you* want," he said. "Either way, you're not going to end up alone. I promise."

"You promise?"

"I don't break promises and I don't repeat them."

"I'm gonna hold you to it," she said, pointing a finger at him before opening the door and slipping back out.

Forrest found an excuse to spend another couple of minutes in the missile silo, then went back to Launch Control, where he found Ulrich smirking in front of the console, watching the grass fires above.

"What the fuck are you smirking at?"

"She didn't seal either door," Ulrich replied. "That tunnel's like a megaphone."

"I'll have to remember that," Forrest said, checking one of the many charts on the wall behind Ulrich to see if the toilet paper count matched the one he'd just taken. "We should probably go ahead and rig some sort of a bidet. Or at least have a plan drawn up for one. There's no way all these women and children are going to conserve enough toilet paper."

Ulrich laughed quietly to himself.

"What's so fuckin' funny, snickers?"

Ulrich chuckled again, saying in an overly manly voice, " 'I don't break my promises, little lady, and I don't repeat them either.' " Then he broke himself up laughing, slapping his hand on the counter. "Fucking priceless!"

Forrest stood looking at the back of Wayne's head, chewing his cheek. "Break yourself up, don't you, Stumpy?"

Ulrich continued to laugh. "Oh, man, wait till Erin hears that one."

Forrest put his finger in his mouth and got it good and wet before sticking into Ulrich's ear.

"You motherfucker!" Ulrich said, grabbing the side of his head and springing from the chair, wiping fruitlessly at the offended ear. "You fuckin' cocksucker!"

"Kinda felt like a monkey's dick, didn't it?"

Ulrich used the tail of his shirt to dry the inside of his ear, chuckling some more. "I'm still telling Erin."

"She'd better keep her mouth shut about it too," Forrest warned, "or I'll stick my finger someplace else."

Ulrich stood tucking his shirt back in, assuming a more serious expression. "You know how goddamn sorry I am about Monica, right?"

Forrest nodded. "She's not hurting anymore, Wayne. And who knows? Maybe they're really together again."

"What a party we'll all have one day, huh? All of us back together?"

"That would be quite a party," Forrest agreed, heading for the other door. "I'm going down to check number two silo. Try not to stir up any more shit while I'm gone."

"Hey, Jack?"

Forrest paused.

"I promise, man."

"Fuck you."

**LATER, FORREST RETURNED** to Launch Control to find Kane and Ulrich listening to the shortwave radio. "Getting anything?"

"Plenty," Kane said. "You should hear some of this."

Andie came into the room and Ulrich quickly switched off the set. "Everything okay?"

"Yeah," she said, masking her curiosity about what was being said on the radio. "Some of us are gathering in the cafeteria for a prayer session. Would you guys like to join us?"

The men shook their heads.

"Are you sure, Jack? You're the leader. It might be nice if you said a few words."

"I'm not exactly God's best representative," Forrest said with a wink. "Besides, I'll be saying plenty in the days and months to come."

"Well, it's never too soon to—"

"Thank you again for the offer," Ulrich said, stepping forward to put his hand on the door. "Be sure to put in a good word for us, will you?"

"Um . . . yeah," she said, backing out of the doorway. "Sure."

"Thank you." He smiled and closed the door, signaling for Kane to switch the radio back on.

" *. . . but it looks like the Dakotas are gone! The sky is black and there's shit raining down on everything! The entire neighborhood is catching on fire! This is the end of the fucking world . . . God's wrath, man . . . Armageddon!"*

"Loon," Forrest remarked, casually lighting a cigarette.

"Should I go get Linus and Oscar?" Kane asked.

Forrest shook his head. "You can fill them in later. I've already told them where I want them and why. Keep the dial moving. We can skip the hyperbole."

Kane turned the dial . . .

" *. . . since it's out all over the city, I should say probably not. First CNN went off the air and then the power went out* *all across town. Nobody knows what's going on. And don't even bother calling 911. There's a lot of smoke outside too. It's blowing in from the west."*

"That's from the flash fire," another replied. *"No telling how far that will spread."*

"No sign here in Maine," said another. *"Still a bright sunny day. We still got TV too. The news is showing fires all over Chicago, Detroit, Cleveland . . . Canada too. People are still rioting in New York City, and the army has pulled out. Wait . . . they're showing shots of the sky now. Looks like it's on fire!"*

*"Where's that?"*

*"Hold on . . . the caption says St. Louis . . . Oh, shit! People are running past the camera in flames!"*

"Keep that channel, Marcus. Sounds like it might be a party line."

*"On fire? In St. Louie?"*

*"It's what it says . . ."*

"Should I lock the door?" Ulrich wondered.

"Dunno," Forrest said. "What do you think? I hate keeping information from the others. Feels a little like communism."

*" . . . Oh, now they're showing somewhere in Southern California . . . It's all on fire—nope, they just lost the feed."*

"This shit here might freak the women out," Kane said.

"I'll lock the door," Ulrich decided. "We'll tell them about it if they ask. People on fire won't play well."

*"My wife just came in from outside . . . she says she can see a darkness to the west. Christ, it's moving fast. We'll be going to the basement soon . . ."*

*"Hey, I'm down here in Jacksonville . . . It's raining like hell here. Loudest goddamn thunderclap I've ever heard in my life . . . and the wind! Jesus, the wind!"*

*"That's from the asteroid, you'd better bet!"*

*"Hey, what about the government? Has anybody heard a damn thing?"*

*"Ha! The government? Remember 9/11? Katrina?*

*They're running for the bunkers . . . or out fishing! We're
on our own, pal."*

*"Nobody's fishing today, ass-wipe . . ."*

*"But he's right. We're on our own . . ."*

*"White Horse calling . . . anyone hear me? This is White
Horse calling . . ."*

*"Go ahead there, White Horse."*

Kane looked over at Forrest. "White Horse?"

"Capital of the Yukon."

*"Earth's quakin' like hell up here, folks. A giant crack
ripped right through the center of town. Power's out too and
it's getting dark. Gonna be a long winter, you betcha . . ."*

The three men listened for the next hour, and the news
was all the same, more or less. The continent was dying and,
for the most part, people were saying their goodbyes in surprisingly calm and dignified ways. By the end of the hour,
Forrest decided to meet with the rest of the population, and
he shared with them much, though not all, of what they had
heard. To his relief, most of the women were satisfied to hear
it from him and made no requests to hear it for themselves,
many of them suspecting things were worse than he was letting on and choosing to remain willfully underinformed.

Later that night, as everyone was milling about getting
ready for bed, Andie cornered Forrest at the end of the hall
near the blast tunnel door as he was reentering the corridor.

"What are you keeping from us?" she asked quietly. "I'd
like to know."

"Ever read Revelation?" he said with a rueful grin.

# BOOK TWO

# TWENTY-EIGHT

THREE MONTHS HAD PASSED SINCE THE ASTEROID STRIKE, and the skies had long since grown dim. The average temperature in the Hawaiian Islands now hovered at thirty-five degrees Fahrenheit, and the ocean life had at last begun to die off. However, there were still fish in the sea to be caught, and the Navy had their hands full protecting the fishing vessels from pirate attack. Admiral Preston Longbottom drew a careful breath before making his response, reminding himself that the people of Hawaii had elected a government, and that a military must exist to serve that government.

"Madam President," he said patiently, "I am not disagreeing with you, but you must understand that we need to patrol the Islands. There are still pirates in these waters."

Ester Thorn, now the president of the United Hawaiian Islands, had reluctantly accepted the office six weeks earlier, and so far she was not terribly pleased with the progress they were making toward securing the future of the Islands. The population of 1.2 million was doing well in terms of cooperation with their newly elected government, but there was growing unease over the dwindling food supply, and the announcement that rations were to be cut again had not been well accepted.

"I don't mean to be obstinate, Admiral," Ester said, "but

I've told you before that your men and their expertise are needed elsewhere. If the pirates attack the fishing boats, by all means blow them out of the water, but don't waste time looking for them. You'll never hunt them out of existence. We're bringing half the vessels back into port and that's my final decision."

Longbottom sat back looking pissed. The idea of taking orders from an astronomer did not ride well with him at all, but the crotchety old bitch had been elected in a landslide. At least her vice president was Barry Hadrian, former twice-elected President of the United States and hugely popular in the Islands.

At first Hadrian had not approved of the idea of canning the old state government in favor of an entirely new *federal* government, but saw that it was inevitable—the vast majority of people in the Islands were demanding a fresh start. When he began to hear talk that the military element in the Islands was considering militarizing the government, he approached Ester and offered himself as her vice presidential candidate. With his support, the other three candidates, all of them lifelong politicians, didn't have a prayer of being elected.

"I think what President Thorn is trying to say, Admiral," Hadrian interjected, realizing that Longbottom was mostly trying to preserve the size of his force and thus maintain his importance, "is that we're in dire straits as far as feeding the population is concerned, and that your engineers and other servicemen will be better utilized trying to solve those much more immediate problems."

Dr. Harold Shipman, here in his new capacity as adviser, smiled at Ester. Neither of them had any illusions about who at the table had actually kept the Navy in check to this point.

"Yes, sir," Longbottom said, still respectful to the former commander-in-chief.

"The wind farms are providing us with enough electricity to run our essential services," Ester continued, "and the natural gas is keeping us warm. But we're not moving fast enough on indoor farming. Which is where we must focus our efforts, gentlemen, until we have solved the problem. We're not going out the way they did at Easter Island centuries ago by devouring one another."

This had been one of Ester's campaign promises, and she never passed up the chance to restate it, understanding how real the possibility was of the food running out. By now most shopping malls and grocery stores—most buildings with fluorescent lighting—were on the way to being converted into greenhouses. But Ester was well aware that once their fluorescent bulbs burnt out, there was no immediate way of replacing them. New technology had to be developed as soon as possible, using resources available within the Hawaiian Island chain.

"Admiral?" she said, having a sudden idea. "How difficult would it be to use the nuclear reactors aboard your aircraft carriers and submarines to power a new industrial center?"

Longbottom sat forward, casting a surprised glance at Hadrian. "What sort of industrial center?"

"I don't know," she said. "That's for you and your engineers to work out. I've already said many times that I don't believe for a single moment there aren't enough resources among these islands for us to sustain ourselves without the sun, but we need men of vision. There are civilian engineers here, but yours are the best and the brightest, and I'm convinced that if we're to be saved by new technologies, your engineers will be the people who develop them. We still need the Navy, Admiral, but we need them to perform an entirely different mission now."

Longbottom drew another breath and sat looking at the table. "Madam President," he said at length, "I'm getting old and I'm afraid I haven't a great deal of faith in new technology."

"I was reading about Golda Meir last night," Ester remarked. "For obvious reasons."

Everyone chuckled, however dutifully.

"And she once said something that I find applicable to our

situation. She said, 'Ability hits the mark where presumption overshoots . . . and diffidence falls short.' Now, we all know that I don't make a pimple on Golda's backside, but I'm smart enough to know that she was right. Your men and women have an abundance of ability, Admiral, and they'll work to solve our problems . . . but I need you on board."

Longbottom sat thinking for a long moment, realizing that fighting against the tide would serve no one's interest.

"Perhaps I've grown too fatalistic about the future," he said slowly. "Perhaps there is a way. I don't know. But I'll put together a committee and—"

"No committees!" Ester said. "Committees are the old way of doing business and we don't have the time. Gather your engineers and your mechanics, your avionics experts and every other expert you've got. Gather them in the hangar of one those floating airports you command out there and tell them I want them—what *we* want them to *think* about! And to start thinking right now! To work to save the life of the human race. And forget about bloody goddamn pirates!"

Hadrian sat smiling in his chair, happy to see that Ester had at last found her way with the Navy. "Does that sound like a great enough challenge for you, Admiral?"

The admiral looked at him, a slight grin coming to him. "Yes, sir, Mr. Vice President. But to be honest, I think I'd rather have to fight the cold war all over again."

"This is a cold war," Hadrian replied, "as cold as any of us can imagine. It snowed right here in Honolulu last week."

"I know," Longbottom said, looking grim. "Dirty, gray snow."

"It's a worthy fight," Ester said. "And we owe it to our progeny to make it."

"I'll do my best, Madam President. You have my word."

"That's all anyone can ask for," Ester said. "Thank you for being here today. I know that meeting with me was the last thing you felt like doing."

"There's something else that Golda Meir once said, Madam President."

"Let me have it," she said glumly.

"She said, 'Being seventy is not a sin.'"

Ester allowed herself to smile at the man for the first time since meeting him. "So then you see, Admiral, why I trust her judgment."

**AFTER THE MEETING** adjourned, Ester sat alone in her office with Hadrian. "You think I'm nuts, don't you?"

"Not at all," Hadrian replied. "Why do you say that?"

"Because you knew what I was trying to accomplish in there even before I did . . . and yet you let me twist."

"You needed to find your own way with him, Ester. You gained some of his respect in there today. Had I done all your talking for you, he'd still be paying us lip service. Whereas now, I think he may actually be with us."

"In other words, you weren't entirely on board before this meeting either."

"This was your sink or swim moment, Ester," he said with a smile. "Every politician has one. Congratulations. You've made it to the edge."

Ester shook her head. "Me a politician. I swear if I ever see that Chittenden boy again, I'll crack him over the head with this cane."

"Who's Chittenden?"

"The astronomer who got me into this unholy mess," she said. "If it weren't for that boy, I'd be rocking in the bosom of my Lord right now instead of having chess matches with admirals."

Hadrian smiled. "It may well be that the human race will one day owe this Chittenden a great debt of gratitude."

"That hope lies with the Navy," she said. "The Navy and a favorable wind."

# TWENTY-NINE

**THE LAST THREE MONTHS HAD NOT BEEN KIND TO PRIVATE** Shannon Emory, who was now the property of a man the bikers called Brutus. He possessed her in virtually every sense that one human being could possess another. She fought savagely every time he came to take her, which was at least once a day, and he always laughed as he pinned her down and forced himself upon her. She had bitten him once on the neck early in her captivity, and he had beaten her for it, promising to bust out her teeth if she ever did it again. So Emory did not try to bite him after that, though she had vowed to bite off anything he put into her mouth, and he must have believed her because so far he had not yet attempted to do so.

She spent most of her days now locked in a motel room in Mesa, Arizona, where the temperature fluctuated between twenty and thirty degrees. There was no heat in the building, so she spent most of her time sitting on the bed wrapped in blankets. She was allowed to keep her uniform and boots, and had so far been fed decent food, but the selection grew poorer over the weeks, and for the past few days now she had been given nothing to eat but cans of creamed corn and lima beans.

She knew the Mongols had recruited more biker types to their cause and that their numbers were now close to a hundred. They were also taking prisoners for food, literally feeding upon the weak. In the early days, from her balcony on the tenth floor, she had watched the flammable parts of the city burned and the populace fleeing south. Few police remained behind, and those who did were quickly killed off by lawless mobs of men looking to rape and plunder away their final days on earth.

Civilized people had banded together and done rather well for the first month or so after the impact, until their food supplies gave out and they grew too weak to fight, either taking their own lives or being overrun by those willing to eat human flesh in order to survive. The males had been killed and eaten straight away, the females abducted and raped and finally eaten as well. Twice, even the biker motel had been attacked. But the Mongols were violent, Viking-like warriors. They fought with everything from pistols and machine guns to axes and machetes, teaching even the local sociopaths to stay away.

A few small convoys of military vehicles had passed through town headed south, and the Mongols ambushed a couple of them, taking the ammunition and food. By the end of the second month, Mesa City had grown bitter cold and become more or less a ghost town, people only emerging at night to scavenge for food. Many of these people fell victim to Mongol traps and became food themselves. The Mongols too had begun to forage, sending groups of well-armed men into the suburbs each day to scavenge anything of use. They went systematically through each neighborhood, moving from house to house, discovering many families who had found ways to survive.

The door to the motel room opened and Emory prepared herself to fight yet again as Brutus stepped in and stood looking at her. He wore his long blond hair in a golden braid and kept his beard trimmed closer to his face than the rest of the gang, but he was every bit as grubby and smelly. He was tall and muscular, with blue, mean-looking eyes, like the archetypal Viking.

"Bad news," he said.

She sat looking at him, hating him intensely. Often, she had considered throwing herself off the balcony, but had so far been unable to bring herself to take that final fall.

"There's nothing left but dog food," he said. "After that, you'll have to eat man meat with the rest of us."

"I'll starve, thanks."

"You'll fucking eat or I'll blowtorch your tits."

He tossed a can of Alpo onto the bed, and she sat looking at it, thinking that the time had finally come to consider the balcony in a very serious way. It would be much easier to do if she were drunk, however.

"Is there any booze left?" she asked. "I'll need something to take the fucking taste out of my mouth."

He grunted and left the room.

She opened the can with her can opener and scooped half of the nasty smelling dog food into the toilet, using the bucket of water to flush it down and getting back into the bed, sticking her spoon into the can and setting it beside her on the blanket. She had fought as hard and as long as she could and hated to give up, but there was nothing ahead now but more and ever greater misery.

Brutus came back into the room with a pair of leg shackles in his hand, and she sprang from the bed like a frog from a hot pan, beating him easily to the sliding door, but he was on her before she could get it open, knocking her to the floor with his great, hairy forearm. She scrabbled to her feet and tried for the hallway, but he caught her collar and swung her around, slamming her hard against the wall, knocking her senseless.

He took hold of her ankle and dragged her across the room, where he used his booted foot to smash apart the heating unit, exposing the radiator pipe. Emory came to as he was shackling her to the pipe and kicked him in the face, knocking him over backward, but it was too late. She was caught fast to the radiator.

Brutus stood back up and wiped the blood from the corner

of his eye, looking at it on his fingers. "This is the second time you've made me bleed."

"Wait till next time!" she said acidly.

He stood on her free leg and began to unlace her boot.

Emory hammered away at him with her fists, but he ignored her as he finished stealing her boots and stepped away, tossing them into the hall.

"I'll fucking kill you!" she swore. "You fucking piece of shit! You fucking biker trash motherfucker! Nothing but a bunch of fucking white trash biker fucks! Eating fucking people! You fucking animals!"

He took the blankets from the bed and tossed them over her. "Didn't have to be like this. All you had to do was go along."

"Fuck you!" she said from under the blanket. "I'm a fucking soldier! You're nothing but a goddamn animal!"

Another Mongol came into the room, a winter parka worn over his colors. His name was Gig.

"Something you might find interesting," Gig said, noticing Emory's shape beneath the blanket. "We found the green Jeep . . . on the east side of town."

"What's the plate number?" Brutus demanded.

"OA 5599," Gig said. "It's him. I've got some men watching the house now. All the curtains are shut, but there's tracks in the dust outside the back door. A dead body under the deck."

Brutus had never gotten a good look at the man who killed his brother, but he would soon be pissing on his dead body. He looked at his watch. It was four o'clock. "Be dark soon. We'll hit him after it gets late."

"You're all animals!" Emory said, still hidden beneath the blankets.

Brutus booted her in the head, not real hard but hard enough to hurt. "Get a house mouse in here to keep an eye on this bitch. I don't want her offing herself."

# THIRTY

THE BASEMENT WAS COLD, BUT MARTY AND SUSAN SPENT most of their time cuddled together beneath lots of blankets, so it wasn't unpleasant. The only time the cold was a genuine bother was when they had to come out from the under the covers to go to the bathroom or to wash up. They usually kept a supply of food by the bed along with the camp stove, so they could keep warm while preparing their meals.

Their time together since the asteroid strike had been good, and they had made love many, many times over the past few months, more times than Marty had in all the rest of his life. By the sixth week Susan was pretty sure she had conceived, but she chose not tell Marty about it. The end was drawing near, and knowing that she was pregnant with his child would only make his job more difficult when the time came.

The food had begun to run low after the first couple of months, and she went to sleep each night hoping never to awaken again, but each morning she awoke to find him there in bed wrapped tightly around her. She did love him, though not in a passionate kind of way, and their lovemaking had been a wonderful way to pass the days and nights. Each Friday night they had even been able to watch a DVD on Marty's laptop until the battery finally went completely dead.

Then one disappointing morning Susan awoke to find that ·
Marty had left the house during the night, to scavenge around
the neighborhood by flashlight in search of food and supplies,
and in doing so managed to scare up enough food to get them
through another week. It had been difficult for her to do, but
she feigned happiness. She felt terrible because she knew how
badly he wanted there to be a future for them, and she knew
he was perfectly willing to live with her there in that basement
for the rest of their lives if that was what it took.

"You do understand," she had gently said the week before,
"that there has to be an end to this, right?"

"I do," he answered heavily. "But will you let me fight for
us?"

"Of course," she said, touching his pained face in the candlelight. "So long as you'll keep your promise to me."

"I will," he said, actually meaning it, for by then he had
seen things on his numerous forays into the neighborhood,
sights that chilled him to his core. Partially butchered
corpses, heads stuck on fence posts, and entire families
gathered together in bedrooms, dead of murder-suicides.
Soon he would be forced to venture too far from the house
at night to risk leaving her alone and undefended.

The light had faded outside the glass block windows, and
Marty got up to cover them so they could light a candle
without the risk of the light showing outside. The nights
were pitch-black now, and the slightest hint of light seemed
visible for miles and miles, though distance was extremely
hard to judge in that kind of darkness. He slipped in beneath
the blankets and wrapped himself around her, placing his
hand flat on her belly where he knew that his child lived.

"Are you hungry?" he asked.

"I'm fine."

"I haven't told you about the time I went to Yosemite with
my scout troop yet. Would you like to hear about it?"

"Absolutely," she said, lacing her fingers through his on
top of her belly and rolling to her side to face away from
him, now realizing that he knew she was with child.

As she listened to him telling her of his trip to Yosemite, tears began to pour from her eyes, for she had sensed a change in him, a change in his tone of voice as he told the story, almost as if he were telling it to a little girl whom he loved very much, and she knew that he had chosen tonight.

Halfway through the story, he stopped and said, "Susan, will you marry me?"

She rolled over, wrapped herself around him and whispered, "Of course I'll marry you!"

He squeezed her and she squeezed him back.

"I love you!" she said suddenly, feeling the emotion more intensely at that moment than she had imagined possible.

"You are my entire life," he told her. "All that I ever was or could ever have been was meant for you."

That was more than she could take, and she began to weep openly, kissing him and wriggling her pajama bottoms down for one last time. They made love by candlelight, their tears mixing together as they kissed and said their vows to one another. They agreed to name the child Purity.

Susan fell into a deep sleep a short time later, and he lay beside her running his fingers through her hair and watching her sleep peacefully in the soft yellow light of the candle. He did not know who had been watching the house all that day, but he knew with absolute certainty that they would never, ever harm his wife or desecrate her body.

"I love you, Susan," he whispered, his throat tight as the tears ran down his face. "And I love Purity. I love you both more than any man has ever loved his family."

He blew out the candle, and Joe's pistol went off a second later.

He then got quickly out of the bed and opened the cans of Coleman fuel, pouring them all over the mattress and the counterpane, knowing his way in the darkness by now as well as any blind man knew his own bedroom. He ran up the stairs and opened the last of Joe's gasoline, pouring it down the stairs. He flung more gasoline around the lower level of the house, then took a road flare from the kitchen counter, popping it alight and tossing it into the basement as he ran for the back door.

The basement erupted in a blast of white flame that shot up the stairs and quickly engulfed the entire lower level of the house. Marty dove from his back porch into the dirt and scrabbled to his feet, grabbing up the carbine and slinging it over his shoulder. He was quick to get out of the light of the flames engulfing the house, running through his neighbor's backyard by the light of the fire. He ducked quickly into the second house over and made his way upstairs, where he took up a firing position in one of the windows, watching for those who had come to eat his family.

When he saw three men in biker colors crossing the street with shotguns over their shoulders, he became so furious with himself for not hiding the Jeep that he nearly jammed Joe's .45 up under his own chin. Instead, he quickly unshouldered the carbine and took aim at the closest Mongol. He squeezed the trigger and the biker jerked as though he had been stung by a wasp, grabbing at his neck and falling to the ground. The other two men turned and ran back across the street, but Marty was pretty good with the carbine now. He shot them down before they were able to make it to cover.

Then something hit him between his shoulder blades, and as he fell over on the floor in agony, he saw a large figure standing over him with crowbar.

Brutus picked him up from the floor with one arm and held him against the wall by his throat. "Now I got you, motherfucker, and you're gonna pay for killin' my brother!" He slugged Marty in the stomach and threw him to the floor.

"I didn't!" Marty gasped. "It was him . . . him!"

Brutus paused before dropping his boot against the back of Marty's neck. "Him who, asshole?"

"Jeep guy," he groaned. "Dead under my deck!"

Brutus remembered that Gig had mentioned a body under Marty's deck, so he jerked him to his feet and threw him into a chair.

"What Jeep guy?"

"Him," Marty choked, his gut feeling as though he'd been run over by a car. "He tried to take my house . . . my wife."

"You're tellin' me you killed the fucker who owns that green Jeep?"

"Jeep sure ain't mine, mister." Marty was still gasping for air, holding his belly. "It's got California plates. He was a Secret Service agent . . . followed my wife back from JPL . . . check his wallet if you don't believe me. He was a total psycho!"

Brutus stood thinking it over. If Marty's story was true, he didn't exactly owe him any favors now that he had killed his three men in the street, but he might be willing to let him live . . . for a while.

"Okay, motherfucker," he said, grabbing Marty's coat and hauling him to his feet. "We're gonna check your story out. If that cat ain't Secret Service, you're gonna wish I'd broke your goddamn neck!"

**FIVE MINUTES LATER** Marty was on his knees in the street in front of his burning house, his hands tied behind his back as Brutus and another biker stood examining Paulis's Secret Service ID.

"Don't make no sense," Gig said. "I saw a broad with red hair at the rest stop getting out of the Jeep. She was telling the Army to shoot us."

"That had to be my wife!" Marty blurted, conjuring his lie off the cuff. "He drove her back from Caltech. Look, I'm an astronomer. I'm the guy who took the story public. My wife worked at the Jet Propulsion Laboratory. The Secret Service gave her a ride home the day before the asteroid hit. A few days later he came back and tried to take her for himself. She's actually the one who shot him, not me."

Brutus and the other biker stood looking at each other.

"This ID sorta proves he's telling the truth," Gig said. "It explains how that bastard was able to kill so many of our bros."

"So where's your old lady now?" Brutus demanded.

Marty started to cry, having blocked it from his conscious thought until that moment. "She's down in the basement," he sobbed. "Our baby . . . I shot her . . . just kill me already. *Get it over with!*"

"Put him in the truck," Brutus said, strangely conflicted. "I'll decide about him later."

# THIRTY-ONE

**LIFE BELOWGROUND FOR FORREST AND HIS FLOCK HAD SET-**
tled into a pleasant, if a little boring, routine within a few
weeks of the impact. The children attended school with
Andie for three hours in the morning and two hours in the
afternoon every day, and the mothers experimented with the
food they were allotted to cook for each meal.

Mealtime, especially dinner, was everyone's favorite because it was story time. They took turns telling stories about
themselves or someone they knew. Sometimes the stories
were funny and sometimes they were very sad, but it helped
them get to know one another and to remember that they
were human beings with histories and memories. And most
importantly, it helped to pass the time.

At other times they read, watched movies, worked puzzles
or played games, and everyone took turns riding the bicycle generators. The women also helped watch the monitors
when the soldier assigned to Launch Control wanted to put
his head down for a nap, or to step out and stretch his legs.
In Forrest's case it was usually to smoke a cigarette in the
cargo bay.

A few of the women were even learning to knit from
Maria Vasquez, a skill she had thought would be important
for the children to eventually learn as well, having seen to

it that a lot of yarn had made its way down into the silo. She had also begun teaching some of the other children to speak Spanish in the evenings.

Late night was the favorite time for the adults. After the children had been put to bed, they almost always played cards, and each of them was allowed either a small bar of chocolate or a shot of whiskey. Almost every mother had someone she shared with, so they could all have a little of each. It wasn't much, but it was something to look forward to. Euchre and strip poker were favorite card games, but it was agreed that no one would strip past their underwear, the married women especially adamant.

There were a few other rare treats held in store, like extra bottles of wine, but Forrest held these items secret in the cargo bay—where none of the civilians were permitted for security reasons—and told them they would have to wait for Thanksgiving and Christmas to find out what they were.

One morning three months after impact, Danzig stepped into the cafeteria where Forrest and Veronica were working on a large jigsaw puzzle with some of the children. "You'd better come have a listen to this, Jack."

"What's up?" Forrest said, getting up from the table. Veronica followed them out of the room and down the hall toward Launch Control.

"Picked up an odd radio signal," Danzig said. "In Morse code, all numbers."

"An encrypted code, probably military."

"Maybe, but Wayne says it's a conversation."

"That is odd."

They stepped into Launch Control, where Michael and the rest of the men were standing around listening to the steady stream of electronic dots and dashes. Ulrich was sitting at the console scribbling down the numbers as fast as they were being transmitted.

"Hey, dude," Forrest whispered into Danzig's ear. "You're getting a little ripe."

Danzig smelled his pits. "It's that crappy deodorant we bought. I'll switch to antiperspirant."

"What do we got, Stumpy?" Forrest said, putting a hand on Ulrich's shoulder.

Ulrich waved at him to shut up, trying to keep up with the telegraphers. "It's a conversation," he said during a brief pause. "Two different hands, both experts."

"Different hands?" Michael asked.

"All telegraphers have a different pace," Kane explained. "Their own rhythm."

"You mean he can tell the difference between who's tapping?" Michael said. "It all sounds exactly the same."

Ulrich shushed him as the transmission began again, and a couple of minutes later the conversation stopped completely. "Looks like that's it for now," he said, sitting back and looking at the stream of numbers on the pad. "They were deciphering during all those short pauses, so they're probably using an agreed-upon text, but we don't have the software to crack a code like that."

"Can I see what you wrote down?" Melissa asked from where she stood in the doorway with Laddie.

"Sure, honey." Ulrich reached between the men to hand her the pad.

"How did you find the signal?" Forrest asked.

"They're using such a high frequency, I almost didn't. It was an accident, really."

"Could they hear us if we tried talking to them?" Michael asked.

"Not sure," Ulrich said. "I've got no way of knowing how far away they are. But it doesn't matter. We're not breaking radio silence."

"We'll continue to monitor that frequency," Forrest said. "You never know."

**LATER THAT NIGHT** Forrest was down in the electrical room preparing for his ride on one of the bicycle chargers when

Veronica came in and shut the door, standing with her back against it.

"Come to take a spin?" he said.

She shook her head. "Missed you at cards tonight."

"I felt like hanging out alone in the LC."

"One of those nights?"

"Yeah, I guess."

She pushed away from the door and walked over to him, putting her hands on his chest. "I've decided what I want."

"Oh? And what's Michael have to say about it?"

"Does it matter?"

"Of course it matters!"

"Why? You said I needed to figure what I wanted . . . Now I have and you're flipping the script on me."

"Flipping the script?"

"Don't dodge the question."

"Much as I wish I felt otherwise, Veronica, I've got a lot of respect for the man. He's a huge part of why we've been so successful to this point. His counseling sessions have probably averted two or three nervous breakdowns already, and I can't believe how popular those stupid jigsaw puzzles are."

She stood looking at him. "Jigsaw puzzles? I'm trying to give myself to you, and you're talking about jigsaw puzzles?"

"I'm talking about respect, honor, integ— No, check that. One man's integrity is another man's bullshit excuse. Loyalty. The man's earned my loyalty."

"So *loyalty's* what's changed since three months ago when you jammed your tongue down my throat?"

He frowned. "That's not what I'm saying."

"You know, you're a real piece of work," she said, stepping back. "You promised me, Jack. Remember? Remember all that bullshit about not repeating or breaking promises?"

"Unfortunately I do," he said, lowering his gaze. "And I'm sorry."

"So I don't rate the same respect that Michael does. Or is it a guy thing? Bros before hos?"

He looked at her. "It sure as *hell* isn't that."

"You're the only reason I'm even down here, Jack. And now I find out it's been one big mind fuck."

"Okay, stop! That's taking it too far. I've never been anything but kind to you."

"Until now. Until you made me feel like a complete fucking idiot." She turned around, walked out of the room and shut the door behind her.

Forrest stood looking at the door. "An absolutely impossible situation," he said in frustration, reaching for his shirt to fish out his pack of Camels.

Veronica came back in just as he was about to light up. She turned to close the door and stood with her back to him, as though she were unsure if she should speak.

He waited, suspecting that she was really going to let him have it this time.

"Do you know what?" she asked quietly.

"What?"

She turned around looking very serious. "You just got punked so fucking bad."

"What the fuck are you talking about?" he said, the cigarette dangling from his lip.

"Michael and I split up, you dope! You haven't heard? He wants to be with Karen."

"I'm the last one to hear about everything down here, and it's giving me a case of the red ass."

"Oh, stop whining. You wanted to be in charge." She came flouncing toward him and fell into his arms. "I'm yours at last," she said dramatically. "Yours at last, Jack."

He stood holding her with a stupid grin on his face, and took the cigarette from his lips. "You laid me lower than whale shit a second ago. That was cruel."

"I couldn't resist," she said, smiling, gazing into his eyes. "I had to see how you'd react. And I'd have been disappointed if you hadn't turned me away, by the way. I'd have kept you but I'd have been disappointed."

"Kept me?"

"You've been mine since the day you set eyes on me, Jack Forrest, and don't even *try* to deny it."

"I seem to remember turning you away a minute ago," he said, his lips only inches from hers now as he stared back into her soft brown eyes.

"And it killed you. I could see it on your face."

"You're the most beautiful goddamn woman I've ever seen," he said, kissing her.

"I want you right now," she said, suddenly wanton. "Right here!"

"But I need to go get—"

"I've come prepared," she said with a grin, pulling a condom from her pocket.

They dropped their pants and Veronica turned around, taking hold of the handlebars on the bike.

"Take me now," she whispered. "Hurry, before I fucking scream."

He entered her from behind and she reached back with both hands, pulling him against her. "Oh, my God!" she whispered.

She began pushing back and forth. After a couple of minutes they were both breathing heavily, their rhythm growing clumsier with each stroke until Veronica gasped in climax, sinking toward the floor barely able to grip the handlebars. Forrest held her up the best he could, finishing only a few seconds behind her, groaning deeply, both of them dropping to the floor where they lay in one another's arms on the cold concrete, their pants bunched up around their ankles.

"Holy shit," she panted. "I almost passed out."

He was holding handfuls of her hair, still breathing hard into her chest. "I never came so hard in my fucking life," he chuckled. "It actually hurt. Fuck, that was a long time coming."

"Again," she said, laughing as she tried clumsily to get up. "We have to do it again."

"Not here," he said. "In the missile silo. I don't want to be interrupted."

"That seems to be the popular place," she said, working her pants back up over her thighs. "Just don't take me to your usual spot."

"What usual spot?" he said, standing and pulling up his pants. "I haven't been with anybody but my wife in twelve years."

"Really?" She grabbed his face and kissed him. "I thought that you and Andie . . ."

"She's never asked and I didn't think it would be appropriate for me to."

"So how long has it been for you?"

"More than two years. Almost two and a half."

"Oh, you poor baby," she said, hurting for him. "Well, let's get you caught up."

They stopped at the door and had a long, tender kiss. "I'm so fucking glad you found me," she said softly.

"It's not fair," he said. "The world's dead and we're down here feeling like this."

"Isn't it what you planned?"

"This? Hell, no. I didn't think we'd survive the fucking impact!"

# THIRTY-TWO

THE NEXT MORNING, MARTY AWOKE IN HIS OWN MOTEL room beneath a pile of musty smelling blankets and lay staring at the ceiling. He had slept fitfully the night before, and he was feeling incredibly guilty for not having killed himself when he'd had the chance. That was an easy situation to remedy, however. The first chance he got, he would grab a gun, shoot a couple more bikers—if he could manage it safely this time—then kill himself.

He couldn't get over how badly they had smelled the night before, all of them crammed into the Humvee together for the ride back into the city. He had also been able to smell what he was sure was human flesh cooking on the way up the stairwell.

He got out of bed, took his winter coat from the chair and pulled on his shoes, then went to the window, seeing the same gray world as the day before, dark and dim as before a heavy rain. There were spits of dirty snow in the air, and it was only late August. He considered jumping off the balcony but thought better of it. That was just too scary.

The door flew open and he spun around, half expecting someone to attack him.

"In the hall," Gig told him.

Marty obeyed and stood in the hall waiting to see what the man wanted.

Brutus stepped from a room a few doors down, pulling a female soldier with dark red hair and stocking feet along behind him. The soldier's hands were tied behind her back, and Marty recognized her immediately as the medic from the highway.

Brutus came up to him and said, "You can go. You killed the sorry fuck who killed my brother, and we made you kill your old lady. Makes us even."

Marty wondered how in the hell that made them even. It was obvious from the look in Emory's eyes that she recognized him, but she didn't say anything or acknowledge him in any way. "Well, can I have my guns back? I won't make it very far without them."

"Gig, get him his shit when we get downstairs," Brutus said, towing Emory toward the stairwell. "Then bring the truck around front . . . but *don't* make it obvious."

"Is something wrong?" Marty asked.

"There's some shit comin' down," Brutus said. "So keep your mouth shut."

They hurried him down ten flights of stairs to the lobby, where a couple of other bikers sat around in blue parkas, each of them with a biker chick in his lap for warmth.

"Hey, Brutus man, is that the dude who killed the Jeeper?"

"Yeah," Brutus said, shoving Emory down in a chair. "Don't get up, bitch!"

"What's goin on, Brutus man? Somethin' up?"

"I'm lettin' this cat go," Brutus said. "Gig's gonna give his ass a ride outta town."

Gig led Marty behind the counter and into an office where they kept the weapons.

"What's goin' on?" Marty asked again, seeing a number of machine guns on the table. He slung Joe's carbine over his back and tucked his .45 into his belt.

"It's time to ditch the rest of these dudes," Gig said. "It's gettin' too hot here."

"Oh," Marty said. "Hey, suppose I can have one of these too?"

Gig thought it over for a second then shrugged and gave him an MP-5 submachine gun, showing him how to operate it. "Ain't hard," he said.

"No, seems easy enough," Marty said, blasting Gig across the room. He grabbed some extra magazines and dashed back into the lobby where the other bikers were jumping up and grabbing for their weapons. He sprayed them with automatic fire and in short order had either killed or wounded each one, the house mice included.

Emory was already running toward him. "Cut me loose!"

He found a pair of scissors in a drawer behind the motel counter and cut the lace that was bound so tightly around her wrists that her hands were a deep crimson.

She flexed her fingers and took the MP-5. "Let's get the fuck out of here!" She ran to where Brutus was crawling on his belly toward a shotgun, hit through both lungs and his spleen, and stepped on his back, taking the hunting knife from his belt.

"Remember me?" she said, grabbing his golden braid and jerking his head back. "This is your last fuck!" She stabbed the knife into his anus and he let out a shriek. Then she gave the blade a twist and jerked it free, using it to scalp him before stomping on his head. She threw his scalp to the floor and whipped around in time to gun down three more bikers who came scrabbling into the lobby to see what the hell was going on.

"Ammo!" she called as they ran for the exit.

Marty gave her the extra machine gun magazines, and she jammed them into the cargo pockets of her trousers.

"What about your feet?" he asked as they burst through the doors and ran down the outside wall of the motel.

"I got worse shit to worry about," she said, dumping the spent magazine from the weapon and inserting a new one. "Like how the fuck I'm gonna tell my kid I scalped its father." She checked around the corner and pulled her head back.

"You mean he got you . . . ?"

"I'm pretty sure," Emory said. "I've been puking every morning for a week."

"Why were they in such a hurry to get out of here?"

"I don't know," she said. "They were spooked about something, though. I think a lot of their people are still asleep. Let's see if we can find a car with some gas."

There was a loud blast, followed by a secondary explosion that took out the lobby of the motel. They spun on their heels to see an M60 tank at the end of the street, a cloud of smoke dissipating before it.

"All right!" Marty said. "We're saved!"

She looked at him. "No, hon, we're in twice the shit we were ten seconds ago."

They took off down the block and hid inside a ransacked Starbucks as troops began surging toward the motel.

Emory crouched inside the door, watching the soldiers fanning out. "Is it true what he said upstairs about your girlfriend?"

"Yeah," Marty said. "I was supposed to kill myself right after . . . but I decided to kill some of those guys first and that Brutus guy jumped me."

"Don't feel bad. She'd want you to live."

"I don't know . . ."

"Don't be stupid. You only killed her to keep her from ending up like I did. Imagine how you'd feel if they'd taken her. She wasn't tough enough to live through what I've been through . . . trust me."

"We got married," he said proudly.

"Really? Who'd you find to do that?"

"We did it ourselves."

"Aw, that's the sweetest thing," she said, turning to look out the window. "Oh shit, get back! Those two are coming in here." She dragged him behind the counter. "Stand here with your hands up. I'll stay down until I hear what they've got to say."

"But—"

She grabbed his carbine and dropped into a crouch.

The two soldiers came into the shop and stood looking at him with his hands in the air.

"Where's the woman?" one of them asked, glancing around the shop. "The GI with long hair."

"She's my sister," Marty said.

"I didn't ask you who the fuck she was!" the soldier said. "I asked where."

"She's in the restroom."

The first soldier went to the back of the shop and stepped into the ladies' room.

Emory stood up and gave the second soldier a six round burst through the neck and face, missing his body armor entirely, then emptied the rest of the magazine through the ladies' room door as the other soldier was scrambling back out.

"Quick!" she said. "Strip that one's armor and ammo . . . and check his boot size!"

Marty ran to the ladies' room and Emory went to the window to make sure no one else had heard the shots.

"These clowns are Air Force troops," she said, checking the dead airman's boot size and seeing that it was nine. "Boot size, Marty, on the bottom of the sole!"

"Eleven!"

"Guess nines will have to do," she mumbled, stripping the dead airman of his boots, then his gloves, armor, combat harness, and weaponry. When she was set, she pulled on the helmet and ran to the back of the shop where Marty was still having trouble shaking the dead soldier out of his harness.

"You look like a monkey fucking a football," she said, shoving him aside.

"How do you people wear all that shit?" he asked. "I've never seen so many buckles and zippers on one human being."

"Shut up. It's not that many. Go strip that other dude's ACU. This guy's a lot bigger than you."

"What's an ACU?"

"Army combat uniform. Come on, Marty, we don't have all fucking day here!"

She had him suited up and looking like a proper soldier five minutes later, with the exception of his sneakers and the bloody mandarin collar. They slipped out the back of the coffee shop, leaving all the other weapons behind save for Joe's Springfield Armory .45.

"Goddamn, it feels good to be back in harness!" she said, punching him in the shoulder. "Full battle rattle! Hooah, Marty?"

"Who what?"

She laughed and grabbed him around the neck with her arm as they walked north up the alley. "Thanks for saving my ass back there," she said, kissing him on the cheek. "You're my fucking hero."

"I'm tired of being a hero," he said wearily.

"Here, hold on a second. I'd better make sure you know how to operate your weapon system before we hit the street again . . . this is an M-4 carbine. It shoots as smooth as that other gun you had, but it's got better range and better penetration. Just look through the scope and put that red dot on whatever you want to hit. Got it?"

"Got it."

She made sure he knew how to load the weapon and they started off again.

"Let's make a pact," she added. "Neither lets the other be taken alive. Hooah?"

"Who what? What is that?"

"It's the Army battle cry. I say, 'Hooah'? You say, 'Hooah'! Got it?"

"Got it, yeah."

"You're a grunt now," she said. "So let's hear it."

"Hooah!"

"Good. So we got a deal?"

"Hooah!" he said again.

"Fuckin' A," she said, slapping him on the back. "We'll probably both be dead by dark, but what the fuck!"

They got to the end of the alley and Emory checked west then east, seeing troops crossing southward two blocks up.

She ducked back. "Okay, listen. Whenever we're moving, it's your job to cover our ass. And whenever we cross a street, we do it one at a time. First I cover you, then you cover me. Got it?"

"Hooah!"

"Don't overdo it," she said. "Now, get across the street and take cover at the corner, then cover me as I come across."

Marty ran across the street and tripped over the curb, falling on the sidewalk. His weapon went off and shot a hole in a shop window on the opposite corner. He got up and ducked around the corner of the building, self-consciously watching up and down the street as Emory came across.

"Nice job, dumbass!" she said, belting him on the helmet. "Keep your finger off the goddamn trigger unless you're gonna shoot!"

When they got to the next corner, they spotted a soldier in the second-story window of an apartment building waving them down.

Emory pushed back against Marty and pulled him down into a crouch.

"What's he want?"

"He's warning us to stay put," she said. "He's Army, but be ready to blow his ass outta that window."

"How do you know he's not Air Force?"

"Because his camo doesn't match yours . . . it matches mine." She double-checked to make sure the M-203 40mm grenade launcher on her carbine was ready to fire.

"Why don't I get the one with the grenade launcher?"

"'Cuz you can't even walk and chew gum at the same time."

The soldier continued to signal for them to hold their position as he watched eastward down the street. A minute later he signaled for them to cross as a pair, and Emory dragged Marty across and into the lobby of the apartment building. They went up the stairs to the second floor, where the soldier met them in the hall.

"In here," he said. "There's bad joo-joo up the street."

Emory saw the blue arrowhead of the Thirty-sixth Infantry Division on his shoulder. On her own shoulder she wore the red and yellow patch of the Arizona National Guard with two arrows crossed over a bayonet. He was a broad-shouldered man with handsome dark eyes, and his name tag identified him as Sullivan.

"You're a long way from home, Sullivan."

"Tell me about it," the trooper said. "But Texas ain't where you wanna be."

"Did you desert or get run off?"

"Depends how you look at it. I wasn't exactly down with the shit they were doin'." He took a second to check out the window. There was a lot of gunfire coming from the direction of the motel now, building to a crescendo.

"So did Mexico attack us or the other way around?" she asked.

"It all went to shit too fast," Sullivan said, turning back to them. "We'd just gotten into Nogales. We were trying to restore order there when somebody said the Mexicans were firing on us across the Rio Grande, but who the fuck knows? They didn't have any tanks, so it was a pretty lopsided battle. Personally, I think we picked the fight."

Sullivan recognized the camouflaged pattern of Marty's uniform but didn't recognize the unit. "How about you, Miller? The Air Force doesn't issue boots anymore or what?"

Marty looked down at his sneakers. "Me?"

"No, the other Miller standing over there."

Emory chuckled. "That's Marty. He's only just enlisted, actually. The real Miller was dishonorably discharged."

"Explains the blood," Sullivan said, checking briefly out the window again. "Closest most of those Air Force jerks down there ever got to combat before this was dragging a can of gasoline over to an airplane."

"They're all Air Force?"

"Yeah," Sullivan said. "From Tinker AFB. They've been probing Mesa all week. Now they're finally attacking some biker gang a few blocks over in that motel."

"We just came from there," Emory said. "You got any food to spare?"

"Got a case of MREs in the closet. I swiped it from the Air Force last night."

Emory showed Marty how to use the chemical heater contained in the MRE pack to warm his food, using a little bit of water from the back of the commode. The heater was a plastic bag containing a simple combination of powdered, food-grade iron, magnesium, and salt. The added water started a chemical reaction that gave off enough heat to warm the ration to more than a hundred degrees.

"This doesn't taste too bad," Marty said.

"I don't know what *you've* been eating these past few months," she said, "but this shit's fucking fantastic. That bastard made me eat a can of Alpo last night."

"What bastard?" Sullivan asked.

"The Mongols had her," Marty said.

"Who the fuck are they?"

"Those bikers you were talking about."

"You were with those animals? They've been kidnapping people all over town. They're *eating* them!"

"That's a fact," Emory said. "So what's your plan?"

Sullivan shrugged. "Keep stealing from the Air Force as long as I can. It's all about the food now."

Emory looked at Marty. "What do you want to do?"

He shrugged dolefully. "I hadn't really thought past getting you to safety."

"Well, I'm safe now," she said with a grin. "So what's Marty want for himself?"

"Nothing. I'll help you two steal from the Air Force. If anything ever happens, I can stay behind and cover your retreat."

"No, Marty. You're not a sacrificial lamb. You're an intelligent guy. You have to have an idea or two rolling around in your head."

"Well, I would like to see the impact crater before I die."

"See what?" Sullivan blurted. "Are you nuts?"

"He's an astronomer," she said, rolling her eyes.

"See the fucking impact crater," Sullivan said. "That's the craziest thing I've heard yet."

"It's a hell of a lot less crazy than people eating people," Marty said. "Which is all that you've got to look forward to—whether it's eating or being eaten. And that crater's going to make the Grand Canyon look like a crack in the sidewalk."

Sullivan looked at Emory. "Where did you find this dude?"

"Look, I'm just talking here," Marty went on. "But there isn't too much of a future in stealing from the Air Force. Why not see the greatest sight of all time?"

"All right, suppose we find a truck," Sullivan said. "Something that can handle rough terrain. And suppose we swipe enough food from the Air Force to get us there. What are we gonna do after that? Sit down and starve?"

Marty shook his head, saying, "Everybody left alive is headed south. They think it's going to be warmer down there, but it won't be enough to make a difference. You were exactly right. It's all about the food now . . . and the food is *north.*"

"You're crazy."

"No, I'm not," Marty insisted. "Everyone's dead up there. Killed by the blast wave or burned alive. But the canned food—at least a percentage of it—is still edible. Scorched and without labels, but edible, buried in the rubble, hidden in basements. You want food? Head north."

"Bullshit," Sullivan said. "You just want to see the crater."

"No," Emory said, "he's serious."

"And I've already got our transportation problem solved," Marty added. "It's even on the way."

# THIRTY-THREE

**EARLY THE NEXT MORNING, VASQUEZ GLANCED UP FROM HIS** book, movement on one of the monitors having caught his eye. "*Puta madre!* Where did that ugly bastard come from?"

Danzig looked up from his *Game and Wildlife* magazine to see a burly looking man with a thick black beard and grubby parka wandering around in the kitchen above. He had a shotgun slung over his shoulder and he was rifling through the cupboards, tossing things about. This was the first sign of life they had seen aboveground since the impact three months earlier. "Better get Jack in here."

Vasquez pressed the button for the P.A.: "Forrest to Launch Control. Forrest to the L.C."

Danzig was busy checking the different camera feeds around the upper compound to see if there was anyone else wandering around up there. "Look at this shit."

A different man in a camouflaged coat stood on the porch, holding a shotgun on two women and a third man. All three of the captives were equally disheveled and filthy, their hands tied behind their backs.

Forrest entered Launch Control tailed by Ulrich and Kane. Many of the others, Veronica and Michael among them, gathered outside the door waiting to learn what had put the urgency into Oscar Vasquez's voice. In addition to being the first sign of life from above, it was also the first excitement there had been since the impact.

Forrest watched the burly man kicking around the kitchen without comment, waiting to see what was going to happen with the prisoners on the porch. The man in the kitchen checked the stove to find that the gas burners still worked and moved quickly out of the room.

Ulrich glanced at Forrest. "That was an oversight. I'll go and remedy that right now." He slipped out the opposite door and went to shut off the gas supply to the house.

"Stay with Black Beard," Forrest said to Vasquez.

Vasquez changed feeds to show that Black Beard was now standing on the porch talking to the man in camouflage. The man in camouflage beckoned to their male captive, apparently ordering him into the house. The captive stepped back, shaking his head, and Black Beard stepped after him. The captive then dove over the porch railing and landed on his back, rolling to his feet as Black Beard ran down the stairs into the yard and tackled him, taking some sort of truncheon from beneath his parka and beating him with it until he stopped fighting. Then he hauled him to his feet by the hair, kicking him in the butt to get him moving toward the stairs.

Forrest noticed the man on the porch covertly snatching the pack of cigarettes he'd forgotten on the windowsill months earlier, jamming them into his pocket before Black Beard came back up the stairs. "Sumbitch took my smokes," he muttered, stepping into the hall to brief the others on what was happening. "Okay, ladies, we've got a couple of scavengers upstairs, but they're no threat to this installation. They haven't found the blast door, and even if they do, there's no possible way for them to open it."

"What are they doing?" Veronica asked.

"Searching the house for food."

"Can we see?"

Forrest looked at her, wishing she wouldn't put him on the spot. "They're pretty ragged and they've got a few prisoners.

It might be a little disturbing. We're taping everything and everybody will be able to view it later if they want to."

He was fine about letting Veronica in to watch, but if he showed her any favoritism, it might cause hard feelings within the group and he didn't need that. Things were going too well . . . or at least, as far as he knew.

"Why don't you let Ronny in to act as our representative?" suggested Joann, the tall black woman. She had a strong personality and she knew the other women would probably not object to her suggestion. Besides, Veronica's relationship with Forrest was easily now the worst kept secret in the silo.

Forrest agreed. "Mike, it may not be a bad idea for you to watch too."

They went inside, and the first thing Veronica saw on the monitor was Black Beard using a steel baton to bash in the skull of his captive, who was now sprawled facedown on the kitchen floor with his hands still tied behind his back.

"Oh, my God!" she said, turning away.

Black Beard then picked the dead man up and laid him across the kitchen table on his belly, cutting his hands free and slitting his coat up the back with a large Bowie knife. He wasted no time slicing into the man's lower back.

"Excuse me," Veronica said, pulling open the door and leaving the room. The moment she came out, the other women could see that she had just witnessed something ghastly.

"What did you see?" Tonya wanted to know.

Veronica looked at the children now gathered about, leaning to whisper into Erin's ear: *"Cannibals."*

"Oh, Jesus," Erin muttered. "Okay, kids, come on. Let's get back to school before Andie comes looking for us."

She took the kids back to class, and Veronica went on to tell the rest of the women in the hall what she had seen. Back in Launch Control the men were still watching as Black Beard stood carving out the dead man's liver, dropping it black and greasy-looking onto the countertop, where he cut it into portions and set them aside. When he was finished, he retrieved the frying pan from the floor and put it on the stove, laying parts of the liver into it and turning on the gas.

"He's about to get pissed," Ulrich said.

The flame burned for almost a full minute before going out. Then Black Beard fiddled with the knobs, realizing there was no more gas in the line. He smashed the chairs into pieces and left the kitchen.

Kane looked across at Forrest. "Captain, I request permission to go up there and blow this asshole's brains out."

"I wish we could," Forrest said, leaving it at that.

By now the man wearing the camouflage jacket had moved the women into the living room and made them sit on the couch, where they huddled together for warmth. They looked alike, sisters perhaps, appearing to be in their early thirties, but with the grime on their faces, it was hard to tell. Black Beard spoke with his comrade, then went back into the kitchen, where he began building a fire in the sink with wood from the broken chairs.

"Those two women aren't for food, you know. What are we going to do if these assholes rape them on camera?"

"Feel bad for them," Forrest said. "If we go up and kill those two assholes, we may as well kill the women too. We sure as hell can't bring them down here. God knows how sick they might be."

Black Beard got a fire going and stood holding the frying pan over the flames.

"That's gotta smell like holy hell," Danzig said, seeing the smoke rising up from the pan.

They all watched as Black Beard stood cooking up the liver, taking a piece for himself. When he was finished, he piled the pieces onto a plate and carried it into the living room, where he sat down on the couch beside the women. His comrade grabbed a handful of the meat and stood eating ravenously. Black Beard then offered a piece to one of the women and she took a bite.

"Oh, Christ, she's eating it!"

"What do you expect her to do? If she doesn't, that bastard will torture her. They want those women alive, dude."

"Let's go up there and waste these dudes, man!"

"Look, we all knew this kind of thing was going to happen," Forrest said peremptorily. "So soldier up!"

"What do *you* think about this shit, Doc?"

"I don't know," Michael said in amazement. "Though I guess it is fascinating in a horrifying kind of way."

"I wonder how long before those women end up as food."

"Well, I can tell you this much," Michael said. "One of those two men is likely to end up as food before either of the women."

They watched as the meal was ghoulishly devoured.

Black Beard left the room and dragged the dead man out into the backyard, butchering him much the way one would butcher a game animal, dumping the intestines and other organs in a pile. He then spent the next couple of hours cooking up the rest of the dead man's flesh on the grill, using the bag of charcoal from the back porch. As he cooked the meat, he dropped it into a black trash bag he had taken from beneath the sink. When he was finished he came back into the house and took a container of salt from the bottom cupboard and poured all of it into the meat bag, shaking it around.

"Who left that salt up there?"

"Must've been up there when we bought the place."

"Oh, shit. Look!"

Black Beard was grabbing one of the women by her hair and dragging her from the room.

"That's caveman foreplay."

"You're sick."

"There's no use letting it get to you, man."

Black Beard took the woman upstairs into one of the bedrooms, pulled down her ski pants and pushed her forward onto the bed with her hands still tied, her pale bottom showing. She made no attempt to escape or to resist as he unbuckled his pants and knelt on the bed behind her. He pumped for two minutes and then it was over.

" 'Least he didn't beat her."

"Check out your man, Doc. He's making his move!"

The camouflage man was sneaking up the stairs with his shotgun lowered. Riveted, Michael stood watching as Vasquez switched the camera feed to keep up with the man now creeping into the bedroom. Black Beard saw him and grabbed for the shotgun lying beside him on the bed but he wasn't fast enough. His comrade blasted him in the face at close range, and most of his head vanished from the beard up.

The gore-spattered woman rolled off the edge of the bed to avoid being hit by the body as it fell over onto the mattress.

"Hooah!" Danzig blurted, and everyone laughed, everyone except Michael, who was simply shocked.

The camouflaged man got the woman to her feet and pulled her pants up, taking her downstairs where he pulled her pants right back down, along with those of the other woman, and over the next half hour he smoked Forrest's cigarettes and took turns at the women on the couch, seemingly in hillbilly heaven. When he was done, he divided the man meat up between four different trash bags, tying them together in pairs and draping them around the women's necks. Once he had satisfied himself that his idea was superior to that of his dead associate, he put the meat bags on the floor and took a dog chain from his rucksack, chaining the women together at the neck and locking it with a combination padlock. The other end of the chain he used to bind their ankles together, locking it in the same fashion with a separate padlock.

"Ain't takin' any chances, is he?"

Next, the man unbound their wrists, presumably to restore the circulation to their hands. He then went up upstairs to take the shells from Black Beard's shotgun, along with the Bowie knife, collapsible baton, and some other items from the dead man's pockets too small to identify. Shoving Black Beard's body onto the floor, he stripped the bloodstained blankets from the bed and went back downstairs, where he curled up on the couch and went to sleep, leaving the women to shiver on the floor. Within thirty minutes it was too dark to see what was happening in the house, and ten minutes after that it was too dark to see anything outside of the house. The time was six P.M.

"I guess that's it for today," Forrest said, looking grim.

"Come on, Captain," Kane said. "I could slip in there and cut that dude's throat so easy it wouldn't even be a trick."

"No," Forrest said, "and I'll show you why. Oscar, run it back to where they were feeding the women. Linus, call West in here."

When Dr. West showed up, Forrest asked him to watch the woman seated on the end of the couch. "She how she's hacking her ass off?"

West stood nodding. "She's sicker than a dog. That could very easily be tuberculosis, which I would expect to see up there by now among so much starvation and deprivation, breathing all that crap in the air."

"But the NBC suits would protect us from—"

"No," Forrest said with finality. "We soldier up and soldier on. Hooah?"

"Hooah!"

**A BIT LATER** Forrest found Veronica sitting with Erin and Taylor in the cafeteria. There were some children about and a couple of other women, but everybody was growing accustomed to the close quarters, learning to block out conversations that didn't involve them in order to allow one another a sense of privacy.

"That sure took a while," Veronica said. "Are they gone?"

He shook his head. "One of the cannibals killed the other and took the women for himself. Now they're sleeping and it's too dark to see anything. It's total darkness up there at night now."

"What if they don't leave?"

"It doesn't matter," he said, shrugging. "They're no threat to us."

"Can we still see the tape?" Erin wanted to know.

"If you really want to, Erin, but it's nothing but raw brutality from start to finish. I don't think it's anything you want in your dreams."

"Believe me," Veronica said. "I wish I'd never gone in there."

"But we are allowed to see if we want to, right?" Erin was making sure.

"Yes, the Freedom of Information Act still applies. Should I go and have Oscar cue it up for you?"

"No," she said with a pleasant smile. "I was merely making sure."

"Christ, I've got the ACLU up my ass," he said with a chuckle, glancing toward the counter to see that the coffeepot was empty once again. "I wonder who I have to fuck in this place to get a cup of coffee."

"Is that your manly way of asking for someone to make you some coffee, King Jack?" Taylor asked.

"No," he said affably. "It's my way of finding out who I have to fuck in this place to get a cup of coffee."

Taylor rolled her eyes and got up from the table.

"Taylor, he can make his own goddamn coffee," Veronica said. "Sit back down."

"No, I've indulged him all these years . . . it wouldn't be fair to turn on him now."

Forrest stuck his tongue out at Veronica.

"Keep it up," she said, less than entirely pleased that Forrest held so much sway with these two women.

"Ooooooh," he kidded.

She got up and walked out of the cafeteria.

"Uh-oh," Erin said.

"She'll be fine," he said with a wave. "She's just upset about those maniacs upstairs—that, and I won't kiss her ass in front of everyone."

Erin shook her head. "You'll never change."

"What makes me such a bad guy?"

"You're not a bad guy, but would it hurt for you to pretend to be a little vulnerable for her?"

"That's what she's pissed about? My lack of vulnerability? E, me walking around down here all weepy-eyed won't exactly instill confidence."

Taylor retook her seat. "Well, I don't think that's the issue, Jackie pie. The issue is that Veronica doesn't know how completely full of shit you are when you do things like manipulate people into making your coffee. I do, so it doesn't bother me. But she thinks that guy's real, and she doesn't know how to reconcile him with the one she cares for."

"And," Erin added, "I don't think it helps that Michael so openly dotes on Karen now. Women like to be doted on, you do remember?"

"So does she want Mike back or what?"

Taylor looked at Erin. "I think his brain is made of clay."

Erin laughed. "He's playing the dullard."

"Forget it," he said. "How soon until that coffee's ready?"

"I'll give you some goddamn coffee," Taylor said. "Go find that girl right now and tell her how much you need her."

He sat looking at her.

"Go and tell her. Now."

"Damn!" he said, getting up. "You two always think you can order me around."

"I'll keep the pot warm, honey."

Forrest found Veronica sitting with Melissa, who was helping a couple of the children with their math homework. Laddie was playing ball with the kids and came over to sniff at his pants pocket, pawing at his leg. Andie had managed to establish a genuine curriculum, and she'd done it with the complete support of the other mothers, which made it a joy for her as a teacher. And giving the children homework to complete outside of class kept them from playing the video games nonstop, allowing the video games to evolve into a kind of reward system.

"You've done an excellent job," Forrest had said to her

weeks earlier. "I was worried it might be tough to keep them occupied once they'd played every video game a thousand times."

"Idle hands are the devil's workshop," Andie had replied with a smile.

Forrest stepped up behind Veronica where she sat at the table, taking a dog treat from his pocket and giving it to Laddie. "Talk to you a minute?"

"I'm busy."

"Taylor won't give me any coffee."

"I don't blame her."

"Are you guys in a fight?" Melissa asked, noting the tension.

"I think so," Forrest said. "I'm not sure."

"My mommy and daddy fight a lot too," one of the children said. "That's why mommy had to get a court order."

Forrest laughed. "You gonna get a court order, V?"

"How would I do that? You're the king."

"Well, that's what I'd like to talk to you about."

She looked up at him over her shoulder. "What's that mean?"

"We can talk about it later, I guess. Sorry I bothered you."

She watched him leave the room, then went back to helping the kids with the puzzle.

"Why do you do that?" Melissa asked.

"Do what, honey?"

"Sit there when you really want to go after him."

"One day you'll know."

"Seems like a waste of time to me. I'd just go see what he wanted."

Veronica looked at her, then got up and followed after Forrest, catching him outside blast tunnel number two. "Step into my office?"

"Sure," he said.

They stepped into the tunnel and shut the door.

"What's on your mind?" she asked.

"Look, I'm sorry if I come off as not needing you. I need

you very much. It's just that I can't walk around down here acting like Mr. Softy. Nice guys don't instill any confidence. These people need to see me acting like nothing fazes me."

"Nothing does faze you."

"Well, so what, Veronica? I've seen untold amounts of heinous shit in my life. What fazes me is you. *You* faze me. I think about you all goddamn day. I'm so fucking grateful that Karen and Mike hit it off that I don't even know how to tell you. I can't even imagine being trapped down here without you now. But I can't walk around down here like I've got Cupid's dick stuck up my ass either."

She smiled and used her thumb to squeeze the tears from her eyes. "Did T and E tell you to say that?"

"The Cupid part or the rest of it?"

"I know the disgusting shit is all you. The first part, the sweet part."

"Of course they told me what to say. I'm too much of a goddamn man to think up mushy shit like that."

She put her arms around him and they kissed.

The door at the far end opened and Tonya stepped into the tunnel from the missile silo, hesitating when she saw them.

"May as well come on out," Forrest announced. "You're busted."

She came down the tunnel biting her lips between her teeth. "I was helping Marcus find the canned corn," she said, averting her eyes.

Forrest laughed. "Well, the corn's over in silo one."

"Must be why we couldn't find it," she said, slipping past them and out of the tunnel.

Veronica slapped him on the shoulder. "That wasn't nice!"

"She's an adult. She doesn't have to apologize for getting shagged. And I don't have to pretend to the look the other way."

A few seconds later the door opened again and Kane stepped into the tunnel, a grin spreading across his face. "Either of you see a cute little black chick pass this way?"

"She said she was looking for the canned corn," Forrest said.

Kane laughed. "I told her to say we were looking for paper towels."

"Well she cracked under the pressure."

"You two are terrible," Veronica said, still hanging against Forrest.

Kane laughed and stepped out of the tunnel, shutting the door after him.

"So are we okay?" Forrest asked. "Or do I need to grovel a little bit?"

She let go of him and pulled her hair behind her ears. "I'm sorry for walking off like I did. I've never been any good at . . . at arguing."

"Don't apologize. That's not a bad thing."

"Yes, it is," she said. "I should do a better job of expressing myself when I'm upset. It's a childhood thing."

He kissed her again. "You're fine."

"Did they do anything terrible to those women upstairs?"

"Yes, they did. And that's as much you need to hear. Let's go get me some coffee."

"Do you think maybe we can go looking for that canned corn later on? I understand it might be missing."

"On second thought," he said, taking her hand, "why don't we go see if we can find it right now?"

**IN THE MORNING,** Forrest arrived with Laddie in Launch Control for a look at the monitors, and the first thing he saw was the man in the camouflage jacket laying faceup on the living room floor with the Bowie knife sticking out of his neck. "What the hell happened?"

"Like that?" Ulrich asked, looking up from a *Popular Science* article on wind power. "That's what we saw with first light. Those girls got loose and did his ass in. They took both shotguns and all four bags of meat. Even the blankets."

"Well good for them," Forrest said. "I was worried that

guy was going to move in for a while. We'd have had to do something."

"Which would have been stupid," Ulrich remarked. "I'm glad they're gone."

"How'd they get those locks open, you wonder?"

"They've probably watched and memorized the combinations by now."

"But how'd they work the combinations in the pitch-dark?"

"First, light must come inside the house before the monitors pick it up," Ulrich said, bringing up the bathroom feed. "See the chain on the bathroom floor? They needed the mirror to work the combination at their necks. One would assume their antagonist was dead by then."

"One would assume," Forrest chuckled.

"We've got another birthday today, by the way. Maria two's kid. She's seven."

Birthdays were good days because everybody got a cake for their birthday, and it cheered everyone up, especially the child of the day who got to play video games while everyone else was in class.

"I'll be back," Forrest said.

He took Laddie with him to the cargo bay where he kept the novelties, sorting through crates of odds and ends until he found a coloring book full of pictures of a sponge named Bob, along with a brand-new eight-pack of crayons. "It's not exactly a GI Joe with the Kung Fu grip," he said to the dog, "but everyone's gotta get something on their birthday, right?"

Laddie grumbled and sniffed around in the box, finding a blue racquetball and trotting off toward the door with it.

"Hey, it ain't your birthday. Come put that back!"

# THIRTY-FOUR

**MARTY AND HIS TWO ARMY BUDDIES FINALLY MADE THEIR** way back to his house on foot. The Air Force was all over town now, and it took the three of them two days to get back to his house and avoid the armored vehicles. Twice during the day, they were spotted and forced to fight a running battle until they finally lost their pursuers. Now Sullivan stood looking over Joe's four-door Jeep Rubicon in the beam of his red light, noting the bad dents left in the hood by meteorite impacts, the hole in the hard top.

"This is about the most aggressive tire tread you can get on a civilian vehicle," he said. "Good call, Miller."

But Marty wasn't paying him much real attention. He was busy looking at the ruins of his home through the night vision device, thinking of his wife and child beneath the rubble, feeling that the weight of his despair might crush him. He wished Emory and Sullivan would take the Jeep and leave without him so he could sit down in the midst of the ruins and blow his brains out—and had he thought for even a moment that he might actually get to be with Susan again on the other side, he would have done exactly that. But he knew better, so he turned around and walked over to Sullivan in the darkness.

"I'd rather you didn't call me Miller," he said quietly. "I'd consider it a personal favor."

"It was just a joke."

"Anything but Miller," Marty said. "I've got his blood all around my neck."

Emory found a roll of duct tape in a garage across the street and used it to black out all of the brake lights and turn signals. She taped over the headlights so that only an inch-wide horizontal space was exposed across the center of each lamp.

Sullivan bumped Marty on the shoulder, and Marty turned around to see him standing there with a red, one-gallon gas can in his hand. "Strip that tunic a minute."

Marty took it as an opportunity to practice stripping his gear, and handed over the mandarin-collared ACU jacket. Sullivan then asked him to hold the light while he poured gasoline on the collar of the jacket and scrubbed it against itself to get the blood out. He then squeezed the excess gasoline from the cloth and gave the jacket back.

"Better?"

Marty shrugged back into the jacket. At any other time in his life, the smell of gasoline on his clothing would have made him sick, but under the present circumstance it smelled wholly appropriate. "Thanks, Sully."

"Sullivan . . . Sully was my dad."

"Hooah," Marty said.

They were on the road a short time later, searching for the best way to refuel the Jeep. By pure dumb luck they came across an abandoned eighteen-wheeled Shell tanker and filled up the Jeep, along with Joe's two remaining fuel cans.

Sullivan drove and Marty rode shotgun. Emory sat in the backseat with her M-203 grenade launcher. Anyone attempting to chase them down would get the shock of their lives.

"This guy Joe," Sullivan said, shifting into drive. "He was a good friend?"

"He was the best friend anybody could ever hope for," Marty said.

"Well, he sure left you a fine set of wheels."

It occurred to Marty then, for the very first time, that he

and Joe had a great deal in common now. "It's a good Jeep," he said.

They drove back into town and Sullivan parked as close to the Air Force perimeter as he dared. "They're keeping their supplies in what they consider to be their rear on their northern perimeter. We can keep to the side streets and walk right up to their supply column like I did the other night. They've still got night vision but they're not keeping up a very good watch."

"What if we swipe one of their chargers?" Marty asked. "Plug it into the cigarette lighter here in the Jeep? That way we could drive without headlights, right?"

"Let's not get greedy," Sullivan said.

"What's one look like?" Marty said. "I'm wearing an Air Force uniform."

"Whoa!" Emory said. "You can't even walk the walk, Marty, much less talk the talk. And you're wearing Adidas."

"Who looks at anybody's feet in the dark?" Marty argued.

"He's a got a point," Sullivan said. "And a charger would be a big advantage. Otherwise, these NVDs will be useless in a day or two."

"He's got a death wish is what he's got," Emory said.

"No, I don't, Shannon. I really do want to see the crater."

Emory reluctantly agreed, then they came up with a plan. They used the night vision devices attached to their helmets to cover the last two blocks, easily slipping through the Air Force perimeter undetected. They grabbed two cases of MREs apiece from the nearest deuce-and-a-half, each case containing twelve complete meals, and hurried back to the edge of the perimeter. There were a number of sentries posted, but they were either sleeping or busy talking, most of them in total darkness with NVDs in the up position on the front of their helmets. Apparently they were feeling invincible now that the Mongol threat had been smashed.

The trio stashed the food in a safe place and made their way back to the supply trucks, searching the cab of each for a charger. Not finding one, they were forced to penetrate deeper within the Air Force perimeter, finally taking cover behind a U-Haul truck near a well-lighted repair station where a number of airmen stood around talking and smoking cigarettes. A large green diesel-powered generator was running at the back of the repair bay, providing heat as well as light to a row of six fifty-three-foot Air Force trailers parked to the right of the garage.

"That's a command car over there," Sullivan said, pointing across the lot to an armored Humvee festooned with multiple radio antennae.

"If they don't have one in there," Emory said, "they don't have one."

"I'll be back," Marty said, and stepped boldly from behind the truck into the light before Emory could grab him.

"He does have a goddamn death wish!" Sullivan hissed, bringing his M-4 to bear, sighting on the group of nine airmen inside the bay.

"I told you," she muttered, doing the same, her finger on the trigger of the M-203.

The airmen glanced in Marty's direction as he strolled casually across the lot with the carbine slung over a shoulder, his hand in his pocket, waving lazily as he passed within a hundred feet of the open door. The wave was returned by a couple of the airmen who went right back to their bullshitting.

"Check that out," Emory said.

"I'm still gonna jerk a half-hitch in his ass . . . *if* we survive this."

Marty walked past the trailers and over to the command car, which sat out of view from the garage, cloaked in shadow. He opened the far-side door and got in, shutting the door and using his red light to have a look around. There was a charger on the deck between the seats, resting on top of a grenade-bearing vest containing a dozen 40mm grenades. In the backseat he saw a medical bag like the one Emory had worn over her shoulder the day he and Susan met her.

The grenade vest was confusing at first, but Marty was

getting the hang of the military's tricky contraptions, so he managed to shrug into it without much trouble. He tucked the charger away in his harness, shouldered the med kit, and got out of the Humvee.

He heard a woman's muted cry and froze. A man laughed. Marty looked up at the windows of the trailers, and his skin tightened into gooseflesh as he realized what the trailers were being used for.

"No more," he muttered, taking Joe's .45 from its holster and stalking through the darkness to the closest trailer. He stepped onto the stairs and slowly opened the door.

**"GET READY TO** run," Sullivan said, watching Marty through his NVD.

"Go ahead, split," Emory said. "I can't leave him."

"You've got a death wish too now?"

"No," she said, resigned to her fate. "But I like the guy. He saved my ass."

"Fuck all," he muttered, sighting down the barrel of his M-4 and getting ready to do battle.

"Go on, Sullivan. You don't need to stay here. You can make a good run without us. There's enough food back there to last you a couple of months."

"Can't do it," he said. "You might be my only chance of ever getting laid again."

She patted him on the shoulder. "In that case, hon, you'd definitely better go. I'm playing for the other team."

He took his eye from the scope just long enough to see if she was kidding. "Still," he said. "I got a pretty good tongue. You might get desperate."

"Hoo*ah*," she said with a chuckle, and prepared herself to meet death standing up.

**MARTY STEPPED INTO** the trailer with the pistol concealed behind his thigh to find an Air Force sergeant sitting at a desk reading *Hustler* magazine. The sergeant pulled himself out of his fantasy and set the magazine aside, having a look at his clipboard and frowning as he flipped to the next sheet of paper.

"You're confused, Miller. You're not up until tomorrow night."

"No, I'm up right now," Marty said, pointing the pistol into the sergeant's face, seeing that his name was Priest.

"What the fuck is wrong with you?" Priest said, cautious but unafraid. "You got shit for brains? You can't wait twenty-four hours? Put that fucking thing away before I report your ass to Moriarty."

"How many men in the back?" Marty asked.

The sergeant gave him a queer look, noting the dark stain on the collar of Marty's jacket. "Who the fuck are you, buddy?"

"Priest, I'm not your buddy. So unless you'd like to die with me, you'd better answer my question."

"Six," Priest said, his mouth suddenly dry. "Three broads to a side."

Marty took a look around, now noticing the six rifles in a rack on the wall behind the desk. "Get the fuck out," he said, stepping aside and waving the sergeant toward the door.

Priest kept his hands shoulder high as he came around the desk, and Marty belted him in the back of the head with the pistol as he passed.

Now, in every movie he had ever seen where a man got whacked in the back of the head with a gun, the guy always fell down; Priest did not fall down. What Priest did was grab the back of his head and spin around, swearing aloud and forcing Marty to belt him again, only this time on the top of the skull, which knocked Priest to his knees, but he still didn't fall over. So Marty bashed him a third time, much harder, and the sergeant finally fell over, but he still wasn't knocked out. He was, in fact, now sobbing like a child.

This put Marty in a serious quandary, mindless brutality not really being his field of expertise.

"Don't hit me anymore," the sergeant whimpered. "I can't see. Jesus, you've blinded me!"

Marty was suddenly feeling so bad for the man that he nearly started crying himself. "Don't fucking move!" he hissed.

"I won't," whimpered the severely injured man. "I swear!"

Marty went down the hall and opened the first door to find a man humping a woman in her mid-forties. She had blond hair and was staring off into deep space.

"What the fuck?" the naked man said, climbing off the cot from between the woman's legs. "Get the fuck—"

Marty shot him in the throat and turned around, kicking open the door to the room directly across the hall, where another woman was being violated. He shot the man in his stomach and turned to face down the hall, shooting each of the three men to emerge from their rooms. The sixth man had obviously chosen to hide, so Marty walked over the bodies and opened the door to find him cowering on the bed with his hands over his head. He was a young airman, no older than nineteen. The woman he had been molesting, even younger than her tormentor, was obviously in a deep fog like the others.

Marty shot him in the head, nearly jumping out of his skin a second later to the sound of a thunderous explosion outside the trailer.

"Kill me," the girl begged. "Please!"

Marty stepped forward, kissing his fingers and touching them to her forehead.

"Close your eyes," he said gently, hearing the sounds of men clamoring out of the next trailer, followed by those of automatic rifle fire. The girl closed her eyes and he did the same as he held the barrel of the .45 near her temple and pulled the trigger. The slide locked back on the weapon as the last shell was ejected, and he turned from the room without looking at her, ejecting the spent magazine and slapping in a new one. He did not look into the other rooms he passed, holstering the pistol and unslinging his carbine as he made for the door, stepping over the sergeant's now lifeless body where he still lay on the floor in front of the desk.

"WHAT THE FUCK'S he doing in there?" Sullivan said as they stood waiting to find out what would happen.

Ninety seconds later three half-naked men came piling out of the adjacent trailer with rifles in hand. Apparently none of the airmen in the garage had been able to hear Marty's shots over the generator, but the men next door had.

"The jig's up!" Emory said. "I got the garage."

Sullivan shot down the men coming from the trailer as Emory fired a grenade into the bay, hitting the generator and blowing the men in the garage to kingdom come. He shot more half-naked men as they came scrambling from the trailers, and he nearly shot Marty too as he came running across the lot with ever more men showing up out of the darkness.

"The fuel truck!" Sullivan shouted, banging Emory on the helmet and pointing far to the right of the trailers. "Burn it down!"

She fired a grenade and blew up the fuel truck, roasting a number of airmen as they were running past it.

Marty made it back unscathed and the three of them slipped away into the night, grabbing up the stashed MREs along the way.

"You stupid fuck!" Sullivan said later, tossing the cases of MREs onto the ground near the Jeep. "What the fuck was that about? Huh?"

"I couldn't find a charger in the command car," Marty lied. "So I decided to check the trailer." He pulled the charger from inside his vest. "I got this med kit, and some more grenades for Shannon's popgun too."

"Never again!" Sullivan said, jamming his finger into Marty's face. "Never again! And I want your goddamn word! You don't have the right to play games with my life!"

"You're right," Marty said, chastened. "It won't happen again. You've got my word."

They put half the MREs inside the Jeep and lashed the other half to the roof with the fuel cans. At first light they decided to stop for some rest and parked the Jeep off the road beneath an overpass in the desert. Emory volunteered to keep first watch because she was too wired to sleep, and soon Sullivan was snoring away behind the wheel with the seat back. Marty sat with Emory on the hood of the Jeep for warmth.

"You should try and get some sleep," she said.

"I'm too wound up."

"I'm getting to know you. You lied earlier. Why'd you really go into that trailer?"

"I heard someone hurting a woman," he said. "Are all military men fucking psycho?"

"No," she said. "And not all those guys back there are psycho either, but if the good-natured guys are outnumbered, what are they going to do? They have to eat."

"They could take off like Sullivan did."

"And I'm sure plenty of them have, Marty. You're talking about a lot of young guys with guns and no worthwhile leadership. It starts at the top. That's what was wrong with our unit. We had a wife-beater for a C.O."

"Think we can trust Sullivan?" Marty asked.

"He made a cute pass at me back there before your little show. I'm pretty sure he's a gentleman."

"Does he have a chance with you?"

"I dunno," she said with a shrug. "Like he said, I might get desperate."

"Can you do that? I mean . . . you know."

She put her arm around his shoulder, pulling him closer. "It's like this, Marty. There's two kinds of lesbians. Those who like intercourse and those who don't really care for it."

"Which are you?"

"Well, I *used* to like it once in a while with the right guy. Now, I dunno. It'll take time . . ."

"Plus you might be—"

"Oh, thanks for reminding me," she said, letting go of him. "I'd actually managed to forget about that. With any luck, I'll have a goddamn miscarriage."

"And if we make it the whole nine months?"

"Well, you're gonna have to deliver the goddamn thing."

"Me? I don't know shit about birthing babies."

"There's plenty of time for me to teach you all you need to know. Now, do me a favor and don't bring it up again."

They sat quietly for a while, then Emory slipped down from the hood and stood looking out across the dim morning expanse of Arizona. "Marty, I don't know what I'll do if it looks like him . . . I might kill it."

"Nine months is a long time to grow attached, Shannon. Let's wait and see how you feel by then."

"What about you? Do you have any kids out there anywhere?"

He smiled sadly and shook his head.

An hour later Marty was dozing in the passenger seat of the Jeep when something woke him up. It was the sound of a rotary winged aircraft, the first aircraft he'd heard in the sky since the impact. Sullivan was still snoring, but Emory was nowhere to be seen. He walked out from beneath the bridge to see her come sliding down the embankment.

"Fuck me!" she shouted. "Gunship coming in along the highway, flying snake and nape!"

"Snake and what?"

"Nape of the earth, Marty. Get outta sight!"

They listened to the helicopter come thundering overhead and on up the highway to the north.

"They're taking a serious risk," Marty said. "There's still too much particulate matter in the air. They'll burn the turbines up."

"Must be why they're flying so low," she said. "That and they gotta be looking for us."

Sullivan had awoken to the sound of the rotors and joined them, watching after the helicopter. "Blackhawk, loaded with rockets. They're definitely pissed." He turned around and pointed at Marty. "This is on you, cowboy."

"I'm sorry."

"Well . . . forget it, we just gotta deal with it."

An hour later the helicopter came back. By now its engines were smoking from sucking in so much dirt and ash, but it swung wide of the highway by a hundred yards for a look beneath the bridge, where Marty had gotten out of the Jeep and stood hidden behind a column. The door gunner immediately opened fire on the vehicle.

Sullivan stomped the accelerator and tore off in the direction of the helicopter. "Don't miss, Shannon, or we're fucking dead!" he shouted.

They had removed the hard top, and Emory was standing in the backseat braced against the roll bar. She opened fire on the door gunner even as machine-gun bullets were hitting the fender of the Jeep. The gunner fell back into the aircraft, and the helicopter swung around to face them directly. Sullivan swerved right against the direction of its turn, hoping to throw off the pilot's aim. The first rocket struck the ground to their left and just behind them, leaving their fate in Emory's hands.

Sullivan straightened the Jeep and she fired the M-203.

Even as the projectile was arcing toward the windscreen of the aircraft, Sullivan was swerving hard to port. The pilot overcorrected and the second rocket struck the ground to their right. A fragment hit Emory in the hip and she fell down in the back of the Jeep as her 40mm grenade detonated against the windscreen of the Blackhawk, killing both pilots.

The aircraft went into a violent spin, whirling around four times before smashing into the desert floor, breaking apart on impact and bursting into flames. Sullivan raced back toward the bridge where Marty stood waiting and locked up the brakes. The three of them raced to reattach the hardtop and quickly tied down the supplies, only to find the front left tire had gone flat. They changed it as quickly as they could, then Sullivan drove back up the embankment onto the highway.

Marty noticed Emory's leg for the first time. "You're bleeding."

"It's shrapnel. Come back here and help me."

He climbed into the back with her and she gave him the curved hemostat she had taken from the medical bag, which was basically a pair of locking forceps normally used for clamping off a bleeding artery or vein.

"Use that to pull the shrapnel out," she said, shrugging her trousers down over her rump to expose her bleeding right hip.

He took hold of the jagged piece of metal and tugged at it, causing Emory to wince. "It's in there pretty tight," he said.

"Don't play with it, Marty. Pull it out!"

He clamped the hemostat onto the metal and gave it a jerk, but it held fast and Emory grabbed the roll bar, shouting in pain. "Fuck!"

"I'm sorry. It's really in there, Shannon."

"Need some help?" Sullivan asked.

"You just wanna play with my butt . . . keep driving."

It was getting too dark to see inside the Jeep, so Marty took the red filter from his light and held it in his teeth while he examined the wound.

"You're going to have to do a cut-down," Emory said, digging in the bag for a scalpel.

"A what?"

"You're gonna cut it out."

"Oh, jeez!" He gripped the light in his teeth and pressed against the wound with the thumb and forefinger of his left hand, holding the skin taut as he drew the razor-sharp blade along the ridge, drawing blood and exposing the blackish metal.

"Okay, good job, hon. Now pull that fucker outta me."

Marty took hold of the metal with the hemostat and had it out with one tug. The piece of shrapnel was half the size of a trading card, cut corner to corner, slightly bent. He tossed it on the floor and Emory poured peroxide over the open wound. Then she took a packet of sutures from the bag and clamped the curved needle between a smaller pair of hemostats. "Sew me up."

He sat looking at her.

"It doesn't have to be pretty. Just keep it as straight as you can."

Marty was sweating. "Can you turn the heat off, Sullivan?"

"It's not on."

"Come on," Emory said. "It's not that tough."

It took him nearly twenty minutes, but Marty got the wound sewn closed and then Emory dressed it and pulled her trousers back up. By then it was total darkness once again, and Sullivan was driving with his night vision.

"Is there enough ambient light for those things to work out here?" Marty asked as he climbed into the passenger seat.

"Not real well," Sullivan said. "I've switched to infrared."

It was a bizarre feeling racing into total blackness, and Marty found it difficult to look out the windshield without feeling terrified they were going to hit something. "You're sure you can see?"

"I can see."

He plugged one of the other NVDs into the charger then closed his eyes and leaned his head back. A second later Emory was tugging at his arm.

"Come back here," she said.

"Something wrong?" he asked, moving into the back again.

She lay over on the seat and put her head into his lap, taking his hand and setting it on her head. "Pet me. I don't feel good."

Marty began to run his fingertips through her hair.

"Somebody talk to me back there," Sullivan said. "Keep me awake."

Marty lifted his head again and drew a deeply disappointed breath, smiling blandly in the dark. He really needed to sleep, but he was apparently in too great a demand.

# THIRTY-FIVE

"RATS?" ESTER SAID IN DISBELIEF. "I ASK YOUR ENGINEERS for new technological ideas and they come up with *rats*? Good lord!"

"It's only a stop-gap, Madam President," Admiral Longbottom tried to assure her. "And the little bastards will eat damn near anything, so breeding them won't be difficult."

"I can't take rat meat to the people," Ester said. "My God, Barry, tell the man!"

"Well, I think it may well be a matter of presentation," replied Vice President Hadrian with the same calm demeanor that had served him so well as President. "If you present them today with some wounded black wharf rat as the answer to our future, they'll throw bricks at you, and understandably so. But if you wait until the food has begun to run low and everyone is afraid . . . and then present them with an entire cash-crop of clean, white lab rats with pink eyes . . . you're a hero."

"Exactly right," said Longbottom, grateful for Hadrian's presence in the Islands.

"Nothing says we have to take the project public. But we are talking about avoiding starvation. And if we start a breeding program now with the lab rats we still have here on the island, we can have a good head start by the time the fish supply begins to run out."

"Okay," Ester said. "So where do you propose we raise these things?"

"Well, we can raise them on the hangar decks of our carriers," Longbottom said, abhorring the idea but feeling the need to offer the concession. "That will keep the population off the island and out of sight. And there are ways the meat could be processed so that eating it won't be such a distasteful idea."

"It's as bad an idea as Soylent Green," Ester muttered. "Anyway, I don't like the idea of using your ships. I'm sure another place can be found, one of the other islands may be perfect. What else do you have for us?"

"I saved the best news for last," Longbottom said with a smile.

"Thank God," Ester said.

"First, my engineers are confident that we can use the reactors aboard our nuclear vessels to supply electrical power to most of Honolulu for twelve hours a day," the admiral began. "On a revolving schedule. It will take time to construct a new power grid but this is a work-ready project. And we won't have to worry about replacing the atomic fuel for a couple years. And by then we should be running largely on tidal power."

"Tidal power? That requires industry."

"Which the Australians have agreed to help us with," the admiral said. "They have been developing the technology for a number of years now."

"What are they asking for in return?"

"Our friendship," the admiral said. "Our future help with any problems they may have. Exchange of engineers and ideas. All of the above. Like you, they view this crisis as an opportunity to get it right."

"But you still don't see it that way, Admiral?"

Longbottom sat back. "I've done as you asked, and I will continue to do my best, but no, I don't agree entirely with the steps we're taking. I think we should be concentrating our efforts on the remaining oil platforms out to sea. The longer we wait, the more they deteriorate out there in the salty air."

"Oil is the past," Ester said. "There's no future in it. We want the sky to clear, not to continue polluting it. I've promised the people a different way forward. It looks like you're making an effort, Admiral, and I thank you for that."

"We still need fuel for our vessels," Longbottom said. "And I'm not sure how much oil the Australians can afford to share."

Ester could sense that Longbottom was expecting a quid pro quo in exchange for his efforts, so she gave it to him, as she and Hadrian had previously agreed she would.

"Very well," she said. "Reopen the closest platform."

"Excellent," he said. "I believe this to be a very wise choice."

"How soon do you expect to see the first tidal turbines installed?" Hadrian asked, making sure the admiral knew that he would be expected to carry through.

"Within twelve months," Longbottom replied. "There's a lot of work to be done."

"And the new power grid will be constructed in such a manner that we will be able to hook the tidal generators right into it," Ester said.

"Well, that will be more difficult," the admiral said. "It would be better to wait until—"

"That wasn't a question, Admiral. Nor was it a request. That was a statement. The new power grid is not going to be a jerry-rig. I want it purpose-built for *future* use with the tidal generators. And whatever 'adaptations' your people come up with will be to accommodate the nuclear reactors. Not the other way around. From now, we build with the future in mind. Is that clear?"

"Yes, ma'am," Longbottom said, pissed because now his engineers would have to go back to the drawing board.

"And I would appreciate it if you would send daily reports to my office," Hadrian added.

"*Daily*, sir?"

"Yes, daily."

"Well, sir, you do realize that we may go for weeks at a time without any real changes in—"

"Daily reports," Hadrian repeated. "And there had better be *some* kind of progress made on every one of them." Then, offering the admiral some wiggle room, he added, "Even if it's only the sketch of a new idea one of your engineers has put forward."

"Yes, sir."

"Now, I understand you also have security concerns," Ester said, continuing their combined assault.

"Yes, well, on the issue of security, Madam President, we have located a site where a number of the pirates seem to be congregating on one of the lesser islands. I would like to know what, if anything, you'd like for me to do about this threat."

Ester had heard these reports already, and though she knew the piracy problem was growing, she pretended not to be concerned. "What would you suggest, Admiral?"

"Cleaning them out, ma'am."

"Then do whatever you deem necessary . . . so long as it doesn't impede the Navy's progress elsewhere."

"Yes, ma'am," Longbottom said, finally feeling some sense of accomplishment.

"Your list of responsibilities seems to be growing, doesn't it, Admiral?"

"It does indeed," Longbottom said.

"And to think you were worried about losing your importance," Ester said with a chuckle. "Will there be anything else?"

"Not right now, Madam President, no."

"I thank you again for your diligence," she said. "And please pass my thanks down the chain of command."

"Yes, ma'am."

When the admiral was gone, Ester rose and went to the window, where she stood leaning on her cane. "Barry, how would you feel about being president again, of the Islands this time?"

"Excuse me?" Hadrian said.

"I'm tired," she said, turning from the window. "And I wasn't kidding about me not making a pimple on Golda Meir's backside. I'm an astronomer, Barry. A novelty act. I wasn't born to lead a society into the new era."

"The Islanders love you, Ester. You're gruff and tough, and that's what they need in a leader right now."

"But what if I die?" she said. "It's better that you're already in office by then. Andrew Johnson had a lot of trouble after Lincoln's death. I think it would better for me to claim ill health and to step aside soon. We'll tell the Islanders that I'm staying on as one of your advisers, and I'll make regular appearances if they really feel they can't live without me, but I worry I may cause more trouble in the long run by remaining in office."

"The people elected you, Ester, and you agreed to take the job for six years. They believe in you. And if you're really that worried about dying in office, I promise right now to do my best to make sure all of your visions come to fruition."

"That's the problem, Barry. This was never my vision. It's the vision of some poor dead idealistic astronomer."

"Don't abandon these people now, Ester. There's nothing that says a lawyer makes any better leader than an astronomer—and you're learning. He didn't show it, but giving the admiral permission to shell that pirate stronghold out of existence bought you a lot of capital with the Navy. Nothing makes a military man happier than getting to take military action." He laughed. "He's probably getting ready to sortie the entire fleet as we speak."

Ester nodded grimly. "He may be, at that."

"But after he takes this pirate stronghold down," Hadrian cautioned, "pretend to lose interest in the pirates we have left. It's too soon to tell, but we may need an enemy to help keep us unified. So we should allow these pirates time to recover a little bit before sending the admiral back out. It's a fine balance you need to strike, Ester."

"See?" she said, pointing at him with the tip of her cane. "That's the type of political evil that would never occur to me."

Hadrian grinned. "That's what you've got me for, Ester."

# THIRTY-SIX

THE BIGGEST TROUBLE FOR MARTY AND HIS FRIENDS DURING their trip had been traveling along I-25 north of the Arizona border. It was jammed with deserted, bumper-to-bumper, ash-coated traffic, all of it pointing south on both sides of the highway. Even in the Jeep they'd had trouble negotiating their way through the logjam of cars and over thousands of ash-coated, frozen bodies along the road.

"What killed them all?" Emory wondered.

"Pressure wave," Marty said. "Those who weren't killed outright likely suffocated in the vacuum."

By the time they reached the outskirts of Denver, the cars were nothing but burnt frames and the bodies no more than grizzled skeletons.

"This is where the firestorm first began to lose its intensity," Marty said. "Everything north of here is likely burnt to a crisp."

They drove into downtown Denver and got out and stood looking at the scorched remains of the once fair city.

"It used to be such a clean town," Emory said. "Now it's an ashtray."

"Smells like one too," Sullivan said, hawking up a mouthful of phlegm and spitting it onto the street.

They drove into the suburbs, where it turned out that

Marty had been largely correct about being able to forage canned food. They saw living people here and there, darting in and out of houses in ones and twos with sacks over their shoulders, all of them ragged and filthy-looking, wretches for the most part. No one came near the trio, however, and there seemed to be very little sense of danger. Still, they kept their eyes peeled. Some of the houses had mysteriously escaped the flames entirely, while others were completely incinerated. They stood talking in the drive of a brick home that had gone largely undamaged, their mouths covered with green triangular bandages against the ash blowing in the breeze.

"Traveling is going to get more difficult from here," Marty said. "We'll still find food but before long the highway's likely to be covered with ejecta."

"Won't be any gas north of here," Sullivan said. "Not with the cars all burned up."

"But there will be in the underground tanks," Marty said. "Beneath the gas stations."

"How do you propose to get it out of the ground?"

"We can go to Home Depot or someplace like that," Marty said. "All I need is some PVC pipe, some glue, and a few other things, and I can make a hand pump."

Sullivan stood looking at Emory.

"We've got nothing better to do, John."

"I disagree," he said. "Okay, he was right about the food. But he's wrong about heading any farther north. We should be scavenging all the food we can. We can hook a trailer to the Jeep, find a place south of here to hole up for the winter, a house near some trees with a big-ass fireplace in it."

"He's right, Shannon. That's exactly what you guys should do."

"What's that supposed to mean?"

"It means I'm pressing on," Marty said. "I'll find a four-wheel drive somewhere in Denver that didn't burn up."

"You're nuts!" Sullivan said.

"I'll be one less mouth to feed."

"Um, no," Emory said. "I don't like that idea."

"I'm not asking you guys to come with me," he said. "But it's the only thing left that makes any sense for me."

"Then I'm coming with you," she said. "John L?"

He shook his head. "No, Shannon. I'm sorry. That way is a total dead end and there's nothing up there I care about. Not anymore."

"*I'll* be there," she said, her eyes grinning over the bandage.

"Sorry," he said. "I've only got so much faith to sustain me."

"Well, if it's a matter of faith," she said, grabbing his belt and pulling him off toward the house.

"Shannon, what the fuck are you doing?" he said, trying to pry her hand loose, but not terribly hard.

She towed him through the door and into the kitchen, pushing him up against counter and reaching down with one hand to unbutton his trousers.

He stood looking at her, his arousal increasing. "Shannon . . . what are you doing?"

She freed his manhood and began to massage him. "Restoring your faith."

"This isn't going to—"

Sullivan drew a deep breath and slid his arm around her, quickly giving in to her touch. He took off her helmet and pulled the bandage down to put his nose into her hair, breathing her in. Even after so many weeks without bathing, there was still the unmistakable essence of a female.

"Goddamnit, that feels good," he said with a sigh.

"I know what guys like," she said, stroking him more vigorously until she got him groaning into her ear.

He gripped her tight against him. "Ohh . . . fuck!"

When he was finished shuddering, she stood back and took a handful of dust-covered paper towels from a roll hanging beneath the cupboard, grinning at him as she wiped her fingers clean. "Too bad you're not coming along," she said. "That's as easy for me as shaking your hand."

He finished buttoning his pants and stood looking at her. "You know it's a one-way trip," he said helplessly. "You have to know that?"

"Go ahead and consider that my thanks for what you've done for us."

"Shannon, think about this. Seriously."

"Already have."

"Jesus Christ," he muttered, grabbing his carbine from the table and walking out of the house. Without saying a word, he walked past where Marty stood in the yard, got into the Jeep and shut the door.

"What's his problem?" Marty asked as Emory came walking out with a self-satisfied smile on her face.

"He's got a crush on a lesbian," she said. "What about you? You need a crank before we go?"

"Stop it," he said, turning away, but she grabbed his jacket.

"I'm a practical woman, Marty. You need one or not?"

"Not today," he said quietly, embarrassed. "But thank you."

She bumped him on the shoulder. "We're buddies, right?"

"Yes," he said. "We're buddies."

"Okay then. Me and you stick together."

"Of course. What about Sullivan?"

"Sullivan . . . well, he's sorta fucked," she said with a laugh. " 'Cuz I play dirty."

**TWO DAYS LATER** Sullivan slowed the Jeep and came to a stop in the middle of a back-country road twenty-five miles north of Cheyenne, Wyoming. The boulder resting in the center of the road was over ten feet tall and twice as wide. "Sweet Jesus," he muttered.

"See what I've been telling you guys!" Marty said, jumping excitedly out of the Jeep and running up to the monolith.

Emory and Sullivan got out and stood looking at the rock.

"That flew up in the sky and then came back down, right?" Emory said.

"Sure as hell did!" Marty answered, running around the side of it, trying to calculate the weight. "Definitely igneous rock," he muttered. "Hey, either of you guys know the unit weight of granite? I'm not sure— no, wait—about a hundred pounds per cubic foot."

They followed him around it and were shocked by what they saw in the distance.

"Now that's a goddamn debris field!" Marty shouted.

For as far they could see to the north, the barren landscape was scattered with boulders, though not all were as big as the first one, and there were great gashes in the earth where they had come to land, inexorably altering the landscape with their presence alone.

"See those cars out there?" Marty said, pointing far off the highway where a dozen vehicles lay scattered like broken toys. "That's where the blast wave threw them. Which means we can cross over to the interstate now. It should be mostly clear." He turned and paced off the size of the boulder. "Finally, some numbers I can work with."

Sullivan looked at Emory. "He doesn't have his head on right."

"Let him go," she said. "He's a got a thing for numbers."

"Just look at it, Sue," Marty was muttering. "Just look at it, honey!"

He came back over to them after nearly fifteen minutes of mumbling to himself and stood scratching his growing red beard.

Okay," he said. "Judging from the size and estimated weight of this monster, speed and angle of attack, we shouldn't be much more than five hundred miles from the point of impact."

Sullivan looked at him disbelief. "You're telling me the explosion threw this fucking thing five hundred miles?"

"That's an estimate."

"Well, shit, how close can we get to the crater before the road's all blown away?"

"That won't be the problem," Marty said. "The road will be buried. But that's what the Jeep is for."

They were towing a trailer now loaded with fuel and food, so they were set for a long drive.

Emory smiled at Sullivan. "You have to admit, it's kinda cool."

He nodded grimly. "My parents were up in Montana."

"Well, for what it's worth," Marty said, "they never knew a thing. It was instantaneous."

"You're sure?"

"Positive," Marty said. "That thing hit with a force equal to five or six teratons of TNT. That's five or six *trillion* tons."

"How did we even survive a blast like that?" Emory wondered.

"Shock cocoons," Marty said. "Small areas of limited damage within a broader area of mass devastation. That's how they explained those firemen surviving the World Trade Center falling on top of them. Shock cocoons even allowed for a few buildings to remain standing after the Hiroshima blast. There can be all sorts of reasons for their occurrence. In our case—meaning Arizona—I'm guessing the Rockies had a mitigating effect on the pressure wave no one ever anticipated. Maybe the Grand Canyon did too. We could probably study this impact for decades and still not know everything. You know, it's kind of like finding a living Tyrannosaurus rex and realizing we were only half right about what they looked like . . . God, I wish Susan were here!"

"Well, can we get going, Mr. Scientist? We're burning daylight."

"Why not?" Marty said. "It's only going to get more interesting."

They crossed back to the interstate, and it turned out that Marty had been largely correct about that too. There were hundreds and hundreds of cars, but most of them had been blown well clear of the highway.

**THE TRIP TO** the Canadian border took another four days and nights of driving over rough and rocky terrain. The interstate was completely covered by the blanket of ejecta that fell from the sky after the impact, obscuring the landscape. Most of the highway signs had been leveled by the blast wave along with every other man-made structure north of the Wyoming border. They kept track of their progress by stopping to brush off—or in some cases to dig up—fallen or buried highway signs.

At last, Sullivan stopped the Jeep and they sat gaping at a massive hole in the earth extending well beyond the horizon north, east, and west, stretching like an empty ocean basin for as far as the eye could see. "Holy Christ," he whispered, awestruck.

Marty and Emory got out. Neither said a word as they walked the thirty yards to the crater's edge and stood looking nearly a mile down into the empty chasm blown in the earth's crust, its sloped and rocky walls lined with the same colorful striations as the Grand Canyon. They saw no sign of a past civilization, heard no sound but the cold breeze in their ears.

There was a tremor in the earth then, and they hurried back from the edge as rocks broke away and tumbled down, hitting speeds of sixty mph before finally reaching the bottom far below, well out of view. The tremor did not last long, and when the earth stood still again they returned to the rim and watched the last of the tumbling rocks and boulders careening out of sight.

"This wound will take a very long time to heal," he said quietly.

"Marty, what's that?" Emory said, pointing roughly three-quarters of a mile around the rim at an orange dot.

Marty trotted back to the Jeep with her on his heels, grabbing his carbine and finding the orange splotch of color through his scope. "It's a tent!"

"You're kidding," Sullivan said, getting out of the Jeep and raising a pair of high-powered binoculars. "Who the hell else would be stupid enough to . . . you're right."

Emory had her own carbine now and was glassing the site as well. "It's an encampment, all right. Is that a truck of some kind in defilade to the right of the tent, dark green maybe?"

"I think so," Sullivan said. "Let's mount up and get a little closer. Everybody keep your fucking eyes peeled for an ambush."

They drove to within four hundred yards of the encampment and Sullivan climbed up onto the roof with the binoculars.

"John, somebody could blow your ass right off there."

"Not worried about me, are you, Shannon?"

She looked at Marty and rolled her eyes.

"Looks deserted," Sullivan said. "There's another tent. It's green."

Emory raised her weapon. "Let's get over there before it starts getting dark."

Marty drove the Jeep slowly along, with Emory and Sullivan walking twenty and thirty yards out in front to guard against ambush. When they drew within fifty yards of the encampment, Sullivan signaled Marty to halt and stay in the Jeep as he and Emory advanced into the site, weapons ready.

"Hear that?" Sullivan said.

"Yeah . . . sounds like gas."

They looked around the corner of the tent and saw a small aluminum camp table with a Coleman stove resting on it, a large propane tank beneath it on the ground. A blue flame hissed beneath a red enameled coffeepot. Emory trained her weapon on what turned out to be a four-door, hybrid Chevrolet SUV. Sullivan advanced on the big orange tent and looked inside, seeing the limbless torsos of a man and a woman, their eyes open, staring sightless at the ceiling of the tent.

"Christ!" he said whipping around. "Look sharp, Shannon! We got bodies!"

Emory dropped into a crouch, never taking her eyes from the SUV. "I got movement, John! Around the truck! Moving to flank us on the left!"

Sullivan moved forward, unable to detect any movement on the uneven, rocky terrain. "I got nothin'."

They advanced together on the truck, drawing close enough to read the words UNITED STATES GEOLOGICAL SURVEY stenciled in dirty white lettering on the door. "You gotta be shitting me," he said.

"The government *did not* send them out here!" Emory said. "Did it?"

"Fuck if I know." Sullivan crept carefully around the front of the SUV, finding a cleft in the earth on the other side. The fissure was as wide and as deep as a man, a trench running from the edge of the crater and winding off across the uneven landscape for what could have been miles.

Emory came around the back of the truck and looked down into the trench. "That's what I saw. Somebody jumping in."

Sullivan slid down into the ditch and poked around until he found a boot print then climbed back out. "Better get Marty in here."

She turned and beckoned Marty into the camp. He drove up to the orange tent, killed the engine and got out. He walked over and lifted the lid from the coffeepot. "It's boiled dry," he said, turning off the flow of propane.

He and Emory had a closer look at the bodies inside the tent, finding their clothes in a pile in the corner.

"Must've taken their arms and legs for food," she said.

"Doesn't make sense," Marty said. "There's backpacking food over there by the stove in a box. Why eat the people?"

Sullivan threw back the flap and stepped inside. "Because you eat the perishable food first. The dehydrated shit will keep."

Marty looked at him.

"People are perishable," Sullivan said, pushing a digital video camera into his hands. "Found that in the other tent. How's it work?"

They stepped out of the tent, and Marty sat on a rock fiddling with the camera while the other two rooted through the surveyors' equipment, searching the truck and the immediate area near the encampment.

"Where are you going?" Emory called.

"To find their latrine," Sullivan answered. "It'll tell us how long they've been here." Shortly, he found a small slit trench about four feet long dug behind a small boulder nearly forty yards away. Near the trench were three rolls of toilet paper in Ziploc bags and a small spade stuck in the ground. He used the spade to uncover the buried excrement, then went back to the encampment where Emory was sorting through the backpacking food.

"Find it?" she asked.

"Either those two were here for at least a week, or there's some people missing . . . probably two or three."

"There's only two sleeping bags."

"Well, there's a lot of shit over there. Maybe somebody swiped the other sleeping bags."

"Three!" Marty called, getting up from the rock and coming over to them. "There's three missing and they're down there." He pointed into the crater. "They apparently died in an avalanche. Check this out."

He played a video clip of two men and a woman preparing to descend the escarpment in full rock-climbing gear. They were happy and excited, all in their early thirties, one white male, one black, and a small Asian woman. The blond woman from the tent was in the video too, but she was not dressed for climbing, and the man with red hair was probably the person holding the camera.

The next clip showed them descending out of sight a hundred yards or so down the face.

After that, the clip showed an avalanche much worse than the one Marty and company had witnessed upon their arrival. The blonde was screaming in the background, and the man holding the camera kept saying, "Oh, my God! Oh, my God!" over and over again for nearly a minute until the avalanche ended. From the look of the video, it did not appear that anyone below could possibly have survived.

"Unbelievable," Sullivan said. "Who in their right mind goes down there?"

Marty shrugged and tucked the camera into his pocket. "Maybe they figured there was nothing else left to do with their lives. They were rock hounds . . . and this *is* the ultimate experience for a rock hound."

"And now it's their grave," Sullivan said. "So, okay, we camp here tonight. In the morning we'll load this food back into their truck and head south. That hybrid will get better mileage than the Jeep. Anybody got a better idea?"

"Don't forget our cannibalistic underground dweller," Emory said.

"We sleep in shifts anyway," Sullivan said. "Nothing's changed."

# THIRTY-SEVEN

IT WAS PITCH-BLACK BY EIGHT O'CLOCK THAT NIGHT, AND Emory sat against a rock with one of the sleeping bags wrapped around her shoulders, unable to even see her hand in front of her face. They had pulled the SUV away from the fissure so they could see the trench unobstructed, and every ten minutes or so she would scan 360 degrees around the encampment through the NVD looking for movement or heat signatures.

A woman's scream split the night, and Sullivan came instantly awake, grabbing the carbine resting across his belly. "Shannon!"

"Here!" she said to the darkness. "It wasn't me." She turned on her night vision device and got to her feet, scanning the trench line.

Sullivan pulled on his helmet and scanned through his own NVD. "How far? Could you tell?"

"Hundred yards maybe."

"What's going on?" Marty said in the inky blackness.

"Ruck up!" Emory told him. "A woman screamed out there."

"Probably a trap," Sullivan said, shrugging into his harness. He could see Marty fumbling around in the dark looking for his equipment, pulling a flashlight from his pocket.

"If you turn that fucking thing on, I'll stick it so far up your ass you'll have light comin' out your ears."

"Well, how the hell else am I supposed to find my shit?"

"Try remembering where you put it!" Sullivan said, walking over and picking up Marty's gear from behind him and shoving it into his arms. Then he grabbed Marty's helmet from a rock and jammed it down on his head. "Try not to forget your dick."

Emory smiled to herself. "He remembered his weapon, John. That's the important thing."

"Hark, his guardian angel speaks."

She laughed. "We'll walk the trench line above ground. Me and Marty on the right, you on the left."

"I say Marty walks down in the trench."

"Sully, fuck off . . . anybody seen my goddamn gloves?"

THEY COVERED ROUGHLY a hundred yards before Sullivan spotted anything telling down in the trench. His fist went up and the other two stopped in their tracks, crouching low to the ground. He peered carefully over the edge of the fissure for a better look, to see what appeared to be a human being lying on the bottom, zipped up in a mummy sleeping bag. Switching to infrared, he saw that it was indeed a trap.

The person in the mummy bag gave off a strong heat signature, so was alive, and there were additional heat signatures as well . . . two sets of footprints glowing eerily in his viewfinder even as they cooled away to nothing, leading away from the bag into a split in the wall of the trench.

"You two in the cave," he called out, not knowing what else to call the little hidey-hole. "Come out with your hands up."

No one answered and no one came out.

"What is it?" Emory asked.

"A goddamn ambush," Sullivan answered. "I think it's the girl from the video down there in the bag . . . Come out, for the last time!" he shouted.

He heard what sounded like someone beginning to dig in, so he aimed his M-203 and a fired a 40mm grenade into the opening, blowing it apart and showering the person in the mummy bag with dirt.

When the dust cleared, two blasted bodies lay mangled in the trench, their heat signatures already fading, and Emory slid over the edge, pulling Marty in with her. She knelt beside the mummy bag and Sullivan kept watch above.

"Get your light out, Marty."

Marty shined his light on an Asian woman's face as Emory unzipped the bag to reveal her badly battered and naked body. Emory began an examination.

"Multiple broken bones," she called up. "Distended abdomen . . . internal bleeding."

"She must have survived the avalanche somehow," Marty muttered in amazement.

"Poor thing," Emory said, zipping the dying woman back up to keep her warm. "John, there's nothing I can do for her!"

Sullivan's face appeared over the edge. "How long does she have?"

"An hour . . . maybe."

The woman found her hand. "My friends . . ." she whispered. "Tammy . . . Ted?"

"I'm sorry, they're gone."

"Find the camera," the woman whispered, trying to squeeze Emory's hand. "There's video of the crater . . . for future . . . future study."

"We have it," Marty said.

"Take it to our friends in Oklahoma . . . an Air Force bunker there. Tell them Yon gave it to you. They're geo . . . geologists . . ."

"There are a lot of Air Force bases in Oklahoma." Emory said. "Which one?"

"Altus," said Yon. "They're at Altus." She lingered another ten minutes then died.

**IN THE MORNING**, they returned to the site and examined the remains of the man and woman Sullivan had blown up with the grenade. Each of them had a pistol and a knife. Another hundred yards down the trench they found a truly surprising sight: a reinforced concrete tunnel in the side of the crater wall.

"Where the hell does it go?" Marty wondered aloud.

"I'm guessing it leads to an old bunker," Sullivan said, stepping carefully around the edge to enter the tunnel without sliding away down the steep wall of the crater. Emory and Marty followed, all of them switching on the flashlights attached to their carbines.

"What kind of bunker?" Marty asked.

"SACOM . . . Strategic Air Command. If this tunnel doesn't lead to a missile silo, it should lead to a command bunker."

They walked along a steel grating until they came to an open blast door, which in fact had been blasted right out of its casement by the asteroid impact. The door itself was now embedded in the concrete on the far side of a twenty-by-thirty-foot living space. The room was scattered with the charred remains of unidentifiable items and a few partial skeletons that lay among the ash.

"Blast wave," Marty said. "This place imploded and they were incinerated instantly."

They found another blast door, also blasted from its casement, and stepped into a perfectly round room filled with scorched and flattened electrical appliances. The remains of a concrete island were in the center of the room, with exposed plumbing sticking up through it.

"That was a sink," Emory said. "This was a kitchen." She pried open a smashed metal cabinet to find little more than ash and some melted glass jelly jars.

They checked the entire level and every room was the same. All of the doors were blasted from their casements, and the rooms were scattered with incinerated remnants of what had probably once been furniture and human beings. In all, they found between fifteen and twenty partial skeletons.

Sullivan kicked a scorched skull across the room. "Our two cannibals must have been living here when the rock hit."

"But how did they survive?" Emory wondered. "All these people were cooked."

Sullivan shined his light on Marty's face. "What do you think, Mr. Shock Cocoon?"

Marty thought for a moment. "Where's the missile silo?"

Sullivan pointed back the way they had come. "The silo was at the other end of that tunnel we came in through . . . vaporized on impact."

"Well, so much for that idea," Marty said. "Okay, so the blast wave was moving laterally through these tunnels, following the path of least resistance . . . which means if our two psychos from last night were in here at the time of impact . . . they must've been beneath this level. So we're looking for a hatch in the floor, probably one that opens *up*."

After another quick search of the facility, they located a round hatch in the center of the floor near the island in the kitchen. They hadn't noticed it the first time because it was hidden beneath a piece of scorched sheet metal. Sullivan turned the round wheel and pulled the hatch upward to open it.

"And voilà," Marty said, shining his light down a red steel ladder.

"Think you're pretty smart, don't ya?" Emory said, hitting him in the arm.

"Simple physics," he replied. "Who's first?"

"I volunteer you," Sullivan said.

Marty shrugged and stepped forward, but Sullivan grabbed him and pushed him aside. "If you got killed, Princess would never let me hear the end of it."

Emory smiled as he climbed down the ladder. "Careful, John."

"Yeah yeah." After twenty feet he stepped onto the floor

at the bottom and shined his light down a short tunnel into intact living quarters. "Bingo!" he called up. "Cocoon Boy was right. It smells like ass down here, but it didn't catch on fire."

He found a battery-powered lamp on a table and switched it on, filling the room with light as the other two descended the ladder.

The twenty-by-twenty-foot living space was a proper mess and smelled of body odor and excrement. A quick look in the lavatory explained the sewer smell, and Sullivan shut the door. "There's no water to flush with . . . they've been shitting in a bucket."

Emory kicked around in the trash on the floor, many empty food cans and wrappers, scattered books and magazines. Sour smelling blankets and clothing.

"Only took 'em five months to turn into animals," Sullivan muttered.

Emory picked something up from the floor. "Check this out."

The men came to stand on either side of her as she flipped through a pamphlet advertising a company called Survival Estates. It showed the renovation process of a decommissioned minute man missile silo and advertised the sale of individual condos within the newly renovated complexes, all of them sharing a common kitchen area and living room.

Sullivan grabbed the pamphlet away from Emory. "Lemme see that fuckin' thing." He stood paging through it. "You gotta be kidding me. Listen to this: 'Feel secure in the knowledge that no matter what happens to the world above, you and your family will be safe and sound in your own personal Survival Estate.' Survival Estate!" He smirked and gave the pamphlet back. "Those sorry fuckers upstairs deserve a goddamn refund."

Emory paged through the pamphlet, shaking her head. "Fucking twenty-twelvers. My God, how stupid. Get this . . . this little room right here . . . it cost them a hundred grand!"

Sullivan looked at Marty. "And I thought *you* were stupid."

"Oh, it gets better," she went on, turning the page. " 'We offer round-the-clock security, state of the art telecommunications, and guaranteed technical support in the event . . . in the event of any malfunction.' " She laughed and tossed the pamphlet aside.

Sullivan chuckled. "I wonder where the repair crew is."

"I'm wondering something else," Marty said.

They looked at him.

"Where are the missing arms and legs?"

"That's right!" Emory looked at Sullivan. "The bodies in the tent."

"Let's get the fuck outta here," Sullivan said, heading for the ladder. "We must have missed another hatch someplace."

Emory was following him closely up the ladder when she heard a pistol shot from above. Sullivan's full weight crashed onto her and she nearly fell from the ladder with him as he dropped to the concrete below. The hatch slammed above them, and Marty jumped off the bottom rung, shining his light to see a stream of blood running down Sullivan's face from beneath his helmet.

"He's hit, Shannon!"

She scurried down the ladder. "Watch the hatch!" she told him, dragging Sullivan clear. "If it opens, shoot!"

She grabbed the lamp from the table, set it down beside Sullivan's head and pulled off his helmet to get a look at the wound.

"Is he dead?"

"Not yet." Her fingers trembled as she probed his matted hair. "John, can you hear me? John!"

She found the bullet wound, and to her utter surprise, the bullet had not penetrated his skull, but was lodged in the bone just above his hairline. "He's gonna be out of action for a while . . . but he'll live."

"Thank God!"

"Thank Kevlar, Marty. His helmet slowed the bullet down." She decided to leave the bullet where it was for the moment, knowing it would help stanch the flow of blood, and got to her feet. "Any ideas?"

Marty took off his own helmet and stood scratching his itching scalp. "We're rats in a barrel . . . and the idea man is out cold."

"Can they lock us down here?"

He shook his head. "It's not that kind of hatch. It's geared in a two-to-one ratio on this side. That means we only have to turn it half as hard as they do to unlock it. The trouble's going to be fighting our way up out of here . . . and that's your department."

"We need a goddamn grenade," she said.

"What about the launcher?"

"There's no way to open the hatch wide enough to fire it without getting shot, and we don't— Hold on a second!" She took a knee beside Sullivan and pulled a yellow-tipped high-explosive grenade from his harness, remembering something she had learned in basic training. "Something about a centrifugal fuse."

"That's what arms it?"

"Yeah, I think."

"Is the launcher barrel rifled?"

"Yeah, the grenade has to spin in flight to be accurate."

He knelt beside her and took the grenade, spinning it nose down on the concrete like a top. He did this many times, spinning it as fast as he could without bumping it against the floor. "That should do it."

"Don't drop it or you'll blow us to shit."

He put the grenade in his pocket and went to the ladder. "I'll need you to open the hatch so I can throw this thing into the room."

He climbed quietly up to the top, and Emory climbed up tight behind him, hooking into his harness with a carabiner so she would have both of her hands free to push the hatch up. Marty hooked an arm over the top rung to keep them both from falling and took the grenade from his pocket. "Okay," he whispered.

She twisted the wheel to unlock the hatch, and though she could feel someone fighting her on the other side, Marty had been right about the gear ratio, so she was easily defeating the other person. She felt the gear come to the end of its turn and whispered into his ear, "I'm pushing up in three . . . two . . . *one!*"

She had to shove with all her strength to lift whoever was sitting on the hatch, and she felt a muscle pop in her shoulder as she strained against the weight, but the hatch lifted nearly six inches before there was another pistol shot. Marty felt a harmless tug at his body armor as he tossed the grenade through the gap before Emory dropped the hatch.

They heard the blast on the other side, and Emory was shoving the hatch upward even before the flash of fire completely dissipated, urging Marty to climb with her because they were still hooked together. They struggled up from the hole as one being and sprawled on the floor with their legs not quite out of the hatchway, drawing their pistols from their harnesses and trying not to choke on the stench of raw cordite. There were panicked voices coming toward them, flashlights dancing on the walls through the smoke as they opened fire on the tunnel way.

Someone screamed and a flashlight fell, shining back into the tunnel to reveal three more wretched looking souls in filthy clothing, one of them a woman, their eyes wild with hate, their gums bleeding with scurvy.

Emory and Marty shot them down without hesitation and quickly reloaded, laying in wait in the gathering silence for close to ten minutes before daring to speak.

"What do you think?" she whispered into his ear.

"I think we got 'em all this time . . . but who knows?"

They waited another minute before Emory set her weapon aside and unhooked the carabiner from his harness. "You stay put . . . I'll go for the M-4s."

She returned quickly and they searched the immediate area, finding six freshly killed bodies. "Wanna look for their hideout to make sure . . . or get the fuck outta here?"

"Let's get the fuck outta here."

She went below and used smelling salts to bring Sullivan into semiconsciousness. "I need you to help climb outta here!" she urged him, dragging him back and sitting him up at the foot of the ladder.

"What the fuck happened?" he moaned. "My head is splitting!"

"Just climb, John L." She pulled him up by the lift strap on his harness and helped him get his foot onto the bottom rung. It took them some time to reach the top, but within thirty minutes they were all in the hybrid and rolling slowly south over the rocky terrain, the video camera locked up in the glove compartment.

Marty drove while Emory removed the bullet from Sullivan's skull and applied a dressing. Sullivan was still only in and out of consciousness, severely concussed.

"So where we headed?" Marty asked, glancing at her in the mirror.

"Might as well head for Altus AFB down in Oklahoma," she said, climbing into the front and grabbing the road atlas. "We can give that camera of Yon's to her geologist friends and see what kind of setup they got, maybe stay with them . . . unless you got a better idea."

"I'm all out of ideas."

She studied the atlas as they bounced along. "Okay. We'll find a highway and drop down to Interstate 80, then cut east across Nebraska and drop down through Kansas by way of Topeka. That'll put us real close to Altus when we hit Oklahoma."

"Kansas," he groaned. "You ever been through Kansas?"

She chuckled and closed the atlas. "One good thing about Kansas, Marty . . . an asteroid strike could only be an improvement."

# THIRTY-EIGHT

MAJOR BENJAMIN MORIARTY PUSHED BACK FROM THE TABLE and sat studying what was left of his decimated officer corps. He was down to four lieutenants now and a mere handful of noncoms, having been forced the day before to put Captains Winterfield, Scarborough, and Phelter—along with ten other enlisted men—before a firing squad after trying them all for sedition and attempted mutiny. The one positive result of the debacle was that the battle for the collective conscience of the men was finally decided, and those few hundred who remained in the ranks now understood that the weak must serve to bolster the strong in whatever capacity was required, and that morality was no longer anything more than a defunct and pointless luxury.

The meal had been meager. A potluck affair of heated vegetables poured from mostly label-less cans scavenged from in and around the city of Denver. The meat had been provided by Captain Winterfield, and it was only the third time the officers were driven to eat another human being. The regular ranks had been supplementing their diet with human flesh for the better part of a month now, but Moriarty and his staff were still in the process of learning that it was an acquired taste, to say the most.

"Lieutenant Ford," he said quietly, picking at his teeth

with a thin sliver of wire. "Direct the cooks to find another way to season the meat."

"Yes, sir."

"Captain Winterfield may have been a candyass, but there's no reason he should taste like one." His men chortled dutifully, all of them having difficulty with the sweet flavor of human flesh.

"Lieutenant Yoder," Moriarty said, noting the bilious look of his most junior officer. "You look a little green around the gills, son."

"I'm sorry, sir. It's still a little hard for me. I'll adjust, sir. Don't worry."

It was no secret that Yoder had been a friend of Captain Winterfield, and Moriarty had chosen Winterfield for their meal with precisely that in mind. "I'm sure you will, son. You're a fine officer and I'm depending on you to set an equally fine example for the men."

"Sir."

"Now, if the rest of you will excuse us, Lieutenant Ford and I have some things to discuss before retreat."

The small hotel dining room cleared, and Ford sat looking at Moriarty through a pair of sagging eyes. He was sallow and gaunt-looking and his gums had begun to recede with the onset of scurvy.

"Eat some more," Moriarty said with a gesture toward the platter in the center of the table.

"I'm fine, sir. Thank you."

"Eat! You're dying before my eyes, damnit, and I need you strong!"

"I'll only throw it up, Ben."

"Should I have put you on trial as well?"

"You know very well that I support you," Ford remarked wearily. "It's not my fault that starvation and cannibalism disagree with me."

Moriarty despised the smaller man's weakness but he needed him too badly, knowing that Ford was the glue between him and the rest of his staff.

"Then I want you eating two cans of cat food a day from now on," Moriarty said, realizing that he was playing right into the lieutenant's hands, but there was nothing to be done about it. Waiting him out wasn't working.

"Yes, sir," Ford said, wanting to shout *Hallelujah!* but concealing his victory.

"You will, of course, be expected to eat the minimum amount of meat before the rest of the staff. If they find out I'm treating you special, we've got more trouble."

"Yes, sir. Have you given any more thought to my suggestion, Ben? The one about those Green Berets back in Nebraska?"

"I've thought about them once or twice. It's too much of a long shot. They're not likely to be any better off by now than we are. We only took them two truckloads of MREs. They're probably long dead."

"I don't think the MREs were the reason for our delivery," Ford remarked.

"Meaning?"

"Meaning what did they need a defense network computer for . . . unless they intended on still being alive to use it when the sky cleared up enough to communicate with our defense satellites?"

Moriarty stared at him, reasoning it out. "A silo could hold a great deal of food. *If* someone had had time enough to prepare."

"And it would be just like the Pentagon to lay an egg that would hatch years later . . . all in the name of being the last nation left standing."

"Fine," Moriarty decided. "We'll send a patrol of trusted men back to Tinker for the silo schematics. The original blueprints will still be on file. When they get back we can begin working our way east, scavenging whatever we can along the way. And we'll need to quietly inquire as to whether there are any demolitions men in the ranks . . . because if that wiseass Green Beret captain *is* still alive, he sure as hell isn't going to open the goddamn door and give us back our MREs."

# THIRTY-NINE

"SO WHAT WAS THE PROBLEM?" FORREST ASKED, LEARNING that Danzig and Vasquez had successfully unclogged one of the facility's three commodes.

"White mice," Danzig said. "The women are flushing their tampons down the toilets, and this old plumbing won't take it. They'll snag in there and clog the whole fucking system, so you have to tell them to stop. Tell them to bag the damn things and we'll keep them in the cargo bay."

"Something else I should have thought of. Thanks. I'll be sure and tell them."

The children were all in class, so Forrest was able to catch a number of women together in the cafeteria. Some of them were talking, others reading. A couple were arguing. About what, he didn't really care to know.

"Excuse me, ladies."

They all looked at him, waiting to hear what sort of law he was going to lay down now.

"Yes?" Erin said patiently.

"We need to not flush our feminine products down the toilets anymore," he said as tactfully as he knew how. "The plumbing down here is very old, so the pipes are rusty inside and if we get another clog and can't get to it . . ."

"Won't be good," somebody said.

"Won't be good, right. So we'll put bags in the bathrooms and store the trash in the cargo bay."

"Message received."

He went back down the hall and into one of the two common rooms where Melissa was sitting on the floor with a pad of paper and a pencil. "Hey, kiddo. Where the hell is everyone?"

"Some are in silo one listening to music," she answered, her attention on her work. "Some are in the other room watching an R movie they don't want the kids to see. One or two are bike riding, I think. And Veronica and Uncle Michael are in Medical talking to the doctors. One of Uncle Michael's fillings fell out or something."

"What are you doing?"

"I'm trying to figure out this code those people are transmitting," she said, flipping through the pages of numbers Ulrich had written down. The transmissions only occurred about three times a week for half an hour or so and not necessarily on the same nights.

"You know about cryptography?" he asked, surprised.

"No, just some basic stuff Wayne told me, but I've been thinking these people probably agree when to talk again before they sign off at night, so I'm looking for patterns of numbers that appear only on certain days. Maybe if I can learn their codes for the days of the week, I can use that information as part of a cipher. Only, I haven't found anything that matches yet and it's pissing me— Oops!" She looked up at him, covering her mouth. "That slipped."

"You're grounded. No leaving the silo for a week."

She smiled, enjoying having him as even a pseudo authority figure in her life. "It's driving me nuts."

"You do know there are literally millions of different algorithms, right?"

"Yeah, but Wayne thinks this one is pretty basic, and I don't have anything else interesting to work on down here. It's killing me not having the Internet. I miss my physics chats."

"Physics chat rooms . . . you're kidding me."

"No. Why, does that sound stupid?"

"Hell, no. I just never heard of it. I guess there used to be a chat room for everything."

"I can't believe it's all gone."

"I know," he said sympathetically. "Hey, before I forget . . . we've been having some trouble with hygiene products in the—"

"I know. Don't flush my tampons down the toilet. I heard you guys in the hall."

"You did, huh?"

"I hear everything that goes on in the hall. I even heard . . . never mind."

"Never mind what?"

She leaned forward, trying to see. "Is anyone out there?"

Forrest double-checked. "No, it's fine. What'd you hear?"

"I heard Oscar and Maria two the other night. They were in the kitchen when everyone else was asleep."

"No, honey, you got it mixed up. Oscar's wife is Maria one."

"I know that," she said. "He was in there with Maria *two*."

Forrest's *Oh, shit!* light began to blink. "You're positive? They look and sound a lot alike."

"I'm positive. I saw her coming back to bed after . . . you know. He was working the late shift in Launch Control."

Forrest crouched down beside her. "So who was in the LC when they were in the kitchen?"

She shrugged. "I don't know, but I don't think anybody was."

"When was this?"

"Few nights ago."

"Don't tell anyone else," he said, standing up. "Let me know when you've cracked the code."

Laddie suddenly came scrabbling around the corner into the room, soaking wet and full of suds, running and jumping all over Melissa and dripping water onto her pad.

"Laddie!" she shouted, holding the pad over her head.

"He's down here!" Karen called down the hall as she came

into the room laughing, her jeans wet from the waist down. "Sorry, honey. Somebody left the washroom door open."

"That's okay," Melissa said, though it bothered her very much.

"I told you washing that dog's more trouble than it's worth," Forrest said, chuckling.

Renee showed up and, with a great deal of effort, the two women wrangled Laddie out of the room and disappeared into the hall, laughing.

Forrest followed after them.

"Jack?" Melissa said.

He stopped. "Yeah?"

"Think you and Veronica will ever get married?"

"I don't know," he said thoughtfully. "Why do you ask?"

She shrugged. "Just wondering."

On his way back to Launch Control, Maria Vasquez stopped him. "I want to ask you about something, Jack."

"What's on your mind?" he asked, preparing himself to lie for Oscar.

"Do you think for Halloween we could turn one of the silos into a haunted house for the kids? Nothing gory. Just spooks and ghosts, maybe some witches."

"You know, I don't see why not," he said with relief. "We'll have to be careful about the lighting, though. We don't want anyone falling on those stairs."

"Great. It's something to do, you know? And the kids should get a kick out of it."

"Sounds fine to me," he said. He had already secretly planned a trick-or-treat for them, and was looking forward to it.

He found Ulrich in Launch Control with his feet up, reading one of his technical magazines. "Erin and Lynette were arguing about something in the cafeteria." He took a chair.

"What about?"

"I didn't pay attention."

"That's a good policy," Ulrich said.

"I've been giving some thought to our future food concerns. Hydroponic tomatoes are only going to get us so far. What do you think about raising rats?"

"Rats?"

"Yeah. We find some rats, breed them in clean cages, and eat them. The damn things multiply faster than rabbits."

"You ever eaten one?"

"Yeah, we ate a few back at Bragg during training. No big deal. Splash a little Tabasco on them and they taste like anything else. Look, meat's meat. And West can show us how to raise them without a big health risk."

"It's a repugnant idea," Ulrich said. "The women will never go for it, and Erin's likely to freak the hell out."

"By the time the food runs out, she won't find the idea so disagreeable."

"So what are you proposing? We catch a few and keep them as pets without telling anybody what they're really for? These broads are smart, Jack. They'll figure it out."

"Well, it may not matter. So far it looks like we've done too good a job of killing them off down here."

Ulrich frowned. "I don't think that's going to be a problem. We've seen a few rats gnawing on the dead guys upstairs. It's only a matter of time before the bodies are gone and they find their way down here again."

"Great, so problem solved," Forrest said, getting up. "Put Oscar to work building some live bait traps."

"I'll put Linus on it. He's better with his hands."

"No, I want Oscar to do it. He apparently has too much fucking free time."

"What's that mean?"

"We'll raise the little bastards in secret," Forrest said, and disappeared into the hall.

Ulrich sat back and returned to his article. "And if I had wheels, I'd be a wagon."

**LATE THAT NIGHT** Forrest was sitting alone in the LC reading *For Whom the Bell Tolls* when Melissa came in and sat down at the console with her paper and pencil. He glanced at the clock to see that it was three A.M.

"Can't sleep?"

"No. Do you think I could scan the radio frequencies?"

He looked at her and smiled. "*That's* why you're up late. Wayne won't let you play with the radio."

She ignored the remark. "I know the code talkers aren't on now, but I want to see if anyone else might be talking."

"Wayne runs a scan twice a day."

"I know, but he's not scanning now . . ."

"Use the bottom set," he told her. "If you mess with his, he'll know and he'll skin us both."

"But that's the junky set," she whined. "Wayne's is digital and its got—"

"Yeah, I know, it's got all the cool lights. I thought this wasn't about playtime."

"Well, digital is better and—"

"Digital is not better. It's newer, and that's not the same thing. You can't fine-tune with digital the way you can with analog."

"What's that mean?"

"What do you mean 'what's that mean'? Aren't you a computer whiz?"

"I'm a physics geek, not a computer geek. Big difference. Huge."

"Okay, well, the dial on the analog set is a rheostat . . . it works like a dimmer switch, so you can fine-tune the frequencies—if you're patient. With the digital set you're either on the frequency or you're off, no fine-tuning."

"But what good's a signal if it's full of static?"

He closed his book, marking the page with his thumb, and sat looking at her. "Well, Wayne, what good is a clean frequency if there's nobody on it?"

She grinned. "So then why does 'Wayne' use the new one if the old one is better?"

"Because he is a bonehead . . . because he is too impatient

for fine-tuning . . . and because he has always trusted the latest technology even when it sucked."

"O-kay," she said sarcastically. "I-think-I-get-the-point." She scooted over to the shelf in her chair and turned on the more simple looking analog set. "How long do I have to wait for this antique to warm up?"

He chuckled as he reopened the book. "It's not that old, you little smartass. And remember to move the dial in tiny increments. Take your time."

After a minute Melissa picked up on a faint signal . . .

*"Mayday, Mayday. This is Genoine Five,"* a scared sounding woman was saying. *"Does anyone copy? Anyone at all? If you can hear me, please, we are in Birch Tree, Missouri. We need your help! We need food and medicine. Mayday, Mayday. This is Genoine Five. Does anyone copy? Anyone at all? If you can . . ."*

"I found somebody!"

Forrest had already heard the transmission many times and did not even look up from the book. "It's a trap, honey."

She turned to look at him in confusion. "How do you know that?"

"Because no one's listening at her end. She's on a loop. Same message over and over. Which either means that everyone in Beech Tree is dead or it's a trap."

"She sounds scared to death."

"I'm sure she is—or was when she made that tape. She's likely dead by now."

Melissa turned the volume down, a scared feeling in the pit of her stomach. "But why would she . . ."

He set the book aside, realizing this sort of thinking was entirely alien to her.

"You take a female prisoner," he explained. "Someone like you or Veronica, maybe. You give her a microphone and a simple script and you tell her to sound scared—which won't be too tough with a knife at her throat. Then you play the recording over the airwaves for every idiot predator with a radio to hear. After that you just have to hope whoever comes to Beech Tree looking for—"

"*Birch* Tree."

"Thank you, *Wayne*. As I was saying . . . you just have to hope that whoever comes to town looking for the woman on the radio has a smaller gang than your gang. If they do, you kill them and take their stuff. If they don't . . . well, you lay low and pray to Christ they leave town without finding your ass."

"No way!" she said in mortified fascination. "For real?"

"For real."

"You've done stuff like that, haven't you?" she said, her eyes shining with an almost prurient enthusiasm. "Uncle Michael says you're *dangerous*."

He smiled, recalling a once younger version of himself. "Your uncle Michael says a lot of things."

"He says that before the boogeyman goes to bed at night he probably checks under the bed for you."

Forrest laughed. "I'll take that as a compliment."

"Tell me something you've done!"

He shook his head, chuckling. "No. That's not the kind of thing I need to be sharing with young ladies."

She bristled. "So it's not my age this time? It's because I'm a girl."

"Maybe I worded that wrong. Some things done during war can sound shameful out of context, and it's not the kind of thing I prefer to talk about with anyone, man or woman."

"Because I might get the wrong idea?"

"More because you might get the *right* idea. War is a bad, bad thing."

"Uncle Michael says we're in a war now."

"Unfortunately, he's right," Forrest said, opening his book and sitting back in the chair.

Melissa sat back too, and watched him for a long moment before returning to the receiver and beginning once again to slowly turn the dial . . .

*"Constantine, go ahead with your traffic . . . over."*

*"Jawbreaker, we cannot make the rendezvous at this time. The entire mountain is on fire and we are cut off. Is there an alternative route that we can try?. . . . Over."*

*"Negative, negative, Constantine. The mountain pass is your best bet. If you try going around to the north or south, you'll be cut to pieces . . . over."*

*"What about the tunnel? . . . Over."*

*"Ambush central, Constantine. I'm afraid it's up and over or not at all . . . over."*

A simple glance over her shoulder told Melissa that Forrest was no more shaken by this transmission than by the first. "Have you heard these guys already too?"

*"We'll try again after dark, Jawbreaker . . . over and out."*

Forrest glanced up from the book just long enough to reply, "We've heard Jawbreaker before, not the other guy."

"So who's Jawbreaker?"

"No one who can help us. Scan on, my child. Get it out of your system."

So she turned the dial some more, picking up another, weaker transmission . . .

*" . . . but my batteries won't last long after my fuel runs out, eh. Plus I won't be able to run my chain saw, and this cabin's gonna get pretty damn cold."*

*"Yeah, well, join the club, eh. We've only got enough firewood left out here for maybe a few weeks. The whole damn forest is burnt down . . ."*

Melissa continued to turn the dial, eventually coming upon another conversation in progress . . .

*" . . . so what I need to know is how to convert this old diesel motor over to vegetable oil. I've got a few thousand gallons of old fryer oil out back."*

*"Well, first you have to install an auxiliary fuel tank with a heat exchanger in it. And it don't sound much like you've got the necessary—"*

Melissa didn't care even a little bit about veggie oil cars so she moved on . . .

*" . . . which is bullshit! You tell your friends over there I*

*don't care how much food you've got left. I've got twenty-five scarecrows on this bus and I'm coming across that god-damn bridge whether they like it not!"*

*"They'll shoot you, Don! I'm not kidding, goddamnit!"*

*"Well, I'm comin'!"*

Melissa waited almost five minutes to hear what happened next.

"You can forget them," Forrest muttered. "They're gone."

She reluctantly turned the dial, realizing she had just heard someone's last words, but another signal caught her attention before she had the chance to dwell . . .

*"We have repelled repeated attacks. Our perimeter is holding. That's not the problem. Our problem is food. We can't survive much longer without you, and you can't survive long-term without our power. We're wasting time even debating this."*

The voice was female.

"Jack!"

"I'm listening," he said, appearing interested for the first time.

*"It's not that simple,"* a male voice replied. *"You're talking about us traveling three hundred miles through extremely dangerous territory. We need to wait. Let the lunatics starve off."*

Forrest set the book aside and moved toward the receiver for a closer look at the radio frequency.

*"If I didn't know better, Patrick, I'd say you were waiting for us to starve so you could take over the facility when you get here."*

*"Valerie, shut up. We could do that anyway."*

*"How long until your heating oil runs out?"*

*"Nine weeks. Maybe less."*

*"Well, we won't last nine weeks without your assistance. We've barely got a month before we start looking at our dogs in a whole new way."*

Patrick did not immediately respond.

"They're gonna eat their dogs?" Melissa mumbled.

Forrest nodded as he marked the frequency on a pad. "It happens."

"*Val . . . I'm not the sole decider over here . . . I'll talk to the council and see what they say. That's all I can promise.*"

"A friggin council," Forrest muttered, tossing the pad onto the shelf.

"*Well, you be sure to tell your stupid council this . . . you tell them that before the last of us shoots herself : . . we'll disable every one of these goddamn mills! You hear me? There won't be enough juice left out here to run a goddamn lightbulb!*"

"*Val, you could hardly disable all those mills. Just try to be patient. Please.*"

"*We can sure as hell destroy this facility . . . and don't think we won't! If you're waiting for us to die off, there won't be shit left when you get here!*"

"*Jesus Christ, Val! Will you please try to understand our situation? Nobody's waiting for you to die off! We've got old people and children to consider here.*"

"*And we don't?*"

"*You're not the only ones who have been attacked, Val. How can we move two hundred people all that way and protect them?*"

"*I'm not suggesting you make the trip in a goddamn wagon train, Patrick. Groups of ten or twelve at time would do the job. Two trucks, moving fast, and you could—*"

"*I gotta go, Val. I'll call you tomorrow at noon.*"

"*Don't leave us hanging, Patrick. Please.*"

"*I'll do what I can. I promise. Over and out.*"

"Maybe *we* can join them!" Melissa said excitedly.

"Settle down there, young communicator," Forrest said, shoving his chair back toward the console. "Grab me the en reel index from the top shelf over there."

"What index?" she said, getting up and walking around the console to the far side of the round room.

"N.R.E.L.," he said, pronouncing each letter separately. "National Renewable Energy Laboratories. It's a map index."

She found the index beneath some manuals and brought it over. It was about the size of a common road atlas, full of colorful maps denoting wind corridors along with the locations of transmission lines that carried power from the nation's many wind farms to population centers.

"You guys thought of everything," she said, setting the index down.

"Hardly," he chuckled. "But we were thinking we might hook into a wind turbine someday. This index is as far as the plan ever got."

"But if these people already know how to make them work and want our help . . . I wonder where they are."

"They could be damn near anywhere," he muttered, flipping through the index. "But it's good to know somebody else is thinking long-term. They took a serious risk staying aboveground, though."

"Maybe we should offer to go and help them," she suggested again. "We could tell her to forget that Patrick guy."

"Their main problem seems to be food," he said. "We can't solve that."

"Shouldn't we at least talk to her?"

"Way too soon," he said, tracing his finger along a power route through Colorado.

"But they need help and if—"

"She sounds desperate, honey, and desperate people are potentially very dangerous—in any circumstance. Though you're right, we haven't heard anything like this before, so it's worth keeping an ear on them."

"There seem to be a lot more survivors out there than you guys have told us about."

"And fewer every day," he said, turning the page. "I wonder if they're out in the San Gorgonio Pass."

"That place is huge!" she said. "My dad drove us through there once. There's like four thousand windmills out there."

"And the land is barren for hundreds of miles," he added

thoughtfully. "Which would make an extended siege difficult at best. You'd have to hit them fast and hard."

"Shouldn't we tell the others about this? It's a pretty big
deal."

"This is a case of what they don't know won't hurt them.
So don't go blabbing."

"But—"

"I'm serious, Melissa. False hopes are bad news, and it's
way too soon to get excited about these people. We have to
be careful with morale."

Just then the floors and walls began to vibrate as if a train
were rumbling beneath them. There was no real movement
because of the shock dampeners that protected the installation, but the rumbling in the earth was unmistakable.

"Whoa," Melissa said, instinctively placing her hand on
the console, though there was no need to steady herself.
"That isn't just a tremor, is it?"

"Doesn't feel like one."

There had been a number of tremors since the asteroid
impact, but none of them had caused so much vibration
within the facility.

"Are we still safe?"

"We're fine," he said. "We're nowhere near any of the
known fault lines, and it would take a major shift to crack
us open."

A couple of minutes later Ulrich wandered sleepily into
Launch Control in his bare feet. "That one woke damn near
everybody up," he said. "What have you two been doing?"

"It sounds like somebody's forded up on a wind farm,"
Forrest said, tapping the index. "I'm guessing San Gorgonio.
My assistant here picked up some new traffic. We'll need to
make sure we're listening tomorrow."

Ulrich cocked an eyebrow at Melissa. "And who said you
could use my radio?"

"I didn't touch your crappy radio," she said, crossing her
arms. "Everybody knows analog's better than digital."

He looked at Forrest. "I guess I don't have to ask where she got that."

"Don't look at me," Forrest said. "I'm not the only one who thinks digital sucks."

"Yeah, well I wasn't talking about the bullshit opinion," Ulrich said, turning for the door. "I was talking about the smartmouth."

When he was gone, Melissa looked at Forrest. "I think I made him mad."

He shrugged and went back to the index. "You may have."

"But . . . but what if he doesn't want to copy down the code for me anymore?"

He looked at her and smiled. "You should have thought of that before you got salty with him."

"But I was . . ."

"But you were what?" he said with a chuckle.

"Well he was the one who . . . He's always such a grouch. Can you fix it for me?"

He laughed and closed the index, picking up his book again. "Your mouth wrote the check, kiddo, not mine."

"But he . . . he was the one who . . ."

He chuckled again as he refound his place in the novel. "You say that like it matters."

# FORTY

EARLY THE NEXT DAY MARIA VASQUEZ AND A NUMBER OF THE
other mothers were busying themselves with the work of
turning silo one into a spook house. They were on the far
side of the silo hanging a number of sheets and black trash
bags to serve as curtains, cordoning off little hiding places
for the witches and ghosts who would soon lie in wait for the
unsuspecting children. Ulrich emerged from the tunnel and
stood on the main deck watching them with his hands on his
hips. He had already been recruited to dress up as a mummy,
and though he felt a little stupid about it, he knew the party
would be a great distraction for the children.

Melissa was in the silo as well, but she wasn't helping with
the Halloween project. She was busy up above with her deciphering project, which had so far yielded nothing in the way
of cracking the code. She listened to Ulrich talking with the
other women and eventually decided she had better walk
down to the main deck and find out if she was on his shit
list. The trip downstairs made her feel like when she was a
little girl and got in trouble with her parents. Only it wasn't
her loving father waiting three decks below but a perpetu-
ally dour soldier who didn't seem to have much in the way
of a paternal instinct.

Ulrich glanced briefly in her direction as she came down the stairs, then went back to talking with Karen and Maria about where they might displace some of the food bundles until after the haunted silo project was finished. She walked over and stood listening, realizing now that Ulrich was definitely annoyed with her because, while his glance wasn't disdainful, it hadn't been exactly pleasant either.

"Very well, then," he said. "Just so nothing falls over on anyone."

"Amen," Karen chuckled.

He turned to walk away without a word to Melissa, and she stood watching him go, debating whether it would even be worth the effort of trying to get back into his good graces. She asked herself whether it would matter if she didn't need him to write out the Morse code transmissions for her. Deciding it would, she trotted after him. "Wayne?"

He stopped and turned to look at her. "Yes?"

"I'm sorry."

"About what?"

"For smarting off to you last night."

Only the slightest of perceptible grins came to his lips. "Realized you need me for the code?"

"Even if I didn't, I still wouldn't want you mad at me. I didn't think before I spoke."

He smiled, understanding she had only been trying to buddy up with Forrest, wishing that he had a better excuse to be pissed with her, disliking his own vulnerability. "I thought you might get Jack to smooth it over for you."

"He said my mouth wrote the check."

Ulrich laughed. "He did, huh?"

"He said I shouldn't have gotten salty with you."

He laughed some more. "Well, you know you're wasting your time with that goddamn code, don't you?"

She shrugged. "I don't have anything else to do, though. I never knew I could get so bored. I don't know what it is . . . nobody else seems to be."

Ulrich reflected that the more intelligent the creature, the more negative the effects of confinement. He recalled briefly his first and only visit to the zoo as a child, the gorillas in their cages with the saddest, most tragic expressions he had ever seen.

"Well, I appreciate the apology," he said quietly. "But the truth is that you've got more than enough of the code now. You're not going to find anything new by continuing to copy it down. Especially if they're altering it."

"Altering it?"

"They may change it from night to night. Just enough to throw off a code breaker."

"Do you think they are?"

"There's no way to tell if the changes are minor. Either way, you're better off sticking with what you've got. Honestly."

"You're not just saying that?"

He shook his head. "If I was mad at you, I'd tell you. Ask Jack."

"Were you before?"

"I was trying to be."

She bit her lip, hesitating a moment, then, "How come you don't let people get close to you?"

He stood looking at her, surprised she had asked. "Because people die."

FORREST WALKED INTO Launch Control and sat on the edge of the console. "Excuse us, Linus."

Danzig gave Vasquez a quick look and got up from his chair. "I guess I can use a break." He pulled the door closed after him, and Forrest sat looking down on Vasquez.

"Look, Jack, before you read me the—"

"Shut the fuck up!" Forrest snapped.

Vasquez sat back in his chair, unprepared for Forrest's anger.

"This isn't a goddamn frat house! Who the fuck do you think you are, deserting your goddamn post?"

"Oh!" Vasquez said. "I . . . I'm sorry. You're right. It won't happen again. I mean I—"

"And who are you diddling besides Maria two?" Forrest quickly demanded, sensing that Vasquez had been expecting to get his ass chewed for an entirely different encounter.

Vasquez hesitated. "Um . . . Renee . . . and Joann."

"Jesus Christ! And none of 'em minds about the others?"

Vasquez shrugged. "I don't think they know."

"You bet your sweet ass they don't know!" Forrest flared. "Because the second one of 'em finds about the other two, they're gonna tell your wife so goddamn fast you won't know whether to shit or wind your watch!"

"I don't think so," Vasquez said innocently. "They ain't like that. I mean . . . they know I ain't gonna be around long . . . you know? And I think they like the thrill of doing something bad . . . seize the day and all that."

"I'm gonna seize something," Forrest told him, standing up from the console and shaking loose a cigarette, "and it won't be your goddamn day. So who's Linus screwing—and don't tell me nobody! He skulked outta here looking guilty as shit."

"Nobody, I swear. He just covers for me sometimes . . . like the other night with Maria two. I didn't abandon my post, Captain. I'd never do that."

Forrest at least took some comfort in that. "It stops now. Understood? If I find it's still going on, I'll tell Maria myself. Got it?"

Vasquez nodded. "But suppose they don't agree?"

"What the fuck does that mean?"

Vasquez shrugged again. "I'm just saying they look forward to it . . . you know?"

"End it, Oscar!"

"Yes, sir."

**HALF AN HOUR** later Forrest's voice announced calmly over the intercom: *"Wayne and Melissa to the LC. Wayne and Melissa to the LC."*

When they arrived in Launch Control, Forrest and Vasquez were sitting in front of the receiver listening intently to a very panicked radio transmission.

"Kiddo, it sounds like your wind farm friends are getting zapped," Forrest said, offering her a chair. "Along with Patrick and his gang."

"Both? But how—"

" . . . *and you're sure you didn't tell anyone where we are?*" Patrick was demanding.

"*Yes!*" Valerie replied in a shout, with gunfire obvious in the background. "*They're hitting us too, goddamnit! I told you! None of our people ever even leave here. One of your people must have said something, one of your scavenging parties maybe. Patrick, you've been double-crossed!*"

"No, he hasn't," Vasquez muttered, shaking his head. "Stupid *pendejos!*"

Melissa stood staring at the radio, almost as if she were watching the drama play out on television.

"*No way!*" Patrick insisted. "*The leak has to be at your end! Can you escape on your own somehow?*"

"*Escape? We're completely surrounded! They've got rocket launchers, Patrick. You've got to come help us!*"

"I don't understand what's happening," Melissa said. "What did we miss?"

"I called you the second I turned it on," Forrest said.

"*I'm sorry, Val. We'll be lucky to save ourselves. I'm hoping they'll let us go once they see we've left the food behind. We're pulling out right now. Gotta go. Good luck to you!*"

"*Patrick, no! . . . Patrick, are you there? . . . Patriiiick! . . . Patriiiiiick!*"

"Turn it off," Ulrich said. "Turn it off, Oscar."

"*Patrii—*"

"But . . . but what the hell happened?" Melissa demanded, clearly crestfallen, her eyes darting between the three men.

"They've obviously been talking back and forth in the blind for some time," Forrest said sadly. "Broadcasting for anyone and everyone to listen in. They were naive."

"But . . . what does that mean?"

"It means that someone's been triangulating their individual signals," Ulrich explained. "Someone with the resources, the muscle, and the patience to arrange a simultaneous assault."

"And that's why we don't talk to anybody without a damn good reason," Forrest said. "There are just enough people left alive out there to finish killing each other off."

"That's sick!" she said in disgust. "They weren't hurting anybody! They were just . . . they were just trying to survive."

"This is also why we don't relate every contact to the other women," Ulrich added, having already discussed the matter of Melissa monitoring the radio in great detail with Forrest earlier that morning, right down to the part about her smarting off, the two of them agreeing to wait and see whether she would apologize. "Too many of these disappointments would irreparably damage morale. So understand that you've been trusted with something very important here today."

With effort, Melissa broke eye contact with him long enough for a glance at Forrest, who confirmed what Ulrich had said with a nod. "You guys knew this would happen," she said quietly, looking at the floor.

"No," Forrest said. "But now you see the trouble we could have been in had we joined in on their conversation last night. It's possible we could have brought this same kind of hell down on ourselves—even though it's likely the triangulation had already been done."

"But not necessarily," Vasquez warned.

"Those women are gonna be . . . they'll be raped, won't they?"

"Let us hope not," Ulrich said quietly. "There are alternatives."

She stood looking at the three men. "So I should keep this a secret?"

"What do you think?" Forrest asked.

"I think we're just buying time down here," she replied, suddenly feeling a new kind of heaviness.

"Do you want the others to start believing that? To start dwelling on it?"

She shook her head. "I won't say anything. I don't feel good. I think I'm gonna go take a nap."

"Okay," Forrest said. "I'm sorry, kiddo."

"Yeah . . . me too."

When she was gone Ulrich dropped down into a chair with a sigh, squeezing his temples between his forefinger and thumb. "So is the military hitting civilians now? Is that what we just heard?"

Forrest switched the set back on just long enough to make sure there was nothing more to hear and switched it off again. "I think we'd damn well better assume as much," he said gravely. "And what's that tell us . . . the military has finally degraded to the point of committing murder?"

"Men are men," Vasquez said. "And men with guns aren't going hungry if they don't have to."

"So you'd kill an innocent for his food—*her* food?"

"If she left me no choice," Vasquez answered without batting an eye. "I've got a family to feed."

"That's too easy," Forrest said. "Say it's just you?"

"Maybe I'd split it with her, offer her a pact like we've made down here. Look, I'm not a murderer and I sure as hell ain't no rapist . . . but a starving person doesn't have any choice about food. Instinct will make him do what he has to do to get it."

"That's bullshit," Forrest said. "Starvation isn't rabies. Gandhi starved himself damned near to death more than once just to make a fucking point."

"Well, I ain't Gandhi either," Vasquez said, and chuckled.

"What I'm saying is that giving up your dignity is a conscious choice," Forrest said. "It's a choice you make ahead of time. You decide that you're either going to throw in the towel after a certain point or you're going to be the last one standing no matter the cost."

"I won't argue that. But if the military hit that wind farm, the common grunt didn't have that luxury."

"Horseshit. No one hit that farm who didn't want to. A man can step back and take stock of himself at any time."

Vasquez sat forward in the chair. "That might be true for you, Captain. You're a leader . . . not all of us are. Some of us are happy to follow, and not all followers are lucky about who they get as leaders. Personally . . . without you two dudes . . . I don't know how I'd handle any of this."

Forrest stood up and tousled the younger man's hair on his way to the coffeepot. "Well, not all leaders are lucky about who they get to follow them either."

Ulrich smiled at Vasquez, hiding his concern about what Forrest referred to as the "insulin habit." He and Forrest had asked Vasquez and Danzig both to come in on the project precisely because they *were* followers. They were not blind devotees, but were highly skilled operatives who could be depended upon to follow orders in a paramilitary setting without a great deal of debate. Kane of course was his own story. He was their noncommissioned officer, the perfect blend of capable and aloof; that he agreed to join them had been as much a compliment as their having asked.

"You're sure you didn't talk to those people last night?" Ulrich said, shifting his attention to Forrest. "We don't need a proper military outfit showing up outside our door."

"Wayne . . . come on "

"I just don't want any surprises, Jack."

"I was only on the air for a few seconds . . ." Forrest kept his face serious.

"What . . . ?"

"Long enough to broadcast our address five or six times." Then Forrest smiled.

Ulrich shook his head, Vasquez grinning.

"Ask a stupid question," Forrest said, sipping his coffee, "and ye shall receive a stupid answer."

# FORTY-ONE

THE HALLOWEEN PARTY, ESPECIALLY FORREST'S SURPRISE
box of candy, was a big hit with the children. The next day,
however, the mothers were a little less than thrilled about
the candy, the first sweets the kids had eaten since coming
to live in the silo nearly five months earlier. They had gotten
into it first thing that morning and were now so hyper that
Andie found herself completely unable to hold their attention during class.

After forty minutes of fruitless effort, she released them
all back into the care of their mothers and went to find Forrest, cornering him below the main facility outside the entrance to the electrical room.

"Do you know what you've done giving out all that candy
at once?"

"Other than putting you mothers on the spot?" he said,
wiping the sweat from his face and neck with a towel.

"Yeah, other than that. There are thirteen kids upstairs
running around like little maniacs on a sugar high. I had to
dismiss class already."

He stood looking at her, struggling to keep the smile from
his face.

"What do they get for Christmas? A bag of cocaine?"

He snickered. "Maybe. You'll have to wait and see."

"Did you give any thought at all to the fact those kids haven't had any sugar to speak of in almost five months?"

"I don't believe you're down here chewing my ass because I gave the kids Halloween candy." He flipped the towel over his shoulder. "What's really got you in a twist?"

"What's that supposed to mean?" she said, crossing her arms in an effort to disguise a sudden insecurity. "Don't try to change the subject."

"Well, to answer your question. Yes. I did give it some thought. In fact, the mummy and I had ourselves quite a laugh about it last night as we were passing it out."

"Well, that was irresponsible as hell."

"Yes, it was, wasn't it?" he said with a grin. "And yet I've succeeded in adding a little bit of harmless drama to all of your otherwise monotonous lives. Even to my own, it turns out."

She bit the inside of her cheek, failing to hide a smile as she recognized his deviousness. "You're a manipulator, Jack Forrest."

"I'm a goddamn wizard, is what I am. This little Halloween stunt of mine will be good for days' worth of conversation and playful recrimination—just like we're having right now. And when it finally wears off, God willing, I'll find something else irresponsible to do in order to keep you women distracted and away from one another's throats. That is unless you decide to go upstairs and blow my goddamn cover."

She laughed, shaking her head in perplexity. "How does Veronica manage you?"

"She doesn't."

"I don't know whether to envy her or to feel sorry for her."

"Oh, yes, you do."

Her eyebrows soared. "Egotistical much?"

"Lady, I goddamn well better be. I'm trying to pull off the coup of the century down here and I need all the juice I can get."

Andie could tell from his body language that all she had

to do to seduce him was say something, anything, to prompt him. Anything that would absolve him of responsibility for something happening between them, however flimsy. Her body ached for a man, her chest constricting. But she couldn't bring herself to tell him how badly she needed him. Was it pride? Or fear of offending Veronica and losing her friendship? In the end it probably came down to both.

"Don't worry, your secret's safe with me," she said quietly, feeling suddenly deflated. "I didn't mean any—"

"You didn't give any. This has been the most excitement I've had in weeks. Feel free to make up a reason to berate me anytime."

Her jaw dropped but she didn't say anything, knowing she was busted and that to deny it would only make her look silly.

"Bring a friend if you like," he added, by way of being a smartass.

"Maybe I will," she said, playfully contemptuous. "You're definitely the man for this job, Jack."

"We all do what we're called to do."

"Oh, that's such bullshit," she said laughing. "You wouldn't be anywhere else and you know it."

HE ENTERED LAUNCH Control later that day—after hearing about his questionable judgment of the night before from at least three other mothers—and sat down beside Kane for a look at the monitors, already bored.

"Snowing a little bit, finally."

Kane looked up from his worn copy of *X-Box Magazine* for a glance at the monitor. "Was only a matter of time."

"How many times can you read the same magazine? Christ, we've got a few hundred books downstairs."

"I'm reading up for the tournament."

"What tournament?"

"Football tournament. Me, Linus, Oscar, and a bunch of the kids. Winner gets to eat the others' desserts for a week."

"You're going to take food from the kids . . . and the women think *I'm* bad."

Kane laughed. "You should hear the smack those kids are talkin', man."

"Any of 'em any good?"

"Oscar Junior can beat his dad six games outta ten. Beats me about half the time. We'll give the others a handicap. It ain't like we're stealin'."

They sat in silence then, Kane reading his magazine, Forrest tapping a pen on the counter.

After a full minute of tapping, Kane said, "Man, I got this. You don't have to be in here. And by the way, Wayne said to tell you there's a big pile of dog shit in tunnel two."

"I saw it," Forrest said, tossing the pen aside. "Stepped right over, in fact. He's right, it's pretty big."

Kane sat staring at him.

"What?"

"Go find somethin' to do, man."

"Hey, Thanksgiving's just around the corner, you know? It's going fast."

"You haven't said nothin' about the turkeys to nobody, have you?"

Forrest shook his head. "Seen those kids running around out there today?" He laughed. "It's a friggin zoo."

"Yeah, and Tonya's not your biggest fan right now."

Veronica poked her head into the room.

"Either of you guys know where Sean is? Melissa's got a bad headache and there's no aspirin left in the common area."

"He's not in medical?"

"Nope."

Forrest had a look at his watch. "I'll come unlock the cabinet," he said, getting up. "He and Taylor might be on an afternoon tryst. Care if I leave you alone a minute, Marcus?"

Kane took a semiexasperated look around the room. "Jack, man, it ain't like we're sittin' on missiles down here. Get him out of here, Ronny. He's makin' me nervous."

Forrest got some aspirin from the medicine cabinet

in Medical, then he and Veronica went to see Melissa in the second common room. The children were still rough-housing, screaming and laughing as they burned off the sugar, and Laddie was jumping around with them, chasing his ball and barking with excitement. A trio of mothers sat about, watching to make sure no one got hurt, a couple of them giving Forrest a collective *you're gonna get it* look as he crossed into the room.

He offered them an innocent smile in return. "What's got these little rascals so wound up today?"

"Like you don't know," Jenny said.

Veronica slapped him on the shoulder. "You're asking for it."

He went to the corner and knelt beside Melissa, who lay back on her bedroll looking very tired. "Got a headache, kiddo?"

"Uh-huh. *Dolar en la cabesa,*" she said, recalling the words from one of Maria Vasquez's Spanish classes.

"As I recall, you weren't feeling so hot yesterday either."

"She's working too hard on that cipher," Veronica said, kneeling and sitting back on her heels. "Why don't you take a little break, honey? Go back to it with fresh eyes in a week or two."

"I will," she said, taking the aspirins from her and sitting up to swallow them with some water. "But I feel like maybe I'm onto something. I've been assigning different letters and words to the sequences. Nothing fits yet, but the more I experiment with it, the more I feel a pattern. I can't explain it, but it's in there."

She lay back down, massaging her neck with her hand. "I'm stiff today too."

"Well, get some rest," Veronica said, kissing her on the forehead. "Let someone know if you need anything."

"Okay. I just need some sleep."

Veronica walked with Forrest down the hall back toward Launch Control. "Think she's really close to breaking that code?"

"I don't know," he said, scratching his head. "The chances are millions to one, but Wayne says it's probably not a complicated code. So who knows? I just wish she wasn't so obsessed with it. That's almost all she's been doing for the past couple of months. I saw her playing with the kids a few days ago but that's been it."

Taylor and Dr. West came around the corner laughing and holding hands.

"Hey, you two," Taylor said happily.

"Hey," Forrest said, extending them the rare courtesy of not teasing them about where they were coming from. "Sean, would you have a look at Melissa? She's got a bad headache. I'm worried she's been driving herself too hard with that damn code."

"She's still got that headache?" West said, surprised.

"And a stiff neck."

"Was her neck stiff before?"

"I don't know," Forrest said. "We're going to have to keep her busy with something else for a couple weeks."

"I'll think of something," Veronica said. "Maybe we can start making Christmas decorations."

"Speaking of that," Forrest said, opening the door to Launch Control, "I've got an artificial tree in the cargo bay. Don't tell anyone else, but I was thinking to set it up the day after Thanksgiving. Get all the juice we can out of the holiday."

"Good idea," West said. "I'll look in on Melissa."

"Talk to you guys later," Forrest said, giving Veronica a kiss. "I'm supposed to be on duty."

"No!" Kane called from inside the room. "Ronny, man, don't let him back in here!"

# FORTY-TWO

DR. WEST AT FIRST BELIEVED MELISSA'S HEADACHE WAS A symptom of the flu, which had been troubling enough, but after she began to run a fever on the third day, her complaints of a stiff neck made him think it might be something much more serious. So he asked for her and Michael's permission to perform a painful spinal tap so he might look at her cerebral spinal fluid under a microscope.

Having brought along as much in the way medical equipment as was humanly practical, he was able to run some basic tests, and though he was unable to diagnose Melissa's affliction with absolute certainty, the elevated number of white blood cells in her CSF gave him cause to believe she was suffering from bacterial meningitis, and he could have named a hundred diagnoses he would have preferred.

He stepped out of Medical into the corridor to talk with Michael and Forrest, leaving Veronica inside with Melissa, who lay in bed covered with blankets.

"So what is it, Sean?" Forrest asked, seemingly even more concerned than Michael.

"I think it's serious," West said. "I'm not absolutely certain but I believe she has bacterial meningitis. And if so she needs intravenous antibiotics; penicillin or vancomycin, possibly even cefotaxime—none of which I've got."

"Wait, you told me you brought every antibiotic you thought we could possibly need."

"In capsule form."

"Why won't those work?"

"Because you can't pick away at an infection this big," West said. "You have to hit a hammer blow, and pills won't do that. I've got her on a broad spectrum of oral antibiotics now to try and slow the infection, but that's not likely to save her."

"So she could die?" Michael asked.

"In all likelihood she will die, and I want you both to prepare for that."

"Now hold on a second!" Forrest said. "Four days ago she was chasing the kids and the dog up and down the tunnels. And now she's in there dying? How does that happen?"

"Some of the children have been passing ear infections back and forth for the past couple of weeks," West explained. "It's possible that Melissa picked up a streptococcus infection from one of them and it spread to her cerebral spinal fluid via the ear. Unfortunately, meningitis is most commonly seen in people between the ages of fifteen and twenty-four—which makes Melissa a prime candidate."

"So are the children at risk or not?" Michael asked, worried about an epidemic.

"It's possible, but they've all had their vaccinations, so we may get away with it. As a precaution, I'm going to put them all on penicillin for a week."

"What's she need?" Forrest said. "Write it all down exactly and I'll go and get it."

"What are you talking about?" Michael said. "You can't go out there."

"I can do any goddamn thing I want. Make me a list, Sean."

"Jack, any intravenous antibiotics still out there aren't likely to be any good by now. They need to be frozen in order to keep long-term, and even in that event they're generally not kept longer than thirty days."

"It's twenty degrees out there," Forrest said. "The whole world's a freezer."

"Jack . . ." West had known Forrest for a long time, and he knew the man just didn't have any quit in him. "Even if you find some that are frozen, they may have thawed and refrozen by now. After five months it's an extremely long shot you're talking about."

"Is it impossible, Sean? If I find some that are frozen, will you use them?"

"There would be very little to lose . . . so, yes, I would."

Forrest and West went to Launch Control, where Vasquez was watching the monitors, and Forrest called for the rest of his men to join them there. After they gathered, West explained what he thought was wrong with Melissa and why. Forrest then told them that his intention was to go to the hospital in Lincoln to gather the items West needed to save her life.

"The entire run should take me less than twelve hours," he concluded.

Not surprisingly, Ulrich was the first to speak out against the idea. "I think you need to consider this very seriously, Jack. As emotionally invested as you are—"

"I'm going, Wayne."

Ulrich looked at the others, who, to his relief, didn't seem overly keen on the idea of Forrest leaving the flock. "I think this is important enough that we need to take a vote," he said regretfully. "There are too many other souls down here depending on you."

Forrest stood looking at him. "You're actually going to challenge me on this?"

"It's not a challenge. This is the command structure we all agreed to. And you're talking about doing exactly what we were all dead set against doing from the beginning."

"You're willing to let that girl die just to stand on fucking principle?"

"Oh, come on, Jack! Principle has nothing to do with this. Sean's not even a hundred percent sure of the diagnosis, for

Christ's sake. And you want to go hunting for drugs that aren't going to be any good anymore."

"Then take your goddamn vote!"

"Hey, Jack," Kane said gently. "We did all agree, man."

Forrest looked at them, wanting badly to overrule them, but this was no longer the U.S. Army and he was no longer their captain. And he had agreed.

"So vote," he said again.

"Before we do that," Kane persisted, "we need to know if you're gonna honor it. Or if you plan to take off in the middle of the night with our only Humvee."

Forrest shook a cigarette from its pack and lit it right there in Launch Control, breaking his own rule. "You guys all know I'd never do that."

"Okay," Ulrich said. "What do you think, Oscar?"

"I think Wayne's right," Vasquez said. "I'm sorry, Jack. We haven't even had to crack the hatch yet and you're talking about lowering the lift elevator."

"You should be more sympathetic than anyone," Forrest argued, referring to Vasquez's finite insulin supply.

"That's not fair!" Ulrich said. "What about you, Linus? What's your vote?"

"If there was a real chance of saving her, Captain"—for Danzig, old habits died hard—"I'd be with you, but I don't think it's a good idea to jeopardize the rest of the group. You're too important down here."

"Well, that's it, then," Ulrich said. "I'm sorry, Jack."

"No, that's not it. I want a show of hands. Who says I stay? Get 'em up!"

Three hands went up, but Kane's remained in his pockets.

"Marcus?" Ulrich said.

Kane stood for a moment looking at the floor. "I'm going with him," he said finally.

"What?!"

"This is a one-man mission, Marcus."

"Either I go, Jack, or you don't get my vote." Only a 4 to 1 vote could override one of Forrest's decisions.

"You're both out of your goddamn minds!" Ulrich rapped, realizing he'd lost.

"The vote's three to two," Forrest said. "I win. I'm going into the bay to prep the Humvee. We'll take two cases of MREs and plenty of water. Marcus, get us two M-4s, six bandoliers of ammo, and a pair of .45s out of the armory."

Kane looked at Ulrich and shrugged. "It was a fair vote, Wayne, and the girl deserves a chance. You on board or not?"

"I think it's a crazy fucking idea, but I don't have a choice. Know this: if you two die out there, I'm gonna put my prosthetic foot up both your asses!"

"You're always gonna do something to somebody's ass when you get pissed," Forrest said. "Why is that?"

"I had a fucked-up childhood. What's your excuse?"

An hour later Veronica caught Forrest just as he was about to open the blast door into the cargo bay. "You were going to leave without even telling me?" she asked, very pissed.

"I'd planned on being back before you knew I was gone," he said with a grin. "Who's sitting with Melissa?"

"Michael's with her. Which is where you should be too. She's only asked for you half a dozen times."

"Tell her I'm running to the pharmacy."

"You're not funny," she said. "You can't save her, Jack, but you can at least give her some comfort while she's still conscious. How am I supposed to tell her that you've gone on a goddamn suicide mission?"

"It's not a suicide mission, for Christ's sake. You sound like Wayne."

"Oh, yeah? Then why aren't you taking Laddie with you?"

The door opened at the other end and Andie came into the tunnel. "Excuse me just a moment," she said to Veronica, moving past her to kiss Forrest on the cheek. "Be careful please?"

"Of course," he said with a smile.

Andie touched Veronica on the arm and left them alone.

Forrest waited until the door was sealed, then said, "See? *That's* how you're supposed to send a man off to battle."

"You know, this is all just one big adventure for you, isn't it?"

"At least I don't look at it as one big social experiment. How's the dichotomy working out for you these days?"

That hurt her feelings, and she turned away so he wouldn't see the tears forming.

"I honestly don't know how Monica did this. How many times did you leave her waiting to hear that you'd been killed?"

"Too many. She was even waiting when Daniel was killed. I can't undo the past, Veronica. And I won't hide down here and let that girl die when I *know* she can be saved. Now turn around and give me a kiss so I can go."

She turned around without opening her eyes, reaching to put her arms around him. She kissed him on the lips and turned away again, going to the door and slipping out of the tunnel, absolutely certain that she had spoken to him for the last time.

People were eating one another out there.

Andie was waiting outside the door for her, and the two of them hugged and went to Launch Control to watch the monitors.

"*I'M READY WHEN you are, Marcus,*" Kane heard Forrest announce in his earpiece.

"Roger that," he said. "Opening blast door number two."

Standing at the top of stairwell, dressed head-to-toe in his NBC suit, complete with gas mask, he turned the lever and opened the door, accessing the security vestibule for the first time since the impact. He went in and Vasquez sealed the door behind him as he made his way to blast door number one.

"Okay," he said. "I'm cracking door number one."

"Roger that."

Kane turned the wheel and pulled the lever to open the door, keeping his .45 at the ready as he stepped from the vestibule into the basement of the house. He pulled the door closed behind him and told Vasquez that it was clear for him to come and seal it.

Vasquez opened door number two and ran down the vestibule, pulling the lever to seal blast door one tight behind Kane and spinning the big red wheel. Then he left the vestibule and resealed blast door two, restoring complete integrity to the silo. "LC, we're a hundred percent again," he announced over the net.

"Roger," Ulrich replied from Launch Control. "Marcus, we've still got zero movement above. You're clear to enter the house."

"Roger." Kane ascended the stairs and opened the door into the house. The first thing he noticed was that the floor was covered with a thin film of grayish black dust not visible on the monitors. "I'm in the hall," he said.

"We've got visual."

"There's a lot of ash in here," he remarked, moving into the living room, where everything looked filthy now and the dead body was mostly eaten away. Outside, the day was gray and overcast, with a dark layer of continuous cloud looming much lower over the ground than he had expected.

Stepping out the back door, Kane scanned the landscape through the scope of his M-4, seeing nothing alive, not even a bird. The only movement was the ash and dust blowing about. The mutilated corpse of the dead man by the grill was frozen and covered in filth. The outside of the house was scorched, the tan vinyl siding twisted and melted by the heat of the grass fires as they had passed. Nothing had regrown and there was no real color anywhere.

He scanned 360 degrees around the house to make sure there were no threats on the horizon, then took a rake from the back porch and went to the garden. "It's all clear up here, Jack."

"Roger. I'm lowering the lift."

Kane saw the garden begin to drop into the earth and stepped back as the sound of the hydraulic lift pervaded the breezy silence. Dirt fell over the edges of the opening as the deck descended fifteen feet to the bottom of the cargo bay. Kane stood looking down as Forrest drove the Humvee up onto the garden-covered deck, which was just big enough to hold a single Army six-by-six truck. Forrest then jumped out of the Humvee and hit a button on the wall.

"Raising the lift," he announced, and ran to jump back onto the lift as it began to rise. It stopped at the top, locking into place, and he drove the Humvee out of the garden and across the yard to the gravel drive. "Lift up and locked."

Ulrich acknowledged the transmission as Kane went to work with the rake, quickly smoothing away the tire tracks in the dirt and raking away the square depression in the soil outlining the edges of the lift. In a few hours' time the wind would do the rest.

Forrest got out of the Humvee and waited for Kane to put the rake away. "Have you tried the air?" he asked.

"No."

Forrest took the Geiger counter from inside the vehicle. "Background radiation is a tad elevated but still in the green. I'm going to try the air."

"That's not a good idea, Jack," Ulrich said over the net.

"I'm not wearing this mask if I don't have to." He pulled the mask from his head and drew a shallow breath, the air smelling to him more like a dirty fireplace than anything else. "There's a lot of particulate matter but I don't think it's volcanic. It's not hurting my lungs."

The two loaded up. Kane got behind the wheel and took off his mask, tossing it into Forrest's lap. "Ready?"

"Definitely. Wayne, we're going off the net, but leave the receiver on until we get back."

"Roger that. Good luck."

"Back before you know it."

Kane put the Humvee in gear, drove down the hill and out through the fence, stopping at the road. "This is some fucked-up shit here," he said, leaning into the wheel and looking out. "It's high noon and look how dark it is. This sky's never gonna clear up before we run out of food, man."

"It has to," Forrest said.

"How's that?"

"Because if it don't, we're fucked."

Kane grunted and stepped on the gas. "This is a dumb idea, Jack . . . just so you know."

Forrest chuckled, lighting up a cigarette. "So why'd you vote with me?"

"Because you're the best officer I ever had . . . and if this is gonna be your last mission, I'm gonna be on it."

# FORTY-THREE

FORREST AND KANE HAD COVERED ALL FIVE MAJOR MEDICAL centers in the city of Lincoln, Nebraska, by late afternoon, and they hadn't found a single frozen bag of intravenous antibiotic in any of the freezers. What they had found were dozens and dozens of dead patients who had been left behind to die.

"I'm sorry," Kane said, getting in on the passenger side of the Humvee. "It was worth the try, Jack."

"I'll drop you back at the silo," Forrest said, hitting the starter.

"Drop me what?"

"I'm pressing on to Topeka."

"I knew you'd pull this shit," Kane said. "Lemme drive."

Forrest watched the highway as they rode, eyeballing various abandoned cars and trucks, remembering Iraq and Afghanistan, where such vehicles were once as likely to explode when you passed as not. Here, though, he was more concerned about an ambush.

There was almost nothing else to see on the ride south to Topeka, only a few buildings and no sign that anyone had passed that way in the last four months. Even the abandoned vehicles looked decades old, covered in grime, some of them burned to the frame, tires melted into the asphalt.

"McCarthy sure as hell got this part right," Forrest muttered.

"Who's McCarthy?"

"He wrote a novel years back about postapocalyptic America. His world was postnuclear rather than postmeteor, but this is almost exactly what he described. He won the Pulitzer for it."

Kane had never been much of a reader, having always preferred to play sports in his free time. "That's why I never liked to read, Jack. Who'd want to know about this shit sooner than you had to?"

An hour later he said, "Did you see that?"

"See what?"

"Over there to the left, way out. I think I saw a flashlight."

"You think or you're sure?" Forrest said, craning his neck to see into the blackness.

"Can't be sure," Kane said, not daring to take his eyes from the highway, his speed no faster than forty-five miles an hour. The headlights of the Humvee did not penetrate far enough into the murk for him to be sure they wouldn't hit some kind of obstruction or debris in the road. Spits of snow had begun to fall as well, adding to the miasma.

"Remember the eighty-four-mile marker," Forrest said. "On the way back we'll want to keep our eyes peeled."

Thirty miles farther on they were approaching the outskirts of Topeka. Along the highway, they began to see signs of past military action, civilian cars armored with welded boilerplate, riddled with .50 cal machine-gun fire, some blown apart—probably by javelin antitank missiles. They passed an M60 tank that had thrown a tread while running over a pickup truck but was otherwise undamaged. They drove slowly through a shattered roadblock, seeing scores of dead bodies strewn about in the dust, all of them strangely mummified now, freeze-dried in the arid cold.

"I'm not sorry we missed this," Kane said. "They slaughtered these people."

"Looks like somebody didn't want them getting into the

city," Forrest surmised. "I'm guessing it was the Forty-fifth I.D."

A mile farther ahead a pair of large spotlights unexpectedly snapped on in the pitch-black, blinding them both. Kane slammed on the brakes and grabbed for his carbine, but Forrest caught his arm. "It's gotta be the Forty-fifth. Give 'em a chance to look us over."

Both men shaded their eyes and waited as a group of soldiers surrounded the Humvee, shouting for them to show their hands.

"Hold your fire!" Forrest was shouting at them. "We're with the Eighty-second!"

"Exit the vehicle!" someone shouted. "Hands in the air!"

Both men exited and stood with their hands up, still squinting against the intense light.

"Hold your fire, guys," Forrest said. "Take it easy. We're on your side."

"Move it!" a soldier said, prodding him forward with the muzzle of an M-16.

They were marched through an opening in a barricade of cars stacked two high, then across an open lot into a Texaco station with blacked-out windows. The inside of the makeshift command post was well lit with military lanterns, and the shelves were empty, all of them jammed up against the walls out of the way.

A black sergeant with a bald head sat in an easy chair behind the counter smoking a cigar. His uniform tag said that his name was Lee, the patch on his shoulder the dingy gold thunderbird of the Forty-fifth Infantry Division, a division reactivated a few years before the asteroid had ever been spotted.

"These men were trying to get into the city," one of the soldiers said.

Lee stood up and came around the counter to Kane, the cigar caught in the corner of his mouth. They were of equal size and height. "You two smell good enough to fuck," he said, puffing at the cigar. "Where the hell you comin' from?"

"I'm afraid that's classified information, Sergeant," Forrest said.

Lee turned to look him over. "That's a term that's lost most of its meaning around here, Captain."

"The fact remains. Who's your commanding officer?"

"These guys are Special Forces," one of the soldiers said, pointing out the patches on their left shoulders. "They must've been in the rear with the gear all this time."

"That so?" Lee asked. "You two a couple of REMFs?" This was an unofficial, pejorative military acronym standing for Rear Echelon Mother Fucker.

"Sergeant, I've already told you that's classified information. I won't tell you again. Now who's your C.O. . . . or are you all that's left after that battle out there?"

Lee stood chewing the cigar. "Colonel Short still commands."

"Then I'll need to speak with him," Forrest said. "In the meantime, Sergeant, I'll be holding you personally responsible for our vehicle and equipment."

Lee glanced at his men and smirked. "Responsible to who, Captain?"

Forrest knew all too well there wasn't much left to intimidate with in terms of a military hierarchy, but if he lost the initiative, they were screwed. He was only now getting a good look at the two men covering them, and they were but mere shadows of the soldiers they had once been, filthy and unshaven, dark circles beneath their eyes. Lee was shaven and better kempt, but he was obviously equally exhausted. "To your C.O. Who the hell else?"

"Got any ID?" Lee asked.

"Just our tags," Forrest said. "Left our AGO cards back at Bragg."

"Lemme see."

Both men took their dog tags from beneath their jackets for the sergeant to read.

"Okay," Lee said, believing they were at least who they said they were. "Turn your pistols over to my men until after you've met with the colonel."

Kane and Forrest took their .45s from their holsters and surrendered them.

"Don't lose them," Forrest said.

"I'll take these cats to the colonel myself," Lee said. "Tell Sergeant Behan he's in charge till I get back."

Sergeant Stacker Lee then grabbed a flashlight from the counter and led them out the back door to a waiting black Cadillac Escalade. He gave the keys to Forrest and told him to drive. "I'll sit in the back. Just follow my directions."

Colonel Eugene Short's quarters were a mile off the highway in a very nice home at the edge of what had once been a wealthy neighborhood. There were four men on guard outside the house wearing night vision devices on their helmets and four more on guard inside. There were more lanterns lighting the inside of the home where Short was sitting down to a meal of heated green beans and canned potatoes. A generator hummed somewhere beneath the floor but there was no electric light to be seen.

"These men were taken into custody at the northern barricade, sir. They're Special Forces with the Eighty-second and claim to be on a classified mission."

Short was a graying man of fifty-two with drifting, watery blue eyes. He was clean shaven and wore a semiclean digitally camouflaged uniform bearing the eagle insignia of a full colonel with the Forty-fifth Division. "A classified mission?" he said dubiously. "I find that rather difficult to believe."

"That's what they claim, sir. They're also very clean and smell of soap and aftershave."

Short stood from the dining table and came over to Forrest and Kane, both of whom stood rigidly at attention.

"At ease, gentlemen," the colonel said, looking them over. "You boys are well fed sons of bitches, aren't you?"

"Yes, sir," Forrest said.

"How is that?"

"I'm afraid I'm not exactly at liberty to say, Colonel. But we're obviously traveling with a well equipped and sizable force."

Short took a humorous glance at Sergeant Lee. "Did that sound like a veiled threat to you, Sergeant?"

"It did, sir."

"It was no kind of threat at all, sir. I was merely attempting to answer the colonel's question without exceeding my mission parameters."

"Take a seat at the table, gentlemen." Short then ordered his personal guards out of the room, leaving the four of them alone as he reclaimed his chair. "You're both Green Berets," he said, forking a potato into his mouth.

"Yes, sir."

"See how the green beanies are, Sergeant? They take themselves too seriously . . . even now."

"Yes, sir," Lee said.

"Captain Forrest," the colonel went on, "would it be safe for me to assume that a detachment of the Eighty-second Airborne has made its way here all the way from North Carolina for purposes unknown?"

"That much would be safe to assume, sir, yes."

"And you came across on Interstate 40?"

"Yes, sir."

"I see," Short said, forking another potato into his mouth and chewing it completely before swallowing, savoring it to the last. "Well, Captain, would you care to hear how I know that story to be complete bullshit?"

Neither Forrest nor Kane made a reply to the colonel's query.

"Of course you would," the colonel went on. "Well, on the night the meteor hit, there were some pretty massive earthquakes around these parts . . . which caused the engineers working over at the Parkersburg nuclear power plant to panic and abandon ship without bothering to power down the reactor. So the core melted down and burned right through the bottom of the plant—China syndrome. Only it never quite made it to China. It hit groundwater and sent a huge cloud of radioactive steam into the air, killing everybody within a fifty-mile-wide corridor east of the plant for a hundred miles. It's a dead zone now, and Interstate 40 runs right through it." He paused long enough to eat a forkful of beans, then said, "What do you have to say to that, Captain?"

Forrest thought it over a moment and smiled. "Actually, Colonel, it wasn't a meteor that hit us. It was an asteroid."

The colonel smiled back. "Indeed it was. Captain, why don't you tell me what the hell you're really up to so I can decide whether or not to let you continue on your way? Otherwise, I'm going to lock you both up and throw away the key for insulting my intelligence."

Forrest knew there was little choice now but to offer at least a version of the truth. "We're living a couple hundred miles north of here, Colonel, in an abandoned missile silo with twenty civilians, mostly women and children. At half rations, we've got maybe enough food left for two months— we're down to mostly flour and rice now. The reason Kane and I are here is that my niece has contracted meningitis, and we're on our way to the hospital to find the antibiotics our doctor needs to save her life."

"Why even bother? So she can eat hardtack and rice for another two months?"

"We're not giving up until the end, Colonel."

"And you're worried I'll lead my division north to rape your women and steal your flour and rice. Is that it, Captain?"

"It's a realistic concern, Colonel, yes."

"Well, you're in luck, Captain. I don't condone rape and neither does Sergeant Lee. As for your rations . . . even if you've lied by half, which I suspect you have, it's not enough food for me to bother with." He finished off his potatoes and directed his attention to Lee. "Sergeant, do you see any reason why we shouldn't allow these men to continue on their way? They're obviously not capable of causing us much trouble."

"No, sir."

"Then pick three men and escort them over to the hospital so they can gather whatever it is they're looking for," the colonel ordered. "After that, return them to the barricade and see them safely on their way with their possessions returned to them."

"Yes, sir."

The colonel rose to his feet and everyone else followed suit.

"You're dismissed," the colonel said.

Both Kane and Forrest snapped him a smart salute and turned an about face, following Sergeant Lee out of the room.

"The hospital's outside our containment zone," Lee explained as he drove them himself deeper into town in the Cadillac. There were soldiers with lanterns and flashlights here and there along the way, all of them armed to the teeth, most of them smoking cigarettes.

"We've got enough food left for maybe a couple months ourselves," he went on. "After that we plan to commit mass suicide. That's why you'll see a grenade around most everybody's neck. It's a sign of solidarity against cannibalism."

"So you've seen them too?" Kane said.

"We've seen plenty of 'em, and we kill 'em whenever we find 'em. Fuckin' wild animals. It ain't no way to survive. You gotta know when it's time to hang it up. Our original plan was we'd all get drunk together before pulling the pins, but then we drank up all the booze." He laughed. "So I guess we're goin' out sober. It's too bad."

"How's the morale otherwise?"

"We've only had a few suicides," Lee said. "But we've had some desertions lately, about twenty. We ain't sure what that's about. The colonel's not keeping anybody who doesn't want to stay. It just leaves more food for the rest of us. Last week ten dudes asked him for a truck and some fuel for a run to the coast. Couple of 'em said they knew how to sail and wanted to try for Australia. Colonel told 'em, 'Good luck.'"

"What the hell's in Australia?" Kane said.

"Beats me, bro. Don't matter no way. I know them dudes, and they ain't sailin' to no motherfuckin' Australia. Them dudes are gonna drown."

"How many men do you have left?" Forrest asked.

"Around a thousand."

"No women?"

"We had some females in the brigade originally, but the colonel ordered them all out with the last airlift to Texas. I think he knew how bad things were going to get here. They'd have gotten raped for sure, man. We got too many young hooligans in this outfit."

"So what's going on down in Texas?"

"Got no idea. We haven't heard from them in months."

"And you chose not to share your food with the civilians here? That's what the battle was over? Food?"

"We distributed plenty of food," Lee said, steering through town on the way to his billet. "That was our primary mission, but the civvies here got carried away. Redneck bastards started showing up at the distribution centers with guns and shooting our men. After that the colonel pulled us into this defensive perimeter and we tried to dispense the food that way. But then local warlords took over outside and started stealing food from those without guns, forming private armies . . . like fucking Somalia, man. At first they traded food for women, and when they finally had all the women, they let everybody else starve.

"After that, the warlords started killing each other off, and that's when the colonel decided to quit distributing food altogether . . . which only forced the warlords into an alliance. Then they attacked us at different places around the perimeter, and they killed a few of us, but we wiped 'em out in the end. What you saw on the road in was nothing. On the city's east side the bodies are piled up knee high for a quarter mile. Things have been pretty quiet out there ever since. The human race has had it, man."

"No word from D.C.?" Forrest asked.

"The last word we got from anybody was months ago," Lee said. "By shortwave—the satellite signals can't penetrate that shit in the sky. We were told the President was dead and that we were all effectively on our own."

"What happened to him?"

"Nobody said, but the colonel thinks there was a coup."

"Doesn't matter anyway," Forrest muttered.

"This is my billet," Lee said, shifting into park in front of a house lit up like Mardi Gras.

"What the hell's going on here?" Kane asked.

"My place is party central. We've got more gas than food now, so we run the generator all night long. We don't have any booze left, like I was telling you, so the guys watch a lot of dirty movies, have circle jerks, play video games. All pretty juvenile shit, but what else is left?"

"We got some gamers too, but we ain't had no circle jerk yet."

Lee chuckled sardonically. "We got a lotta kids in this outfit. You two wait out here while I get my men. I don't need ever'body inside knowing about you guys. It could cause trouble."

Ten minutes later an armored Humvee pulled up behind the Escalade and Lee got out, calling for Forrest and Kane to get in. Their weapons had been retrieved from the barricade and were returned to them, and they were each given a Kevlar helmet with a NVD attached.

"It gets dark as fuck outside the containment zone," Lee said. "There's a moon tonight, though, so the NVDs will light it up good. Inside the hospital we'll have to switch to infrared. These are my homies: Grip, Clean, and Shodo."

Everyone shook hands in the cramped space of the Humvee. All of Lee's "homies" were black men in their thirties, and Forrest was glad he hadn't brought along any of the young hooligans he had mentioned.

At the southern checkpoint, they passed out of the containment zone after giving almost no explanation at all. It seemed that Lee was something of an institution within the brigade and that whatever he said was taken as gospel. Forrest began to wonder how much control Colonel Short actually had over his men, now suspecting that he was little more than a figurehead, which did make sense under the circumstances. In fact, he was surprised to see as much military order as he did. They drove past a parking lot strewn with bodies, fallen one upon the other as if on an ancient battlefield.

Forrest noticed in the red light of the interior that Grip had a pair of very large hands, and it occurred to him that this must have been the origin of his nickname. There was nothing about Clean or Shodo, however, to explain theirs. Clean certainly wasn't at all clean. Two miles from the checkpoint, they pulled up to the emergency entrance of the hospital and piled out, taking time to have a good look around with their night division devices. Nothing moved in the blackish green, and only the sound of the icy wind pervaded.

"So what's it like livin' underground?" Shodo asked as they stepped through the shattered glass door into the emergency ward.

"It's quiet," Kane said, not wanting to make it sound too inviting.

"I bet," Shodo said. "How many other GIs you got?"

"Ten," Forrest lied.

"All green beanies?"

"That's right."

"You all got any women down there?"

"Bro," Lee said, "what I tell you back at the crib?"

"Stacker, man, I'm just curious. Can't a brother at least fantasize a little bit? Shit."

"Get on point," Lee ordered. "Find the fuckin' pharmacy."

They moved in a tight cover formation through the hospital, following the signs on the walls. They were forced to switch over to infrared once they were away from the windows because of the almost total lack of ambient light, which made it impossible to read the signs without having to use the flashlights on their weapons.

"Anybody else smell that?" Kane asked as they made their way up an open staircase to the second floor.

"Yeah," Forrest answered.

"Smell what?" Lee said.

It occurred to Forrest that breathing the filthy air over an extended period of time must have desensitized the others' olfactory systems.

"Smells like burnt meat," Kane said.

The others froze in place.

"I don't smell nothin'," Grip said.

"Me either," said Clean.

"I *think* I do," said Shodo.

"Keep movin'," Lee ordered. "How fresh does it smell, Kane?"

"I don't know. It's not real strong, but I didn't smell it down on the first floor."

They found the pharmacy and Lee's men covered the halls while he and the two Green Berets used their flashlights to search inside. Forrest found a freezer with a padlock on it and bashed it off with the butt of the carbine, pulling the door open to shine his light inside. There were all sorts of frozen drug solutions, but he didn't find any of the names that West had written down for him.

"Jack, got another freezer back here." Kane bashed the lock and Forrest shone his light to find that the freezer contained nothing but antibiotics, including those he was looking for.

"Thank Christ," he muttered, grabbing one of the bags and giving it a shake. The solution wasn't frozen, but it was slushy and icy cold. "How many should we take, Marcus?"

"How many can you fit in the fuckin' ruck, man?"

Forrest packed his rucksack tight. "We're good to go, Sergeant!"

During their egress, the odor of burnt meat became strong enough that Lee and his men were able to smell it very well now.

"Fuck, that's human!" Shodo said, all of them having smelled it before.

"Human?" Kane said.

"Grip, get on point!" Lee ordered in a hushed tone. "Find the source!"

"Guys, I'm not so sure that's a good idea," Forrest cautioned. "We don't know the layout of the building."

"Captain, you and your man cover the rear," Lee ordered, ignoring the warning.

Forrest and Kane had little choice but to comply, both of them relieved that they had grabbed grenades at Lee's behest.

"Cafeteria's just ahead," Grip whispered. "Keep it tight."

All of them could see the heat plume at the end of the hall in their infrared view finders, and they switched over to night vision, realizing there would be ambient light now. They made their way into the cafeteria, which was a proper mess with tables dumped over and chairs scattered about. The vending machines had long been smashed open and raided. The acrid odor of frying meat was mixed with the stench of rotting human flesh, and both Forrest and Kane felt the hair rise on the back of their necks as they shuffled backward along the wall, covering the rear.

Grip could hear the sizzling of meat now as he peered around the corner into the kitchen, seeing a dark hooded figure cooking by candlelight over a Coleman camp stove. He also saw the severed arm and leg of a human being on the counter, most of the flesh gone from both, leaving bare bone, the hand and foot still in tact. Another figure entered the kitchen from the opposite side and spotted Grip peeking around the corner.

"Look out!" he shouted, and the cook jerked his head in Grip's direction, pulling a pistol from his pocket.

Grip fired his carbine and killed the cook but missed the second man, who ducked quickly back out of the kitchen.

"Move!" Lee said, ordering the men forward. "Captain, cover this doorway!"

They cleared the kitchen and had a look around, the eerie blue flame still burning beneath the frying pan, smoke beginning to fill the kitchen. Kane felt his stomach twist at the smell of what he now knew was burning human flesh, and he knocked the pan from the stove to the floor.

"Oh, fuck!" Clean said. "Look at this shit, Sarge!" He grabbed a handful of dog tags hanging from a hook over the counter and held them up for Lee to see.

"Read me the names!" Lee ordered.

"Preston, Sipe, Leskavonski—shit, Sarge, these are our men!"

"They didn't fuckin' desert!" Shodo said. "They got eaten by fuckin' cannibals!"

"Ever'body chill the fuck out!" Lee ordered, peering around the corner after the man who had escaped. The hallway was about fifty feet long with a turn to the left at the far end.

Kane squatted beside the dead man and picked up the .38 revolver, kicking the body viciously in the head to be sure he wasn't playing possum. The dead man was grimy as hell with a thick black beard, and he stunk to high heaven of sweat and shit.

"These people have definitely gone wild," he said to Forrest.

"Sergeant, we need to get the hell out of here," Forrest warned.

"Not before we kill these motherfuckers. We helped you get what you needed, now you help us do what we need done."

"I advise you to go back and gather a company of men first. You've got no idea the size of the force you're going up against or how well equipped they might be. There's a pile of fresh bones in this sink over here big enough to suggest they're feeding a lot of people."

"And suppose they've still got some of our men alive in this shit hole," Lee said. "How long you think they gonna stay that way?"

"Getting killed won't help them."

"We're taking them down. You with us or not?"

Forrest and Kane exchanged glances. Again they didn't have much choice. The six of them carefully made their way down the hall and around the corner. Someone screamed deep within the hospital in the darkness. It was a bloodcurdling cry.

"I'm on point!" Lee said, shouldering his way to the front.

They moved smartly along, clearing any open rooms they passed. There was a flurry of movement at a four-way intersection up ahead and shots were fired. Lee and Grip both returned fire and someone screamed. The six soldiers moved quickly to secure the intersection, where a man lay against the wall wailing in pain, shot through the stomach. He stunk as badly as the cook and lashed out with a knife, trying to hook Shodo behind the knee.

Shodo brought the stock of his M-16 down on the man's head and caved it in. "Fuck you, motherfucker!"

"In here!" Clean called from a nearby room.

The others had a look inside, where one of their missing men was chained to a bed with his throat recently cut.

"Son of a bitch!" Lee swore. "See? Goddamnit!"

"They only got shotguns and revolvers," Clean said, dumping the shells from the cannibal's .357 and flinging the pistol back in the direction they had come. "Let's clean these fuckers out."

Forrest realized that these soldiers had nothing to lose by pressing forward, but he and Kane certainly did. Farther along, a cluster of people burst from a room and dashed across the hall. Lee and his men gave chase.

"Sergeant!" Forrest shouted, but it was no use. He and Kane ran after them, covering the rear as they ran across a large conference room in pursuit of the fleeing figures. The double doors at the far side slammed shut before they could reach them, and the sound of crashing vending machines could be heard on the other side, effectively barricading the doors closed.

"It's a trap!" Kane shouted, turning on his heel to dash back to the entrance. But these doors were also slammed shut before he could reach them, and again the vending machines outside were knocked over to barricade them.

"Goddamnit!" Kane shouted, whirling on Stacker Lee. "See what the fuck you did, motherfucker!"

There were sounds of maniacal laughter in the halls outside, whooping and hollering beyond both sets of doors, and a hail of bullets came through, forcing the soldiers to the floor and up against the walls.

"Now what?" Clean griped.

"I guess this wasn't such a good idea," said Shodo.

"No shit!" Kane remarked.

"Hey, fuck you!" Lee said. "Goddamn green beanie motherfucker! You dudes been livin' underground suckin' on cold beer and eatin' pussy for the last twelve months! Who the fuck are you to tell us jack shit?"

"Cool it!" Forrest ordered. "We have to think our way out of this."

They heard the sound of breaking glass in the center of the room and switched on their flashlights to see a dozen mason jars come dropping through a hole in the ceiling, shattering against the floor and releasing thick clouds of white gas.

"Fuck is that?!" Grip shouted, scooting away along the wall.

"Chlorine gas!" Forrest said.

"Where the fuck they get that shit?"

"Bleach and toilet bowl cleaner," Forrest said, gathering the shemagh from about his neck and tying it over his nose and mouth. Lee's men followed suit by tying green triangular bandages over their faces, and more jars fell through holes scattered all across the ceiling, shattering against the floor to fill the room with the poisonous gas.

Laughter came down through the holes in the ceiling, and more shots were fired through the doors to keep their heads down.

The soldiers started choking and their eyes burned.

"What the fuck are we gonna do?" Lee said. "We don't have much time."

"I have a suggestion," said Kane.

"I'm all ears, man."

"Turn command of this little goat fuck over to my captain so he can get us the *fuck* outta here!"

"What about it?" Lee said tersely. "You want command of the coal train?"

"Sure," Forrest said, grinning beneath the shemagh. "Why not?"

"What you got in mind?"

"First," Forrest said, "we need a fresh air supply. Stick a grenade in that fire extinguisher encasement and blow it outta there. There'll be fresh air inside the wall we can take turns at."

Grip wasted no time sliding over to the empty fire extinguisher box and sticking a grenade inside. "Fire in the hole!"

The grenade exploded and blew the metal encasement open wide enough for them to take turns sticking their heads inside the cinder-block wall for gulps of fresh air.

"Now we blow a hole in that far wall so we can flank these motherfuckers."

"Fuck you gonna use for explosives?" Lee demanded. "Grenades won't do shit to a brick wall!"

"O ye of little faith, Sergeant. Everybody fork over a concussion grenade. Hurry it up! Marcus, tape them together."

Kane took a roll of electrical tape from his cargo pocket and began taping the six grenades together.

"Sergeant, get that jacket off and ball it up," Forrest ordered as he removed the lanyard from his .45.

Lee stripped his combat harness and shrugged quickly out of his body armor. He then took off his jacket and gave it to Forrest, who used his electrical tape to wad the jacket into a ball as Lee shrugged back into his armor and harness.

"Now we'll go knock the cover off that air vent in the far wall."

The two each took a gulp of fresh air from the hole and moved quickly through the cloud of gas across to the wall

Forrest had indicated. Lee used the butt of his carbine to bash the cover from the vent.

"Jam your jacket down inside the wall as far as you can!" Forrest said, choking against the fumes. He then ran the lanyard through the pins of the concussion grenades, lowering them down into the shaft to rest upon the jacket. "Take cover behind that table!"

Lee ran to where the other men had overturned a table and jumped behind it as Forrest jerked the lanyard, pulling all six pins from the grenades at virtually the same time and running for cover.

Four seconds later the grenades exploded in a massive thunderclap, blasting a four-foot hole in the double layered cinder-block wall.

"Move!" Forrest shouted, leaping over the table and sprinting toward the opening with Kane hot on his heels. The two Green Berets reached the opening a full two strides ahead of the others and ran down the hall to the far corner, catching six cannibals stunned and unprepared, machine-gunning them on the move and trampling their bodies underfoot. They continued making their way through the hospital at flank speed by flashlight.

Lee's men caught up and together they fought a running battle back toward the emergency ward.

"Hold up!" Shodo said. "I hear somethin'."

The men stopped and everyone stood listening. They heard the hushed tones of crying children somewhere behind them and around the corner and made their way to a private room where they found fifteen or so ragged women and children huddled together. They were as filthy and sickly looking as the men they had seen, and one of the women took a shot at them with a 9mm pistol, hitting Lee in the chest on his breastplate.

They ducked back out of the doorway and stood looking at one another.

"They sure as shit ain't lookin' to be rescued!" Grip said.

"Fuck you!" a woman screamed from inside. "Bastards!"

Down the far hall they could hear the cannibal men gathering, realizing that a group of their women and children had been found.

Lee took a concussion grenade from his harness.

"No!" Kane said.

"Fuck 'em! You think those motherfuckers see you as anything more than food?"

"We can keep moving," Forrest said. "You gave me command, remember?"

"*Tactical* command, Captain." Lee pulled the pin on the grenade, tossing it into the room, and they all ducked away covering their ears. The concussion from the blast blew out the windows of the room, and a great pressure wave blasted past them down the hall like rolling thunder. No one in the room could have lived.

"Goddamnit!" Kane screamed. "You didn't have to fuckin' do that!"

"It's done!" Lee retorted. "Now what are your orders, Captain?"

"We get the fuck downstairs and find an exit! Shodo, you got point!"

On their way across the lower lobby a shower of Molotov cocktails rained down around them and Shodo was completely consumed by fire, screaming and flailing in a futile attempt to beat out the flames. Forrest shouldered his carbine and shot him dead before any of Lee's men could react, whirling about to spray the balcony above them and driving back the firebombers.

"Forget the emergency ward!" he ordered. "The Humvee's fucked anyhow."

They burst out the main entrance onto the sidewalk to see that the Humvee was indeed burning fifty yards away.

"Looks like we hoof it," Forrest said. "I trust you remember the way, Sergeant?"

"Yes, sir! Grip, on point! I'll bring up the rear!"

Using their night vision, they ran the two miles all the way back to the checkpoint, where they were nearly machine-gunned by their own troops before they could identify themselves.

"Check fire!" Lee screamed from behind a truck. "Check fire!"

"Identify yourselves!"

"Stacker Lee, you dumb motherfuckers! Stacker-fuckin'-Lee!"

It took a minute but they were eventually permitted to advance, and Lee wasted no time telling the men at the checkpoint what had taken place at the hospital. A great fury swept through the men upon hearing that twenty of their comrades had been abducted and eaten. Two full companies of men were quickly assembled.

"At first light we go back there and clean those motherfuckers out," Lee said, gathering a fresh supply of grenades. "Care to lead us, Captain?"

Forrest looked at Kane. "We should be on our way."

Kane agreed.

"In that case, I'll drive you to the barricade," Lee said.

At the barricade he told them to keep their helmets, NVDs, and body armor, and complied with Kane's request for three more sets of NVDs.

Forrest reached into the back of their Humvee and grabbed a bottle of Tequila from a barracks bag, offering it to Stacker Lee. "For that final circle jerk, Sergeant."

Lee smiled a white, toothy smile and accepted the bottle with relish. "And this time I'll save it."

The soldiers all saluted one another, and Forrest and Kane mounted up.

"My guys took the liberty of gassing it up for you," Lee said, shutting Forrest's door for him. They shook hands through the window. "Godspeed, Captain. Sorry I was such a prick."

"Live forever, Sergeant."

Kane started the engine and wheeled the Humvee around, roaring through the gate, headed north.

**BOTH MEN WERE** so exhausted from the fight that neither of them remembered to be alert at the eighty-four-mile marker—until a Molotov cocktail flew out of the darkness and exploded in flames against the windshield.

"Son of a bitch!" Kane shouted, cutting the wheel hard to the left and narrowly missing a car that had been rolled onto the center of the highway. He could barely see where he was going through the flames and ended up swerving into the center median and up a concrete highway barrier, perfectly high-centering the vehicle. "Cocksucker!" he swore, realizing they were stuck fast.

"Dismount!" Forrest said, grabbing his carbine and helmet.

They took cover behind the barrier as shots rang out and bullets began pinging off the Humvee. Forrest could see a number of men across the highway in his night vision and opened fire, killing four with four quick shots. The firing from across the road stopped and the attackers disappeared from their view.

"Guess you saw a flashlight after all," he said.

They could hear hushed voices on three sides.

"They're moving to outflank us."

"We're already outflanked," Forrest remarked. "Soon to be surrounded."

As if to verify that fact, a shotgun slug struck Forrest dead-center in the back panel of his boron carbide body armor, knocking him into the concrete barrier as if he'd been mule-kicked.

Kane whipped around and returned fire, driving the shooter back under cover. "Jack!"

Forrest got to his knees and grabbed his carbine, blinking his eyes to clear his vision. "I'm okay," he groaned. "Christ, that hurt."

"We need to get out of the light of the headlights," Kane said, and they both moved farther down the barrier.

More shots rang out.

Kane grabbed his lower leg. "Shit, I took one!" He and Forrest backed in tight between the barrier and the large steel shovel of a backhoe.

Forrest lifted his head for a look around, switching to infrared. Men were scurrying about in the dark, but there were too many abandoned vehicles to get a shot. They were protected on three sides now from direct fire, but that protection worked both ways, potentially allowing their attackers to creep up unseen and lob a Molotov cocktail directly onto their position. "How many you think we're up against?"

"Feels like about twenty," Kane said. "Give or take."

"Well, let's pick a direction and break out before they tighten the noose."

Another shot rang out, but it was far away and nothing hit near their position. Then they heard another shot from the opposite side of the highway, equally far off, and this time one of the attackers screamed.

"Fuck is that?" Kane said.

"Got me."

They took the chance to raise their heads for a look around, seeing that some of their assailants were now entirely exposed, having taken cover from whoever else was firing. Forrest and Kane fired and killed five more men.

Their attackers began to fire wildly into the night, panicking in the darkness and shouting to one another that they were surrounded. Their firing subsided after a minute, and Forrest could now see that someone was picking their attackers off with apparent impunity, probably from a hundred or more yards away and likely from an elevated position.

"That's gotta be the Forty-fifth!" he said.

The five or six remaining attackers suddenly broke from cover and ran south through the cars in attempt to escape, but the snipers didn't seem inclined to let them go, continuing to fire until they had killed every one of them.

Forrest and Kane kept low as they crept back toward the Humvee, using their infrared to scan the low bluffs east and west of the highway.

"Got one to the west," Kane said. "Moving carefully this way. It's a GI."

"Got one to the east too," Forrest replied. "Has to be the Forty-fifth."

The two men stood near the Humvee and waited for the troopers to approach from opposite sides of the highway.

"It's probably Lee and one of his men," Kane said. "What if they want to join us?"

Forrest took a moment to slap a fresh mag into his weapon. "I'd say they've earned it, wouldn't you?"

# FORTY-FOUR

EMORY SLOWED HER PACE, WAITING FOR MARTY TO APproach the troopers first, prepared to gun them both down if they gave him any shit. Sullivan was not with them. He had a concussion from being shot in the head and was too sick to be tromping around the countryside, so he lay sleeping in the back of the SUV parked half a mile north of their present position.

Emory and Marty had spotted the group of twenty-five road agents earlier in the day and taken cover in the hills around the highway with the intention of picking them off during the night after they were bedded down. The party had stood across their path south, and there was no other way through to Topeka without a long backtrack. Emory had been about to open fire on the snoozing band of marauders when Forrest's Humvee had first gone racing down the highway and stirred them all back up again.

Afterward the bandits stayed awake, taking up positions covering the highway, waiting to see if another Army truck might come by.

After watching the troopers kill six or seven of the bandits on their own, Emory and Marty, keeping in contact now via a pair of USGS walkie-talkies, decided to use the unknown men as a force multiplier and opened fire themselves, eventually killing off the remaining bandits and making the decision to expose themselves.

Marty flipped up his NVD as he walked into the area illuminated by the headlights of the Humvee, noting at once that both troopers were clean shaven. His carbine was slung over his shoulder, but he kept Joe's .45 gripped in his hand as he approached.

"Is either one of you hit?" he asked, trying to sound like a professional soldier.

"My partner is," Forrest said, his own .45 in hand and ready to blow Marty's brains out if he so much as twitched.

"My partner's a medic," Marty said.

"So am I," Kane said, watching Emory through his NVD, realizing she was intentionally hanging back.

"We appreciate you saving our butts," Forrest said. "You're with the Air Force?"

"Not anymore," Marty said, trying to keep his voice as deep as possible. "The Air Force isn't what it used to be."

"You can tell your partner it's safe to come in," Kane said over his shoulder, not wanting to take his eyes off Emory. "We won't shoot if you won't."

"My partner's with the Arizona Guard," Marty said, not yet having enough information to trust them. "Who are you guys with?"

With a speed that seemed inhuman to Marty, Forrest had disarmed him, screwed the barrel of his .45 into his ear and used him as a shield.

Kane was already gone from Emory's view, having taken cover behind the wheel hub of the Humvee.

"Tell your partner to drop his weapon!" Forrest ordered.

Emory shouldered the carbine as she dropped to her knee, sighting on Forrest's head, though not steady enough at fifty yards to be sure she wouldn't kill Marty instead. The speed and skill with which Forrest had moved told her they had come up against a highly trained pair of soldiers.

"Let him go!" she shouted. "Or I'll fire a grenade and kill all three of you!"

Kane quickly sought cover behind a different vehicle. "I got a clear shot, Jack."

Marty drew a breath to scream a warning, but Forrest choked off his air, pulling him closer to ground.

"Now listen up!" Forrest shouted. "We don't want to kill either of you. Just sling your weapon out there and I'll let your man go. This doesn't have to end bloody."

Emory wasn't sure what to do, realizing that Kane must have taken up a different firing position by now.

"How do I know you won't shoot?" she shouted, wanting badly to actually trust another soldier for a change.

"My partner's had you in his sights for ten seconds now and you're not dead! That proof enough?"

She rose slowly and lowered the carbine, waiting for the shots that would kill her and Marty both, but the men did not fire and Marty was released as promised.

"Relax now," Forrest said to Marty. "No sudden moves."

Marty stood in place as Emory came forward. Her carbine was slung, but she was ready to bring it up in a hurry, her finger on the trigger of the grenade launcher.

"She's got her finger on the M-203, Jack."

"That's fair," Forrest said. "Everybody be cool. It's a dangerous world we're living in."

Emory stepped up opposite the concrete barrier.

"Sorry about that," Forrest said, seeing her in the lights of the Humvee now. "But your partner seemed to be stalling. I couldn't take the chance."

"We just saved your asses," she said. "Why would we want to kill you?"

"Good question. Hard to trust anybody these days."

"That's a fucking understatement," she said, her eyes looking for Kane.

"Come on in, Marcus."

Kane stepped out of the darkness. "Thanks for not makin' me shoot you. I've never killed a woman and I wasn't lookin' to start."

"Don't mention it."

Marty wasn't saying much, still too pissed at himself and embarrassed over having been so easily overpowered and nearly getting Emory killed.

"I'm Shannon. That's my partner, Marty. He's an astronomer."

Forrest looked Marty over and offered his hand. "I'm Jack Forrest."

"Marty Chittenden."

"Look, I don't mean to be rude," Forrest said, "but we're trying to save a life, so we have to get this rig unstuck and be on our way."

"We'll give you a hand," Emory said.

While Kane saw to the bullet hole in his calf, Forrest and Emory drew the cable from the winch on the front bumper backward under the Humvee and hooked it into a loop of rebar sticking out of the concrete barrier, enabling the winch to pull the vehicle backward. After a few feet the rear wheels had enough traction to pull the Humvee the rest of the way clear. The whole procedure took less than ten minutes.

"Give us a lift to our truck?" Emory asked. "It's only half a mile north."

"Mount up," Forrest said, squinting against the snow that had begun to fall much more rapidly since their truce.

"Is there anything south of here we need to worry about?" Emory asked from the backseat, wanting badly to know what these men were up to and where they were headed, sensing their reluctance to share much information.

"Stay away from Topeka," Forrest warned from the passenger seat. "It's full of restless young soldiers who haven't seen a woman in a while."

"Great," Marty said gloomily. "As if we haven't seen enough of those."

"You guys said you're trying to save a life," Emory said. "What's that about?"

"A friend of ours is sick. We went to Topeka for some meds."

"We've got a sick friend too," she said. "He's up here in the truck with a bad concussion."

"Sorry to hear that," Forrest said.

Emory could smell the aftershave on these two, so she knew damn well they were living high on the hog someplace and that they were looking to ditch her and Marty as soon as possible. A feeling of desperation welled up inside of her as Kane pulled up alongside their SUV.

"Thanks again for saving our asses," Forrest said, offering Emory his hand.

"And now you're gonna ditch us?" she said, taking his hand.

"It's not like that. You guys were obviously headed somewhere and we're—"

"We're headed toward a long shot," she said, keeping hold of his hand. "And you two smell like an ad in *GQ*, so don't tell me you've got it tough. Look at us. Our luck's about to run out. Don't you think we've earned a break?"

She let go of his hand and gave him a moment to think it over.

"What do you think, Marcus?"

"I think Wayne's gonna pitch a bitch, but if we're gonna do this, let's do it."

Forrest helped them move Sullivan into the back of the Humvee and they were on their way. "What happened to him anyhow?"

"Shot in the head," Emory answered. "But his Kevlar saved his bacon."

"Our doc can take a look at him."

They got back to the silo without any more trouble and Kane pulled the Humvee up to the front porch of the house. Marty and Forrest helped Sullivan inside. He was conscious off and on. Emory saw the mostly eaten body on the living room floor in the beam of her flashlight as they took Sullivan upstairs and laid him down on the bed across the hall from where Black Beard had been killed.

"We'll get the gas and water turned back on for you," Forrest said. "The furnace too. That way you'll have hot water to wash with."

"This isn't where you live?" she asked.

"No, we live underground."

"Wait, this is an old missile installation, isn't it?" She exchanged glances with Marty.

"As a matter of fact, it is. Why?"

"Survival Estates?"

Forrest looked at Kane and laughed. "No, honey. We're not twenty-twelvers. We didn't buy this place until after we knew about the asteroid. How did you hear about Survival Estates?"

Emory and Marty told them the story about the crater and the wiped-out missile installation, then Forrest and Kane went below, promising to send up hot chow.


**THE FIRST THING** Ulrich said when he stepped into the cargo bay to greet them was: "Who the fuck's upstairs, Jack?"

"How's Melissa?"

"Unconscious but hanging in. Who are they?"

"They saved our goddamn lives," Forrest said, handing over the rucksack full of antibiotics. "Get these to West right away. Marcus and I have to clean up before we come in. And have somebody cook up a pot of something hot to eat."

Over the next few hours, Emory and Marty were fed and showered in the house above and given clean clothes to wear before being taken below, where they were asked to shower again and undergo a physical examination.

Sullivan was initially kept in the cargo bay wrapped in a thick arctic sleeping bag until Emory and West were able to give him a sponge bath. West suggested that after a few days of warmth and bed rest he would probably be much improved. For the time being he was given the cot in Launch Control, where he would be safe from the hustle and bustle of everyday life in the silo.

Forrest finally stepped into Medical, and Veronica got up

from the chair beside Melissa's bed, hugging him. She could have cried with joy at the sight of him, but with Michael present she maintained her composure.

Michael shook Forrest's hand and thanked him. By then Kane had related the details of their adventure, and the story had spread throughout the tiny population.

"How is she?" Forrest asked, seeing the bags of fluid now hooked up to Melissa's arms.

"Sean says we should know within twelve hours whether or not the drugs are helping," Michael said.

"They will," Forrest said, willing the antibiotics to be effective.

"I'll give you two some time," Michael said, turning to go.

"Stay put," Forrest said. "I have to go debrief our guests before Wayne gives them the Gestapo treatment." He found Marty and Emory in Launch Control with Ulrich and Kane. Emory was sitting beside Sullivan's cot, running her fingers through his hair as he slept. "How are you doing? Better?"

"It's unbelievable down here," she said quietly, ready to crawl out of her own skin. She was so used to being on the edge twenty-four hours a day that she was having trouble decompressing.

"You knew about the asteroid months in advance?" Marty said from a chair near the wall. "How?"

"A friend of mine at the Pentagon."

"And who are all these people?"

"Some are family and friends, the rest were chosen at random. See you in the hall for a minute, Wayne?"

Ulrich got up from his chair and stepped out with him.

"Recognize the look in their eyes?" Forrest asked.

"They don't know what to do now that there's nothing to fight. Better have Mike talk to them before we try any sort of debrief."

"We'll let 'em sleep in there with their man. They're not gonna want to split up for a while."

"You two fucking near bought it, didn't you?" Ulrich said.

"Twice. But it's over now."

"This makes three more mouths to feed, you know."

"I do. After you crunch the numbers, let me know how many days I've knocked off our lives, and I'll see what I can do to make up for it."

"Oscar and Linus bagged a rat while you were gone. It's in the cargo bay under a tarp. It's a female. Now they need to figure out what to build the cages out of."

"How long can we keep it a secret do you think?"

"I don't know," Ulrich said, "but if you hear Erin screaming like her hair's on fire, you'll know one of the little bastards got in here."

**IT WAS LATE** in the afternoon of the following day that Veronica found Forrest sleeping on the floor in the electrical room. "Jack," she said softly, kneeling to touch his arm.

He opened his eyes and for a moment didn't know where he was. "Yeah?"

"Melissa's awake," she said with a smile. "She asked for you first thing."

Forrest sat up in a flash, throwing back the sleeping bag and pulling on his boots. "What's Sean say?"

"He thinks maybe she's out of the woods."

"See?" he said, suddenly pissed. "Fucking Wayne would have had us watch her die!"

"Hey," she said gently. "I think that's entirely the wrong way to look at this."

"Yeah, you're right," he said, still frazzled from the mission. He got to his feet and kissed her, slipping quickly out of the room and up to Medical.

Melissa was obviously still very weak, but her face lit up the moment he came into the room.

"Hey!" he said softly, taking her hand and kissing her forehead.

"Where have you been?" she asked.

"I've been right here," he said with a smile. "What are you talking about?"

She shook her head. "You went somewhere."

"I'll tell you all about it later. How are you feeling?"

"Better. My head doesn't hurt so bad."

"Excellent," he said with a glance at West. "I'm going to talk with Sean a minute, okay?"

"Are you coming back?" she asked, trying to hold his hand tighter.

"Yeah."

"Promise?"

"Right after I talk with Sean, honey. I swear to God."

Forrest took West down the hall. "No bullshit, Sean. How is she?"

"I think the worst is behind her. The antibiotics seem to be doing their job."

"Could she relapse?"

"Of course," West said. "But she shouldn't, Jack. That's all I can tell you."

To West's surprise, Forrest gave him a hug then slipped back into the room.

# FORTY-FIVE

IT HAD TAKEN A COUPLE OF DAYS, BUT AFTER SULLIVAN IM-
proved to the point where he could sit up and coax Marty
and Emory out of Launch Control, the two slowly began to
adjust to life in the silo. Sullivan had served overseas, and
he understood the impact of post-traumatic stress, realizing
that his friends needed to socialize themselves. Michael
spoke with them briefly, but they hadn't been in the mood
to open up.

Emory took a liking to Veronica and so tagged around
with her for a day before venturing about on her own.

Marty borrowed a laptop from Ulrich and downloaded the
photos and videos of the crater for everyone in the complex
to view. No one could believe the size of the crater, which
looked far larger than a city in the panoramic shots, stretching well beyond the horizon. He had done the geometry and
estimated the crater at fifty miles across, as wide as Lake
Erie, and his tale of their fight with the cannibals living in
a missile complex similar to their own had chilled all of the
women to the bone.

This morning Emory was having breakfast in the cafeteria at a table with Erin and Tonya.

"When are you due?" Erin asked, hoping to engage the

dour-looking soldier in a conversation about something feminine.

"Probably April sometime," Emory replied. "I'm not sure."

"It's kind of exciting knowing there's a baby on the way."

"I guess it's nice somebody's excited about it. I'd like to abort the little bastard."

Tonya politely excused herself a moment or two later and moved to another table.

"Doesn't it get on your nerves living on top of each other down here?" Emory said quietly.

"It took a little getting used to," Erin said. "But you learn to block things out."

"Are any of these kids yours?"

"No, Wayne and I . . . well, we never got around to it, and now . . ." She shrugged.

"Want mine?"

"Excuse me?"

"Do you want mine? Like I told you, I don't want it. I was hoping I'd start to feel something for it but I haven't, and I'm pretty sure I'm not going to."

"It's too soon for you to know how you're going to feel," Erin said, deciding quickly she'd better not let her maternal feelings loose.

"No, it's not. I've been watching these mothers down here, trying to picture myself doing what they're doing. It's not me. I'm a soldier and sooner or later I'm going to have to fight again."

"Well, we can talk about it later. There's plenty of time to—"

"I'm going to talk about it with every woman down here. So if you want it, you might want to speak up pretty quick. Some of these girls seem to *love* being mothers."

"Okay," Erin said, casting caution to the wind. "But I want to know the very second you change your mind. The very second, Shannon."

Emory looked up from her bowl of oatmeal with raisins. "I won't change my mind. So congratulations, you're a mom."

Erin sat looking at her. "Excuse me for a minute?" she said at length.

"Sure."

Erin went to find her husband, locating him in silo number two where he was taking inventory.

"What's wrong?" Ulrich asked, never having seen such an odd look in her eyes.

She covered her face with both hands, looking at him over the tips of her fingers.

"Honey, what's wrong?"

"Shannon just gave us her baby," she blurted, scared to death that he was going be angry with her for not consulting with him. "I'm sorry, honey, but she was going to ask the others and I—"

"Come here," he said, setting the clipboard aside and putting his arms out for her to walk into them.

"You're not pissed?"

"No," he said, stroking her. "Why are you crying?"

"I'm a little overwhelmed, Wayne. I didn't even give it any thought. I was so afraid she'd give it to one of the others if I waited."

"Are you sorry you accepted?"

"No, I'm ecstatic, but I'm scared. I even feel guilty, almost like I'm stealing her baby. I don't know how to explain it. She asked me point-blank, honey. She said she doesn't feel anything for it and doesn't want it."

"Then you've done something good. You've got nothing to feel bad about."

Later, Ulrich found Forrest in the cargo bay talking with Danzig and Vasquez about their rat breeding project. "Can we have a minute, gentlemen?"

Danzig and Vasquez were quick to quit the cargo bay, plainly seeing that Ulrich had a very definite something on his mind.

Forrest started to grin.

"Apparently you've already heard?"

Forrest shook his head. "But I know that look."

"Well, thanks to you, asshole, Erin's adopting a goddamn baby."

Forrest burst out laughing.

"It's not funny!"

"The hell it's not! Serves you right, you prick. You goddamn near killed Melissa."

"Oh, I knew sooner or later I'd have to hear about that!" Ulrich rejoined.

"Bullshit, Wayne. The only reason I'm saying anything now is because you're in here giving me shit about Erin wanting Shannon's baby."

"My vote on that fucked-up mission was the *right* vote! You got lucky, Jack!"

"You're goddamn right I did! And because of it she's alive! You think I'm gonna apologize for that? Fuck you, Stumpy. Erin deserves a baby. You're the selfish motherfucker who told her no all those years. You think I was itching to have a kid before Daniel was born? Fuck, no. But at least I tried to give Monica what she wanted."

"Oh, so now I'm a selfish husband."

"You're a selfish prick, Wayne! You always have been. It's why I'm the only friend you've got."

"Fuck you!"

"Fuck you," Forrest said. "I wouldn't have you any other way myself, but Erin deserves a little bundle of joy for the time she's put in."

"Shit," Ulrich said, turning away. He walked over and took a long look at the burn marks on the hood of the Humvee. "You two fuckers had the time of your lives out there, didn't you?"

"Jealous?"

Ulrich turned back around. "A little."

"Well, now your mission is to make sure Shannon eats right."

"That girl doesn't know who she's gotten herself involved

with," Ulrich said. "Erin's going to be the bane of her existence for the next six months."

By that night Melissa was sitting up in bed and drinking chicken broth through a straw. Dr. West had also given in to her pleading and allowed Laddie to lay in bed with her. Forrest came in to sit with her so Michael could take a break.

"Where have you been all day?" she asked him as he sat down on the edge of the bed and started petting his dog.

"Well, I've been doing my thing, you know. Checking on everybody and seeing to our new members. Cleaning up dog crap. All the usual stuff."

She chuckled. "Wayne cleans up all the dog crap."

"To hear him tell it, yeah."

"What are you guys doing in the cargo bay?"

"Nothing, why?"

"Whatever," she said. "You guys always lie to me and think I don't know."

"Okay, smarty pants. If I tell you, it stays between us. *Nobody else*. Not even Veronica. Agreed?"

She nodded, thrilled to be privy to something so secret that not even Veronica knew about it, thinking it had to do with Christmas, which everyone was looking forward to with great anticipation.

"We're breeding rats."

"Ew!" she said in disgust.

"You wanted to know."

"What for?"

"For in case the food runs out before we think of something else."

"I guess it kinda makes sense," she said after thinking it over. "Can you get me my papers? They're in the room under my bedroll."

"Not until you're well again. You work yourself too hard and you need sleep."

"You and Veronica are ganging up on me with Uncle Michael. Can't I just have one page?"

"Not until you're well. Doctor's orders."

"Then tell me about your trip."

"Can't."

"Oh, God. Why not?"

"Because it was gory and I'm not telling you about gory stuff."

"Did you have to kick some caveman ass?" she asked with a titter.

"That's a good way to put it," he said, smiling.

"Dr. West says you saved my life."

"Dr. West saved your life. All Kane and I did was make a run to the pharmacy."

"I knew you'd make a good dad. See? That's why I picked you."

"Hey," he said softly. "I thought we agreed you wouldn't say stuff like that."

"I didn't agree to anything." She yawned and hunkered down into the bedding, turning over onto her side to face the wall. "Dad, will you scratch my back till I fall asleep?"

He covered his eyes with one hand and began gently scratching her back with the other.

"I love you," she said quietly.

Forrest's face contorted as the memories of Daniel and Monica came flooding back to him in a vivid wave, and the tears ran down his cheeks from beneath his fingers. "Please," he whispered. "Stop."

She turned back over. "Is this why you won't sit with me?"

He nodded, his eyes still covered by his fingers.

"I'm sorry," she said. "I won't ever say it again. I promise."

He opened his eyes, gathered her into his arms and wept openly. "I just miss them."

"I miss my family too," she said, beginning to cry too. "Can't we be a family now?"

"Yes," he whispered. "Of course."

When Michael looked in on them an hour later, Forrest was asleep against the wall and Melissa lay nestled in the crook of his arm with Laddie stretched across the foot of the bed. He smiled, turned out the light and closed the door.

# FORTY-SIX

THANKSGIVING CAME AND WENT WITHOUT A GREAT DEAL OF
excitement, but it was an okay day for everyone, and by
that time the three newcomers had begun to assimilate
fairly well. Emory and Sullivan even began sharing a shift
in Launch Control, and this allowed Forrest and his men
to enjoy shorter shifts of their own. Marty enjoyed talking
physics with Melissa, who knew a surprising amount about
quantum field theory for a person her age, and though
Marty was no physicist, he was able to enhance her understanding of fermions and the latest theories at the time of
the impact.

Now it was Christmas Eve, and the look on the children's
faces when two different Santas came Ho-ho-hoing into the
main room—one black and one white, each wearing a pair
of Blues Brothers sunglasses and carrying a red bag over his
shoulder—was one of utter astonishment. Most of the children had been worried that Santa Claus was dead, but suddenly here he was, and he had brought a friend with him. A
couple of the kids looked suspiciously back and forth at their
mothers, wondering if it was a trick, but they only smiled.

Karen squeezed Michael's hand, whispering, "Look, Terri
thinks they're real."

Michael grinned, pointing discreetly at Joann's daughter. "Look at the discernment on Beyonce's face. She's not buying it for a second."

The Santas began to call the children's names in deep voices, handing out packages wrapped in Christmas paper. The kids tore excitedly into their gifts, delighted to learn after only a few moments that both of the Santas had something for each one of them.

After the children's names were called, the Santas began to call the mothers' names one at a time, and each mother had to sit in Santa's lap before she was given her gift.

Melissa's name was the last to be called, and she was given a brand new laptop computer that had never even been taken out of the box. Her eyes lit up when she opened the box, and even Ulrich was stunned by what he saw.

"Did you know she was getting that?" he asked, leaning into Michael's ear.

"No," Michael said, impressed. "Didn't you?"

The laptop was no run-of-the-mill civilian model. It was mounted in an army green, titanium, rubberized casing just over two inches thick when closed. There was the subdued image of an apple in the lower left-hand corner of the lid.

"No," Ulrich said dryly. "That's a Delta-OSS . . . a military prototype worth a couple of hundred grand. It was designed to interface with any U.S. military satellite system."

"Where the hell did it come from?"

"Jack must have asked Jerry to send it along with that shipment of MREs. There were only a dozen or so of the damn things ever made."

"Will it decipher that code Melissa's been working on?"

Ulrich shook his head. "That kind of software wouldn't have been standard. Ninety-eight percent of what that thing can do, we haven't any use for. Not so long as the satellite signals are smothered by the atmosphere. I'm sure Jack's got the sat receiver down here somewhere."

"That's why he's giving it to her," Michael said. "For the future."

After the presents were given out and the kids had coerced

the Santas into eating six or seven Christmas cookies apiece and drinking two big glasses of lukewarm reconstituted milk, it was time for the St. Nicks to be off. They Ho-ho-hoed their way into the hall heading for the cargo bay, where presumably they would find their reindeer patiently waiting to fly them back to the North Pole.

The children were put to bed a few hours later, and the adults were treated to a few bottles of wine. They played Christmas music and sat around happily talking in the light of the tree. The married couples cuddled together about the room, and though the single mothers found themselves feeling more than a little envious, everyone very much enjoyed the spirit of the evening, wishing that every day could be Christmas.

They all fell asleep in turn, but six A.M. came around quickly and the cooks got themselves up to start preparing Christmas dinner. The children didn't sleep long beyond that, and soon there were some cranky disagreements over who was and wasn't allowed to touch someone else's toys. Those entanglements were cut short, however, by a rare break in protocol when Forrest personally made it clear to the kids that the Santas had not given them their new toys to fight over and that they were expected to share.

After that there was harmony in Toyland.

"You should lay down the law more often," Taylor said, kidding him in the kitchen.

"Oh, no," he said, cocking an eyebrow as Lynette shooed Laddie from the kitchen with an apron. "The Grinch only comes out at Christmas."

Marty sat talking quietly with Emory at the back of the cafeteria. "Did you talk to John about my idea?" he asked.

She ran her finger around the inside of a foil tuna packet, being sure to get every last morsel. "He doesn't want to go," she said, licking the finger. "He says he likes taking a hot shower every day."

"But there's no future down here, Shannon. They're postponing the inevitable."

"Have you seen how much food they've got down here? We're set for another year at least, and in case you haven't noticed . . . I'm getting fat."

"I'm not saying we should leave before the baby's born, I'm—" He looked up as Sullivan stepped into the room.

The soldier stood behind Emory and began to massage her shoulders. This was an unspoken arrangement between them; he massaged her neck and shoulders at least once a day, and she made sure she found the opportunity to help him with his needs a couple of times a week. Emory knew that he had fallen in love with her, but he didn't gush, and when he did say something romantic it was always during one of their intimate moments under the main stairwell between the blast doors.

To her profound surprise, he bent down and kissed the nape of her neck.

"What was that for?" she said, feeling her face flush.

He shrugged and continued to massage her shoulders as though nothing had happened, winking at Marty. "So you want to split, huh?"

Marty took a Christmas cookie from the plate in the center of the table. "Eventually, I think we should, yeah."

"For what?"

"To find those geologists at Altus Air Force Base. Keep things moving forward."

"What things forward to where?" Sullivan said, irritated. "We don't even know if there's anybody alive up there, and even if there is, it's snowing like a bastard now."

"They've got two Army trucks in the cargo bay. We can ask them to give us one."

Sullivan let that pass, shifting his attention to Emory. With the progression of her pregnancy, he was finding her ever more attractive. Unable to help himself, he kissed the nape of her neck a second time, and she whipped her head around, hissing through a mouthful of cookie, "Quit it!"

He chuckled as he sat down beside her. "No one was looking."

She glared the way only a woman can. "You're gonna piss me off."

He rolled his eyes and took a cookie for himself. "I can't help it. It's Christmas . . . and you're gorgeous."

She looked at Marty. "Will you please remind him that I'm gay? He seems to have forgotten."

Marty grinned. "It *is* Christmas. "

"So fucking what? That's doesn't mean I'm—" Ulrich walked up and she stopped talking.

"See you a minute, Marty? I've got another question about those crater photos."

"Sure." Marty got up and followed him into the other room.

Emory made sure no one was paying attention to them, then said to Sullivan, "What's with you lately? You're getting all . . . sappy."

"I'm in love with you."

She gaped at him, unable to believe he had actually said the words.

"Or didn't you know that?"

She took another bite of cookie and turned around. "John, you're gonna ruin this."

"I don't want to ruin anything," he said. "I just want you to know how I feel . . . that's all."

She looked at him. "Then tell me so we can get it behind us."

"I love you and I want you to keep the baby so we can raise it together."

Her eyes filled with tears and she turned away again. "You know that's impossible."

"Yes, I do," he said quietly, touching her hair with affection. "But I wanted you to know my mind."

She put her hand on his leg, said, "Thank you," then got up and left the room.

# FORTY-SEVEN

FORREST HAD GIVEN THE MEN THE NIGHT OFF, BUT EVEN HE was asleep in Launch Control with his head on his arms when someone tapped him on the shoulder. He sat up and opened his eyes to see Andie, Joann, and Maria two.

"I said you could bring *a* friend," he remarked with a tired chuckle, noting the tentative look on Andie's face. "What I am in trouble for now?"

Andie looked at the other two. Then Maria two turned and looked at Joann.

"Okay, I guess it's me," Joann said. "So . . . Jack . . . we have a little bit of a problem."

"What sort of a problem?" he asked, reaching for his cigarettes. "I think Christmas went pretty well, don't you?"

"It's got nothing to do with Christmas. It has to do with the fact you cut us off . . . or rather you told Oscar to. We had a perfectly good thing going with him until you butted in. Now we're climbing the goddamn walls down here, and it's not fair. It wasn't any of your business."

This took Forrest by surprise, and he glanced at Andie, who leaned back against the door.

"Andie's here because she's got a separate issue," Joann said.

"Oh? Why isn't Renee in here too?"

Joann and Maria two looked at each other, obviously confused by the question.

"So you guys didn't know about her," he said, sitting forward and lighting up. "Look, ladies, I wasn't making a moral judgment, and normally this kind of thing wouldn't be any of my business, but Oscar was exercising piss-poor judgment. The last thing I need down here is a civil war . . . married women against the single ones. See what I'm saying?"

"And you thought cutting us off was the way to avoid that?"

Now Forrest saw what Vasquez had meant when he had said, *Suppose they don't agree?* It seemed not even an apocalypse could prevent romantic intrigue. "I'm not exactly sure I know how to respond to that, Joann. Are you saying you have an unalienable right to another woman's husband just because the world has ended?"

Joann looked at Maria two for help.

Maria two said, "We're saying we have needs like anybody else, Jack . . . and Maria takes sleeping pills every night, so she sleeps like a log. That's what we're saying."

"Sometimes you have to make concessions," Joann added, crossing her long arms. "For the sake of keeping the peace."

"It's a small thing," Maria two went on. "We're very careful and Maria isn't going to find out."

"Turns out you're *not* so careful, actually," he said testily, unable to believe he was having such a conversation with two women in the midst of such circumstances. "But let's get past that for a second . . . you're not ashamed of yourselves at all? You don't feel . . . bad?"

"A man wouldn't be ashamed," Joann persisted. "Would you be a bit surprised by this if we were men? I don't think so."

Forrest looked each woman in the eyes. "You're naive to think nobody will tell Maria . . . and when they do, I'll have a huge brushfire to put out down here."

Andie finally spoke up. "Nobody's going to tell her, Jack.

It's terrible to say, but the wife is always the last to find out when she's being cheated on . . . none of the other married women will want to risk their own husbands taking Oscar's place."

"So you're telling me," Forrest said, not quite exasperated, "that you ladies can't maintain any more self-control than this? With an entire *planet* dying above you, you can't be satisfied that your children are safe and that you've got food to eat."

"That's easy for you to say," Joann rejoined, "getting laid four times a week!"

He straightened up in the chair, self-conscious that they knew the exact number.

"You don't think we pay attention?" Joann went on. "You think everybody's happy as pigs in shit down here because nobody fights? Nobody fights because we found a balance . . . that is until you came along and fucked it up."

He sat forward and crushed out the cigarette in the brass cannon shell, exhaling a stream of smoke, feeling disappointed in them. "So what do you want me to do?"

"Lift the embargo," Joann said. "Turn a blind eye. Let Oscar have some fun before he runs out of insulin . . . trust us."

Forrest eyed Andie. "And you?"

She shrugged. "You know what I want."

"So this is an ultimatum," he said. "Either I acquiesce . . . or you start letting your tempers fly down here. Is that about right?"

"It won't be out of spite," Maria two said in earnest. "We're only human. It may not sound like it, Jack, but we're asking for your help."

"All you need to do is stay out of it," Joann said, trying to make it all sound so simple.

Andie finally stepped away from the door. "You can't control every single thing that happens down here, Jack. The tighter you squeeze, the more things will slip through your fingers."

Forrest understood this concept as one of the primary principles of command, but he had never been in charge of a group of women before, nor had he envisioned what seemed to him such an unlikely scenario. "Fine," he said at length. "But you girls had better go *out of your way* to make sure Maria never finds out, and you'd damn well better be there for her when Oscar dies. Understood?" He was applying his military bearing now, and he was glad to see that they were responding in the appropriate manner, both of them straightening up under his gaze and nodding their compliance. "And I will expect to hear all of the appropriate mea culpas in the event that you're caught."

Both women looked at the floor, nodding once more.

"Very well, ladies. Good night."

They thanked him quietly and left him alone with Andie.

"Okay," he said to her, "so what am I supposed to do for you now? Take my pants off?"

Andie's eyes flooded with tears and she turned for the door.

Forrest got up and caught her arm. "I'm sorry," he said gently. "That was uncalled for."

She turned into him and rested her forehead against his chest. "It was cruel."

"It's my way of pouting," he said, lifting her chin. "I'm feeling pretty damn unappreciated at the moment."

She looked at him, loving the feel of being so close to him in private. "I need something only you can give me, Jack. I'm losing my mind down here."

"Why not Oscar?" he suggested dryly. "He's apparently in great demand."

"I'm not attracted to that disloyal little son of a bitch. I'm attracted to you."

"Yet, what you're suggesting would make *me* a disloyal son of a bitch."

"You're not married. And I'm lonely enough for that to be a big enough difference."

They made love carefully and quietly, and when they were

finished Andie no longer looked nor felt like she was about to crawl out of her skin. She lay on top of him listening to the beat of his heart.

"Can I ask you a silly question?" she said quietly.

"Sure," he said, stroking her hair, his mind on fifty other things.

"Do you love her?"

"Yes," he said. "I love her completely."

She got up from the cot and began to dress. "Thank you very much, Jack."

He reached for her hand. "Please don't thank me. You're a wonderful woman, and you deserve an awful lot more than *anyone* down here can give you."


**LATE THE NEXT** morning, Veronica unexpectedly joined him in the shower, pulling the curtain closed. "So how did it go last night?"

"What's that mean?" He was not at all surprised that she knew something had occurred. Probably everyone in the complex knew something had occurred, everyone except for Oscar's wife, of course, which was only because she took pills in order to sleep, the stress of knowing that her husband had less than eighteen months to live having turned her into an insomniac.

"If you're going to play stupid," Veronica said, "we're going to have a fight."

"Fine. I let Andie seduce me."

"And how was it?" she asked calmly, reaching for the soap.

"She's a very lonely person," he said stiffly, not at all sure what to expect from her.

"Or was," she said, turning the soap in her hands. "She looks like a whole new woman today."

"I haven't seen her."

She let the soap drop and slipped her arms around him. "Did I make a mistake?"

"What are you talking about?" he said, resting his hands on her shoulders.

"Last night was my idea," she confessed, trembling slightly. "I knew things were coming to a head . . . and I knew that . . . I knew that concessions had to be made . . . even by me . . . and it all seemed so logical last night with it being Christmas and . . . and now I'm worried I made a huge mistake."

Forrest remembered his warning to her about being too objective. He held her face in his hands. "A mistake how?"

"There's a light in Andie's eyes this morning. So it must have been magical between you. It was, right? You made a connection?"

He couldn't help smiling. "A *connection*? Honey, if there's a light in Andie's eyes today, good for her, but—" He shrugged his shoulders and laughed. "Jesus Christ, you're the only *magic* in this place. Why did you ever send her in there with them?"

"Because it was only a matter of time before something happened between you, and I wanted it to be on my terms, not hers . . . and sure as hell not yours."

He moved her hair away from her face with his fingers. "I'd like to think you're wrong about that . . . but who knows? She does flatter me."

"So what now?" She shifted her weight to one leg, searching his eyes with hers.

"What do you mean, 'what now'?" he asked, puzzled. "Veronica, as far as I'm concerned it never happened."

She smiled and her eyes filled with tears. "If that's true . . . then I made the right choice."

"I love you."

She pressed against him and began to cry, relieved that he was still hers alone.

# FORTY-EIGHT

IT WAS EARLY APRIL NOW, AND WITH THE TEMPERATURE hovering just below forty degrees on the island of Oahu, it was still too cold to even think about growing any kind of food outdoors. Light meters used to measure the amount of sunlight penetrating the cloud layer were indicating a slight increase, which was a hopeful sign, but at the present rate of improvement it would still be years before there would be much actual sunlight. Local meteorologists and other members of the scientific community were still debating whether the rate of improvement would begin to increase exponentially as time passed.

Ester Thorn stood bundled in a coat on the flight deck of the USS *Abraham Lincoln* anchored in Pearl Harbor. With her were Vice President Hadrian and Admiral Longbottom. The admiral had invited them to review the progress made toward converting the aircraft carrier into a power plant for the city of Honolulu. The pier was now replete with transformers and power lines, hooking the carrier into the previously existing lines running along Hawaiian Highway 1 into the city.

Much of the island population had been moved into the capital, because running power all across the island was not going to be practical for some time yet. Personal homes remained private property, but all other structures had become the property of the state in order to provide housing for those moving into the city. No one had to pay for room or board, but everyone had to do their part, however small.

As it turned out, very few people were unwilling to pitch in around the island. In fact, during the early months there were more volunteers than jobs. So a massive recycling program was begun, sending people to scour the islands for anything that might be useful. Scientists and visionaries alike were teaming up in an effort to create new technologies before the clock ran out.

"It's coming along," Ester muttered.

"Yes, ma'am," Longbottom replied.

"But this doesn't exactly look permanent to me," she said.

"No, ma'am. It's not. This is a temporary setup. If you'll look west to Ford Island, you'll see where preparations are being made for the permanent installation of a proper power station. Right now the power is being run directly from the carrier into town, which isn't as efficient as we need it to be. Once we're able to run the power through a series of transformers we'll be able to begin storing some of it."

"And that power station will be ready to accept power from the tidal generators?" Ester asked.

"Yes, ma'am. The Australian engineer has already selected a nearby location to begin installing the first few turbines. Which brings me to another subject."

"Oil, Admiral?"

"Yes, ma'am. The Aussies are asking us to bring a second drilling platform online. They're willing to supply everything needed to get it up and running again if we're willing to do the actual work. They have no one to spare with the know-how and they're struggling with a serious power shortage."

"They need the extra oil to run their mining operations. Yes. I've heard."

"And if they're going to continue the manufacture of the tidal turbines . . ."

"Yes, yes," Ester said. "What do you think, Barry? Is it time to restart another drilling platform?"

"I think we should restart it," Hadrian said. "But then we should show the Aussies how to run it themselves and turn it over to them entirely. Let their navy protect it. Our fleet is already busy enough here in the Islands."

"And piracy does continue to be an ongoing problem," Longbottom said. "I'm sure you've heard that another settlement was attacked last night on the island of Lanai."

Ester cast a glance at Hadrian, the two of them having privately discussed the matter already. "Yes, I've heard. At some point, Admiral, these settlers are going to have to learn to defend themselves to a certain extent. We can't keep a ship lying off the coast of every settlement. It spreads your fleet too thinly and burns too much fuel. Perhaps we could garrison a Marine detachment in each of the settlements. That would give your troops something to do, would it not?"

Longbottom stood thinking it over. "We might try it. I'll speak with the Marine commandant, General Flohr, and see what he thinks."

"Please do," she said. "With no more real wars left to fight, Admiral, it's going to be difficult to keep them busy. And we don't need a bunch of bored young men with weapons just sitting around."

"No, ma'am," the admiral said dryly, noting the veiled smile on Hadrian's face.

# FORTY-NINE

**WITH TWO AND A HALF MONTHS TO GO BEFORE HITTING THE** one-year mark, the silo's food and fuel stores stood at just over half of what they had started with—not counting the truckloads of MREs—so Forrest was pleased with their planning. There were hydroponic tomato plants growing in virtually every available space, and the twenty rats they had bred were all healthy and living in separate cages in order to keep them from reproducing before it was time.

Since agreeing to look the other way concerning Vasquez's midnight trysts with his three girlfriends, the women seemed to be getting along even better than before. Nonetheless, Forrest didn't believe for a moment that Maria Vasquez was the fool everyone else seemed to believe she was.

It was seven in the morning and he was in the middle of getting a shave when every alarm in the installation began to wail. He wiped his face with a towel and ducked quickly out of the shower room, running through the halls to Launch Control. "Whatta we got?"

"Serious fucking trouble," Ulrich said, all the monitors cycling through the many camera feeds. "Multiple targets."

Forrest took one look at the monitors and killed the claxon, grabbing the mike for the P.A. system. "All combat personnel to the LC," he announced. "All combat personnel to the LC. This is not a drill, repeat this is not a drill. Civilian population will move to secure quarters in an orderly fashion . . . Keep calm, people. I don't want anyone hurt."

Emory was the first one to enter the LC, zipping her ACU jacket over her belly.

"What the fuck are you doing?"

"I'm com—"

"No way," Forrest said. "You could have that kid at any minute."

"Don't shoulder me aside, Jack."

"Then . . . take a seat and help Wayne," he said, unlocking the weapons cabinet and strapping on his .45. "Wayne, I want all extra ammo transferred from the cargo bay to blast tunnel number two. Make it happen."

"I'm already on it, Captain!" Vasquez said, crossing through the LC.

Ulrich tapped one of the screens, getting Emory's attention. "This monitor is yours. I want you watching everything that goes on inside the house. Keep moving from room to room. I'll be watching these other two to keep up with what's going on outside."

"Oh, shit!" she said, seeing three slovenly soldiers entering the house through the front door. "It's the Air Force."

Forrest exchanged glances with Ulrich. "What about 'em, Shannon?"

"We've already butted heads with these guys," she said. "They were real bad news back in September. God knows what they're like now. I wonder how they found this place."

Sullivan and Marty arrived dressed in their combat gear, ready to perform whatever task was asked of them. Michael and the other doctors had come too. All of them were understandably disturbed by what they saw on the monitors.

"It's that asshole, Moriarty," Ulrich grated. "He's back for his fucking MREs, Jack. See what getting greedy got us?"

"We don't know it's him, and if it is, we'll deal with him."

"Oh, it's him all right," said Marty. "I'd bet on it."

"What do *you* know about him?"

"I heard that name when I had my run-in with them," Marty said. "And it sounded like he was some kind of hard-ass. These people are rapists, Jack."

"They can't get in here, can they?" Michael asked.

"That depends," Forrest said, concentrating on the monitors as he watched the motley outfit deploying around the grounds and into the house. He was trying to get a head count.

"Depends on what?" Michael said. "You said nobody could get down here."

"These assholes are military," Ulrich said. "If they've got the right shit, they can blow their way in."

"Oh, great!"

"Mike, if you're going to start, you'll have to leave," Forrest said. "Looks like about a hundred men. I count ten transports, five trailers . . . couple Humvees. Three fuel trucks."

"If that's all they've got left," Emory said, "they've lost a hell of a lot of people."

"Yeah, well, eating your own can have that effect."

"Is it time we started thinking about the Broken Arrow?" Ulrich said.

"No," Forrest said, still studying the monitors. "We can only dance that dance once. I'd rather give up the number one blast door first. But keep an eye on those assholes by the trucks. Tell me if they unload any ordnance."

"What's a Broken Arrow?" Michael wanted to know.

"Sean, Price," Forrest said, ignoring the question. "Would you see to the women and children? I'll keep you appraised."

"Let us know if you need us to pick up a rifle," West said.

"We're a long way from having to arm the medical staff, Sean. Sullivan, you and Marty help Oscar and Linus in the loading bay. They'll need help prepping the vehicles for emergency evac."

"Sir!" Sullivan said, turning on his heel and taking Marty with him.

"Before you go, gentlemen . . . what you see in the bay is to remain top secret, is that understood?"

"Sir!"

"Okay, Major Moriarty," Forrest said, turning back to the monitors. "What's on your mind?"

"See these cases here?" Ulrich said, tapping the monitor where a pair of airmen were unloading some large green cases from the back of a deuce-and-a-half. "Those are M-92s, shaped demolition charges. They can use them to blow the blast doors out of their casements."

"I wasn't counting on us going up against professional demolitions people."

"Well, you invited their asses, Jack. Makes it tough to avoid."

"Hey, Wayne, do me a favor and pop the top on an ice-cold bottle of shut-the-fuck-up, will ya?"

Emory snickered.

"Okay, pregnant warrior," Forrest said, moving around behind her chair and putting his hands on her shoulders as he watched the screens. "How were these assholes disposed when you went up against them before?"

"They had an attack chopper, but we shot that down," she said, drawing a look from Ulrich. "Seriously . . . and they had at least one tank and plenty of small arms. That's all we really saw in terms of armament, and this is only a fraction of the transport they had."

"Discipline?"

She shrugged. "Lax at best."

"All right. Then we can assume it hasn't gotten any better."

"Maybe if we offer them some soap and razor blades they'll go away," Michael remarked.

"Wouldn't count on that," chuckled Emory.

"What's this here?" Forrest said, touching the monitor. "Looks like a cage built over the back of this deuce-and-a-half? Are those men locked inside?"

"They're livestock," she said.

"Jesus," Michael muttered, folding his arms and watching Forrest very closely.

When Kane finally entered Launch Control, Forrest looked expectantly in his direction. "We set?"

"All set," Kane said, wiping his hands with an oily rag.

"Looks like we'd better be," Forrest said. "These pricks here are unloading shaped charges."

Kane shrugged it off. "They'll only get the number one door. We'll still have numbers two and three after that."

"How do you know they'll only get one door?" Michael wanted to know.

"Would you knowingly walk into a goddamn blast furnace?"

"Blast furnace?"

"We got our own dragon lives in this cave," Kane said. "You didn't know that?"

"Um, guys?" Emory said, looking into her lap. "I think my water just broke."

"What water?" Ulrich turned around. "Oh, *that* water!"

Forrest looked at Emory and laughed. "You can tell it's Wayne's kid, with the shitty timing."

"Hey, fuck you, Jack. It's not 'my kid.'"

"It will be pretty fucking soon," Emory said, taking Michael's hand as she stood up from the chair. "Good luck with the battle, guys."

Michael walked her down the hall to Medical.

Sean West was in the process of packing an emergency med kit in case they were forced to evacuate the facility when he looked up to see that Emory's fatigue pants were wet. "Stress of the moment?" he said with a smile.

"Musta been," she said. "I started having contractions the second I stood up."

"Help her onto the bed, Michael. And go find Price, will you?"

"Get Erin too," Emory called. "And be sure to tell Marty!" She took off her jacket and lay on her side while West went about preparing a semisterile environment. "Hey, Doc, do you have any of those silver suicide things?"

He turned around. "How do you know about those?"

"I don't think anything's a secret down here, Doc."

A shadow crossed his brow. "What do you want one for?"

"Well, if those bastards get in here anytime soon, I won't be any good for fighting *or* evacuating."

"I'll be taking care of you. Don't worry."

"No offense, Doc, but I've seen things go to shit way too fast in this current reality. I'd feel a lot better if I had one of those things in my jacket pocket right here by the bed."

He stood looking at her, knowing she was right about the fluidity of battle. He opened a cabinet, took a titanium vial not much larger than a tube of chapstick from a steel box, walked over and put it into her jacket pocket. "Once this siege has lifted, I want it back. They're too dangerous to have floating around down here with the kids."

"No problem."

Erin arrived and sat down on the edge of the bed with Emory, taking her hand. "How do you feel, honey?"

"Pissed. I'm supposed to be getting ready for a fight, but I'm in here having a fuckin' kid."

"Do you still feel like you want me to—"

"Erin, don't even *try* getting out of this!"

Erin kissed her hand, suddenly overcome by emotion. "There's no greater gift one woman can give another."

"Bullshit," Emory said, already bored with Erin's sentimentality. "I can think of a few things right off the bat."

"Like what?" Erin asked.

"Some good head, for one thing."

West laughed out loud.

"You're terrible!" Erin said. "You sound like Wayne."

"Must be why he and I get along so good."


**BACK IN LAUNCH** Control, Forrest and the others stood watching as Moriarty walked into the house with a meter-long plastic tube under his arm, strolling into the kitchen like General Patton as he removed his gloves. They recognized him even with the beard as he faced the tiny fiber-optic camera hidden in the smoke detector on the kitchen wall. The fact that the kitchen table was stained dark with blood didn't seem to bother him as he pulled a rolled-up blueprint from the tube and rolled it out on the table.

"Oh, that's just fucking great!" Ulrich said, sitting back in the chair.

"What is that?" Michael asked.

"It's a schematic of this facility," Forrest said quietly. "The Air Force must have still had it on file locally."

"That means we're in big trouble, right? Won't they go right to the lift elevator and blow their way through?"

"No," Forrest said. "And if even they do, they've still got a pair of blast doors to get through—*if* they get past us in the cargo bay."

Ulrich turned around in the chair and looked up at him. "Would you care to tell me what makes you so fucking sure he won't go straight to the lift elevator?"

Forrest took a moment to light up a cigarette with his brass Zippo before replying. "Why would he look for something he doesn't know about?"

"He's got the goddamn schematic right there on the table, Jack!"

"He has the *original* schematic," Forrest said. "See, I do my research, Stumpy. Only two Titan installations were given lift elevators. This one and another one clear the fuck up in North Dakota some place. And *our* lift elevator wasn't added to this installation until two years after it went online. Hence . . . jerkoff up there knows nothing about it."

# FIFTY

**MORIARTY STOOD LOOKING OVER THE SCHEMATIC, SCRATCH-**
ing at himself as Lieutenant Ford came into the kitchen with
a couple of men. "This house obviously wasn't part of the
original plan, lieutenant. So the main blast door must be
located beneath it. You two, go down and check the basement."

Ford waited until the men were gone. "Are you worried
about a booby trap?"

"Better safe than sorry," Moriarty said with a shrug, again
digging at his crotch.

The men returned unharmed and said the entrance to
the silo was indeed located in the basement and that it was
sealed shut.

"Told you," Moriarty said quietly, rolling up the schematic. "It's sealed, which means our Green Beret friends are
still down there eating our food. Mark my words, Lieutenant. Before this is over, I am personally going to feed that
smartass Captain Forrest his fucking liver.

"Sergeant Yoshinaka!" he said, stepping into the living
room. "Are you ready to blow the doors off this beast?"

"They're bringing up the charges now, Major," answered
a Japanese-American male with three dingy blue chevrons
on his arms.

"And you're sure you can do this?"

"These shaped charges were designed for exactly this kind of work, Major. Don't worry. Three big bangs and this place is ours."

"You'd better know what you're talking about," Moriarty said. "Because those six wretches out in that truck are the last of the livestock. After them, we'll have to eat the women, and that won't go over well with the men."

"I still think we should send a foraging patrol ahead into Lincoln," Ford said.

"No," Moriarty said. "We can't afford to risk losing any more men. Find the air shafts. There are two of them on the west side of the compound. Pour diesel oil down them and light them up. It's time to let these jokers know we're here."

Moriarty and his remaining men had spent the last three months in North Platte rooting out the survivors there and scraping by on whatever scraps they could find, but the cities were becoming less fruitful as the months passed due to competitor armies, and their own force had been considerably worn down by attrition through combat, disease, and starvation. They were down to a hundred men, which was a large force to feed but not large enough so they could afford too many more firefights with rival groups. They were also starting to run low on ammunition.

Moriarty placed a great deal of hope in this installation and what they might gain by taking it. If he didn't find a way to feed and reequip his men within the next couple of weeks, they would soon cease to exist as an effective fighting force. He followed Sergeant Yoshinaka and his men into the basement and watched them attaching the linear-shaped charges of composition C-4 to the concrete casement around blast door number one.

The charges were each three feet long with an aluminum V-shaped liner. The opening of the V would be placed against the concrete, which upon detonation would project a superheated explosion in one continuous, bladelike jet deep into the concrete, searing through the steel locking pins within the casement and breaching the underground fortress's first line of defense.

Lieutenant Ford came down the stairs knocking the dirty snow from his boots against a support pole in the center of the room. "We just lit up the air shafts," he said, batting the snow from his trouser legs. "And the exhaust fans kicked right on, so they're definitely down there!"

"And they're shitting their pants," Moriarty said with a smile. "All this time they've been down there thinking they had life by the ass. But it's like General Patton once said, Lieutenant: 'Fixed fortifications are monuments to the stupidity of man.'"

When Yoshinaka was finished setting the charges, the three of them went upstairs and outside into the hip-deep snow where thick black smoke poured out of both ventilator shafts. Crouching in the back of one of the trucks, Yoshinaka attached the wires to the detonator.

"Ready, Major?"

"Blow that fucker, Sergeant."

"Fire in the hole!" Yoshinaka shouted, and pressed the button.

They felt a shock tremor beneath their feet, and a deep boom came from inside the house. The windows did not blow out, however, since Yoshinaka had instructed his men to leave the front and back doors open to neutralize the pressure wave.

"Is that it?" Moriarty asked, having expected an earth-shattering *kaboom*.

"That's it," Yoshinaka said, hopping down from the truck.

"First squad!" Moriarty shouted. "Move up!"

Twelve men with rifles went running into the house, and Moriarty followed, waiting for them to make sure the enemy wasn't coming out to fight.

Even with the dust still settling in the basement, he could plainly see that the steel door had been effectively blasted loose of the concrete casement. A number of men grabbed hold of the door and with gut-wrenching effort managed to pull it over onto the basement floor, where it landed very hard against the cement.

Moriarty shined his flashlight down the tunnel to blast door number two. "Beyond that door, gentlemen, is a stairwell leading down three stories. And that's where we'll find the door to the main complex."

"Think maybe they got some women in there, Major?" asked one of the men.

"They're stupid if they don't, son," Moriarty said, clapping the twenty-year-old on the shoulder. "Now clear the room and two of you go lug another case of charges down here."

"What sort of defense you think they've lined up in there?" Yoshinaka wondered.

"They can line up whatever they want," Moriarty said arrogantly. "Once we put the damn flamethrower to work in their tunnels, they'll be screaming to capitulate. Trust me, Sergeant. This is shock and awe at its finest. We'll go through these assholes like shit through a goose."

Two men returned with a case of explosives and carried it down the tunnel to the second door.

"I'll be outside with Lieutenant Ford," Moriarty called down the tunnel. "All this dust is choking me."

"Won't be long," Yoshinaka called back, going right to work unwrapping the explosives. He handed a flashlight to one of the men. "Hold this light, Sims, so I can see what the hell I'm doing here."

The soldier beside Sims stood ready to fire should someone attempt to open the blast door from the other side. None of them noticed the small fiber-optic camera watching them through a tiny hole in the concrete above the door, but after a few seconds Sims heard a strange hissing sound in the ceiling right above his head.

"What's that noise, Sarge?"

Yoshinaka looked up. "I don't— *Run!*"

The three men dashed for the exit, but they didn't make it. Six jets of flaming, pressurized gasoline shot down from six recessed holes in the ceiling, engulfing the entire tunnel in a scorching pyroclastic cloud of roiling black-orange flame, burning lava-hot to fry the meat from their bones. The charges exploded a few seconds later, the blast expelling the burning bodies from the tunnel.

"What the fuck was that?" Ford gasped outside on the porch, looking to Moriarty for the answer.

"Christ, Yoshinaka must have blown himself up!"

They took three men into the house, cautiously shining their lights down the basement stairs to see that it was filled with black smoke, smelling the stench of broiled flesh mixing with the smell of burnt gasoline.

"That's the end of Yoshinaka," Ford said grimly. "At least we've still got Edelstein to set the charges."

"How did he fuck up?" Moriarty wondered. "C-4 is extremely stable."

"Maybe somebody inside opened the door and tossed in a grenade."

"No, that's not cordite you smell," Moriarty said. "That's burnt gasoline. Something's not fucking right here."

They waited an hour for the smoke to clear, and then five of them went down into the basement with their flashlights and pistols in hand, seeing the three mutilated bodies piled against the far wall.

Moriarty shined his light down the tunnel and saw that the blast door was still intact. "Zeek, get in there and check that door. See if it's been damaged at all."

The young airman walked cautiously down the tunnel to the door and gave it a kick, but the hatch was as solid as a mountain. "It's undamaged," he called back. "Didn't even scratch it!"

When Zeek was halfway back, the jets of flame blasted down into the tunnel again, engulfing him in another roiling ball of orange flame.

"Holy Jesus!" Moriarty screamed, dancing backward to escape the intense heat.

Ford jumped away too, but not before his left arm and

back caught fire. He screamed and flailed around like a madman until Moriarty and the other airman managed to knock him down, using their jackets to beat out the flames. But by then Ford had suffered third-degree burns to both his back and shoulder.

"Medic!" Moriarty screamed up the stairs. "Somebody get the medic down here!"

They hauled the screaming Ford out into the snow and laid him down. The icy cold helped to deaden the pain, but it wouldn't do much to prevent the inevitable infection the man was going to contract.

"Don't let them eat me!" Ford was howling, clutching at Moriarty's jacket, his face black and burned. "Don't let the men eat me, Ben! Please!"

"Nobody's going to eat you," Moriarty said. "Morphine! Get this man some goddamn morphine!"

The medic shot him up with a dose of morphine, and they carried him off moaning to one of the trucks. "He won't survive for very long with those burns," the medic told Moriarty. "How much more morphine do you want me to waste on him?"

"Spread the word around," Moriarty said quietly. "Let the men decide. If it sounds like they want to let him die, bleed him out. Be less of a mess for the butcher that way.

"Sergeant Jeffries!" he shouted, turning around. "Congratulations. You're a mustang lieutenant."

"Thank you, sir!" said a broad-shouldered man of twenty-five.

"Put two men on guard inside at the basement door then meet me in the command trailer. Do *not* let them go into the basement!"

"Yes, sir."

"Edelstein, come with me. We have a puzzle to solve, you and I." They went to the command trailer, where Moriarty dropped into a chair. The interior of the trailer was warm because they still had fuel for their generators, but it smelled like a pigsty. A bevy of malnourished women sat huddled together at the back of the trailer on the floor with their hands shackled behind their backs.

Moriarty told Edelstein exactly what had taken place in the basement. "So tell me this," he said. "How do they know when to squeeze the trigger on us?"

Edelstein lifted his eyebrows. "That's a good question."

"That's the key question," Moriarty said. "Because if we can't disable those flame throwers we're never getting in." He smashed his fist against the table. "Bastards think they're pretty smart. Probably down there laughing their asses off."

"Cameras," Edelstein said suddenly. "Maybe they're watching us."

The obviousness of the idea hit Moriarty like a truck. "Son of a bitch!" he hissed. "I never even considered that possibility. My brain must be addled."

"It's the lack of nutrition," Edelstein said. "It's affecting us all, Major."

"Get out there and tell the men to tear that house apart. If they do find cameras, I don't want them destroyed. I want them covered with tape. Understand?"

"Yes, sir."

When Edelstein was gone, Moriarty walked to the back of the trailer, squatting to look the women over, his face pitiless and his eyes flat like those of a reptile. "Now which one of you ladies wants to improve my mood?"

# FIFTY-ONE

**NO ONE HEARD A SOUND WITHIN THE COMPLEX WHEN BLAST** door number one was blown out of its casement, but there was a subtle trembling that quivered through the facility, making everyone within the civilian population aware that they had taken damage. Forrest immediately went on the air to announce that blast door number one had been breached but that the situation was in hand and not to worry. A short time later they barbecued the demolitions team and watched the monitor as the blast blew the tunnel clean. They waited patiently for the enemy to come back down, and when they were certain no more than one man was reentering the tunnel, they barbecued him as well.

"They won't likely be back for a while." Forrest fired up a smoke.

"We should sneak into the house now," Vasquez said. "Take a few of them out and retreat back inside."

"There's no need to expose ourselves. We still hold every advantage."

Kane stepped into the room and offered Forrest a cup of coffee. "Baby's comin' pretty soon," he told Ulrich. "Erin asked me to send you in."

"Yeah, that's just what Shannon wants," Ulrich said. "Me

in there staring at her snatch. Message received but I'll take a pass. Thanks."

"What's up with the ventilators?" Forrest asked, sipping his coffee.

"We're fine so far," Kane said. "The nonreturn valves we installed worked just like they were supposed to, but we can't draw fresh air until that damn fuel burns off. And they'll probably just pour more down."

"Which means we've got as much air as we're going to get until this is over," Forrest muttered. He turned to the dozens of tomato plants resting on the shelves against the wall. "Breathe, you little bastards."

Michael chuckled sardonically. "Has anyone got any idea how many plants it would take to—"

"Three hundred plants per person," Ulrich said. "Roughly. And we've got about fifty total "

"So how long do we have before we start to suffocate down here?"

"It's tough to quantify," Ulrich said. "But for the sake of argument, let's say about four days."

"Hey, guys," Vasquez said, sitting up in his chair to point at one of the monitors. "I think maybe they're looking for our cameras."

"Well, that didn't take long," Ulrich said.

"Shit, they've got the one in the living room."

The view on the monitor seemed to swing wildly about the living room as the airman pulled the fiber-optic wire from the smoke detector.

"The only camera that matters now is the one in the tunnel," Forrest said. "And they need Superman to get at that one."

"I don't know," Ulrich said, watching the enemy fan out through the house. "I don't like the idea not being able to see what they're up to."

"There goes the kitchen cam," Vasquez said. "Front porch too."

"The aboveground cameras were always a bonus," Forrest said.

"There go the bedroom cams."

"Besides, we've still got the camera on the antenna array if we get into a pinch."

"Which is a onetime deal," Ulrich said. "They'll snuff that motherfucker the second we extend it."

Forrest leaned forward to use the P.A., calling Danzig into Launch Control.

"Linus," he said upon Danzig's arrival. "It looks like we're going to need someone on guard in the cargo bay from now on. We're about to go blind down here. Work out a schedule with Sullivan and Marty, will you? Put those two on the same shift. Kane, you take a shift too. I don't think any of us are going to be getting any sleep for a while."

"OKAY, HONEY, YOU'RE doing fine," West said, his hands resting on Emory's knees. "I can see the baby's head now. You're crowning beautifully."

"Shit!" Emory gasped, gripping the edges of the mattress. "It feels like I'm shitting a bowling ball!"

Erin smiled, wiping the sweat from Emory's forehead with a damp cloth. "You're doing great."

Marty stood in the doorway watching.

"Get in here and hold my hand, Marty. What the fuck, I'm dying in here!"

Marty crossed to the bed and took her hand.

"Okay," West said. "With this next contraction I need you to push for me, Shannon."

The contraction came and Emory pushed as hard as she could, screaming at the top of her voice.

"Good girl!" West said. "Almost there. One more time, honey."

Emory waited and pushed one last time, feeling the baby squirt free of her body and groaning aloud.

"It's a girl!" Erin said, beginning to cry. "It's a girl, Shannon!"

"Thank God *that's* fucking over!" Emory said, her voice trembling.

"Almost," West said with chuckle, handing the baby to Dr. Wilmington so he could tie off and cut the umbilical. The infant began to cry a few seconds later, and after a short while the afterbirth was delivered, allowing West to clean Emory up. Dr. Wilmington cleaned the baby girl and swaddled her in a green cotton Army towel, carrying her over to rest her on Emory's chest. But Emory closed her eyes and turned her head as if some foul-smelling food had been placed before her.

"Marty, who does she look like?"

"You," he said softly, looking adoringly at the infant. "She looks like you."

Emory turned her head slowly and looked at her daughter, at last lifting her arms to touch her. "Hey, you little shithead."

Erin's face was covered with tears.

"Pick her up," Emory told her. "She's *yours* now."

"Shannon, are you sure you don't want her?" Erin said, suddenly sad for the infant. "She's your daughter, honey. Your flesh and blood."

"I like her," Shannon said, holding her gently. "She's cool. But she's yours. I don't want to be a mother. Tell her, Marty."

"She's given this a lot of thought," Marty said quietly. "It's for the best, Erin."

"You'll need to nurse her for as long as possible," West said. "In this environment, she'll need every advantage she can get."

Emory sat against the pillow with the baby in her arms, looking dolefully at him.

"I'm serious, Shannon. It's really very important. We don't have any baby formula down here, and powdered milk isn't going to do at all. Not to mention she needs the immunities only you can give her."

"All right," Emory said reluctantly. "You can go now, Marty. I don't need you staring at my tits." She bared one of her breasts, and West helped her cradle the baby and position the nipple in her mouth. The infant took to the nipple at once and began to suckle like a hungry puppy.

"That's a small mercy," West said with a glance at Erin. "They don't always take to it this fast."

"Hey, that feels pretty good," Emory said with a grin. "It's been a while. Maybe this won't be so bad."

Erin couldn't help laughing. "Shannon, really."

**"WELL THAT'S IT,"** Ulrich said, rising from his chair as the last outside camera was discovered on the roof of the house and wrapped around with tape. "They've blinded us."

"I wonder why they taped them off instead of destroying them," Michael said.

"This way they can communicate with us later on," Forrest said, drinking from another cup of coffee. "Threaten us with imminent destruction." He looked at his watch. "Be dark soon. We can raise the antenna just before sunup, maybe get a quick look at first light and then lower it again before they spot it. It's far enough away, they may not notice."

"I've got an idea I like better," Kane said.

"Which is?"

"Call Broken Arrow about 0400 then go up and finish the job by hand. We're bound to catch a lot of 'em asleep in the house."

"That's what Broken Arrow is?" Michael said. "Engaging them hand-to-hand?"

"Partly," Forrest said. "But I don't like it yet. Those trailers are out of range. We can't risk a protracted firefight."

"But how soon before we're in a use-it-or-lose-it situation?" Ulrich said. "We won't know where they're snooping around up there now. What if they find the lift?"

"I'm not too worried," Forrest said. "Tactically speaking, Moriarty's already fucked up." He set the coffee cup down and shook another cigarette loose. "He *could* have played this like they didn't know about the cameras. They *could* have pretended to prepare for something he didn't really intend to do . . . make us prepare for something that was never going to happen. But this idiot's no tactician. He's a fucking supply officer, and he doesn't scare me. So no Broken Arrow except as a last resort . . . unless you'd like to call for another vote there, Wayne."

"Jack," Ulrich said, pausing before stepping into the hall. "Go fuck yourself."

# FIFTY-TWO

"WHAT IF WE FLOOD THE BASEMENT?" SUGGESTED A MEMBER of Moriarty's staff. "Flood the tunnel and set the charges underwater."

Moriarty sat looking at the man, glancing at Edelstein before sitting forward in his chair. "That's a pretty good idea, Howard—except for the fact we've got no water and no goddamn scuba gear." He pointed at the door. "Get the hell out of here, you moron!"

Howard stood from his chair, saluted and left the trailer.

Moriarty looked at the other four. "The next one of you who comes up with an idea like that, just shoot yourself and save me the trouble. Flood the goddamn basement!"

One of the cooks came in later and set a mess tray of blackish meat on the table. "I put a lot of cayenne on it this time. I think it's better."

Moriarty picked up a piece of the meat and took a bite. "A little spicy but not bad. Who is this?"

"It's Lieutenant Ford, sir."

"Poor fucker," Moriarty said, licking his fingers. "He was a good man."

"Have you come up with a way of getting into the complex?" the cook asked.

"No."

"Too bad we don't have any way of getting that Cat out here," the cook said, turning for the door.

"What Cat?" Moriarty said.

"There was a D-8 along the highway on the way here. We could dig right down to the main complex with it. Blow our way in."

Moriarty looked at Edelstein. "Would that work?"

"The concrete shell is six feet thick," Edelstein said. "It would take a while, but with the explosives we have and a couple of jackhammers . . . yeah, I think it would work. It's worth a try."

"That's it, then," Moriarty said, getting to his feet. "Take a company of men and go get that goddamn bulldozer!"

# FIFTY-THREE

**IT WAS LATE AND MELISSA SAT IN THE HALL WITH LADDIE**
asleep beside her on the deck, her laptop against her knees
as she stared at a simple cipher on the computer screen.

```
          A B C D E F
          G H I J K L
          M N O P Q R
          S T U V W Y
1-1 (Line 1, first letter) = A
4-6 (Line 4, sixth letter) = Y
              etc.
```

The first numeral of a set denoted which line to reference,
and the second numeral denoted which specific letter within
that line to reference. This was the rudimentary alphabetic
cipher Ulrich had shown her months earlier when she first
expressed an interest in trying to decipher the code they
were now listening in on as many as four nights a week. She
had since tried dozens of variations on it, most recently:

```
    A        B        C        D
  E F      G H      I J      K L
 M N O    P Q R    S T U    V W Y
```

She always attempted to match them against the same
string of code that one of the telegraphers signed on with

at the beginning of each transmission: 924913024024812
824012924811636025913013011404925036712036824824.
And always came up with nothing but gibberish.

One of her notable problems—among many others—was
the numeral 9. No matter how she arranged the letters, she
couldn't come up with a workable alphabetical value for the
numeral 9. She asked Ulrich about it, but he hadn't been
very helpful. He told her the 9s could have any one of a
million different values—or even be complete gibberish to
throw off a cryptologist.

She was frustrated with Ulrich, firmly believing that if he
would just help her, they could crack the code.

"Okay, listen," he said to her late one night in Launch
Control when she had resumed work on the code at the
console. "Do you know the Lord's Prayer? 'Yea, though I
walk' . . . and all that."

"That's not the Lord's Prayer," she said, laughing. "That's
the Twenty-third Psalm. The Lord's Prayer is 'Our Father,
which art in Heaven . . .' "

"Whatever. Go get a Bible and copy it down, a line at a
time."

"Which one? The Lord's Prayer or the Twenty-third
Psalm?"

He looked at her and narrowed his eyes, not having the patience with her that Forrest had. " 'Yea, though I walk . . .' "

"Jeez!" she said with another laugh. "You'd better learn to
have some patience if you're gonna be a dad, Wayne."

"Go get the Bible, kid."

"I don't need it," she said, lifting her pencil.

"And always number the lines," he told her. "That will
make it easier for you to reference them as you're deciphering."

"Got it." She wrote out the Psalm from memory.

1. *The Lord is my Shepherd I shall not want.*
2. *He maketh me to lie down in green pastures: he
   leadeth me beside the still waters.*

3. He restoreth my soul: he leadeth me in the paths of righteousness for his name's sake.

4. Yea, though I walk through the valley of the shadow of death, I will fear no evil: for thou art with me; thy rod and thy staff they comfort me.

5. Thou preparest a table before me in the presence of mine enemies; thou annointest my head with oil; my cup runneth over.

6. Surely goodness and mercy shall follow me all the days of my life, and I will dwell in the house of The Lord forever.

"Okay, so now what?" she said, showing him the paper.

Ulrich took the paper and wrote a quick string of code at the bottom of the page:

1-10 / 2-2 / 3-16 / 1-9 / 6-1 / 6-1 / 4-3 __
1-9 / 6-1 __ 4-3 __ 5-5 / 4-3 / 1-9 / 6-11

"Now decipher that," he said. "And keep in mind, the blank spaces are arbitrary. They hold no value of their own. I could just as easily have written it without the spaces, but I'm making it ridiculously easy for you."

It was immediately apparent to Melissa that he had used the line number for the first value of each letter and then just counted spaces for the second value, coming up with:

M/E/L/I/S/S/A_I/S_A_P/A/I/N.

"Ha ha," she said. "I'm telling Erin."

"You probably will," he said with a chuckle. "Look, kid, the point I'm making is they don't have to use a simple alphabetic cipher. They could use *anything*. Any agreed-upon text just like this one here. And the letters in the code they're using don't have to be limited to double-digit values. They could apply to page number, paragraph number, line number, word number, and finally letter number if they wanted to—

which would give each single *letter* in the message a value of *five* digits. So . . . do you see how many possibilities exist just within that single string of code you keep going over? There could be as many as thirty-two letters in it or as few as sixteen—just from that one example."

"But that would take time to translate, and you said they're talking fast."

"That's true," he admitted. "But if they're only using a few pages of the text—which would be logical—they could easily have it memorized by now. So, while I do believe it's a simple code in terms of numerical values, it could still be impossible for a person to crack without a computer program."

"But not necessarily . . ."

"No, not necessarily, but the trouble is we have no way of knowing. So why waste thousands of hours trying to crack a code only to find out that it's impossible? Especially when we already know that it probably *is* impossible."

"But what if these people might be able to help us?"

"Honey, whoever they are, they are in no more of a position to help us than we are to help them. Believe me. And there's a very good chance of them being hostile, so we couldn't risk breaking radio silence before we *at least* knew what the hell they've been talking about all these months."

Melissa had not been even slightly deterred by Ulrich's discouraging opinion of her chances. In fact, she only grew that much more determined. She saw a definite pattern within the code, even if only in her mind's eye. She just couldn't quantify it yet, and she continued to be very frustrated with herself, knowing that with a little more mathematical skill she could crack the damn thing and maybe—just maybe— find them some help before they were forced to eat rat meat in order stay alive . . . or worse, starve.

Forrest stepped around the open blast door and crouched beside her, petting Laddie, who came instantly awake. "I'd feel better if you two were in the common area with the others. The kids are asleep now."

"I can't concentrate with everyone around," she said, her eyes fixed on the screen. "I'm close, Dad. I can feel it."

Melissa had taken to calling him Dad a bit more often now, and it pulled at his heart every time. Veronica had remarked in private that she thought Melissa might have used the moniker to manipulate him in certain instances, which spawned their first genuine argument. She had only meant to imply that all girls manipulated their fathers to a certain degree, but Forrest accused her of being jealous.

"How dare you accuse me of being jealous of a sixteen-year-old girl!"

"She's never made a single unreasonable request, Veronica. There isn't even anything down here unreasonable to ask for, for Christ's sake."

"Never mind," she had said. "You're obviously too sensitive where Melissa's concerned. I won't bring her up again."

After that they hadn't spoken for an entire day.

"I'd like you to move into the common area anyway," he said to Melissa now. "This tunnel's supposed to be sealed in case there's an emergency."

"Can't I—"

"What did I say?" he said, speaking crossly with her for the first time.

She looked up from her work, a hurt expression in her eyes, and closed the computer, gathering her papers together. He offered her his hand and helped her to her feet. Laddie got up with her and stretched.

Forrest sealed the door and they moved into the common area, allowing Laddie to trot deftly ahead of them through the sleeping children. On his way to Melissa's bedroll near the wall, the dog stopped to sniff a couple of the kids, then curled up on his own bed made from folded blankets. Melissa put the computer into its box, unzipped her bag, and sat down to untie her shoes.

"You don't have to go to bed," he said quietly.

"I'm tired," she said, without looking up at him, pulling the flap of the bag over her legs. "Good night."

"Good night," he said, and turned to walk away.

"Jack?"

"Yeah?"

"I'm sorry for making you mad."

"You didn't make me mad. I love you."

"Love you too," she said, and turned over to go to sleep.

Laddie got back up and followed Forrest into in the cafeteria, where Veronica was sitting up with Erin and the infant, whom thus far didn't seem to have a name. Erin had just brought the babe from her feeding in Medical, and now the child was sound asleep, swaddled in Erin's arms. Laddie sniffed at the infant and sat wagging his tail.

"No, she's not yours yet," Erin said with a smile. "You'll have to wait a couple of years."

There was no one sleeping in the cafeteria because the complex was on a war footing. All civilians were to remain in one of the two conjoined common areas at all times except for while preparing food in the kitchen to be served in the common areas.

"So, E, are you an official mom now or what?" Forrest asked, taking a seat beside Veronica.

"Shannon says so."

"You don't seem exactly thrilled."

"Oh, I am," she said. "It just doesn't feel real yet, you know? With Shannon nursing her every couple of hours and those maniacs trying to get in. I feel more like a nanny, I guess."

"Give her to Karen, then," he said. "I know she'd love to have her."

"Over my cold dead body, Jack Forrest."

He laughed. "You sure sound like a mother to me."

"You never pass up the chance to get a rise out of me, do you?"

"Nope." He gave a Veronica a kiss. "How's my girl?"

"Worried," Veronica said.

"Don't be. That's my job."

"Yet you never do."

"That's because it's much more productive to act."

"Well, Wayne's worried," Erin said. "He says not, but I know him. He's as worried as I've ever seen him, in fact."

"He's just a pussy."

Veronica slapped him on the arm.

"He's called Wayne lots worse, V. Believe me. And vice versa. You'd think they hated each other the way they talk to one another. It's disgusting."

"I do hate him," Forrest said, pretending to shake a cigarette from his pack, watching for Erin's reaction.

"You even *try* smoking around this baby . . ."

He tucked the cigarettes back into his trouser pocket and gave Veronica a wink.

"What's going on in the cargo bay?" Erin asked. "Wayne won't tell me."

"We're just making sure nobody cuts through the lift elevator."

"No, before all this," Veronica said. "All five of you have been spending more time in there than normal lately."

"Don't think we haven't noticed, Jack."

"I can describe it in two words," he said with a smile. " 'Top Secret.' "

Erin rolled her eyes. "At least Wayne has guts enough to say it's none of our business."

When Erin left, Forrest said quietly, "You were right about Melissa."

"What do you mean?"

"A couple weeks ago when you said she manipulates me once in a while."

"Oh, well . . ."

"It's not really a big deal, though."

She put her arm around him and kissed his neck. "I never tried to imply that it was. She's a teenage girl. Every woman down here was like that at her age."

"Well, I'd rather think of her as completely innocent."

She laughed and kissed him again. "You and every man who's ever had a daughter."

# FIFTY-FOUR

"MAJOR, YOU'D BETTER COME SEE THIS!" SERGEANT JEF-
fries said, shaking Moriarty awake.

Moriarty let go of the woman he was using for warmth
and rolled over onto his back. "What's happened, Sergeant?"

"The men have found something I think you should see
right away, sir. Something in the snow."

Moriarty swung his feet over the edge of the cot and put
them on the floor. He slapped the woman's backside and told
her to get up and put on his boots for him. After she tied his
laces he stood up, cuffed her hands behind her back, and told
her to go lay down. A few minutes later he was tromping off
after Jeffries through the deep snow with his hands in his
coat pockets. On the far side of the compound a dozen men
stood in a circle with flashlights, shining them on the snow.

"What are they looking at?" Moriarty asked.

"It's weird, sir. You need to see it for yourself."

Moriarty marched up and stood looking at the snow. At
first he didn't see what they were talking about. He was
looking for a specific item, like a frozen arm sticking out of
the snow, but after a moment he saw what they had found . . .
a slight depression in the snow shaped like a nearly perfect
rectangle, about the length and width of an Army six-by-six
truck.

"I'll be goddamned," he said. "You men get some shovels and be ready to dig, but nobody is to step into that area until ordered to do so. Sergeant Jeffries, get the complex blueprints and a compass and meet me in the house! We may not need that goddamn bulldozer after all."

A short time later Moriarty and his staff were gathered around the kitchen table by the light of six army lanterns. "Okay," he said, using the compass to orient the blueprints in the way one would orient a map. "You will notice, gentlemen, there is nothing in these plans to indicate anything located beneath the depression in the snow. Which is because whatever is located there was not added to this installation until after it was commissioned. Does anyone care to take a guess at what it might be?"

"A vent?" Jefferies suggested.

"Even better," Moriarty replied. "It's a hydraulic lift elevator, and below that lift elevator is a cargo bay. A cargo bay that is very likely full of supply, supply that will be ours the very moment we blast our way through the left deck. But what is even better, gentlemen, is that we will once again have unfettered access to a blast door. Now, this blast door will likely be larger and slightly thicker than the one we have already dealt with, but we will still be able to blast our way through it. Isn't that right, Corporal Edelstein?"

"Yes, *sir*!"

"But why is there a depression in the snow?" one of the other men asked.

"Heat," Moriarty said. "There's obviously just enough heat below the deck to cause a slight melt close to the ground, which has dropped the surface level of the snow.

"Now, advise the men to dig slowly and very, very carefully. I'm guessing these cagey bastards have covered the deck with dirt, so when they reach dirt, the men are to put the shovels aside and dig with their hands. And no one—I repeat—*no one* is to step on that deck in anything other than stocking feet. Is that understood?"

"Yes, Major."

"Very good, gentlemen. Let's move with a purpose."

The room cleared and Moriarty stood looking out the kitchen window with Jeffries at his side. He checked his watch. "Still two hours before first light," he muttered. "We need to do this right, Sergeant. Get some men moving around down in the basement with flashlights. Make it look like they're up to something. It doesn't matter what. Just so they have the attention of those bastards below. Keep it mysterious."

"Yes, sir," Jeffries said. "What about the 'dozer, sir?"

"We'll talk with Edelstein about that. Six feet of concrete is a lot to blast through. And assaulting through an opening like that won't be easy."

"What if we wait until the 'dozer gets here, and we let them see us digging on the far side of the compound," Jeffries suggested, "to make it look like we're digging down to the access tunnel for the number two silo? Wouldn't that draw their attention even farther away from the cargo bay? And with the camera angle being what it is, they won't be able to see us working on the lift elevator."

"But they will wonder why we're letting them watch."

"We can show them a note. Tell them to surrender or else. They'll think we're letting them see in order to prove we can back up our threat."

"So the question becomes when to hit them," Moriarty said.

"I think a couple of hours after first light, sir. Give them time to see us and concentrate their defenses on the far side."

"All right. We'll start digging as soon as the 'dozer gets here, and exactly two hours later we'll blow a hole in the lift deck. If there are no defenses in the bay, we'll send two men down by rope to see if there is power to the lift. In the event the bay is defended, we'll rain grenades down on them until there's nothing left but ground chuck."

# FIFTY-FIVE

**FORREST WAS SITTING ON THE JOHN WHEN THE ALARMS** began to sound once again. "Jesus Christ!" he said, pulling a length of paper from the roll and hurriedly wiping his ass. "Every fucking time!"

"Forrest to the LC immediately!" Kane's voice called over the P.A. "Forrest to the LC!"

Forrest sprinted down the hall into Launch Control. "What the fuck is it now?"

"Look!" Kane said, pointing at the monitor. On the screen, a large a D-8 Cat track hoe was digging into the earth on the far side of the compound. Given the depth of the hole, the Cat hadn't made more than a few passes.

Ulrich arrived and took one look at the monitor. "Broken Arrow, Jack!"

Forrest was already on his way to the fuse box. He unlocked it quickly and threw one of two red switches.

Ulrich watched the monitor, hoping to see the ground erupt in a series of heavy explosions. "Nothing!" he shouted, kicking the waste can across the room. "They've already torn up the fucking grid! Goddamnit, Jack, I told you!"

Michael stood in the doorway in his pajamas looking very confused. "What was supposed to happen?"

"We mined the upper compound with TNT," Kane answered. "Everything you're seeing on the monitor right now should have been blown to shit when Jack threw that switch, but that 'dozer has torn up the grid."

"Jack, blow the goddamn house!" Ulrich said, seeing that Forrest was relocking the fuse box. "Once they see the ground was mined they'll check the house sure as shit."

"Not necessarily," Forrest said, moving back to the monitor. "And if we blow the house, we lose this camera feed." He shook a smoke from the pack and fired it up, drawing deeply as he stood thinking.

"At least we'd kill these assholes here," Kane said, bringing up the tunnel feed to point out the flashlights moving around in the darkness deep within the basement. "It's tough to tell what they're doing, but they have to be working on some sort of a countermeasure for the flamethrowers."

"We don't have a lot of time," Ulrich said. "What's it going to be, Jack? Use it or lose it, goddamnit."

"We need to see what they're doing up there, Wayne. The house stays intact."

If he was completely honest about it, Ulrich was glad this particular call wasn't up to him; he was truly at a loss to judge the best move under the present circumstances.

"For now," Forrest said, "we form a human chain all the way to silo number two. We have to transfer every bit of food out of there before we're cut off from it. They're digging down to the access tunnel to blow their way in. Once the silo is empty, we'll use the remainder of the TNT to booby-trap it and the tunnel. Wayne, you're in charge of the relocation. Kane and I will remain here in the LC. Who's on duty in the cargo bay?"

"Sullivan and Marty."

"Get them out and seal it. There's still a shit-ton of supply left in number two silo, and we'll need every swinging dick to move it."

"I'll take care of it," Ulrich said.

Forrest picked up the P.A. "Attention everybody. Our friends upstairs are using a bulldozer to dig down to the number two access tunnel. So we need all of you to pitch in and help move our supplies out of number two silo and into the number one blast tunnel. Everyone stay calm and listen to Wayne. We're going to be okay."

He set the mike down and stood smoking as he watched the Cat plowing through the dirt.

"That last part might be the first lie you've told them," Kane said.

"I know it."

"Those assholes don't have nothin' to do but excavate," Kane went on. "Pretty soon we'll be robbing Peter to pay Paul down here, and we only got four days of air to do that. Even less with everybody workin' their asses off shufflin' shit around."

"I know."

"We're gonna have to go up there and give those motherfuckers somethin' else to—"

"I know it, Marcus, goddamnit!" Forrest stood watching the machine make yet another pass, his mind working to process the entirety of the situation.

"Jack, let me put together an assault team . . . me, Sullivan, and Vasquez. We'll take out those assholes in the basement and clear the house in nothing flat."

Forrest ignored him, trying to gain a sense of how long it would be before the machine unearthed the access tunnel. He estimated it would probably take less than an hour, despite the obvious inexperience of the man operating the 'dozer.

"We need to disable that fucking Cat," he said finally. "That solves our problem."

"Shannon's M-203 will do the trick," Kane replied. "I can hit it easily from the upstairs window."

"Get Sullivan ready to back you up," Forrest said. "I don't want a family man going out there unless it becomes imperative. You two will have to be very fast, Marcus."

"Don't you fuckin' worry about that," Kane said, grabbing for the P.A. to call Sullivan.

"Wait!" Forrest said, having a sudden thought. "Why the fuck are they showing us what they're up to?"

"To scare us."

"But they're giving us time to prepare," Forrest said. "Hold on a second. This shit isn't right. Check the rest of the feeds."

Kane checked through half of the camera feeds before finding that the kitchen camera had been uncovered. All they could see, however, was a close-up shot of a paper plate. Written on the paper plate was a short note: *SURRENDOR NOW OR YOU ALL DIE!*

Forrest shook his head. "Fuckin' idiots misspelled 'surrender.'"

He took the up P.A. "Mike to the LC. Mike, come to the LC."

"What the hell can he do?"

"I don't know. Maybe nothing but I'm having a brain lock."

When Michael returned he was dressed in his street clothes. "What do you need, Jack?"

"Put me inside this asshole's head," Forrest said, pointing to the note on the screen.

"Well, he needs a dictionary. Other than that, I'm not sure what you mean."

"I mean why is he showing me what he's up to?" Forrest said. "The fucking asshole has met me. He knows I'd never surrender. So why is he bothering to ask? A taunt I could understand. But a ridiculous demand? It doesn't make sense to me."

"Okay, I see what you mean," Michael said. "But I'm not sure there's any way to know what he's thinking by this point. I mean, I've never interviewed anyone who's been driven to cannibalism before. His entire psychological profile has been . . ."

"Been what?"

"Well, I was about to say that it's been altered, but no, that wouldn't be right. It's been synthesized. Who he is now is who he's always been . . . just with all the fat boiled off, nothing left to inhibit his true . . . psychopathic nature. He would have to be psychopathic in order to retain command over so many men under these conditions."

"So what's it mean?"

"I think it means he's deliberately coming after us to kill us. He's not one bit interested in our surrender . . . no matter how he spells it. Is that what you're looking for?"

"That's it," Forrest said. "Take care of our girls, okay?"

Michael smiled. "You got it."

Michael left the room and Forrest went back to watching the monitors. He counted the total number of men he could see and came up with only six, not counting however many men were goofing off in the basement with the flashlights, which couldn't have been more than four or five. That left around ninety men unaccounted for.

"Bullshit," he said at length, drawing deeply from his cigarette. "This cocksucker's up to something, Marcus. Something we can't see. Where are we most vulnerable?"

The answer hit them both at the same time.

"Fuck, the lift!"

Forrest grabbed the P.A. again. "All hands under arms to Launch Control now! All hands to Launch Control! Civilian personnel are to seal themselves inside the common area immediately—no exceptions!"

Kane was already up and shrugging into his body armor.

"We need to get to the cargo bay, Jack!"

"Forget it," Forrest said, grabbing for his own armor. "Unless I'm wrong, they're already inside. We're going to lose the first blast door."

"But we don't have a countermeasure for the cargo tunnel."

"We're the countermeasure, my friend. You and me."

"Suits me fine, Captain."

The rest of the combat personnel were arriving in Launch Control and suiting up for battle, including Emory, whom Forrest was not about to argue with under such dire circumstances.

"Shannon, I want you armed and sitting right here manning the goddamn console. You and West will be the last line of defense. Doc, does Price have the box of cyanide capsules?"

"He's got them," West said, accepting a carbine from Ulrich. "He and Mike are both sealed in with the women and children and they know what needs to be done if we lose the complex."

"Okay, people, here's the deal," Forrest said, unlocking the fuse box again. "I'm ninety-nine percent sure we've already lost the cargo bay, and if I'm right, we'll be losing the first cargo door very soon. Marcus and I plan to be in the tunnel when they blow that door. We'll hit them hard the second they make the breach. Under *no* circumstances is anyone to open the second cargo door to try and help us!

"Wayne, the five of you will wait at the top of the stairs inside the main entrance until Shannon flips this switch and blows up the fucking house. At that time you five will enter the main tunnel with Sean sealing it behind you. Sean, you will then haul ass back down here with Shannon.

"Wayne and his assault force will make their way into whatever is left of the house, killing every motherfucker they encounter while en route to the lift elevator from above. Once you've secured the opening to the cargo bay, Marcus and I will meet you in the middle."

"We'll all be dead before that rendezvous ever takes place," Ulrich said, strapping into his harness.

"Men," Forrest said, pulling his helmet on over his head, "those assholes up there are half starved to death. That makes us stronger, faster, sharper, and one fuck of a lot meaner than they are. Hooah?"

"Hooah!"

"Move fast, Stumpy! Take maximum advantage of their confusion after Shannon blows the house."

# FIFTY-SIX

**MORIARTY STOOD IN THE CENTER OF THE LIFT ELEVATOR** looking down through the hole they had blown in the deck as he waited for it to touch down. He then stepped into the cargo bay with twenty-five of his best men and stood looking around.

"They're raising rats down here, Major," said the man who had slid down the rope to lower the elevator for the rest of the team.

Moriarty stood grinning. His plan had worked perfectly. They had taken the cargo bay without firing a shot, and they were about to blow the first blast door with their enemy still entirely unaware of their presence. The fact that the plan had actually been Jeffries's was irrelevant.

"Goddamn textbook!" he said, clapping Edelstein on the back. "Get that fucking door blown, Corporal. Christ Jesus, I think we'll be running through their fucking halls before they even know we're in. Get that goddamn flamethrower ready, Bishop!"

Edelstein and his men went quickly to work setting the linear charges in the shape of a man-door in the center of the much larger three-ton blast door.

"Major!" an airman shouted from across the sixty-by-sixty-foot square bay. "These two trucks are loaded up with MREs!"

"Nobody touches the food until after we've secured this installation!" Moriarty ordered. "Is that clear?"

Suddenly, there was a thunderous explosion outside the lift opening. One of their men standing near the edge lost his balance and fell in, snapping his knee when he hit the deck.

"What the fuck was that?" Moriarty demanded.

"Holy fuck!" the injured man screamed, holding his knee. "They blew up the fucking house!"

"Christ, they're probably attacking!" Moriarty said in fear. "Everyone back on the lift!"

Twenty-five men piled back onto the lift as the twenty-sixth ran to hit the up button.

Nothing happened.

"Major, they've cut the fucking power! We're fucking trapped!"

Moriarty's men fell into instant panic as the sound of automatic rifle fire began to erupt outside the opening and another man fell to the deck, shot through the head.

"Blow that fucking door open!" Moriarty screamed at Edelstein. "We're rats in a goddamn barrel down here!"

Edelstein and his men went back to setting the charges, finishing quickly. "Everybody take cover!"

The men took cover behind the trucks as Edelstein ran backward, reeling out the wire for the detonator. He quickly twisted the wire ends around the leads then shouted, "Fire in the hole!" giving the small handle a twist.

The charges blew with a loud *bang* and the men surged forward to pry the chunk from the center of the door with crowbars. It fell forward onto the concrete, and everyone stood well clear of the opening as Moriarty shined his flashlight carefully inside the tunnel, all of them fearing another horrifying pyrotechnic countermeasure.

This tunnel was of an entirely different construction than the main entrance, made of steel walls and a steel ceiling, supported by I-beam framing every forty-eight inches for its entire length of thirty-two feet. The flooring was made of steel grating, and the walkway itself was suspended from no less than twenty steel-spring shock absorbers, ostensibly to allow the tunnel to survive a near-hit from a nuclear weapon. There were no holes in the ceiling or the walls, and there was nothing in the tunnel except some rubble blown inward by the blast.

"Get to work men," Moriarty said, casting an upward glance at the dim opening in the ceiling, half expecting to see it encircled by enemy riflemen.

As Edelstein and his team hurried down the tunnel with the case of charges, two badly battered Green Berets stood up from beneath the steel grating with blood running from their eyes and ears. They opened fire at near point-blank range, aiming for the necks and faces of the four-man demolition team and killing them instantly.

Both Forrest and Kane then pulled the pins on a pair of grenades each and tossed them down the tunnel after Moriarty's men, who were scrambling for cover with no idea what kind of force they had so suddenly and unexpectedly come up against. The grenades exploded as they bounced clear of the opening, and six of Moriarty's men were killed or badly wounded, the quadruple explosion badly disorienting and rattling the remainder even as they fled.

Forrest and Kane pulled themselves up from the hole in the floor and shuffled to the end of the passage. Neither bothered to speak; it would be days before either would be able to hear at all. They switched on their infrared night vision as they took cover inside the partial doorway, easily seeing many of the men who were relying on the poor light for cover.

They began to fire, hitting Moriarty's men in their exposed legs and arms, shattering bone and picking them apart. There was a lot of return fire but none of it was accurate enough to do much good, as most of Moriarty's men had grown lax about recharging their NVDs. Kane took a hit in his left shoulder and Forrest took a direct hit on his boron carbide chest plate, but both men remained cool, calm, and collected, choosing their targets before squeezing off each three-round burst.

Moriarty lay on the concrete behind a small generator with his arms wrapped over the top of his helmet, his knees pulled tight to his chest in order to make himself as small a target as possible. He was now deadly certain he had fallen into some kind of Special Forces trap and that his middling force was heavily outgunned.

There wasn't much of anywhere for his men to hide other than behind the wheels of the three vehicles, but with them pushing and shoving one another in an effort to get the best cover, they were like ducks in a shooting gallery. Men were dropping their weapons and screaming in capitulation even as they were being shot apart—but no one was listening.

A few moments later the loading dock fell silent, and Moriarty slowly reached to open the flap on his holster, drawing the pistol and pulling his knees beneath him to sneak a peek over the top of the generator.

Forrest was standing there with his M-4 shouldered and ready to fire. "Major Moriarty, I presume?"

Moriarty dropped the weapon, and Kane delivered him a butt-stroke to the side of his head, sending him sprawling across the concrete.

# FIFTY-SEVEN

ULRICH LISTENED FOR THE SHOCK WAVE TO STRIKE THE BLAST door, signaling that Emory had blown up the house. Counting to five, he pulled the lever and swung the door wide, running the twenty-foot length of the tunnel through the smoke and dust until he came out the other end into the dim light of the basement, where three dead airmen lay on the floor with their lungs crushed. A murky sky was visible at the top of the steel staircase, telling Ulrich the house had blown up, out and away—just as he had intended when he set the charges.

He and the other four men—Danzig, Vasquez, Sullivan, and Marty—stormed up the stairs and opened immediate fire on the stunned crowd of nearly thirty men gathered at the opening over the cargo bay, firing from prone positions on the flooring of the house. They shot the airmen down with near impunity as the airmen struggled through the deep snow in a vain attempt to seek cover. The few who tried to return fire were the first to be eliminated, one toppling over backward into the hole.

Sullivan banged Marty on the shoulder, signaling him to help reduce the men on their left flank who were taking up firing positions within the row of trucks and trailers. Marty sprayed them with grazing fire as Sullivan fired a 40mm grenade into the side of a small diesel tanker, killing five in the explosion and flushing many more from the cover of the trucks on either side of the inferno.

Ulrich and the others had eliminated the airmen near the lift elevator and were now adding to the fire directed at the trucks, where there were thirty or so Air Force men left to be dealt with.

Sullivan fired another grenade into the side of the explosives truck, killing or injuring another ten.

"Take cover!" Ulrich shouted, smacking Danzig on the shoulder and pointing toward what used to be the back porch, where the brick foundation of the house would provide them decent cover. "We're too exposed!"

Danzig was crawling backward when he saw Vasquez's head drop face first onto the deck, a round having struck him to the left of his nose and blowing out the back of his head. Danzig grabbed for his friend's ankle, but Sullivan knocked his arm away and shoved him toward cover.

"He's gone!"

Ulrich grabbed Marty's collar and practically dragged him as Marty continued to pour fire onto the enemy, deftly switching out the empty magazine and continuing to fire like a veteran soldier. The two of them toppled off the back porch into the lee of the foundation.

Sullivan fired a grenade and blew up another truck, glancing behind him to his right as he was loading another round, seeing the Humvee ascending from below the earth. He swung the weapon around and was about to fire when Kane's dark face emerged from the gunner's opening in the roof.

The Humvee raced off the deck and swung wide around the compound to the west, outflanking the enemy position. Kane fired into their exposed flanks as Forrest sped through the snow, and within a few seconds the remaining airmen were throwing down their weapons and putting their hands into the air.

"Let's move!" Ulrich shouted, jumping onto the porch and then charging across the floor to the front stairs.

The airmen were walking out to meet them with their hands raised, all of them shaggy and filthy and utterly demoralized.

"Hands on your heads!" Danzig screamed, kicking one of them viciously in the groin. "Down on your fucking knees!"

Soon there were eleven airmen down on their knees in the snow with their hands on top of their heads. Sullivan stalked the row of trucks, shooting the wounded where they lay. Forrest and Kane checked inside each of the trailers for supplies and holdouts, but all they found were two sickly women who had somehow managed to survive the hail of bullets. The truck with the cage on the back of it was in flames, the five men inside, who had been on the menu, now terribly overcooked.

"There's only six of you?" asked a young airman in abject disbelief.

"There were seven of us!" Danzig said, stomping pugnaciously forward to deliver a rifle butt to his face, knocking him over backward into the snow.

"Linus!" Forrest shouted. "Enough!"

"Sir!"

"Weapons and ammo!" Forrest was shouting much more loudly than necessary, his ears no longer bleeding but still ringing like church bells. "We leave nothing of value up here. Kane! Get on the Cat and push that dirt back into the hole." He used hand signals to explain himself and marched off through the snow. He climbed the stairs onto the foundation of the house, knelt beside Oscar Vasquez and turned him gently over onto his back, stripping him of his weapons and ammo. He took the dog tags from around Oscar's neck and put them into his pocket, rooting through his pockets for anything his wife Maria might want.

Danzig came up onto the foundation and began to remove Oscar's boots.

Forrest stared at him.

"We wear the same size, Captain." Danzig got his first look at the ruptured blood vessels in Forrest's eyes, pointing to his own boots so Forrest would know what he was saying.

"Won't be any more boot factories for a while, will there?" Forrest said in a loud voice.

"No, sir."

"What do you want done for him, Linus? We can't let Maria see him with his face shot apart."

"Let's build him a big fire, sir," Danzig said, gesturing with his hands.

"Good idea!" Forrest said, offering him Oscar's dog tags. "It was better this way, Linus. Diabetic coma's no way for a soldier to die."

"Yes, sir. I have a request, sir."

"A what?"

"Request!" Danzig said in a raised voice.

"What is it?"

Danzig pointed at the men still on their knees in the snow, making a shooting gesture with his thumb and forefinger. "I want to do the executions."

Forrest nodded and returned his attention to Vasquez.

Danzig walked off through the snow and took a 9mm pistol from the pile of captured weapons, shooting each airman in the back of the head one at a time. None of the condemned men bothered to plead for their lives until Danzig came to the last one.

"I never touched any of those women!" the man pleaded over his shoulder. "Ask them! I never touched any of them. Ever!"

"I believe you," Danzig said, squeezing the trigger and watching his body fall over into the gray snow.

Afterward, Forrest's men built a large funeral pyre from the debris of the house. It was growing dark by the time they lay Oscar's body in the center of it, dousing it with gasoline and setting it ablaze.

Kane was only just finishing with the landscaping when Forrest walked over and climbed up onto the machine with him. "We have to find a patch to weld over that hole in the lift deck!" Forrest shouted. "Any suggestions?"

Kane backed off on the throttle and sat thinking. His eyes and ears had stopped bleeding as well but both men looked a mess.

"I can cut a patch from the hood of one of the trucks," he said loudly. "It's not as tough as boiler plate but it's better than nothing."

"We'll work until we're finished," Forrest said, patting him on the shoulder with a grin. "And this time we'll cover the lift deck with three feet of dirt!"

It was ten at night before they finished clearing the bodies from the cargo bay and patching the hole in the lift. Dr. West came into the cargo bay to look over the two women, taking Forrest and Ulrich aside.

"They're sick," he said slowly enough for Forrest to make him out, not wanting the women to overhear him. "I don't think it's anything communicable," he said directly to Ulrich, "but I've given them TB tests to make sure it's not tuberculosis. We'll know in three days. Until then, at the very least, they should remain quarantined here in the bay. With some penicillin and hot food, they should be ready to join us inside within a week or two."

He then turned to Forrest and made an OK with his fingers.

"Okay, Sean," Forrest tried to say more quietly. "Thanks. Now would you mind going inside? We've got some dark business to take care of out here, and I don't think your oath allows for you to be present."

"Sure," West said, glancing across the bay to where Major Benjamin Moriarty sat shackled to the fender of a truck before withdrawing to the tunnel.

When West was gone, Forrest walked over and freed Moriarty long enough to cuff his hands behind his back with Sullivan and Kane looking on. Then he shoved Moriarty across the bay toward the two women.

"It's up to you, ladies," he said, keeping a firm grip on the handcuffs. "What sort of justice do you want?"

One of the women backed away, afraid of Moriarty even

now, but the other held her ground. "What do you mean?" she asked.

"I mean tell me what you want done and I'll do it."

Moriarty turned to look him in the eyes and smirked, so Forrest smashed in his front teeth with the frame of his .45, dropping him straight to his knees. "So what'll it be, ladies?"

"Just shoot him," the woman said quietly. "He's not worth another minute of time."

Forrest looked to Ulrich to see what she had said, and Ulrich drew a finger across his throat. He then hauled the battered major to his feet and shoved him over to the lift, knocking him back to his knees. Kane stepped onto the lift beside him, carrying a lantern, and Danzig pressed the up button to send them to ground level.

The lift locked into position at ground level and Moriarty looked up at them. "Fuck you bo—"

Forrest shot him through the mouth and he fell over dead, his spinal column severed. He dragged the body through the snow and threw it onto the pile as Kane climbed back up onto the Cat. Soon the lift was buried beneath three feet of landscaping, and the 'dozer was blown up with a stick of TNT. Both men then went into the basement, where Danzig stood waiting for them, carbine in hand, and the three of them entered the silo, sealing the blast door behind them.

The siege was over.


**WHEN VERONICA AND** Melissa got their first look at Forrest, they both gasped and started to cry as they wrapped themselves around him.

"Shhh," he said softly, holding them tight in each arm. "It's not permanent."

Veronica looked over Forrest's shoulder at Dr. West, who stood against the wall in the corridor. "Is he lying, Sean?"

West shook his head. "He'll likely have some hearing loss, but he looks a lot worse than he is. It was just the pressure wave."

Forrest saw Maria Vasquez coming into the hall and he freed himself from Veronica and Melissa and went to her, folding her into his arms as she cried. "I'm sorry," he whispered into her ear. "It's my fault."

She looked up at him and shook her head. "It's what he wanted," she said carefully, making sure he could read her lips. "And he had a good last year . . ."

# BOOK THREE

# FIFTY-EIGHT

EIGHTEEN MONTHS AFTER THE IMPACT, ESTER THORN AND Harold Shipman were visiting a former shopping mall in Honolulu. It was now a facility for growing hydroponic rice. The horticulturalist giving the tour was a brunette in her late twenties named Sandra Hayes, and it was plain to both Ester and Shipman that she was very proud of the facility she had helped to create.

"And the best part," Sandra was saying with great alacrity, "is that we'll be able to harvest three crops a year."

"Three?" Ester said, stopping to lean against her cane. "Are you sure?"

"Absolutely," Sandra said, smiling brightly. "And there's no reason we can't duplicate this facility all through the Islands. You don't need a giant building like this either. Any building can be converted in this same way, and not just for growing rice. The volcanic soils in these islands are excellent."

"What about the lighting?" Ester asked. "Most of these bulbs were made specifically for growing food indoors, were they not?"

"Lighting continues to be the one problem," Sandra said, turning glum for the first time. "We only have a limited number of them on the island, and though regular fluorescent bulbs can be used, there are still only so many of them available. So unless we can find a way to manufacture lighting domestically . . . we will eventually have to return to the mainland and see if there are any department stores still standing."

Ester turned to Shipman. "We're still up against it, Harold."

"One step at a time, Ester," Shipman said calmly. "We've made an awful lot of progress in a year and a half and these indoor facilities have already begun to contribute."

He turned to Sandra, asking, "Have you worked with the mushroom farmers at all, Miss Hayes?"

"No," she said. "I know Bobbi Pouha from the university in Manoa, but we haven't really been in contact since the big push for indoor farming last year. I know that she's very good. She knows her shrooms, that's for sure."

Shipman chuckled. "I understand they've had a couple of setbacks. I was wondering if you knew anything about that."

"I believe those were mostly climate-related," Sandra said. "And I think they've got things straightened out. Fungus can be tricky."

"I don't know how anyone can eat it myself," Ester said. "But I'm glad it's going to be available. We're only a month ahead of our food demand."

"I honestly think we're going to be okay," Sandra said. "At least for the next couple of years . . . and who knows? We may have sunlight by then. The sky has begun to clear some, even though most of us still need a light meter to tell."

"Thank you very much for the tour," Ester said. "I'm going on the closed circuit television in a couple of days, so I need to collect all the good news I can."

"You're very welcome," Sandra said. "Please come back."

**DURING THE DRIVE** back to the motel where Ester lived on the top floor, she sat staring out the window at the dead palms along the road, the brown landscape. Hawaii had been pretty lucky in terms of snow. Not a great deal of it had fallen, and what little had accumulated melted once the temperature rose into the forties during the second summer. They were heading into their second winter now and the average temperature was closer to thirty-five.

"The Navy has been after me about an expedition to the mainland," she said with a sigh.

"You're still opposed to the idea?" Shipman asked.

"They're asking to disconnect one of the carriers from the power grid, the idea being that they can fit more men aboard and bring back more supplies. Which I'm not entirely opposed to, but it would mean asking Honolulu to cut back even further on its power consumption, and people have become somewhat spoiled these past six months. Not to mention that the crew would need to take a large portion of the dry goods we have in reserve."

"But the general public isn't aware of that reserve. The Navy's kept it under lock and key belowdecks. What does Hadrian think about the idea?"

"He's not opposed to it," she said. "But he's suggested sending a destroyer first to reconnoiter the shoreline, dispatching shore parties all up and down the California coast."

"What about *Boxer*?" Shipman asked.

"Who?"

"Not who," Shipman chuckled, "it's a *what*—the USS *Boxer*. It's a small aircraft carrier meant for helicopters and amphibious landing craft. And it's not nuclear powered."

"Which must be why the Navy hasn't suggested it," Ester said, perturbed. "That Longbottom is trying to hoard his fuel for the big war he thinks he's going to have someday with God knows who. Well, that's what we'll do, then. We'll send the *Boxer* and one destroyer escort . . . Oh, and the volcanologists are already after me to send an expedition to find the impact crater. Have you heard this insanity?"

Shipman smiled. "Yes."

"Like we have the time and the resources to mount such a frivolous expedition."

Shipman chuckled. "Is this the same Ester Thorn who got so angry with the government thirty years ago for refusing to allocate more money to keep an eye on the Great Beyond?"

"Oh, shut up, Harold. It's not even remotely the same."

"How can you say that? You're a scientist."

"The U.S. government had more than enough money to fund such a project, and it would have directly benefited mankind—which was exactly what I told them!"

"Well, I can't argue that point," he said, glancing at the dead countryside.

"Allowing them to mount an expedition like that now wouldn't be any different than sending them to the gallows."

"Well, you know geologists, Ester."

"Yes, I do," she said. "And I understand their desires, but they're just going to have to wait until we've gotten these islands more than a couple of weeks ahead of our food consumption. I wonder what old Longbottom's going to say when I tell him to send the *Boxer* out. You know, Harold, I need a liaison to the Navy who I can trust, someone to tell me about things like the *Boxer* so I know what types of resources we truly have."

"That person may be tough find," Shipman said. "Longbottom has a pretty tight rein on most everyone who knows anything about their internal affairs."

# FIFTY-NINE

**WITH THE SIEGE A DISTANT MEMORY, THE SILO POPULATION** was preparing to celebrate their second Christmas belowground. Forrest and Kane had both recovered from their injuries with minimal hearing loss, and Emory's baby was quickening nicely, still nursing regularly at her breast. Erin was unquestionably the baby's mother, however; Emory behaved as little more than nursemaid to the child, and was already being referred to as Aunt Shannon.

The installation remained secure. The antenna array was raised every morning so the men could watch the countryside with the robotic camera, and lowered each night after dark. Thus far there had been no further signs of life aboveground. It did not snow a great deal over the summer, but no more than half the snow had melted, and flurries began to fly again with the coming of autumn.

The rat population now stood at thirty-five mating pairs and, amazingly enough, was still a secret kept among the men, Melissa and Emory the sole exceptions. The food stores were holding out better than Forrest had any right to expect, but he knew that by late March they would have to begin incorporating rat meat into their diets if they were to stretch the rest of the food through the summer—which meant it was time to start letting the rats breed at will, and they still hadn't figured out what to use for cages. So far they had partitioned off four empty fifty-gallon fuel drums cut down the middle, but the little critters were escape artists, so Danzig and Kane had an almost full-time job just keeping them wrangled. Fortunately, the loss of the bay's first blast door provided an excuse for keeping a man on duty within the cargo bay at all times without raising suspicion.

Ulrich tossed his pen down and sat back from the console with a brief glance at the monitors. "No matter how I crunch these numbers, Jack, we're down to rat meat and the occasional tomato by the first of September. And we still don't know what the fuck we're going to do for breeding cages. The little sons of bitches can chew through damn near anything."

"Okay. So maybe we need to forget the rats altogether," Forrest said, thinking they might need to make a break for it before the food ran completely out. "Those figures of yours don't include the MREs, do they?"

"You ordered me not to, so no, but each truckload only buys us an extra month at one MRE per day per person, which isn't exactly a feast."

"So, come the first of September we load into the trucks and roll south with the MREs."

"South to where?"

"Maybe Altus Air Force Base." Forrest grinned. "Marty seems to think it's teeming with geologists."

"That's a pretty huge maybe, Jack, and we'll only have a month to find a safe haven."

The door opened and Erin came in carrying Emory Marie Ulrich, named after her birth mother Shannon Marie Emory, though everyone called her Emmy. Laddie got up from where he lay on the floor near Forrest's chair and sat watching as she offered the infant to her husband.

"Would you hold Emmy for a little bit, honey? I need to eat."

Ulrich sat up straight in the chair and put out his arms. "You mean with all those women out there you can't find anybody else to hold her?"

"Everyone else is eating lunch," she said. "It's not going to hurt you. You are her father, right?"

Ulrich accepted the baby with a nod, and Erin smiled, kissed him on the lips and left the room. "That's a buncha bullshit," he grumbled. "Those broads fight over this baby."

"She wants the kid to know you're her father," Forrest said, scratching the dog behind his ears. "What's wrong with that? You're supposed to be doing this for your wife. Remember?"

"Oh, shut up," Ulrich said, holding the baby delicately, almost as if he were afraid of hurting her. "Pretty thing, though, ain't she? I can't believe Shannon still doesn't want her."

"She's got reason enough," Forrest said. "Marty told me she went through some pretty heinous shit. Maybe not as bad as Liddy and Natalie, but bad enough."

The two women they had freed from Moriarty—Liddy and Natalie—were neighbors before the asteroid, and their families had been captured together in a basement by Moriarty's men. Both women saw their husbands and children killed and eaten over a period of weeks, and if not for their mutual support of one another, Forrest was certain they would have killed themselves by now. Even after eight months of safety belowground, they rarely left one another's side, as if still afraid of being violated. Michael doubted they would ever completely assimilate, both women still suffering from severe post-traumatic shock and horrible nightmares.

The baby began to fuss, so Ulrich stood from the chair and took her for a walk in the halls, talking softly to her and hoping that one of the other women would offer to take her off of his hands, but none of them did, and he began to suspect a conspiracy. There was no sense in trying to find out for sure, however. The women had grown thick as thieves over the last eighteen months.

He found Melissa in one of the blast tunnels, one of her favorite haunts, where she sat reading a book. He had not seen her working on the code for a few months now and was glad she had finally given it up.

"Good book?"

"It's okay," she said with a shrug, leaning against the steel bulkhead, knees drawn up. "Nothing great. I'm reading the ones that look boring first."

"Good plan. Hey, wanna hold the baby for a while?"

She grinned and shook her head, confirming his suspicions.

"See if I do you any more favors."

"She needs to know you're her dad, Wayne."

The remark struck him differently coming from Melissa, knowing that she had lost her father. "I suppose you're probably right."

"Can I ask a question?"

"Shoot."

"Are we going to have to eat the rats pretty soon?"

"I'm afraid so."

"I won't have to help butcher them, will I?"

"No. The men will take care of that."

"Thank God," she said, going back to her book.

After he was gone, she read for a while longer then checked her watch and saw it was time for the second half of the school day to begin. She closed the book and went to the classroom to help Andie with the day's reading lesson, like she did every other day.

Today Andie was focusing on phonics. Most of the children were already reading at a third-grade level, but she wanted to enhance their understanding of the sound values for individual letters because some of the students were having a difficult time sounding out multisyllabic words.

"So what are the vowels again?" she asked them, preparing to write them out with a blue marker on her dry-eraser board.

"A . . . E . . . I . . . O . . . and U," the children said together as Andie wrote them out.

"And sometimes Y," one of them added.

"That's, right," Andie said, "and sometimes Y."

Melissa looked up from the lesson she was preparing to help with, her mind's eye suddenly seeing a stream of numeric code. "Vowels," she muttered. "What's the most common vowel?"

She excused herself, slipped out of the room and into the adjacent common room, taking her laptop from the box beneath her bedroll and disappearing all the way to the very top level of silo number two, where she often went to be alone. She sat down in her private nook between two stacks of cardboard boxes and opened the file containing the cipher work she had done on the code months before.

The first thing she did was bring up the same stream of code she had been working on since the beginning: 9249 130240248128240129248116360259130130140492503671 2036824824.

Next, she brought up one of the very first ciphers she had created on her own, the same cipher now flashing in her brain for reasons she did not yet understand:

```
    A       B       C       D
  E F     G H     I J     K L
 M N O   P Q R   S T U   V W Y
```

Then she sat staring at the code and instinctively broke it up into units of three for perhaps the two hundredth time:

```
924-913-024-024-812-824-012-924-811-636-025-
913-013-011-404-925-036-712-036-824-824
```

She scanned the string of numbers just as she had so often before, allowing her brain to process them with something specific to focus on this time, her subconscious thought no longer hindered by Ulrich's discouraging remarks about the infinite number of possible algorithms.

"The most common vowel is E," she muttered, pulling on her lower lip. "So is it zero-two-four? It does appear twice."

But what about 824? she wondered. That appeared twice as well, and both sets appeared in tandem, so they might just as easily be consonants. L's perhaps.

She set the computer aside, ran back down the stairs to the tunnel, then down the tunnel to the main corridor and into the first common room, to retrieve a sheaf of worn papers from inside the computer box.

"What are you up to?" Taylor asked her with a smile.

Taylor had been talking with Jenny and Michelle when Melissa had left in a hurry before with the computer, and she could sense that Melissa was still in a hurry even though she was trying not to look it now. Her query drew the attention of some of the other adults in the room, and Melissa was suddenly acutely aware of how crowded the complex was; she normally kept everyone largely blocked from her conscious thoughts by daydreaming of things like string theory and dark matter. Even her uncle Michael was looking at her funny.

"Nothing," she said curtly, and walked out of the room.

When she got back up to her nook she sat down and began scanning the myriad pages of code, mentally dividing the numbers into groups of three, seeking out the digit sequence of 024 and spotting it over and over again, whereas she saw the occurrence of 824 only very rarely.

"So 024 has to be the letter E. How did I not see it before?"

The question was easy enough to answer—she had been thinking too far outside the box—and only partially on account of Ulrich's gainsaying. Sometimes straightforward solutions to complicated issues simply avoided her, something her father had enjoyed teasing her about.

Now she needed to come up with a cipher in which E was equal to 024. She decided to add a numerical value directly to each subgroup of the early cipher merely as a jumping off point.

| 0 | 1 | 2 | 3 |
|---|---|---|---|
| A | B | C | D |
| E F | G H | I J | K L |
| M N O | P Q R | S T U | V W Y |

Then she assigned E a value of 022 as a place to start: Group 0, second row down, second letter in the subgroup. She could just as easily have assigned it a value of 021: Group 0, second row down, first letter in the row, but she needed to start somewhere and one place was as good as another.

After deciding she was in the right neighborhood, it occurred to her for the first time to invert the subgroups within the cipher.

```
        0          1          2          3
      M N O      P Q R      S T U      V W Y
        E F        G H        I J        K L
        A          B          C          D
```

And suddenly there it was: E = 024. Group 0, second row down, fourth letter in the subgroup.

"Okay," she muttered, her stomach filling with an eager anxiety, "but how do I find values for all these stupid *nines, eights,* and *sevens*?"

Her mind began to clutter again, so she closed the laptop and drew a breath to clear it before opening the lid for another look. And just like that she saw the numerical values in her mind's eye.

```
        0          9          8          7
      M N O      P Q R      S T U      V W Y
        E F        G H        I J        K L
        A          B          C          D
```

"Yes!" she said, jumping up to do a quick dance before sitting back down to decipher the initial string of code.

```
   G    R    E    E    T    I    N    G    S
924-913-024-024-812-824-012-924-811-636-
                                         ?
F    R    O    M      H    A    W    A    I    I
025-913-013-011-404-925-036-712-036-824-824
                  ?
```

"Holy shit!" she said, her face splitting into a grin. "That's it!"

She grabbed the papers and began to decipher them as rapidly as she could. Oblivious as the hours passed, she didn't stop to come up for air.

"Melissa!" Forrest shouted from three stories below.

She looked at her watch and was surprised to see how much time had passed. "Up here!"

"It's time to eat!"

"Not hungry!"

"Too bad. Get down here!"

"No!"

She heard his boots trotting up the four flights of steel stairs and sat grinning until his face emerged over the deck. Laddie came trotting over and licked her face.

"I *know* I misunderstood you," he said, a wry grin on his face. "Because from way down there it sounded like you told me no."

"I can't stop right now," she said.

"You're back at that goddamn code, aren't you?"

"Can I please skip dinner just this once? *Please?*"

"Melissa . . . that code is going to drive you insane."

"Dad, will you please trust me this one time?"

He saw a new kind of determination in her eyes now, something that said to him she finally had a legitimate reason for wanting to skip dinner. "Okay. I'll put a plate in the oven for you. I want you to eat when you come down. Understood?"

She gave him a little salute, making him laugh as he turned and went back down the stairs.

"Laddie, you comin'?"

The dog sat beside Melissa and watched him, cocking his head to one side.

"Communist," he said with a chuckle, and trotted down the stairs.

"Hey, know what?" she called when he stepped onto the deck below her, looking down at him through the grating.

"What?" he said, looking up.

"I'm gonna be seventeen pretty soon."

"I know that," he said with a smile.

"What are you getting me?"

"What do you want?"

"A car."

He laughed and said, "I'll see what I can do."

When Forrest got back to the cafeteria he sat down beside Veronica, across from Karen and Michael. "She says she's busy," he said, lifting his fork from the steel tray.

The other three exchanged looks.

"You've never let her get away with that excuse before," Karen said, grinning. "What's different about today?"

Melissa was famous for trying to skip dinner a few times a week, and Forrest would never allow it.

"I've got a feeling she's close to cracking that goddamn code," he said quietly. "But don't say anything to Wayne. She'll want to tell him herself."

"For real?" Michael asked, surprised.

Forrest shrugged, saying, "She didn't actually say it, but I could tell by the light in her eyes."

"Well, good for her," Veronica said. "She's sure lost enough sleep over that damn thing."

After the children were put to bed that night, Forrest asked the women to join him, Ulrich, and Dr. West in the cafeteria for a meeting. Emory and the rest of the men stayed behind to watch over the sleeping children in the common rooms.

Melissa was still in the silo.

Formal meetings were rare events, so there was a lot of whispering as the women speculated over what it was about. The general consensus was that Forrest was going to announce a cut in the daily food allowance, a step that had not yet been taken and that most of them realized was probably long overdue.

"So," Forrest said with a dubious kind of smile. "I suppose you're all wondering why the three of us have gathered you here tonight."

There were some chuckles.

"Okay, as I'm sure you're all aware, we've consumed well over half of our original food stores. And I'm afraid that in order for us to stretch what we've got left through to the end of the summer, we're going to have to take certain . . . certain measures."

He glanced at the other two men sitting beside him to see if either of them wanted to jump in, but Ulrich only smiled at the women, and West maintained his usual passive demeanor.

"We know you're going to reduce our rations," Erin said, burping the baby over her shoulder, having only moments before gotten her back from Emory. "Just tell us by how much."

"I'm afraid the measures are going to be a bit more radical than that, actually," he replied. "At our present rate of consumption, we'll be out of food around mid-May—which makes nearly two years. So we've done an excellent job of conserving while at the same time keeping everyone well nourished. But in order for us to stretch the food through the summer, we're going to have to cut back to *below* what would be considered healthy by even minimal standards, which would put us all in jeopardy if we didn't find a way to supplement our diet."

"You've got plenty of vitamins stashed away," Andie piped up from the back row.

"That's right," he said with a chuckle. "And you can believe we'll finally be breaking them out, but I'm afraid vitamins alone aren't going to do the trick."

The women began to murmur, their mutual concern steadily rising.

"And as we all know," Forrest continued, "the skies have not cleared enough to—Okay, everyone, cut the chatter and give me a second to finish. We do have a plan. But it's going to sound somewhat repugnant to you when you first hear it, so I want you to brace yourselves."

He was trying to make the plan sound a tad worse than what he hoped it actually was, in order to keep the truth from coming as too great a shock.

"We've been raising a certain kind of animal in the cargo bay. And we're pretty sure we can breed them fast enough to provide us with a viable source of nutrition through the winter. So long as we start a full-fledged breeding program right now."

Not one of the women made a sound. None of them wanted to even speak the word *rat*, but there was no other animal Forrest could possibly have been talking about in this postasteroidal world.

Erin got up from her seat and took the baby with her into the common area without even meeting her husband's eyes, furious with him for keeping such a disgusting secret from her.

"Look, these animals aren't the demons they have been stigmatized to be," Forrest said quietly. "In fact, they're actually rather affectionate if they're handled from birth, and they're as clean as their environment will allow."

No one was speaking up yet, so he continued.

"The babies are called pups, and a female is capable of producing twelve litters a year with an average of ten or so to a litter. A female is able to begin breeding after just three months, and at the moment we have thirty-five breeding pairs and two extra females."

"My God, that's fifty-two of those . . . *things*!" Lynette said, standing up, half expecting to find one of them running under foot. "You can't honestly expect us to eat them!"

"I'm afraid that starvation is our only other option at this point," Forrest said, making brief eye contact with Price, who stood just inside the common room doorway.

The doctor looked embarrassed, and Forrest felt sorry for him, of course. But when a man marries a woman based largely upon her looks, he takes a calculated risk, and Forrest had warned him before he'd taken that final plunge.

"No!" Lynette said. "I'll fucking starve! I'm sorry."

"That will of course be your decision," Forrest replied. "But I have seen starvation up close—in time of war—and you will be very surprised at what you can eat by the time your belly begins to swell from hunger. And I would like to remind everyone that these animals were eaten as part of the regular diet in many Asian cultures and treated with great respect, particularly in India, where they were actually worshipped, rather than eaten."

"Next you're going to tell us they taste like chicken!" Lynette lashed out, her flesh continuing to crawl.

Forrest could see her hysteria beginning to spread to some of the other women, so he signaled for Price to come into the cafeteria.

"Oh!" Lynette said, growing angrier. "So now I'm going to be treated like a fucking head case, is that it?"

"Honey, please try to calm down," Price said. "This isn't going to help anything, and no one is going to make you eat anything you don't want to eat."

"I want out!" she said, continuing her harangue. "Give me my share of the food and let me the fuck out! I'm sick of living on top of each other down here anyway! At least out there I'll be able to fucking breathe!"

Forrest remained calm, seeing Emory and the other men gathering outside the doorway, Emory clearly ready to physically subdue Lynette if Forrest so much as crooked a finger.

"Lynette, are you sure that's what you want?" he asked her with a stern military bearing. "Because I will load you up right now with all the food you can carry. You'll actually be doing the rest of us a favor. Because you won't be able to carry even a fraction of what you'll eat should you choose to stay. I'm even willing to supply you with a weapon. But remember one thing: I will *not* let you back in when that food runs out."

Lynette's irate bluff had been called, her punk card drawn, stamped, and given back to her just that fast, and she was suddenly afraid that she might now be expected to make good on her threat. She could already see Ulrich's cold blue eyes cutting into her, the faintest hint of a sinister smile on his face.

So she did the only thing a woman of her breeding knew how to do in such a situation; she sat back down and began to bawl, and Price went to her, pulled her to her feet and walked her down the hall.

The rest of the women sat staring at Forrest, unsure what to say or even think; the prospect of having to subsist on rat meat was a lot to digest.

"In response to Lynette's supposition," Forrest said with a smile, "I did have the pleasure of eating a few of these delectable animals during my time in the military, and yes, they do taste a little bit like chicken, particularly with a dash of Tabasco."

Andie laughed, and that seemed to break the tension.

"Don't we have to worry about them making us sick?" Karen asked.

"Like Jack said," Dr. West joined in at last, "these animals will keep themselves as clean as their environment will permit. But they've got bad bladders, so they tend to pee a lot, which will make keeping their environment laboratory-clean something of a challenge. And while a ra—*the animal*—is capable of carrying diseases that are communicable to people, we're hoping our animals are at minimal risk. This is because they're all the progeny of the same original breeding pair—which were local animals living in the fields around the silo, rather than some New York City sewer drain."

**LATER THAT NIGHT.** Forrest was sitting in Launch Control with his feet up, smoking a cigarette. He and Ulrich were reminiscing about their younger days of whiskey drinking and womanizing and other forms of youthful wickedry. It was taking all of his self-discipline not to check on Melissa, who had yet to emerge from the silo, or envisioning her falling from the top deck to the bottom of the silo in a freak accident. If Laddie hadn't been with her, he'd have long ago checked on her.

He was about to finally give in to his fears when she at last stepped into Launch Control. Laddie came trotting around the console and jumped up to put both of his feet into Forrest's lap, whining and licking his face.

"Oh, so she's not all she's cracked up to be, huh?" Forrest said with a smile, rubbing and squeezing the dog's face.

Melissa was smiling more brightly than he had ever seen her smile as he watched her put a single sheet of paper on the console in front of Ulrich.

```
A B C D E F
G H I J K L
M N O P Q R
S T U V W Y
```

"See that?" she asked.

"That's the first cipher example I showed you," Ulrich answered, noting her unmistakable glow. "The first one I checked the code against. The first cipher any cryptographer would check it against."

"And they know that," she said. "That's why they're using it. They've been hiding their cipher right in plain sight."

"What are you talking about?" he said, noting the proud grin on Forrest's face now. "Are you saying you've cracked the damn thing?"

"I'm saying more than that." She put another piece of paper down in front of him.

```
   0      9      8      7
 M N O  P Q R  S T U  V W Y
  E F    G H    I J    K L
   A      B      C      D
```

Any group of three numbers beginning with a digit <u>lower</u> than 7 is either a space or "gibberish" intended to throw off the cryptographer.

G  R  E  E  T  I  N  G  S
924-913-024-024-812-824-012-924-811-636-
                                        ?
F  R  O  M    H  A  W  A  I  I
025-913-013-011-404-925-036-712-036-824-824
            ?

Ulrich studied the cipher, matching each letter for himself against the cipher. "Well, I'll be a son of a bitch!" he said, seeing the other papers in her hand. "And this works throughout? You've deciphered every conversation I copied down?"

"Yep! And you were right—you can memorize a cipher pretty fast. By the time I got to the last few pages, I didn't have to look at the cipher anymore."

"Well, let's see the other sheets," he said enthusiastically.

"Whattaya give me?" she asked, hiding the pages behind her back.

"Jack, tell your wiseass kid to give me those papers."

"You're on your own," Forrest said, rocking back in the chair with his hands behind his head. "She begged you to help her with that damn thing for months and you kept blowing her off. Now you want her to just hand it over? I think she's entitled to something from your private stash."

"What private stash?" Melissa asked, instantly scandalized, her eyebrows raised.

Ulrich glowered at his friend. "You got a big mouth, Forrest."

"I want something from your private stash!" she said, dancing around the console to hide behind Forrest.

Ulrich got slowly up from his chair, eyeing them both. "You two may have the upper hand tonight," he said, moving toward the spiral staircase, "but the tables will turn."

He spiraled down and out of sight.

"What's he got down there?" she asked in a whisper.

Forrest smiled and shrugged.

Down below, Ulrich worked the combination on a big red steel case with TOOLS spray-painted across the lid in black.

A few seconds later they heard the lid slam, and Ulrich slowly reemerged with a vacuum-sealed silver package in his hand. The package was about the size of a slice of French toast, and he offered it to Melissa with a veiled smile.

She reached for it, but he held it tight. "Give me the papers."

"At the same time," she said, offering the papers with a tight grip.

Each let go of their trade item at the same time, and Melissa backed away, reading the print on the foil package: ICE CREAM, FREEZE DRIED / U.S. GOVERNMENT / NASA CENTRAL STORES.

"No way!" she said in awe. "Jack, look!"

"See?" Forrest said, knowing exactly what goodies Ulrich had stashed away in the toolbox. "You can't trust this guy as far as you can throw him."

He looked up at Ulrich, who stood scanning Melissa's work.

"What's it say there, Wayne?"

Ulrich continued to read for a spell, then turned and looked at Melissa, saying, "Come here, kid."

"No way."

"Give the ice cream to Jack and come here."

She gave the ice cream to Forrest and stepped suspiciously forward. "What?"

Ulrich hugged her tight. "Forgive me," he said quietly, almost reverently. "I've failed to support you twice now, but I will not again . . . I promise."

Forrest sat up and set the ice cream down on the console, having only seen Ulrich comport himself with such respect a few times in all the years he'd known him, and all three times Ulrich had been in the process of placing a folded American flag into the hands of a fallen soldier's widow.

"What the hell does it say, Stumpy?"

"It says there's hope," Ulrich said, letting go of Melissa— who didn't quite know what to think—and handing him the papers. "Excuse me. I have to go hug my wife."

Ulrich left the room, and Melissa stood looking at Forrest. "What was that about?" she asked, totally confused.

Forrest sat skimming over the translations. "He's probably feeling a little bit ashamed."

"But he didn't know the code was breakable."

"Well, honey . . . the night you got sick, he very nearly convinced the others to vote against me going after your medicine. So if it hadn't been for your uncle Kane . . ."

"I'd be dead?"

"Maybe. And from the looks of this here, kiddo . . . well, you just might have saved every damn one of us, Erin in particular. So Wayne owes you personally now. You've given him a reason to finally have some hope, which is something he hasn't had since the night my buddy Jerry called about the asteroid."

"Don't you mean the *meteor*?"

He laughed, saying, "Well, don't tell Wayne, but I actually do know it was an asteroid."

# SIXTY

THE NEXT MORNING FORREST WALKED INTO THE SHOWER room and jerked back the curtain on Marty's shower stall. "You ever hear of an astronomer named Ester Thorn?"

"Jesus Christ!" Marty said, covering himself. "Ever hear of privacy?"

"Well have you?"

"Yeah. Why?"

"Meet me in Launch Control when you're finished jerkin' off . . . and that's too big a weapon for you, by the way."

Forrest and Ulrich were working to connect a linear amplifier to the wireless transmitter when Marty joined them in the LC. He saw Ester's textbook on the console and picked it up. "If this is what you want to know about, there's not much she can do for us now."

"That's what you think," Forrest said, peering over the top of the set. "Read those papers there. Melissa deciphered the code last night."

"You're kidding me."

"Nope."

Marty read the transcriptions and sat down, staring at them in disbelief.

"What do you think?" Forrest asked.

"It's unbelievable. She's a friggin president? This can't be for real, can it?"

"What's she like?"

"I don't really know her all that well. I only met her once." He went on to share with them for the first time his story of discovering the asteroid and his visit with Ester Thorn. Forrest and Ulrich stopped their work and looked at him.

"Are you fucking serious?" Ulrich asked him in disbelief. "Or are you jerkin' us off?"

"No, honest to God."

"You're telling us that *you're* the son of a bitch who sent her off to Hawaii and got her to go on CNN?"

"That's me," Marty said. "I can't believe she's their friggin president, though. She didn't seem the type at all. Are these dates correct?"

"They're correct," Ulrich said, going back to work on the transmitter, "but they're still transmitting three to five nights a week. They should be on the air tonight, and we'll try to get some up-to-date information."

"Think she'll remember you?" Forrest wanted to know.

"That's kind of a stupid question."

"Okay, I guess a better question is whether you think she'd be willing to send a rescue party to pick your ginger ass up."

"No, the question is whether they've got the resources," Marty said, still befuddled. "But if they do, I'd like to think she'd feel at least something of an obligation. Hey, the crater photos! If Ester's not interested in sending anyone for me, the Islands' scientific community will definitely be interested in getting their hands on those pictures."

"Maybe we could use the photos to start a bidding war between the Hawaiians and the Aussies," Forrest joked. "First ones to rescue us get the pics."

"I don't care if they send a canoe full of Aborigines," Ulrich said. "So long as the damn thing floats. I just hope that his name and those photos are enough to tempt somebody into taking the risk. That's one hell of a voyage."

"Are you guys sure you can even reach Hawaii with that transmitter?"

"No," Ulrich said. "That's why we're working to boost its power."


**ERIN WAS SITTING** with Emory at the back of the cafeteria, where Emory was finishing up with the baby's morning feeding.

"Is Wayne warming up to her at all?" Emory asked.

"He's doing a little better," Erin said with a wan smile. "He's got an awful lot on his mind."

"Are you still pissed at him for not telling you about the, uh . . ."

"Rodents? Well, a wife has to pick her battles carefully down here. He says he was only trying to avoid upsetting me. He knows how horrified I am of the damn things."

"Here he comes," Emory said, covering her breast as Erin took the baby.

"Good morning," Ulrich said, walking up to the table. "How's our little girl this morning?"

Erin almost fell off the seat. *Our* little girl? "Um, she's fine. She's just finished feeding, actually."

"Can I have her?"

"Um, well, she needs to be burped."

"Let me give it a try," he said, putting his arms out across the table.

"Are you sure, Wayne?"

"Would you rather I didn't? You don't think I can do it?"

"No, it's not that . . ."

"Then let me give it a try."

"Okay," she said, a little unsure as she offered him the baby.

"You'll need this," Emory said, standing up to put a towel over his shoulder.

"I've had worse shit on my clothes than baby puke," he said.

"Haven't we all," Emory muttered.

"Where are you going?" Erin asked as he turned to walk away with the baby resting against his shoulder.

"Outside for a walk in the snow."

Erin sat watching as he left the cafeteria patting the baby gently on her back.

"What's *that* about?" Emory wondered.

"Beats me," Erin said, getting up to go after him.

"Where ya goin?" her friend Taylor said, coming around the counter, wiping her hands on her apron.

"To see what Wayne's—"

"No, you're not," Taylor said, putting her arm around Erin's waist and walking her back toward the table. "The quickest way to ruin it is to make him feel like you don't trust him with the baby. Trust me. I've been there. You wanted him to take an interest. So now you'll just have to—"

"But that wasn't like him, Taylor, and you—"

"E, name one fucking thing we've done down here in the last year that's been like any of us."

"But—"

"He's not going to hurt that baby. Now, sit down and finish your reconstituted egglike breakfast and let your husband get to know her."

Ulrich walked down the hall and into Launch Control. "Put that cigarette out, will ya?"

Forrest glanced up and crushed out the cigarette in the cannon-shell ashtray. "Since when are you Father of the Year?"

"Since the whiz kid made me start to think we might actually live through this bullshit." Ulrich heard the baby burp in his ear.

"That's a dangerous way to think," Forrest said with a smile.

"Tell me about it. It's only been twelve hours, and the worrying's already got my appetite fucked up."

Forrest laughed. "You'll get used to it, Stumpy. Hope is a love-hate relationship."

"How many times is this kid supposed to burp?"

"Get a good one yet?"

"Pretty good."

"Give her a bit longer, but she might be done."

"I'd like to get *me* some of that milk," Ulrich muttered, casting a careful glance over his shoulder to make sure there was no one in the doorway.

Forrest chuckled. "You're the father, all right . . . already looking to bang the babysitter."

"I would too."

"Lyin' ass."


THAT NIGHT, FORREST and the rest of the fighting men were gathered in Launch Control waiting for the transmissions to begin. Melissa was there too, nervously biting her fingernails.

"Think you can keep up with me?" Ulrich asked her.

"No, not that fast, but I won't be far behind."

"Are we going to try to contact them tonight?" Marty asked.

"Depends on what they've got to say," Forrest said, "but I don't think we should waste any time."

Forty minutes later the transmissions began.

"That's the Hawaiian," Ulrich said, recognizing the telegrapher's hand and grabbing his pen.

Melissa looked on as he wrote out the string of numbers, going straight to her decoding, having long memorized the cipher and seeing the numbers themselves almost as words now.

"There he goes," she said. " 'Greetings from Hawaii.' "

Forrest watched over her shoulder.

"Don't," she said, pushing his leg with her hand. "You'll mess me up."

He curled his upper lip, backing away with a grin at Kane, who crouched in the corner petting the dog.

The first transmission was finished in a very short period of time.

"That's it," Ulrich said, sitting back. "The Australian should answer within a minute or so."

"He should already be done translating," Melissa said, handing the message off to Forrest. "I am."

"Well, give the guy time to digest what he's reading."

"He's not digesting anything," Melissa said. "If I can read it in my head almost as fast as you're writing out the numbers, these two guys should know what it says without even consciously deciphering it. What he's doing is letting someone else read it."

Ulrich looked at her. "He is, is he?"

Forrest was sitting in a chair now, allowing Marty and the other men to read over his shoulder.

```
Greetings from Hawaii / mostly good news
tonight / will not be eating rats after
all / hurray / latest quartermaster re-
port indicates now one month ahead of
food consumption / meteorology now be-
lieves will be sufficient sunlight for
limited farming within ten years / sub-
ject to change / oceanography reports
previously unknown plankton species ex-
tra sensitive to ultraviolet light be-
ginning to thrive / believes this could
be very good news for oceanic life / now
for bad news / surprise pirate raid along
shoreline near kapaau left nine men dead
and six women kidnapped / et has given
navy free hand throughout island chain /
how are things down under . . .
```

"The Navy is still operational," Forrest said. "That's damn good news! Maybe we won't have to rely on those Aborigines of yours, Wayne."

"We'll see," Ulrich said feeling his pulse quicken as he and Melissa began to intercept the Australian response.

```
Salutations from land down under / news
of plankton life very encouraging / will
begin own studies here asap / meteorol-
ogy here not so optimistic about sun-
light / will discuss further at future
date / piracy here also growing problem
/ launching all out offensive this week
/ oil production here up / food stores
remain shallow / only one week ahead of
consumption / great white shark reported
off barrier reef yesterday / raises in-
teresting questions / chinese war ves-
sel spotted in torres strait north of
queensland / any ideas what this could
mean . . .
```

"That's curious as hell," Marty said. "What's a shark eating?"

"Screw the shark," said Sullivan. "What's the Chinese navy up to?"

"This discussion is a good sign overall," Ulrich said. "They don't seem nearly as concerned about their long-term survival as they were in the last conversation we recorded. I think we need to break into this conversation, Jack."

"Jump in there," Forrest said, indicating the prepared message on the console.

Ulrich began tapping out the encoded message.

```
Greetings from Nebraska / only recently
able to decipher your transmissions /
wish to join conversation / in posses-
sion of impact crater photos . . .
```

Within seconds the Hawaiian telegrapher was rapidly tapping out a signal in blind Morse Code.

```
−··/·−·/−·−·/−·−/−···/··/·−··/·−··/·/−··/
·−−·/·−··/·−/−/−·−−/·−−·/·−−/···
```

Which Ulrich translated effortlessly: *duckbilledplatypus.*

"Shit!" he said, throwing the pen down.

"What the fuck does that mean?" Sullivan said over his shoulder.

"It means the Hawaiian just told the Aussie to switch to another fucking code. A code that not even our little genius here has a prayer of cracking." He put his arm around Melissa and kissed her on the side of the head. "No offense, honey."

"But how do you know that?" Sullivan said.

"Because they're switching to a three-layered emergency encryption. I'm guessing our signal is only strong enough to reach Hawaii, which means the Australian didn't hear us. So right now the Aussie's down there waiting with bated breath to find out why the Hawaiian just declared an emergency."

"So that's it?" Marty said. "They won't even talk to us?"

"Give them time," Forrest said easily. "What did you think they were going to say? 'Hey, guys, join the party'? They need a minute to figure how they want to handle this."

Ten minutes later the Hawaiian sent a lengthy message to the Australian, and it was nearly half an hour before the Australian got back to him.

Forrest took Ulrich's pen and scribbled out a message: *Nebraska standing by.*

"Send that in Melissa's code," he said quietly.

Ulrich tapped it out and two minutes later they got a reply: *confirmed nebraska.*

"See there?" Forrest said, patting Ulrich on the shoulder. "Relax. It's going to take a little time. That's all."

They listened to the telegraphers communicating slowly back and forth for nearly two hours before the Hawaiian got back to them directly:

```
Greetings nebraska / understand you have
reconnoitered impact zone / is this cor-
rect . . .
```

Ulrich told them that it was and that they were requesting *extraction* from the American west coast.

```
Unable to respond to your request at this
time / state size and location of impact
crater . . .
```

"It's approximately fifty miles across and nearly a mile deep," Marty said. "Just north of the Montana border."

Ulrich relayed the information.

```
State radiation levels / seismic activ-
ity / level of damage to surrounding
areas . . .
```

"Radiation minimal," Marty said. "Seismic activity moderate to heavy. Damage—total."

Ulrich sent the information, and then at Forrest's direction, added: *Please tell Ester Thorn that Martin Chittenden sends his regards and looks forward to seeing her again soon. Nebraska signing off. Attempt to contact same time tomorrow.*

"Wait," Marty said. "Why are you signing off?"

"I don't want them treating us like a bunch of goddamn stepchildren, that's why. The more desperate we sound, the less we have to offer and the less likely they'll be to send someone to pick us up."

```
Confirmed nebraska / will comply . . .
```

They listened to the Hawaiian and the Australian talking privately for another hour before the airwaves fell silent.

# SIXTY-ONE

**HAROLD SHIPMAN PLACED HIS HAND ON ESTER'S SHOULDER,** gently shaking her awake at 4:40 A M. "Ester?" he said quietly.

"What?" she said, coming awake quickly. "What's happened?"

"Nothing bad," he said. "Are you awake?"

"Well goddamn, Harold, I'd better be. I'm talking, aren't I?"

Shipman chuckled. "May I turn on the lamp?"

"Of course," she said, pushing herself up against the headboard. "What is it?"

Shipman turned on the lamp and sat in the chair beside her bed. "You won't believe it," he said. "I'm not even sure I do, but our wireless operator has heard from a group on the mainland who has not only cracked his code, but also claims to have been to the impact crater. They say that it's a mile deep, fifty wide, and that there is heavy seismic activity in the area."

"What's so hard to believe about that?" she said, drywiping her face with her hand.

"For one thing, it's difficult for me to believe that anyone civilized is still functioning anywhere near the impact area."

"Well, that was Marty Chittenden's plan," she said. "For someone to survive and carry on."

"And that's the irony of it, Ester. These folks claim that Martin Chittenden sends his regards and that he hopes to see you soon. They're asking to be evacuated off the West Coast."

"My God!"

"That's what I said."

Ester threw back the blanket, revealing her blue flannel pajamas. "When did we get this message?"

"A couple of hours ago."

"Why I am only now hearing about it?"

"Apparently, no one was quite sure whether or not to wake you," Shipman said. "Had I not gone down to the lobby for a stroll, they would have waited until morning."

She took her cane from against the nightstand and crossed to the walk-in closet, switching on the light. "Can we get them back on the air?"

"I don't know," he said. "They signed off asking that we contact them at the same time tomorrow night."

"They did, huh?"

She reemerged from the closet a few minutes later dressed for the day in black slacks and a salmon colored button-up sweater. "Well, let's drive up the mountain and see if we can't get them to answer. I don't believe for a goddamn minute they won't be listening."

# SIXTY-TWO

FORTY-FIVE-YEAR-OLD CAPTAIN WILLIAM J. BISPING stood drinking a cup of coffee on the flight deck of the USS *Boxer* LHD 4, a Wasp Class amphibious assault ship capable of accommodating 1,200 crew members and 2,100 battle-ready Marines. In addition, the *Boxer* was capable of carrying up to forty-two helicopters and a number of amphibious landing craft. For the purposes of this cruise, however, it was carrying fewer than eight hundred crewmen, a detachment of only four hundred Marines, two F-35B Lightning VSTOL fighter jets, four attack helicopters, and five EFV, or expeditionary fighting vehicle, amphibious landing craft.

Steaming just off of *Boxer's* starboard bow at one thousand yards was her escort vessel, the HMCS *Algonquin* DDG 283, an Iroquois Class Canadian destroyer, one of only a few foreign vessels the Hawaiian navy had permitted to join them at Pearl Harbor.

With Bisping's month-long mission to the Americas now at an end, both ships were en route back to Pearl Harbor. The naval port of San Diego, more than twelve hours in their wake, the *Boxer* hangar deck was loaded stem to stern with thousands of boxes of fluorescent bulbs of all sizes, shapes, and varieties. She was also laden with tons of medical and mechanical supplies, critical to the longevity of the Hawaiian population.

Ashore, the sailors and Marines had encountered a few violent cannibal groups, but the Marines were heavily armed, and the ever-watchful attack helicopters on station in the air above prevented any surprise attacks as the sailors moved methodically from store to store up and down the coast, collecting every lightbulb they could lay their hands on and loading them onto trucks for transfer to the ship. They had taken no casualties, though it was necessary to kill a few dozen starving male civilians intent on eating them, most of whom had been too sickly and malnourished to be effective in pitched battle.

Bisping had remained aboard the *Boxer*, which did not actually go into port until it was time to load the cargo collected on the pier. The reports and digital photographs the division commanders brought back, however, gave Bisping a horrific impression of what had taken place in Southern California during the early months after the impact. Freeze-dried, mummified corpses littered the streets by the thousands, and nearly everything made of wood or that was otherwise flammable had been burned to ash.

*Boxer* communications officer, Lieutenant jg Brooks, stepped out of the conning tower and walked across the flight deck to where the captain stood watching the sea. "Message from Pearl, Captain."

"Thank you, Mr. Brooks," Bisping said, reading the printout. "Have Mr. O'Leary meet me in my cabin."

"Aye aye, sir."

First Officer Commander Duncan O'Leary rapped at the captain's door five minutes later.

"Enter."

"You wanted to see me, sir?"

"Have a look at this, Duncan."

O'Leary read the printout and gave it back. "Extract who, sir?"

"Beats the shit out of me," the captain said. "Get up to

the con and inform *Algonquin* of the change in orders, then bring us about a hundred and eighty degrees. I'll make an announcement to the crew shortly."

"They won't be happy, sir. This means we're going to miss Christmas."

"We're not going to miss Christmas, Duncan. We're going to be celebrating the birth of our Lord right here aboard *Boxer*."

"Yes, sir," O'Leary said with a smile. "I'll be sure to point that out to them."

"Please do."

When O'Leary was gone, Bisping sat down on his bunk and took a Bible from beneath his pillow. It contained the only photos he had of his wife and three children, the only photos he would ever have. He touched his wife's face and sat looking at her.

The temptation to jump ship and head off across the country on his own to look for them had been difficult enough to suppress the first time. Now, with the change of orders, he would be forced to endure the temptation for another indefinite period. He would, of course, never actually abandon his ship or his crew, but it was an agonizing temptation nonetheless. He told himself that Atlanta was too far to travel anyhow; he told himself that his family was long dead; and most important, he told himself it was better not to know exactly what had happened to them.

Chief Petty Officer Gordon, the senior aircraft mechanic, reported as instructed, informing Bisping that the particulate matter in the air was thin enough that it didn't seem to have affected the turbines of the helicopters.

"Good," Bisping said. "The precipitation must have brought a lot of it down. We're heading back to Cali, Chief. So make sure that all of our aircraft can be ready on a moment's notice."

"Aye aye, sir."

Bisping announced the change of orders to his crew over the MC then laid down for a short nap. He had not been napping more than twenty minutes when the ship's claxons began to sound.

"Captain to the bridge. Captain to the bridge."

Bisping took the phone from the wall, getting O'Leary immediately. "What is it?"

"A pair of Lanzhou Class destroyers, Captain, steaming right at us out of the north at twenty-five knots, distance thirty-two hundred meters beyond visual range. There wasn't anything on the scope until just now, sir. They're coming out of a squall."

"Turn into them!" Bisping ordered. "Scramble the F-35s and advise *Algonquin* that they are to take whatever action necessary to sink both vessels. I'm on my way up."

Bisping couldn't imagine what a pair of Chinese destroyers was doing in American waters, but twenty-five knots was very near their top speed, and both vessels carried the Hai Ying antiship missile, lethal within a range of well over a hundred miles. *Boxer* and *Algonquin* would be engaging them at less than twenty.

By the time Bisping reached the bridge, the *Algonquin* had already been struck once and there was a fire on his own ship's flight deck, where a firefighting team was already in action.

"What the hell happened?"

" The fuckers launched a full spread the second you hung up the phone, sir."

O'Leary was watching the northern horizon through a pair of large binoculars. "Our phalanxes knocked two missiles down but we each took a hit. *Algonquin* took one to her bow cannon and we lost a chopper on the deck." A phalanx was a radar-equipped weapon system based on the M-61 Vulcan Gatling gun, capable of firing its 20mm cannon at a rate of 4,500 rounds per minute, roughly seventy-five rounds per second. They were the ship's last line of defense, and the *Boxer* had four of them, two mounted on the stern, one to starboard, and one to port. The *Algonquin* carried one on the foredeck.

"How many missiles did *Algonquin* get off?"

"Two, sir. I don't see any smoke on the horizon yet but there are no more missiles inbound at this time."

The flight officer was requesting permission to launch both of the F-35 Lightning fighters, and permission was given. As vertical/short takeoff and landing aircraft, the F-35s could take off regardless of the burning helicopter on deck.

"I don't want any more goddamn missiles hitting my ship. Is that clear, Mr. Ryder?"

"Aye, sir!" answered the weapons officer, knowing he would be getting his ass chewed later on.

"Mr. Brooks, what's happening aboard *Algonquin*? Did their missiles hit or not?"

Brooks was on the phone to their escort within seconds.

"*Algonquin* believes they scored a hit on each vessel, sir, and they're about to launch another pair. There was a problem with their weapon system, but they've got it back up."

A second pair of SM-2 antiship missiles were fired from the *Algonquin*'s deck and went streaking toward the horizon just fifty feet off the surface.

"Four more Chinese missiles inbound!" Ryder announced.

This time four Sea Sparrow antiaircraft missiles were launched from the *Boxer* to intercept them. Seconds later Bisping saw three explosions just off the water some 1,600 meters out.

"One got through," Ryder announced. "Port and starboard phalanxes have a lock!"

Each phalanx fired a single two-second burst and the missile was destroyed a thousand yards out.

By then both fighter jets were closing on the Chinese destroyers, reporting that both vessels were hit and smoking. It was unclear whether they were still capable of launching missiles, but the ships were still steaming south at better than twenty knots.

Bisping took the mike from the comm officer. "Ghost Rider, this is the captain. Your orders are to sink them. Is that clear?"

*"That's affirmative,* Boxer. *We are beginning our attack run now . . ."*

Both F-35s carried a pair of joint-strike missiles designed for holing enemy ships at or near the waterline. One fighter broke to the east, the other west, as they dropped to a mere two hundred feet off the water, cutting sharply back toward the Chinese destroyers to attack them full abeam. At one mile, both launched their missiles, then broke hard to the right and climbed, hitting full afterburners and firing countermeasure flares in case the Chinese tried to shoot them down. But the Chinese antiaircraft systems had been knocked out as a result of previous missile strikes.

All four antiship missiles struck home, hitting the vessels at the waterline, and soon both ships began to list, quickly going dead in the water. The F-35s made a number of strafing runs with their 25mm cannons, then returned to the *Boxer.* One sailor aboard the *Algonquin* had been lost to the missile strike, and the *Boxer* had lost two helicopter pilots.

"Mr. Brooks!" Bisping said.

"Yes, sir?"

"Get a message off to Pearl. Message is to read: 'Attacked by two Chinese Lanzhou destroyers six miles out of San Diego. Sank same.'"

"Aye aye, sir."

"Let me know if they change our orders. I'm going down to the flight deck to see about our men."

# SIXTY-THREE

THE WOMEN WERE GATHERED ONCE AGAIN IN THE CAFETERIA, and Forrest stood before them with his usual smile. "Ladies," he said happily. "How are we this evening?"

A quick glance told him that Lynette was not in attendance; she had been avoiding him like the plague since their last exchange.

"Fine," many of them answered, having no idea why the hell they were being called together again so soon, and most of them dreading it.

"Do we have to eat scorpions this time?" Erin asked with a dry smile.

"Only you, E. The rest of us get caviar."

There was some laughter and then everyone quieted down.

"As of last night, we have a brand new plan," Forrest announced. "And you will all be happy to know that it does *not* involve any scorpions, mice, or any other kinds of creepy crawlies. What it does involve, though, is a great deal of risk. As you all know, Melissa has been working very hard to decipher the encrypted transmissions we have been picking up for a long time now. And I am happy and very proud to report that her diligence has finally paid off."

This sent a tremor of anxiety through the group, everyone suddenly aware of what such a development could mean.

"As a result of this new knowledge," he went on, "we are now in contact with the Hawaiian Islands, where they seem to be making a hell of a lot of progress toward building a future."

A wave of enthusiasm swept over them, hesitant smiles on their faces.

"In another odd twist of fate," he continued, "Marty happens to be a personal acquaintance of Hawaii's new leader. And, as luck would have it, this leader of theirs seems to value Marty's life enough that she has agreed to send a ship to rescue us."

The women let out a collective cheer and there was general pandemonium.

"Hey! Ho!" he said, after a sharp whistle. "Allow me to finish before you get too carried away."

The women settled quickly, smiles still plastered to their faces.

"They're sending a ship," he said, "not a convoy of trucks, which means it's up to us to get ourselves to the California coast by the first of the year. This gives us just over two weeks. And we have no idea what kind of obstacles lie between here and there. The trucks we have will drive through some pretty deep snow, but there's no telling how much snow has fallen in the mountain passes. It could be ten feet deep for all we know. We've got two months worth of MREs to take with us, but they won't do us much good if we get snowbound and miss our window for extraction.

"So here's the deal. The only personal items you may bring with you are what you can put in the pockets of your coats. Everything else stays, no exceptions. With all the food and fuel and ammo we'll be hauling, there won't be room for anything else. As it is, we are going to be sitting quite literally on top of one another in the vehicles."

"When are we leaving?" Andie asked.

"The men are prepping and loading the vehicles as we speak."

"Jesus, that fast?" said Maria two.

Everyone began talking at once.

"Shut up!" Joann shouted, throwing the room back into a startled silence.

Forrest chuckled, thanking her. "Okay. There's no need to go scrambling around the complex like cats on fire. No one's going to be left behind, so everybody stay calm, take your time and be careful. We've come too far for somebody to get hurt now. Make sure the children are bundled up in their winter clothes because we're only taking one blanket per person. There won't be room for many sleeping bags."

The group broke up, and Melissa caught Forrest in the corridor. "What about my computer?" she asked.

"Well, I've always been a little bit superstitious," he said with a smile. "Suppose we left it here as a sacrifice to the gods of war? It might help guarantee us a victory."

"I love my computer."

"I know you do, sweetheart, but you're going to have your hands full helping with the children and helping me to look after Laddie. And I think maybe it's served its purpose."

# SIXTY-FOUR

**TRAVELING WEST IN A PAIR OF ARMY M35, SIX-BY-SIX** trucks, it took the group almost forty-eight hours to travel 180 miles through two and half and sometimes as much as three feet of snow to the city of Denver. Even with snow chains on all of the tires, it was slow going, with one truck occasionally bogging down and being pulled free by the other. Kane and Forrest drove the lead truck; Sullivan, Emory, and Marty were in the second; and Ulrich and Danzig followed in their tracks due to the Humvee's lower ground clearance.

"We've got what, about three hours before dark?" Forrest said, standing on the hood of his truck watching the ruined city through a pair of binoculars. "Maybe we should wait until then before we try to get through. Our night vision should give us an advantage over anyone we happen to come up against."

"Why not wait until morning?" Ulrich suggested. "This snow's getting deeper, and Denver may be the best chance we get to switch the trucks out for some snowcats."

"Good point," Forrest said. "Switching vehicles in the dark would be a pain in the ass. But we've still got a thousand miles to go, and I hate to waste even an hour sitting still."

"I hear you."

"Let's get in there before dark and try to find the address for a local snowcat dealer. Any objections?"

"None."

They stopped at the first gas station they came to and found a phone book behind the counter. The station looked like it hadn't been open in fifty years, its windows shattered, trash and filth and a few hundred dollars of now useless currency swirling around in the wind. There was not a single morsel of anything edible to be found. Not so much as a stick of gum or a bottle of water.

Ulrich found an address then snatched a map from the rack near the busted register and looked up the street, tracing his finger from where they were at the corner of Tucker and Cisco to Chester Avenue on the other side of town. "Looks like the dealership's about eight miles up the road."

He dropped the phone book on the floor and went out through the broken storefront window.

It was getting dark by the time they made it to Vann's RV dealership, where they found a pair of used red Bombardier GT300 twelve-passenger snowcats in the back lot alongside a new orange fifteen-passenger Tucker 1600. The vehicles were behind the building and out of sight of the road, and thus had not been tampered with.

Forrest told Sullivan, Emory, and Marty to take up positions on the roof of the dealership, then asked Kane for an assessment on getting the trucks up and running.

"Shouldn't take long," Kane replied. "Unless the batteries are dead, which is possible. Wayne and Linus are in the garage gathering some tools."

"Let's make it happen," Forrest said, starting back to the trucks to inform West and Price of their find.

Trudging through the hip-deep snowdrifts behind the dealership, he heard the women and children suddenly begin screaming, and he bolted toward the corner, knees high and his weapon at port arms. There were rifle shots, and the screaming reached a crescendo as his legs churned through the snow. Marty bashed his way through a locked glass door to join him at the run.

They rounded the corner to see a cluster of the women gathered near the back of a truck, all of them pointing into the dimness at two men scurrying away in tattered parkas where the snow was only knee-deep. Joann and West were giving chase, but the interlopers were outpacing them, and one carried a screaming child gripped in his arms.

Forrest stopped and sighted on the man lagging behind, who was trying to shield the abductor from West's rifle. He fired and hit the man in the small of the back. The abductor, however, was too far off to risk hitting the child, so Forrest continued running for the truck, knowing he'd never catch the man before he disappeared into the night.

Marty fired at the interloper's legs and missed.

"Marty, no! It's too far!"

"But if he gets to those houses, we'll never catch him before he kills her!"

Forrest could see two dead men in the snow near the trucks now, where Price was staggering to his feet, holding his head.

"The dog!" Forrest screamed. "Price, the dog!"

Price whirled drunkenly around and scrabbled onto the running board of the truck where Laddie was barking savagely to get out. He pulled the handle to open the door and fell away as the dog leapt from the cab and went tearing off through the snow, quickly overtaking Joann and West as he gave chase into the shadowy neighborhood.

"Save my baby!" Joann shrieked as she stumbled, then fell forward into the dirty fluff. "Laddie, please save my baabyyyy!"

"Jack, I'm sorry, they came outta nowhere!" West shouted as Forrest and Marty ran past him. Emory and the other men were responding now, but they were still fighting their way through the deep snowdrifts.

"That way, Marty! Flank his ass to the right around those houses!"

The light was fading fast and there was no time to go back for their night vision goggles. They could still hear Beyonce screaming for her mother somewhere ahead of them, but they knew it wouldn't be long before her captor put her to death to silence her screams.

RUNNING FOR HIS life, the raggedy man felt his muscles burning, fear and exhilaration gripping his heart. He was nearly home free, but he needed to shut the kid up fast or those bastards with the guns would catch him even in the dark. His stomach twisted as he weaved his way through the yards, feeling the child's plump and tender limbs through her coat and pants. His salivary glands were already working, smelling her soapy scent, already tasting her juicy, fire-roasted meat, salted and sweet in his mouth.

He had dropped his knife during the scuffle, having underestimated the tall black broad's strength. What had these people been eating all this time? How were they so healthy? It didn't matter. They had obligingly seen fit to kill his three cohorts for him, so if he could just make it to the sewer, he'd be free and clear with enough meat to last him for the next couple of weeks.

He decided to jam his thumb deep into the child's eye socket to kill her on the run, but she was struggling and he mistakenly jammed his thumb into her mouth. Beyonce sank her teeth to the bone, and the raggedy man gritted his teeth and swore in anger as he bounded down the alley toward the open manhole, clouting her clumsily about the face and head until she let loose. The path through the snow here was well traveled and the going was fast.

At last he arrived at the manhole, laughing in victory as he held the child by her ankles over the opening, certain the twenty-foot fall would shut her up for good. But before he could drop her, he was slammed from behind by a 110-pound German shepherd moving at top speed. The man and the girl both flew clear of the hole, and the dog sank its teeth deep into his emaciated thigh, thrashing its head back and forth like an angry mako shark, easily separating muscle from bone, severing the femoral artery.

The man screamed in agony and beat at the dog's head in the dark, having no earthly idea what sort of beast was killing him. Was it a bear? No! It was a fucking wolf! Holy hell! Where the fuck did a wolf come from? And why was it eating him instead of the child?

**FORREST STUMBLED ONTO** the well-traveled path and raced along it, following the sound of Beyonce's continued screams. Marty hurled himself over a backyard fence and fell in behind him, flashlight in hand to light the way.

"There!" he shouted, spotting the screaming child ahead of them on the far side of the manhole.

Laddie was sitting beside her, licking her face in a desperate effort to give her comfort while she continued to shriek.

In a fury, Forrest leapt past the girl to land on the raggedy man's body, caving in his skull with the butt of his carbine. Marty snatched the child up, asking her if she was hurt, but all she did was scream.

"I think she's okay. Can't tell for sure."

"Get back!" Forrest ordered, directing Marty and the dog away from the open sewer, slinging his weapon. He stuffed the man's fetid carcass into the hole and dropped a phosphorus grenade in after it.

"Fire in the hole!" he shouted as Kane and Sullivan arrived on the scene, all of them ducking as a white flash of light erupted from the chasm with a muffled bang.

"Is she okay?" Sullivan asked, his chest heaving.

"I think she's fine," Marty said over her cries. "She's just terrified."

"What about you?" Kane asked, shining his own light on Forrest, seeing the dead man's blood on his uniform.

Forrest nodded. "Get that child back to the truck before she draws more of these animals."

"Let's go, John," Marty said. "This kid needs her mama."

Forrest watched them go. "See how fucking close it was?" he shouted at Kane, pointing at the hole, shaking with rage. "Jesus fuckin' Christ! What the fuck were they doing, Marcus? Playing grab-ass?"

"Man, I don't know. They're just doctors."

"I told 'em, *watch the fuckin' kids!*" Forrest howled, remembering the blasted bodies of the children in the Afghan desert, the missing arms and legs, the endless pleading for their mothers who had almost always preceded them in death.

"It's cool!" Kane shouted. "The dog saved the fuckin' day, man. That's all that matters."

Forrest dropped to his knees and wrapped his arms around his dog, burying his face in its fur and thanking the animal for doing what he and his men had failed to do.

West met them on the way back, nearly in tears with shame. "Jack, I—"

Forrest threw his arms around the doctor and clutched him tight, kissing him on the cheek and speaking into his ear. "Let it go. It's not a mistake you'll ever make again."

When they got back to the truck, Joann jumped down from the back to hug the dog, bawling with gratitude in the light of the Hummer's headlamps.

Forrest pretended not to notice that Veronica was watching him teary-eyed from the back of the truck. He gave orders for the battered Price to lay down and rest and for the vehicles to be moved around back while the snowcats were prepped.

"That guy's still alive over there," Marty said quietly. "The one you shot."

"Is he, now?" Forrest turned and walked through the snow to where the man lay on his back, with West kneeling alongside him examining the exit wound to his belly. Emory knelt opposite, holding a green cyalume stick to provide light enough for him see. "That's enough, Sean."

"I'm just—"

"That'll be all, Doctor."

"Sir!" West replied, got to his feet and moved off.

"Make sure Price is okay. Go with him, Shannon."

"What are you gonna do?" she asked, rising.

He grinned and took a pack of smokes from his breast pocket. "You know? For a soldier, you don't take orders for shit."

She smiled in the green light. "Orders my ass. What are you gonna do?"

He shook another cigarette from the pack, lit it off of the first and knelt in the snow to put it between the dying man's chapped lips. "How's that, partner?"

"It's good," the man croaked, holding the cigarette in the corner of his mouth and feeling the nicotine hit him quickly. "Been a long time." He was bearded and his skin was covered in open sores. The eyes were hard and there was no fear in them.

"How many more of you pricks I gotta worry about?"

"We're the last of the—" The man shook with a tremor of pain and held his exploded belly. "—of the holdouts."

"No military types about?"

"Not anymore. Moriarty's animals pulled out last year . . . with all the food."

Forrest took a long drag. "You'll be happy to hear I shot Moriarty in the face."

Smiling crookedly now, the man said, "Then this was a good day to die." His eyes glassed over and he was gone.

Forrest stood and turned to Emory. "You and Marty join Sullivan up on the roof, keep watch through the infrared in case this prick was lying."

"Sir!"

"Anything moves out there, anything at all . . . kill it."


AN HOUR LATER both of the used Bombardiers were running like a pair of tops, but the Tucker didn't want to fire up, and it took another hour of tinkering with the engine to get it running. After they had all three snowcats running, the food, fuel, and equipment were transferred into the larger, four-track orange Tucker vehicle, then the women and children were moved into the heated cabins of the red Bombardiers. It was still a snug fit, but far preferable to sitting scrunched and cold in the back of the canvas-covered Army trucks.

The Tucker was twice as tall as the Bombardiers, so it would bring up the rear, with a pair of lookouts to keep watch over the small convoy as it slipped through the outskirts of Denver to the south, and headed up into the mountains along Interstate 70.

They drove all that night without lights at roughly thirty miles per hour, and by first light it was time to recharge the NVDs. They had crossed over the mountains by then, through spots where the snow was ten feet deep or more on the highway, and had to drive around the big green highway signs. They did not encounter a single living creature. Much of the forest had burned away, and all that remained for mile upon mile were the blackened trunks of charred trees.

By the time they crossed into Utah the depth of the snow was back down to three feet and it was time to stop and refuel.

"That's the last of the fuel," Kane said, wiping his hands with a rag as the seven fighting personnel gathered into a loose group. "But it's more than enough to get us to the coast."

"Who besides me expects trouble once we start getting close to the ocean?" Forrest asked.

Everyone lifted a hand.

"Good," he said, lighting a cigarette. "Then there shouldn't be any surprises."

Price came dragging himself through the snow.

"Something wrong?" Forrest asked.

"Lynette needs to go number two," Price said. "Do we have time for her to use that Porta-John over there?"

"Sure," Forrest said. "Might not be a bad idea for everyone to go again before we get moving."

They continued talking as Lynette wrestled her way through the now thigh-deep snow to the Porta-John in the center median near an earthmover. She kicked the snow away from the door with her legs then went inside.

A second later she came back out screaming hysterically. The screams seemed to carry for miles across the barren snowscape.

"Somebody shut that bitch up!" Ulrich hissed.

"Easy," Forrest said, watching Price running toward her through the snow.

Lynette threw herself into his arms and stood blubbering into his shoulder. After he calmed her down, he took a look inside the Porta-John, then walked her back to the snowcat. He came over to tell Forrest and the others that there was a woman's head in the frozen slop at the bottom of the toilet.

"How's *your* head?" Forrest asked, taking a drag from the cigarette and pointing at the goose egg on Price's forehead.

"I'll live," he said. "I'm sorry Lynette's been such a pain."

"She hasn't been a pain for any of us," Forrest said. "She keeps it interesting."

Price let out a sardonic chuckle and made his way through the snow back to the snowcat where his wife sat trembling in Taylor's arms.

Forrest got the map out and took a bearing with a compass. From this point they would no longer be following the interstate. The snow was deep enough for them to drive straight overland toward San Diego, which would save them a great deal of time and mileage as they crossed southern Utah. Forrest also hoped it would decrease their chances of being ambushed by the type of people who chopped off women's heads and dumped them into Porta-Johns.

It had grown dark again when they reached the Nevada border, where it was time to make a decision: Cross the Hoover Dam or keep heading south to skirt around it?

"I don't think we want any part of that pass," Marty warned. "Suppose the dam's still operationa—"

"The crews would have split ages ago," Ulrich said, almost dismissing him.

"Yeah, but suppose somebody's figured out how to run the place? We're talking about an endless source of heat for that facility, a good place for an army of cannibals to make their home. Tell 'em, Shannon."

"He's got a point," Emory said. "It's a safe bet that some military unit took it over early on."

"And what do you suppose they're doing for food two years into a global famine?" Ulrich asked.

"I don't know," she snapped. "Maybe they're getting fat off the people who are too fuckin' stupid to stay away!"

Forrest laughed, holding his red light over the map where he crouched in the snow at their feet, tracing his finger southward. "I don't know what they'd be eating, and I've got no interest in finding out. We'll take your advice and cross the river farther down . . . closer to Needles."

By first light they were crossing into California, and the Tucker began to have engine trouble again, finally stalling completely and refusing to restart.

"I don't know what the hell it is," Kane said after trying for half an hour to get the engine running. "Damn thing's brand new. If I had to guess, I'd say there's ice in the fuel line. It can't be much over five or six degrees out here today."

"Do you recommend we leave it?" Forrest asked in the middle of playing fetch with Laddie. "Or do you think it's worth trying to fix?"

"If I'm wrong about it being ice in the line, we could spend another two or three hours and have nothing to show for it."

"Then screw it," Forrest said, wrestling the stick away from his dog. "Pack everybody into the Bombardiers and let's get the hell outta here."

By the time it was dark they had reached the now deserted U.S. Marine Corps training grounds north of Twenty-nine Palms, where Forrest brought them to a halt.

"Okay," he announced. "We're three hours from Oceanside, where the USS *Boxer* is supposed to be anchored just out of sight from the shore."

"We goin' in tonight or waitin' for first light?" Kane asked.

"I'm open to suggestions," Forrest said, having already made up his mind to press on.

"I think daylight only increases our chances of being spotted," Emory said. "We should keep taking advantage of our NVDs."

"That's where I come out too," Sullivan said, a glance around telling him that everyone else felt the same.

"Who needs Benzedrine?" Forrest asked.

Everyone needed it, so he dumped three capsules into everyone's hand.

"Only one at a time," he reminded them. "The other two are for emergencies only. If all goes well, you'll be aboard ship long before you ever need them."

Then he climbed aboard the first cat with Dr. West.

"Okay, ladies, I want you all to listen carefully and not make a sound," Forrest said, taking one of the titanium vials from his pocket and holding it up for them all to see in the light of the cab. "I'm not going to spell out its purpose for obvious reasons, but there is one NASA approved cyanide capsule inside each one of these vials. Every mom gets one for herself and one for each of her kids. You will keep them in your pants pockets, and you will not take them out unless there's an emergency. Is that understood?"

The mothers nodded with fearful looks in their eyes, but said nothing for fear of upsetting the children.

"What is that for, Mommy?" one the little girls asked as Dr. West was doling out the vials.

"It's astronaut medicine, honey. In case we get exposed to some really bad germs."

Forrest left and gave the same presentation to the mothers aboard the second snowcat, and then they were off.

No one realized that it was Christmas Eve.

# SIXTY-FIVE

"CAPTAIN TO THE BRIDGE. CAPTAIN TO THE BRIDGE."

Captain Bisping trotted up the ladder and onto the bridge less than a minute later. "What do you have, Mr. O'Leary?"

"*Algonquin* reports a Chinese sub coming to periscope depth ten miles off the port bow, sir."

"Jesus Christ!" Bisping said, stepping to the far window for a look. "Make sure this ship is blacked completely out. How did a sub get so goddamn close without *Algonquin* hearing it?"

"It's a Song Class, sir. Diesel-electric."

"Shit," Bisping said in disgust.

"Bridge, Radar," came the voice of the radar operator. "Periscope out of the water ten miles off the port bow. She's not moving, sir."

"Duncan, I want a pair of Sea Kings armed and in the air yesterday—and without lights."

"Aye, sir."

"Mr. Brooks, find out if *Algonquin* is disposed to destroy that submarine. I can't see her in this ink."

"Sir, *Algonquin* advises she has loaded war-shot into her tubes, but she's not at optimum angle for launch. She's asking if you want her to come about."

"Negative!" Bisping said. "I don't want anybody doing

anything to tip them off. *Algonquin* isn't to even flood her tubes."

"Aye, sir . . . *Algonquin* advises she is standing by."

"We're a sitting duck," Bisping muttered. "Be sure that *Algonquin* advises us the second that sub moves or opens its outer tube doors."

"Aye, sir."

"Duncan, quietly spread the word that I want the crew ready to abandon ship," Bisping ordered.

"Aye, Skipper."

"We can't even run the engines up to full power without them hearing us," Bisping grumbled. He took the phone from the wall and called down to the engine room.

"Chief, it's the captain. Listen, there's a Chinese electric resting at periscope depth ten miles off our port bow. She's got us dead-nuts with both bow anchors on the bottom. We can't even slip the chains without tipping them off. I want you to do everything you can down there without making any goddamn noise so you'll be ready to get those engines up and roaring in full reverse the second I give you the word. Understood?"

"I'll have her ready to pull a hole shot, Captain."

"That's what I wanted to hear, Chief." Bisping hung up the phone and grabbed the one next to it. "Radar, I want to know if that periscope moves even an inch. Understood? . . . Good."

He went back to the window, making doubly sure no was smoking down on the flight deck.

"Captain, both Sea Kings report ready for takeoff."

"Get them into air."

"Captain! *Algonquin* reports the submarine is blowing ballast and coming to the surface! . . . And she's opening her outer tube doors!"

"Stay those helicopters!" Bisping ordered. "That sub captain so much as hears a rotor blade and he'll launch."

Bisping stood trying to figure a way out of the mess. We

can kill them, he thought to himself, but not before they've killed us.

"Maybe they don't want to fight," O'Leary said. "They've had plenty of opportunity to fire."

"After what we did to their destroyers? I find that very hard to believe."

Ensign Allister Miller cleared his throat. "I don't think she knows we're here, sir."

Bisping turned to him in the red dim. "Explain yourself, Mr. Miller."

"Well, sir, we've been resting quietly at anchor all day," Miller replied. "Only *Algonquin*'s had her boilers up to steam, so she's the one the bastards are likely homing in on. They're probably hoping she'll lead them to us in the dark. And they can't go on active sonar without tipping their hand any more than we can power up or launch our choppers without tipping ours."

"Which is why they've come to the surface," Bisping said. "To use their eyes and ears. Very good, Mr. Miller. You're a lieutenant jg now. If we get out of this without losing the ship, I'll promote you to first."

"Thank you, sir."

"Duncan, get Commander Reese up here on the double."

"Aye, sir."

Reese was the commander of the ten-man SEAL team aboard the *Boxer*. He was a short, hard-bodied sailor who had been in the Navy since John Paul Jones was a baby, and he was known for getting the job done under very sticky circumstances.

He stepped onto the bridge, announcing: "Commander Reese reporting as ordered, Captain."

"Mr. Reese, has your team ever rehearsed the taking of a Chinese submarine resting quietly on the surface?"

A grin spread across the commander's face. "Not exactly, sir. Though similar scenarios have come up in conversation once or twice."

"So you have some ideas on how such a feat of arms might be accomplished?"

"Oh, I've got some very definite ideas, Captain. How close is she?"

"Ten miles at the moment, but I expect that to change as soon as this captain I'm up against begins to grow some balls."

"If their hatch is open, Captain, I guarantee we'll take the con. What I cannot guarantee is taking it before they fire their torpedoes."

"What do you need?"

"We've got everything we need in our kit. We can power right out to the boat below the surface on electric motors."

"This kind of darkness won't be a problem?"

"For the Chinese, yes. Us, no. All we'll need from *Boxer* is a comm link to find out whether the sub is moving. I'll break the surface every ten minutes to check in on that."

"How soon can you be in the water?"

"From this moment? Less than twenty."

"How long to the sub?"

"If she stays right where she is, an hour."

"Let me know when you're ready to get wet, Commander."

"Aye aye, Skipper."

Bisping noticed the concern on Commander O'Leary's face. "Something on your mind, Duncan?"

"No, sir."

"If we're torpedoed, Duncan. They're going into the water anyhow, only *without* their wet suits."

"Aye, sir."

**Forty minutes later** Commander Reese carefully broke the surface of the water in total blackness to check in with the *Boxer* about the position of the Chinese submarine.

"Be advised, *Aqualung*, the target has closed to within five miles and is sitting still once again."

"Clear," Reese murmured, raising his infrared scope to

see that the sub now lay only a couple of hundred yards ahead of them. "I have visual."

He then slipped silently back beneath the water.

Below the surface, neither Reese nor any of his men were able to see anything that wasn't lighted or glowing, and with the murk of ash and sediment now spoiling the seas, they weren't even able to see that beyond ten feet or so.

He wrote a short message on a diving board in fluorescent chalk telling his men that the target now lay only a couple hundred yards ahead of them. He then wrote in a kind of shorthand that they would motor past the sub fifty yards off the port side, then circle around to approach her from the stern.

# SIXTY-SIX

**ABOUT THE SAME TIME THAT COMMANDER REESE AND HIS** SEAL team were first getting wet, Forrest and his flock were turning down a side street in the outskirts of Oceanside. They were still running without lights to avoid being spotted as they drew closer to the shore, all of the fighting men wearing NVDs. The snow was only inches deep in Southern California, but the snowcats ran equally well on dry land.

The women in the lead transport began to notice a dim glow illuminating the street ahead of them.

"What's that light?" someone in the lead vehicle said as they rounded a corner.

"What light?" Forrest answered, reaching to lift his night vision device so he could see what they were talking about.

A Molotov cocktail exploded on the roof of the snowcat. Another exploded on the hood of the vehicle behind them, momentarily engulfing both cats in bright orange balls of flame.

Laddie started barking furiously, and the women and children screamed in horror as both Forrest and Ulrich applied full throttle in an attempt to get clear of what was obviously an ambush.

Ulrich shouted for everyone aboard his cat to get down, even as Sullivan, Emory, and Marty were shooting out the windows and pouring fire into the three-story apartment building on the left side of the street.

"How are they seeing us?" Marty shouted, spotting a man step from a doorway and taking careful aim at the lead snowcat before pulling the trigger on a hunting rifle.

Sullivan flipped up his NVD and looked around, now seeing that every building along the both sides of the street had been painted with a fluorescent green paint, which even late into the night was casting a dim glow over the entire street.

"Wayne, back up!" he shouted, realizing that to continue down the street would spell certain death. "The street's illuminated!"

"What?" Ulrich flipped up his own NVD, immediately seeing the paint. "Jesus Christ!"

He got on the radio and told Forrest what was going on, but it was too late. Grenades went off beneath the engines of both snowcats and knocked them out.

"Everybody out!" Ulrich shouted, seeing their worst nightmare unfolding before his eyes. Bullets struck him in the center of his back, impacting against his armor, but none of the women or children were hit as they jumped from the vehicle. "Sullivan, they're targeting the men!"

The fire was coming from the left side of the street, so they were momentarily shielded in the lee of the snowcat. Ulrich could hear Laddie barking down the street as he took a quick head count and saw that he was missing two civilians. Ducking quickly back aboard, he found that both Liddy and Natalie had bitten into their cyanide capsules.

"Goddamnit!" he muttered, scrambling back to the sidewalk.

"We gotta get under better cover," Sullivan said, scanning the darkened street around the corner with the NVD. "Wayne, there's a pharmacy around the block. It looks deserted."

"Get the women and children to cover," Ulrich ordered. "I'm going to try to link up with Jack's group."

"Sir!"

Sullivan, Emory, and Marty began to herd Erin, Taylor, Lynette, Tonya, Maria two, Jenny, Michelle, West, Price, and all of the children around the corner toward the pharmacy.

Ulrich didn't make it more than a step down the street before taking a round in the gut just below his armor. He dove behind a stack of trash cans and began crawling down the sidewalk toward Forrest's group, where Laddie was still barking wildly. They were all still trying to work their way back to the corner, moving from parked car to parked car, but then they came to a gap far too wide for them to cross.

"You're cut off, Jack," Ulrich told him over the radio.

"Any suggestions?"

"Take cover in one of the buildings on this side of the street and escape out the back. We'll try to link up with you on the next street over."

"Roger that," Forrest said, signaling for Kane to break into one of the buildings. "Watch your ass, Stumpy. They're only shooting at the men."

"I know," Ulrich said before getting painfully to his feet and scrambling back to the corner and down the block to the pharmacy where Sullivan and the others had taken cover.

"We won't last here," Sullivan said. "They're already taking up positions across the street."

"We need to get out the back and link up with Jack's group on the next street over," Ulrich said. "Otherwise we're looking at a complete goat fuck here."

The women and children were in the dark again, so the soldiers gave them a couple of red lights, telling them not to shine them unless they were moving and needed to see where they were going.

Ulrich and Sullivan went to the back door and opened it to a hail of bullets.

"Fuck!" Sullivan said, reeling away from the door. "Got my fuckin' arm!"

"Well, I'm already gut shot," Ulrich said.

"You're shitting me!"

"Jack," Ulrich said over the net. "We're cut off. Stuck inside the pharmacy."

"Don't feel bad," Forrest replied. "We're stuck inside a goddamn porn shop. Never seen so many dildos in my goddamn life."

Everyone on the net chuckled in spite of the tense situation.

"Listen, Stumpy," Forrest said. "You have to get out of there on your own somehow. Work your way to the beach and declare Rotten Dog."

"Why me?" Ulrich said. "You're half a block closer and I'm missing a fucking foot."

"The three of us are already shot up too bad down here," Forrest said. "And Mike just isn't the man for the job."

"Listen, Jack, I'm gut shot. I'll never make the beach. I'll have to send Sullivan."

Forrest was silent for a moment, asking finally, "How bad, Stumpy?"

"Bad enough. The Navy's our only chance now, Jack. We'll never fight our way to the beach with all these women and children."

One of the women screamed from the front of the store.

"Gotta go, Jack."

Ulrich and Sullivan moved to the front of the store to find West and Price kneeling behind the counter beside the bodies of Tonya and her son Steven.

"Everyone needs to move into the back now," Sullivan said quickly, herding the others into the storeroom.

The baby was crying in Erin's arms, and Taylor was hovering close by her, keeping her own two children close. Marty and Emory covered the front of the store from behind a makeshift barricade of overturned shelving.

"What the fuck happened, Sean?" Ulrich asked, painfully taking a knee beside West in the red glow of two flashlights.

"She used the cyanide," West said quietly.

"Goddamnit," Ulrich swore. "Liddy and Natalie did the same fucking thing. I'm taking it away from the others."

"No," West said, grabbing his arm. "It's their right, Wayne. We all agreed."

"But goddamnit!"

"What's going on with Jack's group?"

"We're all cut off from the beach. And we're cut off from each other. Sullivan's going to make a run for the beach."

"No, I'm not," Sullivan said, standing in the doorway. "I just lost the use of my right hand."

West examined his wounded arm to find that the bullet had shattered his ulna.

"I guess that leaves Marty," Ulrich said. "Unless you want the job, Sean."

"I can't leave Taylor or the kids," West said. "I promised them. Besides, Marty's better with a weapon than I am."

"We have to send Shannon with him," Sullivan said. "Marty won't make it alone. His instincts aren't good enough. But he listens to Shannon."

"All right, then," Ulrich said. "You and Sean replace them up front and send them back here."

"Just how bad are you, Wayne?" West asked, pissed that Ulrich hadn't told him he'd been shot.

"It's bad enough that I'll croak if we don't make it to the ship," Ulrich said.

"How much Benzedrine have you taken?"

"Enough to see this through one way or another."

West asked Price to take his place up front so he could bind Ulrich's belly wound.

Emory and Marty came around behind the counter where a blanket now lay over Tonya and her son.

"You two have to make a break for the beach," Ulrich said. "Find lifeguard station number six. A SEAL team has buried a radio in the sand beneath it. Our call sign is Halo. Be sure and tell them that our condition is Rotten Dog. That will tell them to send the Marines in, expecting a fight."

"Got it," Emory said. "Come on, Marty, let's rock and roll these motherfuckers."

She took him into the stockroom to check him over with a flashlight. "Nothing rattles and nothing shines. Got it?"

"I'm cocked and locked," he muttered. "Let's get the fuck outta here."

"The back door is no joy," Sullivan said. "You'll have to go out the front. But we'll pop smoke both front and back to keep them guessing."

"Fuck it," Emory said. "You can hardly fucking see out there as it is."

"I think there must be one or two out there with night vision," Ulrich said, grunting as West bound his middle with a cotton wrap. Erin came from the stockroom and knelt beside him, crying into his neck. "Where's the baby?" he asked.

"With Taylor."

"Well, get on back there," he said. "I've still got work to do out here. And don't worry, I won't be dying in the next ten minutes."

"I have O-negative blood," Erin told West.

"If he ends up needing it, honey, I'll get some from you. I promise."

A pair of smoke grenades were tossed out the front and back of the store a short time later, and gunfire filled the air as the clouds began to grow.

Emory grabbed hold of Marty's jacket at the shoulder. "When they stop to reload, we move."

"Right behind you."

The firing slacked off and they made their break, running left down the sidewalk into the darkness.

A shot rang out and hit the sidewalk, a piece of a bullet ricocheting up into Marty's rump. "I just got hit in the ass!" he swore, grabbing at the seat of his pants.

"Better than your balls. Keep moving!"

They stopped at the end of the street to catch their breath. "You know what?" he said, panting. "We can see better with the night vision now than we could last year. That means there's more ambient light. The sky's beginning to clear."

Emory raised her NVD and held her hand up in front of her face, unable to see it.

"Whatever you say, Marty."

Half a block down they spotted a band of six men using a single weak flashlight to make their way toward the porn shop where Forrest and his group were holed up. They were a motley crew, dressed piecemeal in military clothing, but there was no telling whether they had ever been Marines. They were scrawny and wore long scraggly beards. One of them had a LAW rocket slung over his shoulder.

"We have to take them out," she said. "That rocket will kill everybody in Jack's building."

The two of them hustled off through the snow after their prey, and Marty stepped on a soda can beneath the snow, its muffled crunch just loud enough for the men to hear.

They spun around as Marty and Emory dove for cover behind a burned out car.

"Who's behind us?" one the men asked the others, their flashlight too dim to penetrate into the murk. "Any of our people?"

"Maybe Wallace and Cutter. I ain't sure."

"Wallace!"

"What?" Marty shouted.

"You comin', asshole?"

"Go ahead! Sprained my fuckin' ankle!"

The men moved on, and Emory punched Marty in his helmet, hissing, "You ever do that again, I'll kick the shit outta you!"

By the time they worked their way to within fifty feet of the men, the man with the rocket was down on one knee, about to fire it into the back door of the porn shop. Emory fired a burst from the hip in a vertical arc, stitching the rocketeer up the spine. The man folded over backward and the rocket went streaking off into the sky over top of the buildings, detonating three or four blocks away.

"Wallace, you dumb fuck!" shouted the man with the flashlight.

Emory shot him next, and the flashlight fell into the snow, leaving the remaining four to fire blindly into the black. Emory and Marty lay prone watching their prey make idiots of themselves. They each fired two quick bursts and sprang to their feet.

More men came running toward the sound of the fight, dim beams of light searching wildly about, but Emory and Marty withdrew to slip away undetected. They quickly covered the half mile to the beach, meeting no further resistance before reaching the surf and running to the closest lifeguard station.

It was number nine.

"North or south?" Emory said. "You pick."

"North."

The next station they came to was number eight, and within a few minutes they arrived at station six. They kicked away the snow and Marty began digging in the sand while Emory kept watch. A foot down he found a sealed, black polymer case the size of a large tackle box and pried it from the ground.

"You keep an eye out," Emory said, kneeling in front of the case to open it. She turned on the radio and took out the hand set, holding it to her head the way you would a regular phone and depressing the button. "This is Halo calling *Boxer*. Do you read? Over."

There was no reply.

"Halo calling *Boxer*. Our condition is Rotten Dog. Repeat. We are Rotten Dog. Do you read? Over . . ."

"Maybe you should try switching channels."

"No, Marty, you don't fuck with a preset frequency. It's probably just some squid asleep at the radio. They don't have anything else to do out there."

"Halo calling USS *Boxer*. Do you read? Over . . . Halo calling *Boxer*. Do you read . . . ?"

# SIXTY-SEVEN

ABOARD THE *BOXER*, CAPTAIN BISPING WAS QUITE BUSY—OR at least he had a hell of a lot on his mind. For one thing, he was still feeling very much like a sitting duck on an open pond. The *Boxer* had enough ordnance aboard to kill the Chinese vessel dozens of times over, but if he so much as flinched, the submarine's passive sonar would pick up the sound, and the Chinese captain would beat him to the trigger by more than five minutes—the approximate time it would take to get an antisub warfare helicopter into position to drop a depth charge. Not even the *Algonquin* could be in position to fire in under a minute, her tubes aimed over ninety degrees in the wrong direction.

"Captain! I've got Halo on the emergency band. They're declaring Rotten Dog."

"You've got to be shitting me!" Bisping declared. "Now, of all goddamn times!" He looked to his executive officer. "Who is it, Duncan, who keeps insisting there are no more wars left to fight?"

"I believe that's President Thorn, sir."

"Mr. Brooks, get a message off to Pearl."

"Yes, sir. "

"Message to read as follows: 'Engaged in battle by land and sea. Merry fucking Christmas.'"

"Word for word, sir?"

"Yes, Mr. Brooks. Word for fucking word. And somebody call Gunny Beauchamp to the bridge. Talk about fighting a battle with both hands tied behind your goddamn back."

He took the handset from Brooks. "Halo this is *Boxer*. Over."

"*Boxer, be advised we are Rotten Dog. Our main force is pinned down half a mile inland from lifeguard station number nine. Over.*"

"Halo, say again all after main force. Over."

"*Pinned down half a mile inland from lifeguard station number nine. Over.*"

Bisping gave O'Leary an ironic grimace and muttered, "That's what I thought she said."

"Stand by, Halo. We are presently engaged in a sea battle but will send Marine detachment ashore ASAP. Over."

"*What is their ETA? Over.*"

"Stand by, Halo."

"*Don't keep us waiting too long, Boxer. Our tit's in the wringer!*"

"We read you," Bisping said, giving the handset back to Brooks. "Her tit may be in the wringer but my balls are on the block."

Beauchamp came onto the bridge and saluted crisply, snapping immediately to attention. "Gunnery Sergeant Beauchamp reporting as—"

"At ease, Gunny."

"Sir."

"Are your devil dogs ready to go ashore?"

"That's affirmative, sir."

"Well be advised, Gunny, you and your men will be going very soon, and your condition will be Rotten Dog. Our evacuees have apparently gotten themselves pinned down half a mile inland from lifeguard station number nine."

"And if we're torpedoed, sir?"

"Then you'll be going ashore indefinitely. Either way, Gunny, you're on in less than ten."

"Oorah, sir."

**FIVE MILES OUT** to sea, as Commander Reese and his men were creeping toward the sail of the Chinese submarine, they felt the boat lurch forward, its electric motors kicking on to propel the submarine very slowly through the water, barely raising a wake.

Through the murk at that distance, Reese was just able to make out the *Boxer*'s silhouette lying some five miles distant, but only because he knew exactly where she was and what to look for. In a very short time, however, the Chinese officer watching eastward through his own night vision scope from atop the sail would be making a positive identification and calling below to his captain, who would then—in all likelihood—give the order to launch a full spread of torpedoes at both the *Boxer* and *Algonquin*.

There were no ladder rungs on the almost thirty-foot-tall sail of a Song Class submarine the way there were on old fashioned subs, which meant that Reese and his men had to form a human ladder in order for him to reach the rear sail plane jutting backward twenty feet above the pressure hull. Even from atop the sail plane it still took two men standing on one another's shoulders for Reese to climb the final ten feet. Once atop the sail, he moved quickly forward to the observer's station, where the Chinese officer was studying the pitch-black shoreline.

Reese heard the man draw an excited breath and saw him reach for the phone, obviously having just spotted the *Boxer*. He dropped down into the observer's station and grabbed the officer from behind, gripping him under the jaw with his left hand to twist his face away, jamming a killing knife up through the base of his skull and giving the blade a sharp twist, leaving Reese holding a veritable rag doll. He lay the man down and signaled over the net for the rest of his men to join him.

The next man to reach the top of the sail lowered a knotted rope for six others. Two SEALs would remain down on the hull to kill anyone attempting to escape through the bow or stern hatchways.

As expected, the observer's hatch was sealed from inside, so Reese signaled for Chief Petty Officer Chou to do his thing. Chou picked up the phone, saying in a sickly voice to whomever it was that answered: "Man, I just got a real bad case of the shits!" Or whatever the Cantonese equivalent of that was.

The wheel began to turn on the hatch, and the SEALs prepared to do battle.

The somewhat bemused Chinese sailor below was standing in a compartment illuminated only in dim red light, and he was opening the hatch into absolute darkness, so he didn't see the silencer of the MP-5 submachine gun Reese was aiming down into his face.

Reese squeezed off a single round and shot the sailor straight through the forehead, dropping him to the deck with a dull thud. He was down the ladder in a split second, moving rapidly into the next compartment, where he gunned down two more unsuspecting sailors standing at the periscope. He waited until the rest of his men were formed up behind him before sliding down the ladder into the next compartment. From there, half of the team made their way forward toward the control room. The other half remained in position to prevent their line of retreat from being blocked.

Reese and the other three walked boldly into the con and opened fire. The startled Chinese sailors screamed as they died, but the captain of the boat kept his head, leaping for the launch buttons.

Reese fired and killed him, but not before the captain managed to launch a single torpedo.

"CAPTAIN! *ALGONQUIN* REPORTS hydrophone effect! One torpedo in the water—it's got us dead-bang!"

"Slip both anchors!" Bisping ordered. "All engines full reverse!"

"Launch helicopters!" O'Leary announced simultaneously over the MC. "Launch amphibious craft! All hands rig for impact!"

Having also been prepared for this eventuality, the *Algonquin* had long since off-loaded the majority of her crew into lifeboats, leaving only the captain, the sonar officer, and a few engineers aboard. The engineers applied full power to the destroyer's propellers, then scrambled up to the weather deck as the *Algonquin* captain put his ship into full reverse. She had good power but was starting from a dead stop, so she didn't move quickly at first. Even so, her captain was hoping against heaven and hell to get the *Algonquin* into the torpedo's path before it could detonate beneath the *Boxer*'s hull and break her spine.

Bisping stood on the bridge watching the other ship through a pair of NVDs as the *Boxer* oh-so-slowly began to back away. We're moving as fast as mechanically possible, he thought, but we'll never make it.

"Captain!" Brooks shouted. "Commander Reese reports he and his men have taken the con." Bisping got on the radio immediately, ordering the helicopter pilots not to attack the submarine.

"All landing craft away, sir," O'Leary announced. "The Marines should be ashore within five." But Bisping didn't hear him. He was once again watching to see whether his ship was going to be blown out from under him.

"Captain, *Algonquin* reports it's going to be close."

In the same moment, the torpedo passed directly beneath the screws of the *Algonquin* and, sensing her magnetic field, detonated, blowing off the destroyer's stern in a huge white flash of froth and fire.

A cheer went up on the *Boxer*'s bridge.

"Knock it off!" Bisping ordered. "We just lost half our task force and this battle's not over. Get me Commander Reese on the radio!"

A few seconds later Bisping was talking to Reese. "How do you want to play this, Commander? I want that sub sunk!"

"We can set demolition charges here in the con, sir, to destroy her controls. After that we can abandon ship, allowing you to sink her at your leisure. One of the helos can lift us out of the water."

"How do you keep the Chinese sailors from killing you after you make it into the water?"

"I intend to leave this boat in flames, Captain. They'll be too busy fighting the fires to bother with us. They haven't even tried to retake the con yet, for Christ's sake."

"Very well," Bisping said. "Get off that boat as quickly and safely as you can so I can sink the damn thing!"

"Roger that."

Bisping then looked at O'Leary. "Launch two more ASWs," he ordered. "I want them in position to provide covering fire for Reese and his men as they're being picked out of the water. Then I want that pig sent to the bottom."

"Aye aye, Captain."

# SIXTY-EIGHT

FORREST, KANE, AND DANZIG WERE ALL PRETTY BADLY SHOT up. Only by the grace of God had the hits missed their vital organs; their body armor had done its job many times over, but they were all bleeding from multiple limb and shoulder wounds. Forrest was the worst for the wear, one round having penetrated his thigh and another having shattered his right ankle. Kane had bound the joint for him, wrapping an elastic bandage tightly around the canvas boot to help immobilize the foot and to stem the flow of blood, but the pain was intense when he applied any weight to the leg. So far, he had refused morphine, needing his head clear for the ongoing fight.

Veronica sat in the back corner behind the counter with Andie, Joann, Jessie, Renee, Maria, Karen, and the children. Michael, armed with a carbine, was lying in the hall covering the rear entrance, which they had barricaded with a desk and a filing cabinet.

Andie had been nicked in the chest and face by a ricochet, and Maria Vasquez had a bullet wound to her backside. A couple of the children were badly bruised up, and a few of them cried continuously.

Melissa sat in the dark beside Veronica, keeping Laddie on a short leash.

By now they had received word that Tonya had already taken her own life, as well as that of her son Steven, and the women were aghast. Kane had remained silent on the issue but Forrest knew he was blaming himself.

"Hey, she had eighteen happy months," Forrest said, bumping Kane on the shoulder. "So did the boy. It's more than what they would've had."

"I told her not to worry," Kane said quietly, not wanting the others to hear him. "That I'd come for her if anything happened."

"Maybe we see it differently, partner, but from where I sit, she bailed before you could make good on that promise."

"Don't make me feel no better."

"Ain't tryin' to make you feel better. I'm tryin' to keep your head in the game."

"My head's in the game, Captain."

Forrest crawled forward to peer up at the top balcony across the street. The building was only coated in fluorescent paint on the first floor level, so he still needed the NVD to see the upper levels. "I haven't seen any movement over there for ten minutes. They're up to something."

"Yeah, but what?" said Danzig, crouching in the opposite corner.

They only had to wait a few seconds for the answer. The fuse popped on a grenade right outside the window to the left. Neither Forrest nor the others made a sound. All of them knew from experience that to shout a warning would only prevent them from hearing where the grenade landed. The steel orb hit with a *thunk* inside the showcase, where they were unable to grab it, but they did dive clear of the blast and were already bringing their weapons up as the first attackers came charging in through the smoke.

The women remained surprisingly quiet as Forrest and the others kept up a withering fire, effectively piling bodies up in the showcase window. By the time the enemy realized their surprise assault had failed, they had lost five men. The rest retreated around the side of the building.

Kane and Danzig moved quickly to strip the dead of weapons and ammo as Forrest kept an eye on the apartment across the street with Kane's M-21 sniper rifle; Kane's shoulder was too badly wounded for precision sniping. The first enemy to sneak a peek from the second floor balcony took a .308 through the center of his face, and Forrest just missed another the next level down, driving the man back inside. After searching the bodies and stacking them in the window, they retook their positions to either side.

"We can't let them keep creeping up on us," Forrest said. "If they come to the well like that enough times, they're gonna get in."

A Molotov cocktail landed on the sidewalk in front of the window and exploded, setting the clothing of the dead bodies on fire and illuminating the inside of the store.

"Everyone stay down! They're trying to see in!"

Two men ran up on either side of the window and tossed in another pair of grenades, blasting the showcase apart and filling Danzig's left side with shrapnel. He screamed in agony, and Jessie and Veronica both jumped from cover to drag him to safety.

"Stay down!" Danzig shouted, not wanting his wife to get herself killed, but they ignored him and finished pulling him behind the counter where the children were all screaming and the dog was going wild at the end of his leash.

"Jack, what the fuck is going on over there?" Sullivan's voice sounded over the radio in Forrest's ear.

"They're storming the goddamn castle! Let me talk to Wayne."

"He's unconscious. Stand by. I'm coming to assist."

"Negative! Hold your position. There's nothing you can do for us!"

**But Sullivan hadn't** heard him, having already peeled off the headset and given it to West. He ducked out of the pharmacy and ran to the corner. Scanning the cluttered greenish-black street through the NVD, he saw two men rifling the second snowcat for the MREs and shot them dead, dropping into the snow and taking aim, left-handed, on seven more men lining up outside the porn shop window, preparing to make another assault.

He opened fire on their legs, knowing many of them wore armor of their own, and the attackers danced about on the sidewalk in an almost comic display as the bullets tore the meat from their bones. They fell, scrabbling for cover through the snow on their hands and knees, but a grenade was lobbed from the porn shop window and it exploded in their midst, ripping many of them apart, though only killing two. The survivors lay in a bloody, screaming tangle on the walk.

As Sullivan stood to withdraw to the pharmacy, he was jumped by two stinking, hairy men. The NVD was bashed from his helmet and the carbine pried from his grip. Someone kicked him in the groin and he buckled, grabbing a grenade from his harness and pulling the pin with his teeth before stuffing it down the pants of an assailant.

The man cried out and let go of him, presumably to pull the grenade from his pants, but it was too dark for Sullivan to know for sure. His other attacker was still struggling to subdue him when the grenade went off. Sullivan felt himself fly through the air. He landed hard on his back, the left side of his face and neck full of shrapnel, his left arm nearly severed at the elbow and his left leg in tatters.

He blacked out.

He came to in total darkness a short time later, feeling hands probing his wounds, and grabbed ineffectually with his crippled right hand for the knife on his belt.

"Easy," West said, gently catching the arm.

"You're safe now," Taylor said softly into his one good ear. "Sean brought you back in."

"Jack's group," Sullivan murmured. "Are they . . . ?"

"They're secure for the moment." West was working feverishly beneath a flashlight to stanch the flow of blood from

Sullivan's wounds. "Whatever you did seems to have bought them some time."

"You have to finish it," Sullivan whispered, feeling the morphine carrying him away. "Finish it now . . . too many to hold off . . . saw them in the flash . . ."

West looked at Price, both of them realizing what that meant, and picked up the headset. "Jack, it's Sean. Over."

"Go ahead."

"Jack, Sullivan says we're about to be overwhelmed. He says we should all finish it now."

"How does he know?"

"He's unconscious but his exact words were 'finish it now, too many to hold off.' "

"Can he make it?"

"No."

"Go ahead and establish your own protocol there, Sean. We're going to hold out here to the last possible moment. Tell T and E that I did my best, will ya?"

"They know that, Jack. We all know."

"Wish I did, goddamnit. Godspeed, Sean."

"What's going on?" Taylor asked, panic in her eyes, her voice trembling.

"Go on in the back with the kids, sweetheart. I'll be back to join you in a minute."

"What are you going to do?" she asked, starting to cry. "Sean, what are you going to do?"

"Price?"

"Come on, honey," Price said gently, helping Taylor to her feet.

"Don't, Sean. Please . . ."

West took one of the titanium vials from his jacket pocket and twisted off the lid, shaking the glass capsule into his hand. "God," he said quietly, slipping the capsule between Sullivan's molars. "Allow me to commend this man's spirit into your good hands."

He pressed upward on Sullivan's jaw to crush the capsule between his teeth. Sullivan's body tensed for an instant and then relaxed. West stood up and went into the back room.

"Erin," he said gently. "We need to see about Wayne."

"No, Sean!" Erin said, holding the baby in her arms and beginning to cry. "You're not allowed. He's *my* husband!"

"I won't do anything without your permission, honey, but it's time to make some decisions. We may only have seconds left."

The other mothers were crying as well, their hands trembling as they took the vials from their pockets. By now the children realized the true purpose of the astronaut medicine and they were all crying as well.

"This is bullshit!" Lynette said in disgust. "To get this close—"

"Lynny . . ." Price said quietly.

West sat down with his kids and took Taylor's hand. "There's no reason for us to be afraid. We're in God's hands. Now everyone put a capsule under your tongue and join hands."

Everyone did as he said.

"Will it hurt?" one of the little ones asked, sobbing.

"No, baby doll. You'll just go to sleep and wake right back up in heaven with God. I promise."

Erin couldn't hold anyone's hand, however; she would need them both for pinching capsules into the mouths of her husband and infant daughter. Jenny offered to help her but she refused.

"Can we all agree to wait until they come into the building?" Taylor asked through her tears. "Can we do that? I love you all so much!"

"I like that idea," Michelle said, gripping her son's hand. "Okay, baby? We're all going to heaven at the same time, so make sure you wait for Mommy."

"Okay, Mom," the little boy said, seemingly unafraid.

West began to recite from the Twenty-third Psalm: " 'The Lord is my shepherd. I shall not want. He maketh me to lie down in—' "

Without warning Lynette let go of her husband's hand and

sprang to her feet, dashing for the front of the store, gripping a flashlight.

West let go of Taylor's hand and jumped up to chase after her, but Price all but tackled him in the doorway.

"Price, what the hell are you doing?"

"You can't catch her," Price said, hearing Lynette scampering over the barricade. "Your place is here, Sean. She's my wife . . ."

Lynette ran down the street and froze at the corner, shining the flashlight on a disbelieving horde of barbarous-looking men, who for a moment might have believed they were seeing an angel with flowing blond hair, were it not for the grenade she gripped in the opposite hand.

"Catch!" she said, lobbing it into the air over their heads and turning to run back toward the pharmacy.

"Fuckin' bitch!" one of the men shouted as they scattered in the dark, none of them having any idea where the grenade would land. When it did land it rolled beneath a car where two men had taken cover, wounding them both upon detonation and prompting their comrades to move in and finish them off quickly in accordance with the laws of the wild.

Lynette stumbled in her dash for the pharmacy and was caught from behind by her hair and shoved into a lamppost, knocking the flashlight from her hand. She struggled to keep her feet, tussling in the blackness with a surprisingly weak and apparently shorter man, gnashing her teeth lest she accidentally spit out the capsule of cyanide she still kept in her mouth. She slashed with her fingers, found the soft gelatinous orb of the attacker's eyeball and grabbed him close, thrusting her thumb into the socket to claw it out. The man screamed and reeled away, but as she turned to run once more, she was struck by a vicious uppercut from an unseen fist that fractured her jaw, dropping her to her knees. She was not even remotely aware of the broken slivers of glass in her tongue as she fell forward onto her face.

Her body was lifted in the darkness as four men attempted to haul her off across the street, all of them thinking she was merely unconscious, but Price shot them down from behind then turned the carbine on the rest of the mob, which had reformed and was on the move. He was struck by a hail of bullets, the men trampling his body in their renewed assault on the pharmacy, kicking and pounding at the barricade to get inside.

"Not yet!" West told the women, breaking away from their prayers, his instinct for survival overriding all common sense as he grabbed his carbine and leapt into the doorway, firing into the mob at forty feet.

The attackers screamed and pulled back onto the walk, returning his fire.

Outside, the street erupted in a fusillade of automatic weapons fire and the attackers fell back from the pharmacy in confusion. West stood listening as the gunfire reached a crescendo, then he slammed the storeroom door and moved to cover the bodies of his wife and children with his own, shouting for everyone to spit out their capsules of cyanide.

Seconds later there was a cacophony of rapid 40mm cannon fire followed by the roaring sound of an 850 horse power Motoren-und Turbinen-Union diesel motor as it went rumbling past the building toward the corner.

"In here!" they heard Marty shout from the front of the store. "They're in here!"


"WHO BROUGHT THE forty mike mike?" Danzig mumbled through a fog of morphine, his head resting in Jessie's lap where they hid behind the counter in the porn shop.

"Jack!" Veronica shouted toward the front of the store. "What's going on?"

Forrest climbed painfully up into the showcase and stole a quick glance west toward the corner. "Jesus Christ!" he said jumping back down and landing painfully on his bad ankle. "Everybody spit those fucking capsules out! Melissa!"

"I already did!"

"Is it the goddamn Marines or what?" Kane asked, sticking his head down from a crawl space in the ceiling. He and Forrest had decided that he would be the last one left alive, surviving them all just long enough to rain their last six grenades down upon their attackers after the shop had finally fallen and filled up with the enemy, an enemy that might rape the bodies of the women.

"Everybody stay ready," Forrest cautioned, girding himself for the next onslaught, an old instinct telling him the fight was not yet over. "Kane, get down here!" he said, dropping to a crouch and shouldering his carbine.

A mob of men came pouring from three different apartments across the street, maybe twenty in all, hurling a grenade at the shop front.

Forrest and Kane fired into them even as the grenade exploded on the sidewalk. Laddie broke away from Melissa and bound past them, leaping over the bodies and out into the street, tearing into the first man he saw and ripping him screaming to the ground. The rest of the attackers recoiled in a moment of awe, astonished to see such a large dog, half expecting a pack of hungry wolves to come streaming out of the building.

One of them raised his weapon to shoot the animal but his head instantly exploded as a 230 grain, .45 caliber bullet blasted through his brain and slammed into the man behind him, killing them both.

Forrest stood defiantly among the many dying men at his feet, firing point-blank into the faces of the savages who would dare try to kill his son's dog. Screaming as he charged into them, he grabbed up an empty carbine, swinging at their heads and splitting skulls as they reeled away in panic, their combat reflexes horribly degraded by starvation and disease.

Not all of them had lost their wits. One was returning his fire and scoring hits on Forrest's armor and limbs, tracking him as he pivoted to the right, about to squeeze the trigger to blow out his brains. But suddenly, and to his horror, the dog sank its teeth into his testicles, frenziedly ripping them from side to side.

Kane smashed the man's skull with the barrel of his carbine and grabbed the dog's leash to haul him back inside. Glancing over his shoulder to see that Forrest had gone down, he dragged Laddie, snarling over the stacked bodies, and handed the leash to Melissa. He turned to dash out, but an unseen concussion grenade exploded just outside the window and hurled him back across the storefront into the counter, knocking him senseless. He tried to rise but collapsed and fell unconscious.

Bleeding badly, Forrest rolled beneath the hull of a pickup truck and blacked out as the Marines came charging up the street, supported by a second EFV, its 40mm cannon blasting away at the apartment building and killing all who ran for cover; killing all who stood to fight.

Veronica screamed for Michael and he abandoned his post in the back hall, running to the front and firing into the small group that sought to take cover inside the shop, killing a few and fumbling to reload. The women were about to put the capsules back into their mouths when they heard again the staccato blast of a 40mm cannon and the screaming of Marines as they surged past the shop. They were driving the few remaining killers before them toward the end of the block, where the other EFV and two more Marine platoons were waiting to gun them down.

When the last barbarian fell, the Marines let out with a roaring *"Oorah!"* and the street fell strangely silent, save for the occasional coups de grace being delivered to a wounded, sneering cannibal.

**IN THE LIGHT** of a magnesium flare held high above her head, Emory came through the Marines with a medical bag over each shoulder, spotting at once the bright red, white, and blue patch of the Eighty-second Airborne Division on the arm of a dead soldier stuffed beneath the rusted hulk of a pickup truck. She ran toward it, grabbing the wrist and dragging the body out into the light.

Forrest's lifeless body was covered in blood, his face lacerated and his uniform torn to tatters.

"Oh, no," she whispered, taking a knee beside him as men of the Third Marines shuffled around her and into the porn shop, shouting for survivors. She heard the women screaming from within that they were alive, and a surge of excitement swept through the Marines.

"They're alive!" someone shouted. "Get Beauchamp!"

"Corpsman!"

"Hey, Emory! They're alive!"

With a heavy heart, Emory rose to her feet to go see who had made it.

"Fuck you goin'?"

She whipped her head around to see Forrest looking up at her through one very swollen eye. "Oh, Jesus!"

"Can't you see I need a fuckin' medic?"

"Corpsman!" ripped from her throat as she dropped to her knees, then tore into one of the med kits. "More corpsman up front!"

"Who taught you to take a pulse?" Forrest mumbled, head spinning, his body coming alive with pain.

"I didn't bother taking your pulse," she said, digging out the compression bandage she would have to apply to his leg to prevent him from bleeding to death. "You sure as fuck know how to play possum!"

"Good thing. Else one'a those damn jarheads may've shot my ass."

"You're probably gonna lose that foot," she said, seeing that it was bent nearly forty-five degrees.

"Figures."

Veronica was climbing out through the window of the shop now and screaming his name. "Jack! Jack!"

"Here!" Emory called.

"Oh, Christ," he murmured. "Knock me out, Shannon. I can't take her right now."

Emory smiled and took a syrette of morphine from the pocket on her upper arm. "See how good I follow orders?"

She stuck him in the leg, and he was unconscious by the time Veronica and Melissa and the dog came scrambling around the rear of the truck.

"Oh, my God!" Veronica shouted. "Is he alive?"

"Just a little banged up."

"A little banged up!" She dropped to the ground beside them. "He looks like he's been hit by a truck, Shannon!"

Emory looked up to see Melissa gripping Laddie's leash in one hand and covering her mouth in abject terror with the other, the sight of Forrest's wounds shattering her. She punched Veronica in the shoulder, pointed up at the girl and gave her a shove. "How about trying to help!"

"Oh!" Veronica shook off her own sense of shock and jumped up to grab Melissa into her arms. The girl stood bawling into her bosom as Laddie began to lick the blood from Forrest's face.

Gunnery Sergeant Beauchamp appeared and stood looking down. "This one gonna make it, Emory?"

"He'll make it, Gunny. We need to get him to the ship ASAP."

"They got one bad wounded around the corner," Beauchamp said. "Medevac's loading him up now. Five dead."

"Five?" The number had startled her.

"Two men, two women, and a boy," he said, then walked off shouting orders to his men.

As Emory was finishing with Forrest's IV a short time later, Marty squatted beside her on his haunches, face pale, eyes full of dread.

"No!" she said, realizing her fear had come to pass. "Don't you fucking tell me that, Marty!"

"I'm sorry," he said, starting to cry. "Sean said he probably saved a lot of lives. Maybe everyone's."

Her eyes filled with tears, making it hard to see what she was doing. A corpsman joined her and she asked him to finish for her and got to her feet. "Where is he?"

"In a . . . in a bag on the sidewalk around the corner."

"Stay here."

She walked off through the milling Marines and made her way to the front of the pharmacy, where she knelt beside the largest of the five dark forms on the sidewalk. Taking out her flashlight, she drew a breath then unzipped Sullivan's bag. She saw his shattered face and for a moment was sick to her stomach, certain she was going throw up and shame herself, but then a Marine called her name and pulled her back from the brink: "Emory! What do you want done with your dead?"

"I . . . I . . . Can we take them aboard ship? Bury them at sea?"

"Don't see why not," the Marine said, stepping back from the doorway as they were bringing Ulrich out on a stretcher to load him onto the EFV medevac.

Erin and the baby came out right behind him. "Oh, my God, Shannon!" she called. "Thank God you made it, honey!"

Emory waved and smiled mirthlessly, it never occurring to her that the baby in Erin's arms was her own daughter. She reached into the bag to take hold of Sullivan's hand. It was cold and lifeless and did not feel anything at all like the soldier's hand it had once been. "I loved you," she whispered. "Not the way you wanted, but I loved you."

She took one of his dog tags and sat there lost in thought until she heard the crunching of glass and looked up to see that the other bodies had already been loaded onto the deck of the EFV and the Marines were waiting for her. She tucked Sullivan's arm back into the bag and zipped it up, then she got to her feet and stood away. "Gently, guys. Please?"

"Sure," one of the Marines said, crouching at the foot of Sullivan's bag as another grabbed the handles at the head.

Marty came up beside her and put his arm around her, and in return she slugged him. "Not in front of the Marines, you idiot!"

"Sorry," he groaned, holding his ribs.

They watched until Sullivan was loaded and then walked around the corner, passing their snowcat on the way.

"The bastards must have taken Liddy and Natalie," Marty said. "Their bodies are gone."

"I hope they try eating them," she muttered, feeling an emptiness she'd never known. "See how the bastards like cyanide poisoning."

# SIXTY-NINE

THE USS *BOXER* WAS NOW THREE DAYS INTO HER FOURTEEN-day voyage back to Pearl Harbor. Forrest and his three wounded compatriots—Ulrich, Kane, and Danzig—all shared the same hospital bay, and though Ulrich had very nearly died of his gut wound, Dr. West and the Navy surgeon managed to repair the damage to his intestine. So far they were keeping septic infection at bay, and West was hopeful about Ulrich's recovery. Forrest had only just managed to keep his foot, and the ankle would need to be operated on again once they arrived in Hawaii. His other many wounds were healing satisfactorily.

During the evenings, the curtains were pulled around their beds and their wives or sweethearts were permitted to spend the night at their sides if they so desired.

The unmarried women aboard had of course quickly become the belles of the ball, and by the end of their third day at sea, Captain Bisping felt it necessary to call a meeting with them in the pilots' ready room.

"Ladies," Bisping began, pulling the door to the room closed. "I understand that you have all been . . . *alone* for some time now, and I can appreciate what that must have been like for you. However, I must remind you that this is a warship and there are certain activities that are forbidden aboard a man-of-war—and all for very good reason."

A few of the women snickered, and Bisping looked to Emory for help. "Am I not making myself clear?"

"In other words, guys, the captain doesn't want anyone getting laid aboard his ship." The women started to laugh. "How's that, sir?"

"That's fine, thank you," Bisping said dryly. "So . . . if you ladies are unable to restrain yourselves for the remainder of the voyage, I will have to confine you to a smaller area of the ship, forbidding you to mingle with the crew. And this would be as much for your own safety as for any other reason."

"Damn!" said Maria two. "All we did was trade one military dictator for another."

Again the women started to laugh.

"Does that mean you cannot be trusted?" Bisping asked, cocking an authoritative eyebrow.

"They can be trusted," Emory said, looking hard at the others. "He's serious about confining us, you guys."

The others rolled their eyes but no one made any argument.

"So are we all in agreement?" Bisping asked them.

"Yeesss," they said in practiced unison.

"Thank you," Bisping said with a smile. He left the room, but was not far down the passageway before he heard his name called.

"Captain Bisping?"

He turned to see Andie coming toward him. "Yes, ma'am?"

"We haven't met formally," she said, offering him her hand. "I'm Andie Tatum."

"William Bisping," he said. "Pleasure to meet you."

"Bisping is an English name, isn't it?"

"Yes, ma'am, though my family's lived in the States for generations."

"You've been a Navy man all your life, I assume?"

"Yes, ma'am. Is there something I can do for you? I don't mean to be rude, but I have a ship to run."

Andie hesitated for a moment then thought, to hell with it. "I've noticed you don't wear a wedding band, Captain, and I've been wondering whether there is anyone waiting for you back at Pearl?"

"Excuse me?" he said, startled.

"I apologize for being so forward. Especially after that, um, *announcement* you just made. It's just that I've hesitated before and ended up wishing I hadn't. Being lonely isn't easy and it makes you do things you wouldn't otherwise."

Bisping swallowed. "Yes . . . I suppose it does. To tell you the truth, Andie, I haven't really . . . Well, I lost my wife and two daughters to the asteroid. So, no, there's no one waiting back at Pearl or anywhere else."

"I'm very sorry," she said. "I lost my husband to the Taliban five years ago. Our daughter barely got to know him."

"We seem to have some sad things in common."

"They may not all be sad."

"I'm sure they're not, but I'm afraid I have a ship to run. Now, if you'll excuse me." He turned and walked off down the passageway, leaving Andie watching after him, feeling like a complete fool, her self-esteem in a sudden tailspin. She thought of what her dead husband might think if he could see her at that moment and very nearly started to cry.

"You know what?" Bisping said, turning around and coming back down the passageway.

"What?" she said, swallowing and attempting to smile prettily.

"What's wrong?" he said, seeing her eyes.

"Nothing. What were you going to say?"

"I was going to say that I was full of crap just now. There's no reason we can't have dinner in my cabin later if you think you might like to."

"I'd love to," she said, a warmth spreading through her.

"Perhaps you could bring your daughter?" he suggested.

"As a chaperone?" she asked with a smile.

"There are no secrets aboard a ship, Andie. And it's important that I lead by example."

"Of course."

"I should also warn you, though . . . in case we find that we do have other things common. I'm the permanent captain of *Boxer* now, which means I'll be at sea whenever she's at sea, and I've got no idea how often that's going to be. Particularly if there is more trouble with the Chinese. We sank three of their vessels on this cruise, and we have no idea how much of their navy is still active or what their intentions may be."

"William, as long as this ship is the only woman I'd have to share you with, I'll take my chances."

"Very well, then. I'll send someone for you after a while."

"Looking forward to it," she said with a smile.

**FORREST SAT HOLDING** Melissa's hand, his head resting against the pillow, the curtain drawn around his bed. "So are you going to tell me what's wrong?" he asked, giving her fingers a squeeze.

"Nothing's wrong," she said, lowering her eyes.

"Do you think I'm stupid?"

She shook her head.

"Well, tell me what it is. You and I don't have secrets from one another."

Her eyes filled with tears and she turned her face toward the foot of the bed.

"Don't hide your face. Talk to me."

"I can't," she whispered.

"Since when?"

She shook her head again, saying, "You'll think I'm . . ."

"I'll think you're what?"

"Bad."

"Oh, bullshit. Look at me . . . Look at me . . . There's nothing you can do to make me think you're bad. If you took a shit in church, I'd find a way to excuse it. And what's worse than shitting in church?"

"Lots of things."

"Well, nothing having to do with you. So tell me."

"I'm jealous," she softly, almost ashamedly, tears running down her face.

"Of Veronica?"

She closed her eyes and nodded, lowering her face to the mattress, and he let go of her hand, running his fingers through her curls, petting her. Melissa felt the heat spread through her, the body ache that she had never known until her feelings for him first began to change, making her feel dirty and ashamed.

"Why?" he asked her gently.

"Because I love you," she said in a barely audible whisper.

"I love you too."

But she shook her head, whispering into the sheet that it was not the same.

"How do you know?" he said softly, touching her face.

She sat up and looked at him.

"Hmm?"

"I don't think you understand what I mean." She wiped her nose with her fingers.

"I understand exactly what you mean. Wanna run off and get married as soon as we get to Hawaii?"

"No," she said, shaking her head. "It's not like that . . . I can't explain it."

"Can I be honest with you?" he said, giving her hand another squeeze.

She nodded.

"You're conflicted because there aren't any young men around. When we get to Hawaii that will change, and that feeling you have won't confuse you anymore."

Her eyes grew big and she felt her face grow hot.

"See?" he said with a smile. "I know what you're going through. And I've never pulled any punches with you, so I won't start now. It's completely natural, what you're feeling. We just have to find you someone your own age to feel it for, that's all."

"And what if I don't?" she said quietly, worried that Ulrich or one of the others might hear.

"Then I'll dump Veronica," he whispered, "and we'll run away together up into the mountains and live in a hut."

She snickered. "Nuh-uh."

"Oh, don't be too sure. She'll be old and ugly pretty soon, and you'll still be young and beautiful."

"Shut up," she said, laughing softly. "You're not going to tell her we had this talk, are you?"

"Nope."

"Promise me."

"I swear on my hope of being reborn a cat that I will never tell her we had this conversation."

"You don't want to come back as a cat!"

"I never told you that?"

"No," she said. "Why the hell would you want to be a cat?"

"Have you ever seen a cat take any shit from anybody?"

"No," she laughed.

"Well, next time around I ain't takin' no shit from nobody."

She stood and slid her arms around his neck, then blushed and leaned over to kiss him chastely on the lips. "I love you, Jack."

"Love you too, honey."


**WHEN SHE WAS** sure Melissa was gone, Veronica stepped out from behind Kane's curtain and stood looking at Forrest. "It scares me how easily you handled that."

"What was hard about it?" he said. "All I had to do was tell her the truth. And you know what they say about the truth."

"Well, you're committed to living in a hut if this doesn't work."

"Oh, stop it. She'll have ten boyfriends by this time next month."

Captain Bisping entered the sick bay a few moments later and stood outside Forrest's curtain. "Knock, knock."

"Come on in," Forrest said.

Bisping pulled the curtain aside to see Veronica sitting on the edge of his bed. "I had to have a little talk with the single women in your crew."

Forrest chuckled. "And how did that work out for ya, Captain?"

Bisping, feeling a little light-headed over Andie, smiled and said, "I'm guessing you've had your hands full these past eighteen months."

"Women respond to kindness, Captain. Remember that."

Veronica hit him in the head.

"Hey, I'm wounded, you know!"

"Not as bad as you're gonna be."

Bisping shook his head. "I've received word from Pearl. Our leadership is particularly concerned about the health of you and your men."

"Well, that's awfully nice of them, Captain."

"Turns out," Bisping went on, "that the four of you are going to be the only Green Berets of fighting age in all the Hawaiis."

"Well, we're retired."

"No," said Bisping, "I'm afraid you *were* retired. You see, everybody's got a job to do in Hawaii these days, *Captain*. And President Thorn is going to be asking for your assistance with a little piracy problem we've been having. Our settlements along the coasts are being raided. Most people live in Honolulu now, but the settlements are important for protecting the infrastructure of the Islands for future repopulation. So the settlers are actually caretakers, and we need someone qualified to teach them how to defend themselves . . . and since the training of indigenous troops is a big part of what the Special Forces were all about . . . Well, it speaks for itself, doesn't it?"

Forrest looked up at Veronica. "First cannibals and now pirates. Jesus Christ, you'd think I was a goddamn sailor."

# Epilogue

THERE WERE DOZENS OF GULLS IN THE SKY AS MARTY CHIT-
tenden and Shannon Emory disembarked from the *Boxer*,
walking the ladder leading down to the pier. They stood off
to the side watching the birds for a long time, unable to take
their eyes off them. The only other wild creatures they had
seen in the last year were rats, and the sounds of the gulls
were like sweet music.

"Nobody knows where the damn things came from," said
a voice from behind. "They just showed up one day."

They turned around and there was Ester Thorn, bundled
up in her coat and leaning against her cane.

"Holy shit," Marty muttered, a grin coming to his face.
"It's really you!"

"Who is she?" Emory asked.

"It's Ester," he said, walking over to the old woman and
giving her a hug.

"You look ten years older, boy. Turned you into a man,
hasn't it?"

"Not the kind of man I ever wanted to be," he said, turning
toward Emory. "Ester, this is someone I'd like you to meet.
Shannon Emory. She's the best friend I've ever had. We've
been taking turns saving one another's lives."

"Pleased to meet you," Ester said, taking her hand.

"Pretty thing." Then she turned and gestured with her cane at all of the construction taking place around the harbor. "Take a look at the new power grid we're building! It'll be the most efficient grid there's ever been. Of course, for now we remain largely dependent on the Navy's nuclear reactors to pick up where the wind farms leave off, but it won't always be that way. We're harnessing the tide, Marty. Our engineers believe we'll be drawing up to eighty percent of our power from the sea within the next five years. After that, who knows?

"Of course, I won't be here to see it," she added. "But you will, Marty, and don't worry about a thing. Everyone in these islands knows who you are now, and they know they've got you to thank. I've made sure of it."

"Ester, all I did was spot the rock."

"No, son, you did a lot more than that. You got this grumpy old woman up off her ass and sent her to Hawaii to carry out your vision. *Your* vision, Marty. This sure as hell wasn't mine. I would have said to hell with it all. And now, with a little honey here and a little honey there . . . you'll keep the Naturalist Party in power for the next twenty or thirty years. The Federalists are growing weaker every day now."

Marty laughed. "I don't have any idea what you're talking about."

"You will, son. You will. There's a lot to do—a lot for you to live up to! This is your baby as much as it is mine, and now you'll have to help me raise the damn thing. I didn't turn the Navy around and give up one of my destroyers for you to sit on the beach and watch the lava cool."

Emory chuckled and bumped Marty with her shoulder. "Told you," she said. "There's still a need for your skinny ass."

"Captain Bisping!" Ester said suddenly, a scowl coming to her face the moment she spotted him coming through the crowd.

Bisping touched Andie's arm and asked for her and Trinity to wait for him. "Madam President?"

"Captain Bisping, I'd like to know just who exactly that goddamn *Christmas* greeting was intended for!"

"Well, it was intended for you, Madam President," he replied equably.

Ester laughed aloud and clapped him on the shoulder. "Old Longbottom thought it was meant for him!" she cackled, leaning heavily into her cane. "Boy, you should have seen the look on his face. He got so red I thought he was going to have himself an apoplexy. Honest to God! I told him, though. I said, 'Oh, Admiral, don't think so damn much of yourself! That message is meant as an affront to me. I'm the fool who sent him out there with only one escort! Not you!'

"I've apparently got a lot to learn about military matters, Captain, but you and I, we know how to talk to one another. There's no messing about with you. We'll get this fleet allocation business worked out in a way that we can all live with. Don't you worry. You're hugely popular now, Captain. A bona fide hero of the deep!"

By now Bisping was grinning, seeing easily into Ester's political stratagem. "Yes, ma'am."

"I don't suppose I can talk you into giving up the *Boxer* for a cabinet position, can I?"

"Madam President, I'd rather be keel-hauled."

She cackled some more, saying, "Well, then I'll get as much mileage out of you as I can whenever you're ashore. How's that?"

Then she took him aside, saying in a low voice for only him to hear: "Maybe you could suggest to the admiral that he send his *requests* through you in the future. It might keep things running a little more smoothly—provided he thinks it's your idea."

"Ester," Bisping said, "suppose we let him think it's *his* idea?"

She laughed and squeezed his hand. "We're going to get along fine, Captain, you and me. Be sure to come by the hotel in the morning, will you? I've got a meeting with Longbottom about this supposed Chinese threat, and I want you there for it. I'm half worried he thinks we should invade."

"The admiral may have some extreme ideas," Bisping said, "but he knows the sea."

"The sea!" Ester said, pointing at him. "He knows the sea, sure enough. But the man's got no vision. We need people of *vision* in these islands. I keep saying it!"

She turned around and put her hand on Marty's shoulder, dismissing Bisping almost out of hand. "Marty, I haven't felt this good in years," she said, taking his arm and leading him up the pier toward a waiting black limousine. "Now, I want you to come along with me. We're meeting Harold Shipman over a late lunch—he's the man who put me into office—and I don't want you to worry about your friends. They'll be fine. You're all staying in my hotel for the first few weeks until we get the kinks ironed out. The people want to see you all and to get to know you. And I want you to tell me about these Green Beret friends of yours too. All of Honolulu's talking about the five heroes who built some kind of an ark beneath the ground. It's craziness, I know, but the people need heroes these days, Marty. They need the inspiration to keep them working!"

Marty looked back over his shoulder at Emory, shrugging in a gesture of helplessness.

Emory laughed and waived him goodbye as Ester pulled him into the backseat after her, still talking a mile a minute as Marty closed the door.